Thomas L. Wilson

Sufferings Endured for a Free Government;

Thomas L. Wilson

Sufferings Endured for a Free Government;

ISBN/EAN: 9783337284466

Printed in Europe, USA, Canada, Australia, Japan

Cover: Foto ©Andreas Hilbeck / pixelio.de

More available books at **www.hansebooks.com**

Yours Truly
Thos G Wilson

SUFFERINGS

ENDURED FOR A FREE GOVERNMENT;

OR,

A HISTORY

OF THE

Cruelties and Atrocities of the Rebellion.

"Facts stranger than Fiction."

BY

THOS. L. WILSON.

PUBLISHED BY

1865.

CONTENTS.

1*

INTRODUCTION.

OUR country, during the last four years, has been the theatre of a rebellion, which, in point of magnitude and enormity, has scarcely a parallel in the world's history. Conceived in sin and born in iniquity, it has been, from the beginning, a monstrous exhibition of human depravity, and characterized by cruelties and atrocities supposed to be peculiar to barbarians only. These atrocities, although beggaring description, and almost exceeding belief, are yet substantiated by evidence abundant and superabundant.

To give an account of these atrocities, is the design of the following work. The author was led to its preparation by what he has seen and suffered. A Southern man by birth and education, he was on his way homeward at the breaking out of the rebellion. At Richmond, Virginia, his progress was suddenly arrested, by acts of violence and threats of incarceration, on account of his refusal to take the oath of allegiance to the rebel government. With difficulty he effected his escape, and succeeded in reaching Washington, D. C. Thrown out of employment—cut off from his resources—cast among strangers—suffering keenly in many ways, and sympathizing deeply with the persecuted Unionists of the revolted States—he was naturally led to think much of the causeless character, and enormous wickedness, and hideous barbarism of the revolt. In this course of thought the present work had its origin.

At first, the author's ideal was somewhat indefinite; but as he thought, and read, and wrote, it gradually assumed shape and grew into its present proportions.

(7)

The author makes no pretensions to literary eminence. He has aimed only at a simple and truthful presentation of facts, and has taken great pains to insert nothing but well-authenticated facts. Comments he has generally avoided, although strongly tempted thereto by his own feelings, preferring to let the facts speak for themselves. He is fully persuaded that his book gives only a faint picture of the reality. This is confirmed by the concurrent testimony of thousands upon thousands of refugees from the land of bondage—of men who, on account of their love for the Union which our fathers formed, have been driven from the revolted States, leaving home, and kindred, and the accumulations of years, perhaps of a lifetime. They tell us that the whole cannot be told—that the reality exceeds our conceptions.

But why, it may be asked, present to the public such a revolting picture of cruelty and crime? How else is the animus of the rebellion, which has filled the land with sighs and tears, with broken hearts and stricken households, to be brought out to view and placed in a clear light? How else is the character of the conspirators against a beneficent government, which made them the chief recipients of its favors, and loaded them with its benefits, to be unfolded and made fully manifest? How else are measures to be adopted, wisely and effectively, for subduing a revolt of such immense proportions and enormous wickedness? How else is sympathy to be awakened, and relief secured for our suffering soldiers, taken captive in battle, and groaning, starving, shivering, dying in Southern prisons—and for the persecuted Unionists of the rebellious States, robbed of their property, driven from their homes, hiding in dens and caves, hunted with bloodhounds, forced into the rebel service—subject to every species of indignity and wrong if suffered to live? Have they no claims upon us? Have we no duties in regard to them? How else is it to be known what it has cost them, and what praise and admiration they deserve for adhering to the old flag? To adhere to the Union has cost us comparatively little; but what has it not cost the Unionists of East Tennessee and Texas? And for it, will they not deserve to be held up for admiration, in all ages and generations? But how can this be made known or properly estimated, without a recital of the atrocities to which they have been subjected?

How else are men to learn what is the natural fruit of that institution, which has so long been paramount in the revolted states, penetrating all the relations of life, underlying all measures, and overshadowing all interests, giving shape and tone to society in all its departments, and manifestations to its civilization, its literature, and even its religion? These atrocities are the natural outgrowth of slavery, and show it to be barbarous in its tendencies and results, as well as in its origin. Such an institution, trampling upon the rights of man, ignoring the social relations of husband and wife, of parent and child, reducing one class to a state of chattelism, and making irresponsible despots of another, cannot but foment the worst passions, and be productive of violence and bloodshed. This, in substance, was long since affirmed by the illustrious author of the Declaration of Independence, and it is confirmed by the present rebellion. In these atrocities may be seen, what is the state of society which it produces, what is the civilization it admits of, what is the Christianity to which it gives shape.

But it may be said that atrocities have been committed on the Union side. This is doubtless true.* But they have been comparatively limited in number and enormity, and have usually met with exemplary punishment when detected. Our people and our Government, our officers and our soldiers, have been slow to retaliate, when deeds of barbarism have been committed by the rebels. It may be questioned whether they have not forborne when forbearance ceased to be a virtue. Fort Pillow, which will constitute one of the bloodiest pages of history, remains unavenged. The starving and shooting and bayoneting of prisoners of war, so common by the rebels, have never been imitated by us. While Unionists in the revolted states are hunted down like wild beasts by blood-hounds, Secession sympathizers among us are usually unmolested and allowed freely to utter their sentiments.

It may be said further that these atrocities are in many cases the work of guerrillas. But when or where, have they been repudiated and condemned by the rebel authorities? When or where have the authors of them been punished on account of them? In how many cases have they been commended and extolled, and rewarded with the honors and emoluments of office?

But it may be said, still further, that the atrocities recorded in this book are isolated and extreme cases, and do not present a fair view of the matter. Would that this were true! But so far is this from being true, that the picture, as already intimated, is altogether too faint. The atrocities related in this book are only specimens; mere selections from an immense mass of hideous deeds of barbarism. Were the whole to be recorded, the mind would tire of, and recoil from the recital; were the whole to be recorded, volumes would be required. Barbarism has characterized the rebellion from the beginning to the present hour, in every state, and county, and town, and village, and hamlet. It originated in barbarism; has been prosecuted with barbarism; and may its overthrow be the overthrow of barbarism, and give place to a higher civilization, and a purer Christianity!

Believing that these atrocities should be held up for the execration of mankind; that they illustrate great and fundamental truths in morals and politics; that a brief record of them is necessary for the instruction of his countrymen, the author commits the work to the public, in the hope that it may be of some little service to the country and the world.

PART I.

TREATMENT OF PRISONERS OF WAR BY THE
REBEL GOVERNMENT, AND ITS
AUTHORIZED AGENTS.

TREATMENT OF PRISONERS OF W

BY

THE REBEL GOVERNMENT.

PRELIMINARY.

THE advancing civilization of centuries, the cultivation of literature, the diffusion of knowledge, the extension of commerce, the increasing intercourse of nations, and above all, the prevalence of Christianity with its benign and subduing influences, has not been without effect on the treatment of prisoners of war. Once it was the rule that they should be slain without mercy, or reduced to a state of abject bondage. But now we are horrified by the accounts of such conduct which have come down to us from past ages, and execrate the memory of the cruel and bloody men who showed no mercy to the unfortunate prisoner of war. Even a Roman triumphal procession, however imposing, is to us revolting, on account of the position and treatment of the captive.

Now, it is required among civilized and Christian nations, that prisoners of war should be treated hu·

2 (13)

manely; that, in ordinary cases at least, their lives should be spared, their persons protected, their feelings regarded, their wounds dressed, their pains assuaged, and their wants supplied. The opposite of this is justly regarded as barbarous, and branded as infamous. How all these rules have been violated by the Rebel Government and its authorized agents, the following pages will show.

How differently have Confederate prisoners of war been treated by our own government! Instead of being subjected to indignity and wrong, how generally have they been treated with great kindness! As yet Fort Pillow remains unavenged, although the cry runs through the revolted States, "Repeat Fort Pillow!"

BULL RUN ATROCITIES.

That barbarities of a hideous nature were perpetrated by the Rebels upon the Union soldiers who fell into their hands at the battle of Bull Run; that prisoners of war were shot and bayoneted; that the wounded and dying were treated with neglect and inhumanity; that the dead were outraged, and the very grave was desecrated and despoiled, in a manner supposed to be characteristic only of savages; are abundantly confirmed by the sworn testimony of men of the highest standing—such as Senator Sprague of Rhode Island, General James B. Ricketts, Mr. Daniel Bixby of Washington, D. C., Surgeons J. M. Homiston and William F. Swalen, Fourteenth New York Volunteers, Dr. James B. Greeley, Rev. Frederic Denison, and Frederic Scholes, Esq., of Brooklyn, New York.

I was made prisoner on the field, and immediately taken inside the enemy's lines. I told them that my wish was to attend to the wounded men, there were so many of them wounded and crippled; that I had remained voluntarily with them for that purpose. I asked as a privilege that I should be permitted to attend them. Two of the surgeons then permitted me to go to work and attend to the wounded. I did so until dark, when a guard came up and said that I must accompany them. I told them that it was my wish to remain on the field; that I desired to remain all night with the wounded men, as there were so many who needed attention, and some of them in a very helpless and painful condition, and suffering for water. I protested against being sent from the field at that time.

They became very rude, and talked in a very ugly way, and insisted on my going with them. They marched me, with a party of prisoners, mostly privates, to Manassas; they did not offer us even water, let alone anything in the shape of food; we stood in the streets of Manassas about an hour with a guard around us; a crowd collected about us, hooting and threatening, in a very boisterous way, what they would do with us. We were finally put into an old building, and left to sleep on the floor there, without anything in the shape of food being given us. In the morning, those of us who were surgeons, were brought before the medical director, as he was called, who took our names, and then sent us back to the battle-field; there were three of us in that party. We told them we were already faint and exhausted, having been without food for twenty hours. They gave us some cold bacon, and sent us back to the battle-field.

When we reached the battle-field they took us to the
Lewis House, as it is called; they had commenced bringing the wounded in there, mostly their own. They finally
allowed us to have an ambulance, and we commenced
picking up our wounded, and bringing them in ourselves,
a guard all the while accompanying us; we were then
ordered to report ourselves to a Secession surgeon, a Dr.
Darby, of South Carolina. He said he had been sent
there by General Beauregard to take charge of the
wounded. He would not allow us to perform operations
upon our own men, but had them performed by his assistants, young men, some of them with no more knowledge of what they attempted to do than an apothecary's
clerk. They performed the operations upon our men in
a most horrible manner; some of them were absolutely
frightful.

It was almost impossible for us to get anything for
our wounded men there to eat; they paid no attention to
us whatever. We suffered very much on account of the
want of any kind of food for our men. They would not
even bring water to us. On the Monday night after the
battle, all the wounded in that old house were lying there
upon the floor as thickly as they could be laid. There
was not a particle of light of any kind in the house to
enable us to move about among the wounded. They were
suffering very much for water; but with all the persua-
sion I could use they would not bring us any water, and
the guard stationed about the house prevented us from
going after any. Fortunately, I might say, it rained
that night, and through the open windows the rain beat
in, and ran down the floor among the wounded, wetting
and chilling them; still I was enabled, by setting some
cups under the eaves, to catch a little water for our poor
soldiers to drink, and in that way I spent all the night,

catching water from the eaves, and carrying it to our wounded to drink. As there was no light in the house, it being perfectly dark, I was obliged to crawl on my hands and knees to avoid stepping on their wounded limbs. It is not a matter of wonder that the next morning several had died there during the night. They seemed to be perfectly indifferent to the sufferings of our men—entirely so. There was occasionally a man here and there, who seemed to have no connection with the army at all, who appeared desirous to extend some kindly assistance to our wounded; but those connected in any way with their army seemed to try to do everything to show their perfect indifference.

Some of our wounded lay upon the battle-field until the Wednesday after the battle. More were brought in Tuesday night and Wednesday morning with their wounds completely alive with larvæ deposited by flies. They had lain out there through all the rain-storm of Monday, and the hot, sultry sunshine of Tuesday, and their wounds were completely alive with larvæ when they were brought in on Tuesday night and Wednesday. Our dead lay upon the field unburied, to my knowledge, for five days.

TESTIMONY OF SURGEON SWALEN.

I was at the Lewis House from fourteen to fifteen days. One afternoon Captain Withington and myself took a walk over the battle-field. This was some ten or twelve days after the battle. As we walked around, I saw some of our men still unburied, and some entirely naked— shoes, stockings, everything they had on stripped from them, and their bodies left exposed naked on the field. Yet I saw a great many women, ladies I suppose they called themselves, walking about the field at that time,

2 *

apparently entirely unmoved. I should judge that I saw ten or twelve of the Fourteenth New York Regiment unburied, many of the Seventy-first Regiment, and a number of others whose regiments I did not recognise.

At the time I went for two wounded men, on the Wednesday morning after the battle, I saw them (the rebels) digging some trenches, and saw some two or three Union soldiers buried. They paid no attention as to how they put them in, but put them in face downwards, or in any other way, just as it happened. They buried a number in a ravine that had been washed out by the rains, throwing the bodies into the ravine, and covering them up with the earth. In going over the battle-field subsequently, I noticed where some of the graves had been opened by pushing rails down under the bodies and prying them up. Many of the negroes said that they had seen the soldiers doing that. The object, as I was informed, was to make-drinking cups of the tops of the skulls, and rings of the bones.

Dr. Ferguson, of New York, was taking his ambulance for the wounded, when he was fired upon. He took off his green sash to show his calling, and his handkerchief, as a sort of flag of truce, and waved them. A party rode up to him and asked him who he was. He told them that he was a surgeon of the New York State Militia. They said they would take a parting shot at him, any way. They fired at him, and shot him in the leg. He was taken prisoner and laid in the ambulance. He had his boots on, and his spurs on his boots, and as, they drove along, his spurs would catch in the tail-board, causing him such agony that he screamed out. One of their officers rode up to him, and placed his pistol at his head, and threatened if he screamed again he would shoot him. This was on Sunday, the day of the battle.

A party of rebels passed by where I was lying wounded on the battle-field, and called out—referring to me—"Knock out his brains, the d——d Yankee!"

I could from my room (in Richmond) overlook the place where they buried our dead. I know they were buried in the negro burying-ground, among the negroes. They had no funeral service over them, but they were just taken out and put in the ground in the most unfeeling manner.

The general treatment of the prisoners there, I thought, was very bad indeed. We were very much crowded. Our diet was very meagre indeed. I subsisted mainly upon what I purchased with my own money, which my wife brought me.

There were a number of our men (prisoners) shot. On one occasion, there were two shot, one was killed and the other wounded. * * * * * I heard of a great many of our prisoners who had been bayoneted and shot. I saw three of them, two of them had been bayoneted, and one of them had been shot—one of them was named Lewis Francis, of the New York Fourteenth. He had received fourteen bayonet-wounds; and he had one wound, very much like mine, on the knee, in consequence of which his leg was amputated after some twelve weeks had passed. And I would state here that, in regard to his case, when it was determined to amputate his leg, I heard Dr. Peachy, the surgeon, remark to one of his young assistants, "I won't be greedy, you may do it;" and the young man did it. There was a man named Briggs, of a Michigan regiment, who has a scar on his hand now from a bayonet-wound. He says he saw the rebels coming, bayoneting and pillaging the pockets of the dead. He had a little portmonnaie, with about eight dollars in it; he put it inside his shirt, and let it fall down his back, and lay down on it; he was wounded, shot below the knee somewhere. When they came to him, they asked for his money, and commenced thrusting a bayonet at him—he caught it in his hand, and as they withdrew it his hand was cut by it.

I heard a doctor on the steps below my room say that he wished he could take out the hearts of·the d—d Yankees as easily as he could take off their legs. * * * *

My wife, in the first place, joined me while I was at the Lewis House, on the field of battle. The first rumor she heard was that I was killed. When she heard that I was alive, but wounded, she started with her carriage and horses to come to me. · She almost had to fight her way out there, but succeeded finally in reaching me on the fourth day after the battle. There were eight persons in the Lewis House in the room where I lay, and my wife for two weeks slept in that room on the floor by my side without a bed. When we got to Richmond there were six of us in a room, among them Colonel Wilcox, who remained with us until he was taken to Charleston. There we were, all in that one room. There was no door to it; and in the hot summer months the stench from their wounds and from the utensils they used was fearful. There was no privacy at all, because, there being no door, the room could not be closed. The hospital was an unfinished building, one half of the windows being out of it; and there we were, a common show. * * * The people would come in there and say all sorts of things to us and about us. In fact, people that I knew, would come in and commence discussions, until I was obliged to tell them that I was a prisoner and had nothing to say. When we went down to Richmond in the cars from Manassas, wherever we stopped, crowds of people would gather around and stare at us. At Gordonsville, particularly, crowds of women came around to see the prisoners and the Yankee woman. They would ask my wife if she cooked, if she washed, and how she got there. Finally, Mrs. Ricketts appealed to the officer in charge, and told him that it was not the intention that we should be subjected to this treatment, and that if it was continued she would make it known to the authorities. He then said that he would stop it. General Johnston took my wife's horses and carriages away from her at Manassas, and kept them, and has them yet for aught I know. When we got down to Richmond I spoke to several gentlemen about it, and so did Mrs. Ricketts. They said that of course the carriage and horses would be returned. But they never were. Instead of that, when I was exchanged, and we were about to leave, they refused Mrs. Ricketts a transportation ticket to Norfolk, obliging her to purchase it. Dr. Gibson, who was in charge of the hospital, when he heard of it, said that such a thing was very extraordinary in General Winder, and that he would speak to him about it. I said that it made no difference, though I thought as General Johnston had taken her carriage and horses and left her on foot, it would be nothing more than fair to give her a ticket to Norfolk.

I must say that I have a debt that I desire very much to pay, and nothing troubles me so much now as the fact that my wounds prevent me from entering upon active service at once.

TESTIMONY OF SENATOR SPRAGUE.

In that part of the field where I was, our wounded were taken to two different places—one was a storehouse at the point where the engagement first took place, the other was about three-quarters of a mile in the rear of the battle-field. Colonel Slocum and Major Ballou were taken to a position at the rear. When the retreat commenced, we had in this hospital, as it was termed, several wounded rebel officers; and there were also several of our men there, who were promised, if they would stay with them, that they should be released. They did remain. When I went out there a few days since, I took three men with me to designate the places where these officers had been buried. On reaching the place, we commenced digging for the bodies of Colonel Slocum and Major Ballou at the spot which was pointed out to us by those soldiers.

While we were digging there, some negro women came up, and asked whom we were looking for; and at the same time said that "Colonel Slogan" had been dug up by the rebels—some men of a Georgia regiment— his head cut off, and his body taken to a ravine some thirty or forty yards below, and there burned.

We stopped digging, and went to the place thus designated, where we found coals, ashes, and bones, mingled together. A little distance from these we found a shirt, and a blanket with large quantities of hair upon it. Every thing indicated the burning of a body there.

We then returned and dug down at the spot indicated as the grave of Major Ballou, but found no body there. But at the spot designated as the place where Colonel Slocum was burned, we found a box, which, upon being raised and opened, was found to contain the body of Colonel Slocum. The soldiers who had buried the bodies of Colonel Slocum and Major Ballou were satisfied that the grave had been opened, and that the body taken out, beheaded and burned, was that of Major Ballou, because it was not in the spot where Colonel Slocum was buried, but to the right of it. They at once said that the rebels had made a mistake and taken the body of Major Ballou for that of Colonel Slocum. The shirt we found near the place where the body was burned, I recognised as one belonging to Major Ballou, as I had been very intimate with him. We gathered up the ashes containing the portions of his remains that were left and put them in a coffin, together with his shirt, and the blanket and the hair found upon it, and some hair also that was brought to us by a civilian who had expostulated with the rebels against this barbarity.

After we had done this we went to that portion of the field where the battle had first commenced, and began to dig there for the remains of Captain Tower. We had brought a soldier with us to designate the place where he was buried, who had been wounded at the battle, and had seen from the window of the house in which he was placed the spot where Captain Tower was buried. On opening the ditch or trench where he was buried, we found it filled with bodies of soldiers all buried with their faces downward. After taking up some four or five of them, we discovered the remains of Captain Tower, mingled with those of the men, and took them and placed them in a coffin and brought them home.

Question.—The position of these bodies was such that you were satisfied that they were buried intentionally with their faces downward?

Answer.—Undoubtedly, beyond all controversy.

Ques.—Did you consider that that was done as a mark of indignity?

Ans.—Yes, sir, as an indignity.

Ques.—What could have been their object in doing what they did with what they considered the body of Colonel Slocum?

Ans.—Sheer brutality; nothing else. They did it on account of his courage and chivalry in forcing his regiment fearlessly and bravely upon them, and destroying about one-half of that Georgia regiment which was made up of their best citizens.

Ques.—Were these barbarities perpetrated by that regiment?

Ans.—By that same regiment, as I was told. We saw where their own dead were buried, with marble head and foot stones, and the names upon them, while ours were buried in trenches.

TESTIMONY OF DANIEL BIXBY, JR.

I went out in company with Mr. G. A. Smart, of Cambridge, Massachusetts, who went to look for the body of his brother, who fell at Blackburn's Ford, in the action of the 18th of July, 1861. We took with us one who was there at the time, to point out where he fell. We found a grave there, which was opened. The clothes there found were identified as those of the brother of Mr. Smart. * * * * We found no head in the grave, and no bones of any kind—nothing but the clothes, and portions of the flesh of the body. We also saw the remains of three other bodies together that had not been buried at all, as we concluded from their appearance. The clothes were there, which we examined by cutting them open, and found some remains of flesh in them, but no bones. A Mrs. Pierce Butler, who lived near there, said that she had seen the rebels boiling portions of the bodies of our dead in order to obtain their bones as relics, the rebels not waiting for them to decay so that they could take their bones from them. She said that she had seen drum-sticks made of "Yankee shin-bones," as the Rebels call them. Mrs. Butler also said she had seen a skull that one of the New Orleans artillery had, which he said he was going to send home and have mounted, and was going to drink a brandy-punch out of it the day he was married.

TESTIMONY OF FREDERICK SCHOLES, OF BROOKLYN, N. Y.

I proceeded to the battle-field of Bull Run on Friday, April 4th, 1862. We passed across the battle-field, and proceeded to the place where I supposed my brother's body was buried. * * * * We then proceeded to the house of a free negro, named Simon, or Simons, and had a long conversation with him. He said he was a sutler, or rather kept a little store, and supplied the rebel soldiers with eatables. He said the rebel soldiers would come into his store with bones in their hands, which they showed to him, and said they were bones of Yankees which they had dug up. He said it was a common thing for the soldiers to exhibit the bones of "the Yankees" which they had dug up.

I went over to the house of a free negro named Hampton, as I understood that he assisted in burying some of our dead. * * * .I spoke to him about the manner in which these bodies had been dug up. He said he knew it had been done; that the rebels commenced digging up the bodies two or three days after they were buried, for the purpose at first of obtaining the buttons on their uniforms; afterwards they dug them up, as they decayed, to get their bones.

I went over where some of Mr. Lewis's negroes were, and inquired of them. Their information corroborated fully the statement of this man Hampton. They also stated that a great many of the bodies had been stripped naked on the field before they were buried; others were buried with their clothes on. They said that numbers

3

of them had been dug up through the winter, and even shortly after they had been buried.

A party of soldiers came along, and showed us part of a shin-bone, five or six inches long, which had the end sawed off. They said they had found it, among many other pieces, in one of the cabins the rebels had deserted. From the appearance of it, pieces had been sawed off to make finger-rings. As soon as the negroes noticed this, they said that the rebels had had rings made of the bones of our dead, and that they had them for sale in their camps. The soldiers said that there were lots of these bones scattered through the rebel huts sawed into rings.*

BARBAROUS TREATMENT OF TWENTY-TWO PRISONERS NEAR CHATTANOOGA.

OFFICIAL REPORT OF JUDGE ADVOCATE GENERAL.

JUDGE ADVOCATE GENERAL'S OFFICE,
March 27th, 1863.

Sir: I have the honor to transmit for your consideration, the accompanying depositions of Corporal William Pittinger, Co. G, Second Regiment, Ohio Volunteers; private Jacob Parrott, Co. B, Thirty-third Regiment, Ohio Volunteers; private Robert Buffum, Co. II, Twenty-first Regiment, Ohio Volunteers; Corporal William Reddick, Co. B, Thirty-third Ohio Volunteers; private William Bessinger, Co. G, Twenty-first Ohio Volunteers; taken at this office on the 25th instant, in compliance with your written instructions, from which the following facts will appear. These non-commissioned officers and

---

* See Report of the Committee on the conduct of the war.

privates belonged to an expedition set on foot in April, 1862, at the suggestion of Mr. T. J. Adams, a citizen of Kentucky, who led it, and under the authority and direction of General O. M. Mitchell, the object of which was to destroy the communications of the Georgia State Railroad between Atlanta and Chattanooga.

The mode of operation proposed, was to reach a point on the road where they could seize a locomotive and a train of cars, and then dash back in the direction of Chattanooga, cutting the telegraph wires, and burning the bridges behind them as they advanced, until they reached their own lines. The expedition consisted of twenty-four men, who, with the exception of its leader, Mr. Adams, and another citizen of Kentucky who acted on the occasion as the substitute of a soldier, had been selected from the different companies for their known courage and discretion. They were informed that the movement was to be a secret one, and that they doubtless comprehended something of its perils; but Mr. Adams and Mr. Reddick alone seemed to have known anything of its precise direction or object. They, however, voluntarily engaged in it, and made their way in parties of twos and threes, in citizen's dress, and carrying only their side-arms, to Chattanooga, the point of rendezvous agreed upon, where twenty-two out of the twenty-four arrived safely. There they took passage, without attracting observation, for Marietta, which they reached at twelve o'clock on the night of the 11th of April. The following morning they took the cars back again toward Chattanooga, and at a place called Big Shanty, while the engineer and passengers were breakfasting, they detached the locomotive and three box-cars from the train, and started off at full speed for Chattanooga. They were now upon the field of the perilous

operations proposed by the expedition, but suddenly
encountered unforeseen obstacles. According to the
schedule of the road, of which Mr. Adams had possessed
himself, they should have met but a single train on that
day, whereas they met three, two of them being engaged
on extraordinary service. About an hour was lost in
waiting to allow these trains to pass, which enabled their
pursuers to press closely upon them. They removed
rails, threw out obstructions on the road, and cut the
wires from time to time, and attained, when in motion,
a speed of sixty miles an hour; but the time lost could
not be regained. After having run about one hundred
miles, they found their supply of wood, water, and oil
exhausted, while the rebel locomotive, which had been
chasing them, was in sight. Under these circumstances,
they had no alternative but to abandon their cars and fly
to the woods, which they did under the orders of Mr.
Adams, each one endeavoring to save himself as best he
might.

The expedition thus failed, from causes which neither
reflected upon the genius by which it was planned, nor
upon the intrepidity and discretion of those engaged in
conducting it.

But for the accident of meeting the extra trains, which
could not have been anticipated, the movement would
have been a complete success, and the whole aspect of
the war in the South and South-west would have been
at once changed.

The expedition itself, in the daring of its conception,
had the wildness of a romance, while in the gigantic and
overwhelming results which it sought, and was likely to
accomplish, it was absolutely sublime. The estimate of its
character entertained in the South, will be found fully
expressed in an editorial from the "Southern Confede-

racy," a prominent rebel journal, under date of the 15th of April, and which is appended to, and adopted as, a part of Mr. Pettinger's deposition. The editor says: "The mind and heart sink back, appalled at the bare contemplation of the awful consequences which would have followed the success of this one act. We doubt if the victory of Manassas or Corinth were worth as much to us as the frustration of this grand *coup d'état.*" It is not by any means certain that the annihilation of Beauregard's whole army at Corinth would be so fatal a blow to us as would have been the burning of these bridges at that time by these men."

So soon as those men, comprising the expedition, had left the cars and dispersed themselves in the woods, the population of the country around turned out in their pursuit, employing for their purpose the dogs which are trained to hunt down the fugitive slaves of the South. The whole twenty-two were captured. Among them was Private Jacob Parrott, of Co. K, Thirty-third Regiment Ohio Volunteers. When arrested he was, without any trial, taken possession of by a military officer and four soldiers, who stripped him, bent him over a stone, and, while two pistols were held over his head, a lieutenant in rebel uniform inflicted, with a rawhide, upward of a hundred lashes on his bare back. This was done in the presence of an infuriated crowd, who clamored for his blood, and actually brought a rope with which to hang him. The object of this prolonged scourging was to force this young man to confess to them the object of the expedition, and the names of his comrades, especially. that of the engineer who ran the train. Their purpose was, no doubt, not only to take the life of the latter, if identified, but to do so with every circumstance of humiliation and torture which they could devise. Three

3 *

times, in the progress of this horrible flogging, it was suspended, and Mr. Parrott was asked if he would not confess; but steadily and firmly to the last he refused all disclosure, and it was not till his tormentors were weary of their brutal work, that the task of subduing their victim was abandoned as hopeless. This youth is an orphan, without father or mother, and without any of the advantages of education. Soon after the Rebellion broke out, though but eighteen years of age, he left his trade, and threw himself into the ranks of our armies as a volunteer, and now, though still suffering from the outrages committed on his person in the South, he is on his way to rejoin his regiment, seeming to love his country only the more for all that he had endured in its defence. His subdued and modest manner, while narrating the part he had borne in this expedition, showed him to be wholly unconscious of having done anything more than perform his simple duty as a soldier. Such Spartan fortitude, and such fidelity to the trusts of friendship, deserve an enduring record in the archives of the Government, and will find one, I am sure, in the hearts of a loyal people.

The twenty-two captives, when secured, were thrust into the negro jail of Chattanooga. They occupied a single room, half under ground, and but thirteen feet square, so that there was not space enough for all of them to lie down together, and part of them were in consequence obliged to sleep sitting and leaning against the walls. The only entrance was through a trap-door, in the ceiling, that was raised twice a day to let down their scanty meals, which were lowered in a bucket. They had no other light or ventilation than that which came through two small grated windows. They were covered with swarming vermin; and the heat was so oppressive that they were often obliged to strip themselves entirely of their clothes to bear it. Add to this, they were all handcuffed, and with trace-chains, secured by padlocks around their necks, were fastened to each other in companies of twos and threes. Their food, which was doled out to them twice a day, consisted of a little flour, wet with water, and baked in the form of bread, and spoiled pickled beef. They had no opportunity of procuring any supplies from the outside, nor had they any means of doing so, their pockets having been rifled of their last cent by the Confederate authorities, prominent among whom was an officer wearing the rebel uniform of a major. No part of the money, thus basely taken, was ever returned.

During their imprisonment at Chattanooga, their leader, Mr. Adams, was tried and condemned as a spy, and was subsequently executed at Atlanta on the 7th of June. They were strong, and in perfect health when they entered this negro jail, but at the end of something more than three weeks, when they were required to leave it, they were so exhausted, from the treatment to which they had been subjected, as scarcely to be able to walk; and several staggered from weakness as they passed through the street to the cars.

Finally, twelve of the number, including the five who have deposed, and Mr. Mason, of Company K, Twenty-first Ohio Volunteers, who was prevented from illness giving his evidence, were transferred to the prison of Knoxville, Tennessee. On arriving there, seven of them were arraigned before a court-martial, charged with being spies. Their trial, of course, was summary. They were permitted to be present, but not to hear either the argument of their own counsel, or that of the judge advocate. Their counsel, however, afterwards visited the prison, and read to them the written defence, which he made before the court in their behalf. The substance of that paper is thus stated by one of the witnesses, Corporal Pittinger. He, the counsel, contended, being dressed in citizens' clothes, was nothing more than what the Confederate Government itself had authorized, and only what all the guerrillas in the service of the Confederacy did, on all occasions, when it would be of advantage to them to do so; and he recited the instance of General Morgan having dressed his men in the uniform of our soldiers, and passed them off as being from the Eighth Pennsylvania Cavalry Regiment, and by that means succeeded in reaching a railroad and destroying it. This instance was mentioned to show that our being in citizens' clothes did not take from us the protection awarded to prisoners of war. The plea went on further to state that we had told the object of our expedition; that it was purely a military one for the destruction of communications, and as such lawful according to the rules of war. This just and unanswerable presentation of the case appears to have produced its appropriate impression. Several members of the court-martial afterwards called on the prisoners, and assured them that from the evidence against them they could not be condemned as spies; that they had come for a certain known object, and not having lingered about, or visited any of their camps, obtaining or seeking information, they could not be convicted. Soon thereafter all the prisoners were removed to Atlanta, Georgia, and they left Knoxville under a belief that their comrades who had been tried either had been or would be acquitted. In the mean time, however, the views entertained and expressed to them by the members of the court were overcome, it may be safely assumed, under the prompting of the remorseless despotism at Richmond. On the 18th of June, after their arrival at Atlanta, where they joined their comrades, from whom they had been separated at Chattanooga, their prison-door was opened, and the death sentence of the seven, who had been tried at Knoxville, was read to them. No time for preparation was allowed them. They were told "to bid their friends farewell, and to be quick about it." They were at once tied and carried out to execution. Among the seven was Private Samuel Robinson, Company G, Thirty-third Ohio Volunteers, who was too ill to walk. He was however pinioned, like the rest, and in this condition was dragged from the floor on which he was lying, to the scaffold. In an hour or more the cavalry escort, which had accompanied them, were seen returning with the cart, but the cart was empty. The tragedy had been consummated.

On that evening and the following morning, the prisoners learned from the Provost Marshal and guard that their comrades had died, as all true soldiers of the Republic should die in the presence of its enemies. Among the revolting incidents which they mentioned, in connection with this cowardly butchery, was the fall of two victims from the breaking of the ropes, after they had been some time suspended. On their being restored to consciousness, they begged for an hour in which to pray and prepare for death; but this was refused them. The ropes were readjusted, and the execution at once proceeded.

Among those who thus perished was Private Alfred Wilson, Company C, Twenty-First Ohio Volunteers. He was a mechanic from Cincinnati, who, in the exercise of his trade, had travelled much through the States, north and south, and who had a greatness of soul which sympathized with our struggle for national life, and was in that dark hour filled with joyous convictions of our final triumph. Though surrounded by a scowling crowd impatient for his sacrifice, he did not hesitate, while standing under the gallows, to make them a brief address. He told them that, though they were all wrong, he had no hostile feelings toward the Southern people, believing that not they, but their leaders, were responsible for the rebellion; that he was no spy, as charged, but a soldier regularly detailed for military duty; that he did not regret to die for his country, but only regretted the manner of his death. And he added, for their admonition, that they would yet see the time when the old Union would be restored, and when its flag would wave over them again. And with these words the brave man died. He, like his comrades, calmly met the ignominious doom of a felon, but happily ignominious for him and for them only so far as the martyrdom of the patriot and the hero can be degenerated by the hands of ruffians and traitors.

The remaining prisoners, now reduced to fourteen, were kept closely confined, under a special guard, in the jail at Atlanta, until October, when, overhearing a conversation between the jailor and another officer, they learned and were satisfied that it was the purpose of the authorities to hang them, as they had done their companions. This led them to form a plan for their escape, which they carried into execution on the evening of the next day, by seizing the jailor when he opened the door to carry away the bucket in which their supper had been brought. This was followed by the seizure of the seven guards on duty—and, before the alarm was given, eight of the fugitives were beyond the reach of pursuit. It has been since ascertained that six of these succeeded in reaching our lines. Of the fate of the other two nothing is known. The remaining six of the fourteen, consisting of five witnesses who have deposed and Mr. Mason, were recaptured and confined in the barracks until December when they were removed to Richmond.

There they were shut up in a room in Castle Thunder, where they shivered through the winter, without fire thinly clad, and with but two small blankets, which they had saved with their clothes, to cover the whole party. So they remained until a few days since, when they were exchanged. And thus, at the end of eleven months, terminated their pitiless persecutions in the prisons of the South,—persecutions begun and continued amid indignities and sufferings on their part, and atrocities on the part of their traitorous foes, which illustrate far more faithfully than any human language could express it, the *demoniac spirit* of a revolt every throb of whose life is a crime against the very race to which we belong.

Very respectfully, your obedient servant,

J. HOLT,
Judge Advocate General, U. S. A.

To Hon. E. M. STANTON, Secretary of War.

TREATMENT OF UNION PRISONERS AT RICHMOND.

BELOW is an official statement, from a Committee of Surgeons liberated from Libby Prison, to the President of the United States. It was prepared on their way from Richmond to Fort Monroe, and presented to the President on their arrival at Washington.

STEAMER ADELADE, CHESAPEAKE BAY,
November 26th, 1863.

At a meeting of the Surgeons of the United States Army and Navy, lately confined in prison in Richmond,

Virginia, of which S. P. Ashman, Surgeon Thirty-ninth Ohio Volunteers, was chosen Chairman, and I. McCurdy, Surgeon Eleventh Ohio Volunteers, Secretary, it was

Resolved, That a committee of seven be appointed to prepare a report on the condition and treatment of the Federal prisoners in Richmond, Virginia; also its prisons, quality and quantity of the rations, and treatment of our sick and wounded.

The following committee was appointed:—Daniel Meeker, Surgeon Seventeenth Ohio Volunteers; O. Q. Herrick, Surgeon Thirty-fourth Illinois Volunteers; W. M. Houston, Surgeon One Hundred and Twenty-second Ohio Volunteers; H. J. Herrick, Surgeon Seventeenth Ohio Volunteers; J. Markum Rice, Surgeon Twenty-fourth Massachusetts Volunteers; John T. Luck, Assistant Surgeon United States Navy, and Augustine A. Mann, Assistant Surgeon First Rhode Island Cavalry.

The following report was presented by the president of the committee, which was read, received, and adopted unanimously; after which the committee received the thanks of the meeting, and were then discharged.

The Committee appointed by the United States Army and Navy Surgeons, recently imprisoned in Richmond, Virginia, to report the past and present condition and treatment of Union prisoners, now held at that place, submit the following facts, derived from personal observation, and the statements of fellow-prisoners, in whose veracity they have implicit confidence. The officers, about one thousand in all, and representing nearly all grades of both branches of the service, are confined in seven rooms of Libby Prison, a building formerly used as a warehouse. Each room is forty-three feet wide, and one hundred and two feet long, affording each prisoner about two hundred and seventy-six cubic feet of air.

The rooms have unplastered walls, partitions, and ceilings, but few of the windows are glazed, being open either to the full sweep of cold winds, or closed with boards or canvas, rendering the rooms dark and cheerless.

One of the rooms is used exclusively as a kitchen and dining-room, while portions of others are necessarily devoted to the same purpose, and all of them are scantily furnished, and medium-sized cook-stoves supplied the prison. The officers have to do their own cooking, and the supply of wood for this purpose is often insufficient, and occasionally, for half a day, none at all is sent in. A privy and sink render foul and disgusting one end of each room, polluting, at times, the air of the entire apartment. None are permitted to leave this building of accumulated and accumulating horrors, till borne to the hospital, or happily exchanged.

The enlisted men are confined in various places. At the time the surgeons left Richmond, there were about six thousand three hundred soldiers held on Belle Island, on James River, near the city, and about four thousand soldiers, and fifty sailors and marines, in buildings similar to, and in the immediate vicinity of, Libby.

In the buildings, the condition of the men is about the same as that of the officers in Libby, only they are much more crowded. The condition of those on the Island is much worse. An insufficient number of tents is furnished to protect them from the cold and rain, and no blankets or any other bedding have been given them by the rebels.

Only one surgeon is assigned to Belle Island, and he makes but one visit a day, during which he does not enter the enclosure where the men are kept, to see those too sick to walk, but attends to those only who are able

4

to come to him. When the neglected men are sent to the hospital, it is often too late.

None of the privates in the prisons about "Libby" are furnished with bedding of any kind. A member of this committee received a letter from a man belonging to the same command, and confined in the building opposite Libby, worded thus: "Doctor, we beg of you to try and get us something, either clothes or blankets, to keep us warm. We have no fire in the building to warm us; have nothing either to lie on or cover us, and suffer greatly from cold."

In Libby, stoves for heating purposes have recently been put up in some of the rooms, but no fuel has yet been given to render them useful.

At one time the rations issued consisted of about three-fourths of a pound of wheat bread, one-fourth of a pound of fresh beef, and two ounces of beans, and a small quantity of vinegar and salt for each prisoner per day. Subsequently, the same quantity of corn bread, made of unsifted meal, and rice instead of beans, was issued; or, in lieu of half rice, two or three sweet potatoes, and quite often, more particularly during the past two weeks, absolutely nothing, except three-fourths of a pound of corn bread, has been issued to each prisoner to satisfy the gnawings of hunger for twenty-four hours. On the 10th of this month, the men on Belle Island did not get a morsel of anything to eat until four o'clock P. M.

The Committee unanimously agree that the rations furnished our prisoners by rebel authorities at Richmond are not sufficient to prevent the prisoners from suffering from hunger, and thus becoming debilitated and very susceptible to disease. Some of the committee have seen men brought from Belle Island to the prisoners' hospital *literally starving to death;* and a United States officer of

high rank and undoubted veracity, then and now a prisoner in Libby, told a member of the committee, that,
while on a visit to Belle Island recently, whither he went
by permission of the rebels, the prisoners there followed
him in crowds as he walked around the enclosure, and
cried to him, with eager voices: "We are hungry! send
us bread! send us bread!" Were it not for supplies received from home, none of them confined in Libby and
other prisons would escape the pangs of hunger.

On arriving at the prison, the officers are searched,
and, in addition to articles contraband of war, their money
and other valuables are taken from them. A few got all,
and some the greater portion, but others none of their
money returned, while all other articles are retained. All
money arriving in letters and express packages for the
prisoners, from whatever source, is taken and deposited
with the rebel Quartermaster of Richmond, and the
owner is permitted to draw it in limited amounts, in
rebel paper, though they allow seven dollars in Confederate currency for one dollar in United States money.
Some of the signers, released yesterday, on applying for
the money taken from them in various ways, but always
with the promise that if released with any remainder on
deposit it would be returned in kind, were civilly told
that the aforesaid Quartermaster had exchanged all their
money, and they must take "Confederate" or wait.

The treatment received by the privates is of the greatest severity. For looking out of a window, three nights
since, one was shot and instantly killed. Those having
trades, and also some who have none, are taken out into
the city and compelled to work, guarded, and restrained
from all liberty, by sentries. It was no uncommon sight
to see squads of our men coming back to their prison-
house at night carrying their implements of labor, be-

spotted with whitewash, or showing other signs of having been at work. About thirty of our men are now employed in Richmond making shoes, supposed to be for the rebel army.

Some of the officers have been compelled to scrub the floors, clean the water-closets of the prison, and perform other menial services. All are, and have been at all times since their imprisonment in Libby, subjected to insults and brutal treatment on the part of prison subordinates; and the captain and inspector of the prison, when applied to, not only does not rebuke these subordinates, but encourages them to further offensive conduct.

Upon the most trivial charges, officers have been confined from twenty-four hours to several days in damp dungeons under the jail, and there fed on only bread and water. An officer, for doing that which certainly did not merit the term offence, was put in one of these dungeon-cells, though at the same time convalescent from typhoid fever and too weak to do anything. Not more than two hundred blankets have been given to the prisoners in Libby by the rebels. Were it not for those received from home, and furnished by the Sanitary Commission, all would suffer very much. Twice in the past week, the floors of the prison-house have been scrubbed at sundown, and during the cold night following, with no fire to drive off the moisture, officers have been compelled to lie on these disease-engendering floors, or walk the floor until the morning brought relief by bringing light.

On two other occasions the floors were scrubbed nearly half an hour before the officers were ready to rise from their beds; and thus, in various ways, did the authorities seek to make our condition not only uncomfortable, but dangerous.

After their arrival at the hospital, the sick are not unkindly treated, and the rations given them are a shade better than those issued to them while in the prisons But so enfeebled have they become by the deprivation of food, and so stricken by exposure previous to their admission, that the mortality is great.

The number of deaths among the prisoners at Richmond and on Belle Island, together, have reached the startling number of fifty in a day. All the prison hospitals are insufficiently supplied with medicines for the proper treatment of the sick.

Finally, the members of this Committee individually asseverate, that no prison or penitentiary has ever been seen by them in a northern State which did not surpass in cheerfulness, in healthiness, and abundance of rations issued in them, either of the military prisons of Rich mond, Virginia.

Respectfully,

DANIEL MEEKER, Surgeon U. S. Volunteers.

O. Q. HERRICK, Surgeon 34th Illinois Infantry.

WILLIAM M. HOUSTON, Surgeon 122d Ohio V. I.

H. J. HERRICK, Surgeon 17th Ohio Vol. Infantry.

J. MARCUM RICE, 24th Massachusetts Volunteers.

JOHN T. LUCK, Assistant Surgeon U. S. Navy.

AUGUSTINE A. MANN, Surgeon 1st R. I. Cavalry.

G. P. ASHMAN,

Surgeon 93d O. V. I., Chairman.

J. McCURDY,

Surgeon 11th O. V. I., Secretary.

Rev. George H. Hammer, Chaplain of the Twelfth Pennsylvania Cavalry, who was incarcerated in Libby

4*

Prison, in reference to the treatment of our prisoners, says:—

Many sunk under it, and falling away into living skeletons were passed over to the hospital, in the end of the building, where they lived or died, as circumstances might decide. How often have I seen this? So often that it had long ceased to call forth special attention. Did men fall down exhausted upon the floor, those stronger picked them up, and strove to have them removed to the hospital. Did they die, their bodies were carelessly thrown to one side until convenience suited them to hurry them under ground. During this time the heat was intense, and the suffering from this cause alone very great.

Speaking of their rations, he said: The bread was very unpalatable and unwholesome; the beef oftentimes tainted, and sometimes evidently diseased, as we could see where tumors had been extracted. If, in lieu of rice, we obtained beans or peas, we received no small quantity of animated life in the form of worms, fat and plump. If by any means we offended his supreme highness (the commandant of the prison), our supply of water was cut off for half a day and night, and this during the suffocating weather of summer, or, to vary the punishment and give zest to the regimen, we would be left without wood for three-fourths of a day wherewith to cook our food. I have seen a captain of cavalry, for the simple offence of missing the spittoon, and spitting on the floor, thrown into a dark, damp dungeon for two days and nights, on bread and water, causing serious inflammation. Lieutenant Welch, of the Eighty-seventh Pennsylvania Infantry, lay for six weeks in a dungeon under the building, because, as an orderly sergeant acting under appointment as a lieutenant, although not mustered in, he had rightly classed himself with the enlisted men. When brought up among the other officers, his clothes and shoes, &c., were covered with green mould. Lieutenant Dutton, of the Sixty-seventh Pennsylvania Infantry, has been doomed to a dungeon until the close of the war, and is now suffering for a similar offence, with the additional fact that he assumed the name of another. Colonel Powell, of the Twelfth Virginia Union Cavalry, wounded severely in the back from a window in Wytheville, and left behind, was carried to Richmond, and placed in the hospital. A few days after, one of the Richmond papers railed out against him in a most brutal manner, and suggested he be executed. The prison inspector entered the hospital, and ordered him to get up off his bed and follow him. He was placed in one of the dungeons spoken of, and, upon asking him what were the charges against him, he was answered, God d—n you, you will soon find out. Here, with a ball in his back, he remained five weeks and four days, part of the time without a blanket, rarely receiving any medical care, and sometimes his rations withheld. While he was confined there, the entry-way was frequently blocked up with dead bodies remaining there for several days, and this during the heat of summer. This entry performed another important part, being the place where men and women were brought in to receive their lawful allowance of lashes at the hands of the prison inspectors.

I have so far only given an outline of the treatment and condition of the officers, which in comparison was a favoured one. I cannot describe the condition of the enlisted men. Hunger, bad treatment, and exposure have done their work too surely for many brave souls who have gone to testify at the bar of God to the barbarities practised upon them. Many of them, also, were shot by the guard upon the most frivolous pretences. I have seen our men marched through the city of Richmond barefooted, bareheaded, without coats, and with only the remnants of other articles of clothing. I have seen them brought from this island in the evening, to ship them in the morning for City Point, so weak from hunger and disease that they were unable to stand upon their feet. One of the many nights spent in Libby is engraven upon my mind. A free negro of Philadelphia, nearly white, captured while serving in our navy, received three hundred and twenty lashes. His loud cries and pleadings penetrated every part of the building, as blow followed blow. He was then wrapped in a blanket, saturated with salt and water, and cast into one of the dungeons for a month or so. Such scenes and cries were frequent.

Major Houstain and Lieutenant Von Weltrien, who escaped from Richmond in November, 1863, stated, in a conversation at Fort Monroe, that the cries of the prisoners for food were piteous, and the ravings of the men, rendered insane in many instances by the pangs of hunger, sounded through the Libby building night and day. One man in the room with Major Houstain was so prostrated by want of food, that when a piece of bread was thrown to him by his brutal jailor, he had not the strength to eat it, and died with the scrap in his hand, clutching in death the very staff of life. Rev. James Harvey, Chaplain of the Hundred-and-Tenth Ohio Volunteers, who was taken prisoner at Winchester, Va., says: After spending three days in connection with our hospitals in gathering up our wounded, I found in the dead-room of one of our hospitals files of men who were lying in a state of decomposition. The nurses told me that they could not be taken out, as the stench was such that the room could not be entered.

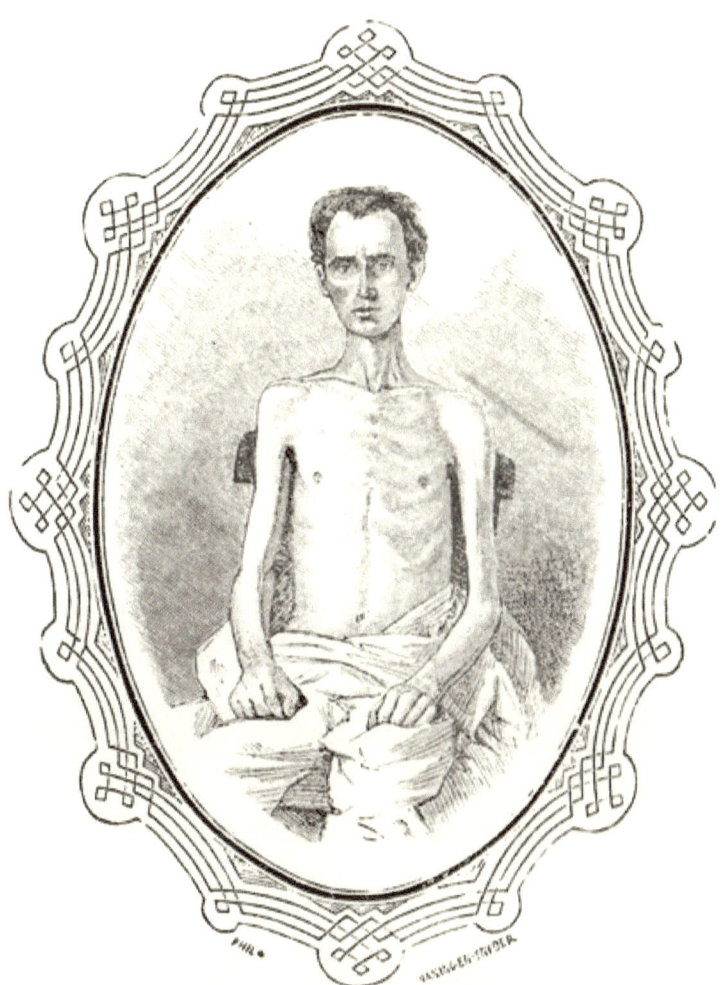

PRIVATE GEORGE H. WIBLE,

Company F, 9th Maryland Volunteers, Admitted from Flag-of-truce boat,
April 18th, 1864.—West's Building Hospital, Baltimore, Md.   35

WRETCHED CONDITION OF UNION PRISONERS, RELEASED FROM RICHMOND.

THE following is a simple statement of facts from a gentleman of undoubted veracity :—

The flag-of-truce boat New York arrived at the Naval School wharf, Annapolis, Maryland, this morning, October 30th, 1863, from City Point, with one hundred and eighty-one paroled men. Eight of the men died on the boat, on its way hither. They had literally been starved to death. Never, in the whole course of my life, have I witnessed such a scene as these men presented. They were living skeletons; every man of them had to be sent to the hospitals, and the surgeon's opinion of them is, that more than one-third of them must die. They are beyond the reach of medicine.

I questioned several of them, and all stated that their condition has been brought on by the treatment which they have received at the hands of the rebels. They have been kept without food, and exposed, a large portion of the time, without shelter of any kind.

To look at the attenuated and squalid condition of these poor men, and listen to their tales of woe and agony, as to how they have been treated, one would not suppose they had fallen into the hands of Southern Chivalry! but rather into the hands of savage barbarians, destitute of all humanity or feeling.

The following is a letter addressed to the editor of the Daily Chronicle, of Washington, by Rev. E. W. Hutter, Pastor of St. Matthew's Lutheran Church, New Street, Philadelphia, in regard to the prisoners referred to in the above.

ANNAPOLIS, MARYLAND,
December 1st, 1863.

Dear Sir: Although the statements respecting the extreme wretchedness of the Union prisoners returned from Richmond, seemed to me to be so well authenticated as to preclude all possibility of doubt or mistake, I yet resolved to satisfy myself of their truthfulness, or otherwise, by actual personal observation. To this step I was prompted by no desire to gratify a mere idle curiosity, but to render to those poor men, if possible, all the good that might be in my power. "He that knoweth to do good," says St. James, "and doeth it not, to him it is sin." Nor are we, in our ministrations of mercy, to wait until occasions for their exercise present themselves at our doors, but, in imitation of our blessed Redeemer, we are to seek them out.

Actuated by motives such as these, I paid a visit to the Government Hospitals at Annapolis, and proceed to furnish you with a statement of the condition of the prisoners recently returned from Richmond. In my visit there, I was most kindly assisted by Rev. H. C. Henries, the laborious and self-denying chaplain in charge of that place. Be assured, it is not possible to exaggerate the scenes there presented; they defy the descriptive powers of language. The pictorial representation in Harper's Weekly, so far from being an exaggeration, affords but a very inadequate view of these scenes of wretchedness. In my pastoral experience, I have stood at the bed-side of many dying sufferers—often have I seen the human frame painfully reduced by the ravages of consumption—but never before have my sensibilities been so shocked as at Annapolis. To look upon men who, a short time since, were robust and stalwart men, not brutes—immortal men, created by a com-

mon Father, and redeemed by a common Lord—to see
such reduced to wasted and bony skeletons, by withhold-
ing from them the "daily bread," for the production of
which the Lord of heaven and earth sends his genial
sunshine and his refreshing rains—Oh! this was a
scene which, in this land of plenty, enriched by the
superabundant goodness of God, I never expected to
witness. Such scenes I did witness only to-day, in the
hospitals at this place—men, from emaciated bodies,
breathing out their spirits into the hands of God, whose
death has been literally wrought by the murderous process of *starvation.* An unspeakable satisfaction to me
was it, to be permitted, in company with the beloved
Chaplain, to point a number of such dying starvelings to
"the Lamb of God who taketh away the sins of the
world." In every instance, when it was in the power of
these poor men to speak, the last lingering accents or
their lips consisted of petitions to Christ for the remis-
sion of their sins, and in the supplication of blessings
from the Almighty Ruler of the world on their beloved
country. Very few of these men, after their arrival here,
have been able to articulate; they could only signify
their wishes by *looks* and signs. From the few who
were able to speak, it is a noteworthy fact, that I did not
hear a solitary murmur of complaint that they had enlisted in the service of their country, or that, by the
mysteriousness of Providence, they had been doomed, for
such a cause, to die even so ghastly and horrible a death.
Like the Apostles of our Lord, these heroic men seem
content, in the prosecution of their noble work, to endure
even worse things than a baptism of blood and a martyrdom of fire—even a horror not confronted by the Apostles themselves, viz., *Starvation.*

In my intercourse with these famishing victims of

Southern barbarity, I was exceedingly anxious to learn
their own impressions as to the causes that underlie the
action of the Rebel Government toward themselves,—
whether the treatment they had received at Richmond
was voluntary or compulsory. If the former, it would,
of course, be the fault of their enemies; if the latter,
their misfortune. With one accord, the answer was, that
their dreadful condition was mostly voluntary, the result
of a system of wanton and deliberate cruelty. The Richmond conspirators, our prisoners admit, are in straits, and
have it not in their power to bestow upon them even a
tolerable degree of care and attention; but their condition is not so desperate, that they might not, if they
wished, afford them at least as much daily food as would
serve to sustain life. Their own destitution the rebels
seize upon, not as a real and truthful justification of
their inhumanity, but as a pretext; and this they do, not
in sorrow, but in the intense maliciousness of diabolism
itself. They gloat over it, that, for the display of their
fiendish cruelty, they have an argument plausible enough
to quit themselves in their own wicked foregone con-
clusions, however transparent its flimsiness to all the
world beside. I stood at the bedside of a dying youth,
from Tennessee; I kneeled at his bedside in prayer; he
claimed to have made his peace with God, through faith
in Jesus Christ. In the very article and hour of death,
when all purposes are honest, and all secrets are revealed,
I asked him: Do you think, my young brother, that the
men in Richmond have starved you to death from choice,
or were they driven to it from necessity? His answer
was, "God forgive them, they might have done better if
they wished." The utterance of another was, "I know
they could have given us more food than they did, from
the amount they gave to the guards; but they wished us

to starve." One of their leading men said to me, "Libby Prison and Belle Island are our best generals—they are killing off more men than Bragg and Lee!"

One other fact I learned most discreditable to the rebel authorities. Bell Island is a contracted patch of ground, consisting of only three or four acres, on which thousands of prisoners are crowded, with scarcely a foot of intervening space. The water they are compelled to drink is in close proximity to the sinks, and necessarily polluted and poisoned. This the prisoners are compelled to drink, in very sight of clear and wholesome water, which is running in perennial streams before their eyes. Their hardships are thus purposely aggravated, and under them, an iron constitution melts away as frost before a summer's sun. This, indeed, is the very refinement of cruelty.

From another of the dying men, I learned the astonishing fact, that since the incarceration of our poor prisoners at Richmond, in no solitary instance has a woman appeared in their midst to minister even to our wounded and dying. From the "gentler sex," ordinarily so noted for the finer and better sensibilities of human nature, not one of our prisoners has received as much as a "cup of cold water"—nothing but insults and reproaches. How strikingly this contrasts with the kindness lavished by the ladies of the North on the suffering rebels whom the "accidents" of war have thrown into our hands! After the battle of Gettysburg, numbers of ladies from Philadelphia and elsewhere hastened to the scene, and distributed stores, to the amount of thousands, indiscriminately—between the parties they made no distinction. Had they been monsters in human shape, they might then have suffered thousands of rebels to die of neglect; but it sufficed for them to know, that although engaged

5

in a gigantic iniquity—such as has not been paralleled in the annals of crime since the crucifixion of Jesus on Calvary—these misguided men were nevertheless of a race of our universal manhood, redeemed by the blood of Christ. This consideration alone sufficed to secure them a passport to the enlarged sympathies and the most generous and substantial aid of our Christian ladies. This, as thousands can and do attest, was spontaneously rendered, "without respect of persons," in no pharisaical spirit, but in that of unsophisticated truth and soberness. May we, who espouse the cause of the Union, thank God that such cruelty and inhumanity as are now under re view may not be charged to us!

To the conduct of the rebel conspirators it adds monstrous aggravation, that these barbarities are being enacted in Richmond, under the immediate cognisance of the so-called "Confederate" authorities Had they ever occurred in the wilds of Arkansas or Texas, or among the Sioux savages on the Pembina, they might challenge some degree of palliation; but, when we call to mind that the voluntary starvation of defenceless men is occurring at Richmond, within the sound of the voices of Jefferson Davis, Judah P. Benjamin, and their associates in crime, then does the bogus Confederacy itself become responsible for these atrocities to God and man; and impartial men, all the world over, who use all efforts to bewilder the human mind, by leading it into a mazy labyrinth of doubt, will reach the inevitable conclusion, that these men deserve the scorn of the civilized world, not to speak of the just vengeance of Heaven. Surely, surely, the vengeance of an incensed Omnipotence must ultimately overtake them!

Very truly, your friend,

E. W. HUTTER,
Pastor of St. Matthew's Lutheran Church, Phil'a.

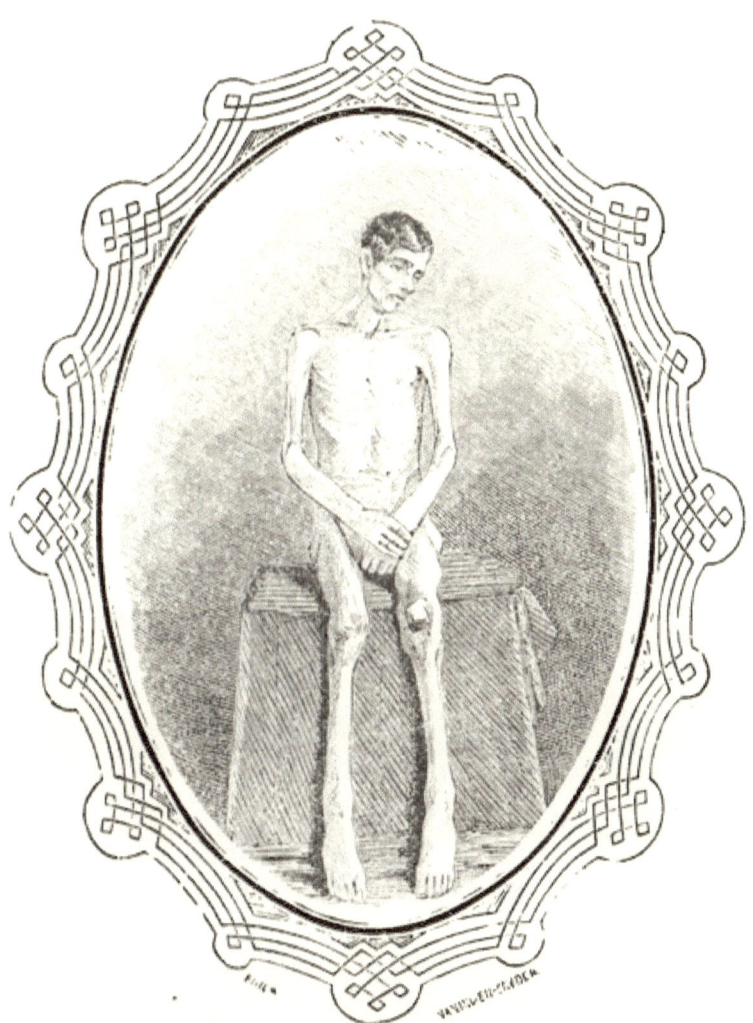

PRIVATE L. H. PARHAM.

Company B, 3d West Tennessee Cavalry, Admitted per Steamer New York, from Richmond, Va., May 2d, 1864. Died May 10th 1864, from effects of treatment while in the hands of the enemy.—U. S. General Hospital, Div. No. 1, Annapolis, Md.   51

RELEASED PRISONERS.

REPORT of the Committee on the Conduct of the War on the condition of our released prisoners, after their confinement in the dens, and prisons, and unsheltered fields, at and near Richmond :— -

IN SENATE,
Wednesday, May 9, 1864.

Mr. Wade, from the Joint Committee on the Conduct and Expenditures of the War, submitted the following Report, with the accompanying testimony :—

On the 4th instant your committee received a communication of that date from the Secretary of War, enclosing the Report of Colonel Hoffman, commissary-general of prisoners, dated May 3, calling the attention of the committee to the condition of returned Union prisoners, with the request that the committee would immediately proceed to Annapolis, "and examine with their own eyes the condition of those who have returned from rebel captivity." The committee resolved that they would comply with the request of the Secretary of War on the first opportunity. The 5th of May was devoted by the committee to conclude their labors upon the investigation of the Fort Pillow massacre. On the 6th of May, however, the committee proceeded to Annapolis and Baltimore, to examine the condition of our returned soldiers, and took the testimony of several of them, together with the testimony of surgeons, and other persons in attendance upon the hospitals. That testimony, with the communication of the Secretary of War, and the Report of Colonel Hoffman, is herewith submitted.

The evidence proves, beyond all manner of doubt, a determination on the part of the rebel authorities, delibe-

rately and persistently practised for a long time past, to
subject those of our soldiers who have been so unfortunate as to fall into their hands, to a system of treatment
which has resulted in reducing many of those who have
survived, and been permitted to return to us, to a condition, both physically and mentally, which no language
we can use can adequately describe. Though nearly all
the patients now in the Naval Academy Hospital, at An
napolis, and in the West Hospital, at Baltimore, have
been under the kindest and most intelligent treatment
for about three weeks past, and many of them for a
greater length of time, still they present literally the
appearance of living skeletons—many of them being
nothing but skin and bone. Some of them are maimed
for life, from being exposed to the inclemency of the
winter season on Belle Isle—being compelled to lie upon
the bare ground, without tents or blankets—some of
them without overcoats, or even coats—with but little
fire to mitigate the severity of the wind and storms to
which they were exposed.

The testimony shows that the general practice of their
captors was to rob them, as soon as they were taken pri
soners, of all their money, valuables, blankets, and good
clothing, for which they received nothing in exchange,
except, perhaps, some old worn-out rebel clothing, hardly
better than none at all. Upon their arrival at Richmond
they have been confined, without blankets or other covering, in buildings without fire, or upon Belle Isle, in
many cases with no shelter, and in others with nothing
but discarded army tents, so injured by rents and holes
as to present but little barrier to the winds and storms.
On several occasions the witnesses say they have risen
in the morning from their resting-places upon the bare
earth, and found several of their comrades frozen to

death through the night; and that many others would
have met the same fate had they not walked rapidly back
and forth through the hours which should have been devoted to sleep, for the purpose of retaining sufficient
warmth to preserve life. In respect to the food furnished
to our men by the rebel authorities, the testimony proves
that the ration of each man was hardly sufficient in
quantity to preserve the life of a child, even had it been
of proper quality, which it was not. It consisted usually,
at the most, of two small pieces of corn bread, made in
many instances, as the witnesses say, of corn and cobs
ground together, and badly prepared and cooked; of
perhaps two ounces of meat, usually of poor quality,
and unfit to be eaten; and occasionally a few black,
worm-eaten beans, or something of that kind. Many of
our men were compelled to sell to their guards and others,
for what price they could get, such clothing and blankets
as they were permitted to receive and have furnished for
their use by our Government, in order to obtain sufficient food to sustain life; thus, by endeavoring to avoid
one privation, reducing themselves to the same destitute
condition, in respect to clothing and covering, as they
were in before they received any from our Government.
When they became diseased and sick, in consequence of
this exposure and privation, and were admitted into the
hospital, their treatment was little if any improved as to
food, though they doubtless suffered less from exposure
to cold than before. Their food still remained insufficient in quantity, and altogether unfit in quality. Their
diseases and wounds did not receive the treatment which
the commonest dictates of humanity would have prompted.
One witness, whom your committee examined, who had
lost all the toes of one foot, through being frozen on
Belle Isle, states that for days at a time his wounds were

5 *

not dressed, and that they had not been dressed for four days when he was taken from the hospital and carried on the flag-of-truce boat for Fortress Monroe. In reference to the condition to which our men were reduced by cold and hunger, your committee would give the following extracts from the testimony:—

One witness testifies—I had no blankets until our Government sent us some.

Quest.—How did you sleep before you received those blankets?

Ans.—We used to get together just as close as we could, and sleep spoon-fashion, so that when one turned over we all had to turn over.

Another witness testifies:—

Quest.—Were you hungry all the time?

Ans.—Hungry! I could eat anything in the world that came before us. Some of the boys would get boxes from the North, with meat of different kinds in them, and after they had picked the meat off, they would throw the bones away into the spit-boxes, and we would pick the bones out of the spit-boxes, and gnaw them over again!

In addition to this insufficient supply of food, clothing, and shelter, our soldiers, while prisoners, have been subjected to the most cruel treatment from those placed over them. They have been abused, and shamefully treated, on almost every opportunity. Many have been mercilessly shot and killed when they failed to comply with all the demands of their jailors; sometimes for violating rules of which they had not been informed. Crowded in great numbers in buildings, they have been fired at and killed by the sentinels outside, when they appeared at the windows for the purpose of obtaining a little fresh air. One man, whose comrade in the service and in captivity had been so fortunate as to be among those released from further torments, was shot dead as he was waving with his hand a last adieu to his friend. Other instances of equally unprovoked murder are disclosed by the testimony.

The condition of our returned soldiers, as regards personal cleanliness, has been filthy almost beyond description. Their clothes have been so dirty and covered with vermin, that those who have received these men have been compelled to destroy their clothing, and re-clothe them with new and clean raiment. Their boots and hats have been so infested with vermin that, in some instances, repeated washings have failed to remove them, and those who have received them in charge, have been compelled to cut all the hair from their heads, and make applications to destroy the vermin. Some have been received with no clothing but shirts, and drawers, and pieces of blankets, or other outside covering; entirely destitute of coats, hats, shoes, or stockings; and the bodies of those better supplied with clothing have been equally filthy with the others, many who have been sick and in the hospital having had no opportunity to wash their bodies for weeks and months before they were released from captivity.

Your committee are unable to convey any adequate idea of the sad and deplorable condition of the men they saw in the hospitals they visited, and the testimony they have taken cannot convey to the reader the impressions which your committee there received. The prisoners we saw, as we were assured by those in charge of them, have greatly improved since they have been received in the hospitals, yet they are now dying daily, one of them being in the very throes of death; and your committee stood by his bed-side and witnessed the sad spectacle

there presented. All those whom your committee examined, stated that they have been thus reduced and
emaciated entirely in consequence of the merciless treat
ment they received while prisoners, from their enemies
Physicians in charge of them—the men best fitted by
their profession and experience to express an opinion
upon the subject—all say that they have no doubt the
statements of their patients are entirely correct.

It will be observed from the testimony, that all the
witnesses who testified upon that point, state that the
treatment they received, while confined at Columbia,
South Carolina, Dalton, Georgia, and other places, was
far more humane than that they received at Richmond,
where the authorities of the so-called Confederacy were
congregated, and where the power existed, had the in-
clination not been wanting, to reform these abuses, and
secure to the prisoners they held, some treatment that
would bear a feeble comparison to that accorded by our
authorities to the prisoners in our custody. Your committee, therefore, are constrained to say that they can
hardly avoid the conclusion expressed by so many of
our released soldiers, that the inhuman practices herein
referred to, are the result of a determination, on the part
of the rebel authorities, to reduce our soldiers in their
power by privation of food and clothing, and by exposure, to such a condition that those who may survive,
shall never recover so as to be able to enter into effective
service in the field; and your committee accordingly ask
that this report, with the accompanying testimony, be
printed, with the report and testimony in relation to the
massacre of Fort Pillow—the one being, in their opinion,
no less than the other the result of a predetermined
policy. As regards the assertions of some of the rebel
newspapers, that our prisoners have received at their

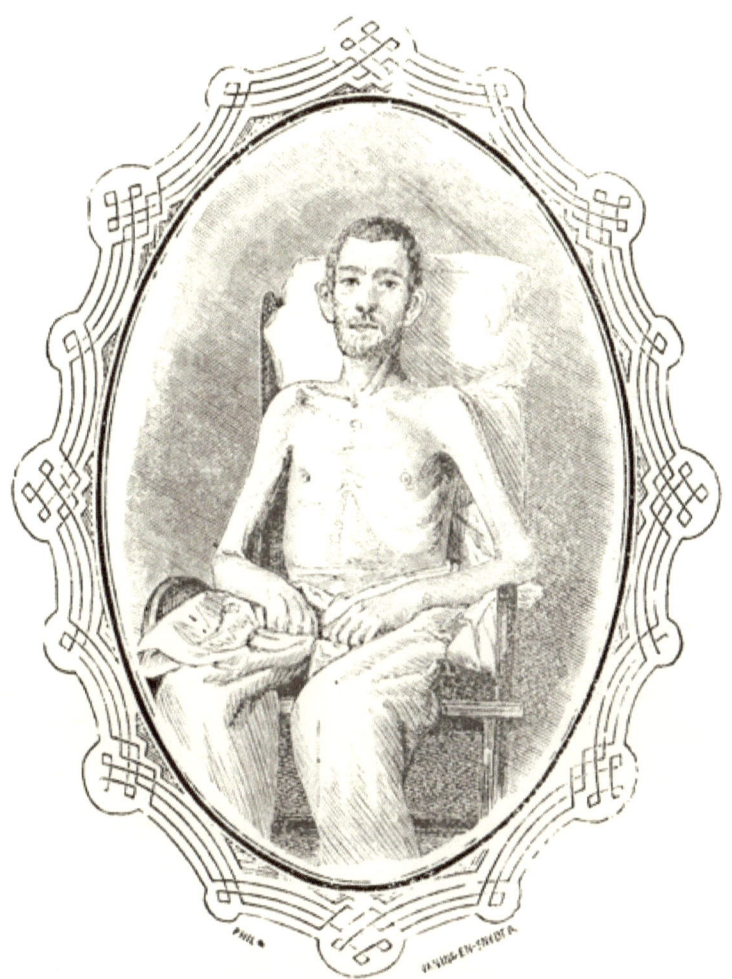

PRIVATE EDWARD CUNNINGHAM.

Company F, 7th Ohio Cavalry, Admitted from Flag-of-truce boat, April
16th, 1864.—West's Building Hospital, Baltimore, Md.   35

hands the same treatment that their own soldiers in the
field have received, they are evidently but the most
glaring and unblushing falsehoods. No one can, for a
moment, be deceived by such statements, who will reflect
that our soldiers who, when taken prisoners, have been
stout, healthy men, in the prime and vigor of life, yet
have died by hundreds under the treatment they have
received, although required to perform no duties of the
camp or the march; while the rebel soldiers are able to
make long and rapid marches, and to offer a stubborn
resistance in the field.

There is one feature connected with this investigation
to which your committee can refer with pride and satisfaction; that is, the uncomplaining fortitude, the undi-
minished patriotism exhibited by our brave men under
all their privations—even in the hour of death. Your
committee would close their report by quoting the
tribute paid these men by the Chaplain of the hospital
at Annapolis, who has ministered to so many of them in
their last moments, who has smoothed their passage to
the grave by his kindness and attention, and who has
performed the last sad offices over their lifeless remains.
He says:—

"There is one thing I should wish to state. All the
men, without any exception, among the thousands that
have come to this hospital, have never, in a single instance, expressed a regret (notwithstanding the privations and sufferings they have endured) that they entered
their country's service. They have been the most loyal,
devoted, and earnest men. Even in the last day of their
lives, they have said that all they hoped for was just to
live and enter the ranks again, and meet their foes. It
is a most glorious record in reference to the devotion of
our men to their country. I do not think their patriotism has ever been equalled in the history of the world."

TREATMENT OF PRISONERS CAPTURED AT THE BATTLE OF CHICKAMAUGA

DIARY OF A SOLDIER.

STEWARD'S HOSPITAL, September 20th, 1863.

AT nine·o'clock this morning, I was wounded and captured by the rebels; was hurried to the rear as fast as possible, with quite a number of our wounded. We were taken to the Steward's Hospital, some three miles from the battle-field; were put out upon the ground, with no shelter whatever, and a great many of us had no blankets. There were some eighty of our wounded at this place. Dr. Hamilton (rebel) came round and examined our wounds. Some of the worst cases were washed, and partially dressed. Toward evening, all that were able were marched off—Captain McWilliams and Lieutenant Cole, of the Fifty-first Illinois Infantry, were among them; about sundown we were forced to believe our troops were falling back. The rebels are jubilant; they say they have captured half of Rosecrans's army.

September 21st.—To-day the rebels have been so jubilant on what they term the "Yankee rout," that they have taken no notice whatever of the men lying weltering in their blood, suffering beyond description.

September 22d.—To-day we had a man die. Dr. Story (rebel) has been put in charge of all the Yankee wounded. He appears to be a gentleman, but as yet there has been nothing done for the wounded, who are suffering intensely.

September 23d.—To-day the doctors dressed most of the wounds. Many of the men have shattered limbs, and are suffering beyond description. We have had nothing to eat since we came here.

September 24th.—Two of our men died to-day. They had shattered limbs, and the worms had got into their wounds. Had they had proper attention they probably could have been saved.

September 25th.—The rebels say they have driven Rosecrans over the river, also Burnside out of East Tennessee. The 'doctors are having a spree over it—no attention has been paid us to-day; there are two or three hundred rebel wounded here that have to be attended to first. One man died to-day.

September 26th.—To-day we drew the first rations we have had since we came—a ration consisting of half a pint of corn meal and two ounces of beef, a miserable pittance for a hungry man. No doctor has been near to-day. Some of the men are suffering intensely; the rebels don't seem to care how many of us die. Heavy firing heard in the direction of Chattanooga.

September 27th.—We lost one man by death to-day. Two of the boys have had limbs amputated—both will probably die. The boys are suffering a great deal from their wounds; mortification has taken place in many instances, while some have worms in their wounds. Many are very sick; no medicine to be had.

September 28th.—We lost two by death to-day; arteries burst, surgeons absent—bled to death! We have nothing to eat to-day. I believe they mean to starve us to death. It is a pitiful sight to see the haggard countenances of the men. To-day they have sent two hundred rebel wounded to the hospitals.

September 29th.—Dr. Hamilton told us, this morning, that arrangements have been made to send all through our lines. We drew rations to-day.

September 30th.—To-day our boys are trading their pocket-knives and everything they can for rations.

There is scarcely five dollars among us. The miserable thieves robbed us of everything we had. To-day has been a day of intense suffering among our men. It has rained all day, and we have no shelter.

October 1st.—It rained all last night; we look like a set of drowned rats. Some of the boys are very sick; many must die with such treatment. The sergeant of the guard procured a tent for eight of us. Dr. Story does all he can for us. We drew our pittance of corn meal to-day.

October 2d.—We expect to leave here to-day. I sincerely hope we will; I long to be in God's country once more, and behold the good old flag again. The lice and filth here are intolerable.

October 3d.—No signs of leaving yet. Dr. Story is doing his best to make us comfortable, but we have no bandages with which to dress our wounds. Two deaths to-day.

October 4th.—To-day is very cold; we have no blankets, hence there is a great deal of suffering from cold. Our rations have run out, and taking all things into consideration it would be hard to embitter our condition.

October 5th.—Heavy cannonading has been going on in the front all day. The Rebels say they are shelling Chattanooga. We learned to-day that the armistice was over, and that we would have to take a trip to Richmond; the trip will doubtless kill quite a number of us. We got our mush to-day. Intense suffering from cold nights.

October 6th.—We expected to leave here to-day for Atlanta, but for some reason the ambulances have not come. All we have to eat is mush, with little or no salt in it. Many are suffering from diarrhœa.

October 7th.—To-day we drew rations of flour. Captain Foster, Forty-second Illinois, is baking bread. One of our men died to-day. We have lost fourteen by death since we came here.

October 8th.—At nine A. M., this morning, we were stowed in lumber-wagons and hauled to Ringgold, a distance of eight miles, over the roughest road I ever travelled; many of the men were so sick that they could not raise their heads.

October 9th.—Last night they put one hundred and eighty of us into box-cars and brought us to Dalton, where we stopped for the night. We had to sleep in the cars; and they gave us no supper. The night was very cold; it was heart-rending to witness the suffering among the sick and wounded. This morning, we left for Dalton without breakfast, and arrived at Atlanta, Georgia, at six A. M. We were then taken to a military prison, where we now lie upon the ground, with no shelter and no fires. Our wounds have not been dressed for three days. The stench is awful.

October 10th.—We are under the charge of our own doctors here, but the rebels won't furnish bandages to dress the wounds. I never suffered so from hunger in all my life. They have been promising us rations all day, and now they tell us it will be here early in the morning. The boys are selling their rings and everything they have for something to eat.

October 11th.—We are a little more comfortable to-day; the surgeons have amputated several limbs, and dressed all the wounds. One man died this morning. On the 7th instant, one of our men was shot by the guard for going too near the fence. One of our officers is here, carrying around a thirty-two pound ball and chain. Several of the men are handcuffed.

October 12th.—Two men died last night; the wounded

6

are doing pretty well under treatment of our surgeons. We get a little better rations, but not enough. Later— All the wounded that were able, were taken out of prison and put in tents. Things are much more comfortable here.

October 13th.—This morning the names of all those who are able to travel were taken. We start for Richmond to-morrow. We drew five days' rations to-night— ten crackers and half a pound of pork to a man.

October 14th.—At two A. M. we fell in, marched down to the depot, a distance of one mile; many of us had to go on crutches. There were over two hundred of us, and we were put into five box-cars. Only those who have experienced it know how we suffered on the train; for eight days we were jammed up in these cars. One of our number died, and we had to leave several at hospitals on the road. Our five days' rations lasted only two, and those who had no money had to share with the rest. Bread was a dollar a loaf, and pies sold as high as two dollars. The 15th, 16th, 17th, 18th, 19th, and 20th were spent in the cars.

October 21st.—Arrived at Richmond, and were put in Libby. Although we found this a miserable hole, it was much better than the filthy, lousy cars. When we got to Libby we were as nearly starved as men can be, and navigate. We drew our rations here, and got our wounds dressed, although no surgeon was there.

October 22d.—To-day they have stopped our rations for punishment. Four men escaped from Castle Thunder last night. We got grub from our officers, who are confined above, but we have to be very sly, as they allow no communications to be held between us and them.

October 23d.—They still keep our rations from us. The wounded are doing pretty well, but we are all so dirty and filthy it is a wonder we don't catch some contagious disease; we can get no soap to wash with.

October 24th.—This morning all the wounded were taken to the Alabama Hospital, and all those that were not wounded were sent to Belle Isle, to remain there until exchanged or starved to death, the latter the most probable.

October 25th.—We are much more comfortably situated than we were in Libby. We have a very good room, yet we have no blankets, and have to sleep on the floor. There is no medicine even here.

October 26th.—Nothing of importance to-day.

October 27th.—To-day they took the names of one hundred and eighty-five of the worst wounded to exchange at nine P. M. We were put in a scow, and started for City Point.

October 28th.—We are now on the flag-of-truce boat New York. The stars and stripes float proudly above us, yet it is a sorrowful sight to see the poor boys look like skeletons. I venture not more than ten of our number will weigh one hundred pounds. I fear quite a number of the boys will die; they are beyond medical skill.

October 29th.—I feel like a white man, now, the first time since I was captured. We are now in St. John's College Hospital. Each one of us had to take a good scrub, and were put into a clean shirt, after which the most welcome of all things came—a beautiful roast. I trust our troubles are ended for a season.

THE FORT PILLOW MASSACRE.

REPORT OF THE COMMITTEE ON THE CONDUCT OF THE WAR.

MESSRS. WADE AND GOOCH, the sub-committee appointed by the Joint Committee on the Conduct and Expenditures of the War, with instructions to proceed to such points as they might deem necessary for the purpose of taking testimony in regard to the massacre at Fort Pillow, submitted the following report to the joint committee, together with the accompanying testimony and papers.

In obedience to the instructions of this joint committee, adopted on the 18th ultimo, your committee left Washington on the morning of the 19th, taking with them the stenographer of this committee, and proceeded to Cairo and Mound City, Illinois, Columbus, Kentucky, and Fort Pillow and Memphis, Tennessee, at each of which places they proceeded to take testimony.

Although your committee were instructed to inquire only in reference to the attack, capture, and massacre of Fort Pillow, they have deemed it proper to take some testimony in reference to the operations of Forrest and his command, immediately preceding and subsequent to that horrible transaction. It will appear from the testimony thus taken, that the atrocities committed at Fort Pillow were not the result of passions excited by the heat of conflict, but were results of a policy deliberately decided upon, and unhesitatingly announced. Even if the uncertainty of the fate of those officers and men, belonging to colored regiments, who have heretofore been taken prisoners by the rebels, has failed to convince the authorities of our Government of this fact, the testi

mony herewith submitted must convince even the most
sceptical that it is the intention of the rebel authorities
not to recognise the officers and men of our colored
regiments, as entitled to the treatment accorded by all
civilized nations to prisoners of war. The declarations
of Forrest and his officers, both before and after the capture of Fort Pillow, as testified to by such of our men as
have escaped after being taken by him; the threats contained in the various demands for surrender made at
Paducah, Columbus, and other places; the renewal of
the massacre the morning after the capture of Fort
Pillow; the statements made by the rebel officers to the
officers of our gunboats, who received the few survivors
at Fort Pillow—all this proves most conclusively the
policy they have determined to adopt.

The first operation of any importance was the attack
upon Union City, Tennessee, by a portion of Forrest's
command. The attack was made on the 24th of March.
The post was occupied by a force of about five hundred
men, under Colonel Hawkins, of the Seventh Tennessee
Union Cavalry. The attacking force was superior in
numbers, but was repulsed several times by our own
forces. For the particulars of the attack, and the circumstances attending the surrender, your committee
would refer to the testimony submitted. They would
state, however, that it would appear from the testimony
that the surrender was opposed by nearly if not quite all
the officers of Colonel Hawkins's command. Your committee think that the circumstances connected with the
surrender are such that they demand the most searching
investigation by the military authorities, as, at the time
of the surrender, but one man on our side had been
injured.

On the 25th of March, the enemy, under the rebel

6 *

Generals Forrest, Buford, Harris, and Thompson, estimated at over six thousand men, made an attack on Paducah, Kentucky, which post was occupied by Colonel S. G. Hicks, Fortieth Illinois Regiment, with six hundred and fifty-five men. Our forces retired into Fort Anderson, and there made their stand, assisted by some gunboats belonging to the command of Captain Shirk, of the navy, successfully repelling the attacks of the enemy. Failing to make any impression upon our forces, Forrest then demanded an unconditional surrender, closing his communication to Colonel Hicks in these words: "If you surrender you shall be treated as prisoners of war. But if I have to storm your works you may expect no quarter." This demand and threat was met by a refusal on the part of Colonel Hicks to surrender, he stating that he had been placed there by his Government to defend that post, and he should do so. The rebels made three other assaults that same day, but were repulsed with heavy loss each time; the rebel General Thompson being killed in the last assault. The enemy retired next day, having suffered a loss estimated at three hundred killed, and from one thousand to twelve hundred wounded. The loss on our side was fourteen killed and forty-six wounded.

The operations of the enemy at Paducah were characterized by the same bad faith and treachery that seems to have become the settled policy of Forrest and his command. The flag of truce was taken advantage of there, as elsewhere, to secure desirable positions which the rebels were unable to obtain by fair and honorable means; and also to afford opportunities for plundering private stores as well as Government property. At Paducah the rebels were guilty of acts more cowardly, if possible, than any they have practised elsewhere. When the attack was made, the officers of the fort and of the gunboats advised the women and children to go to the river, for the purpose of being taken across out of danger. As they were leaving the town for that purpose the rebel sharpshooters mingled with them, and, shielded by their presence, advanced and fired upon the gunboats, wounding some of our officers and men. Our forces could not return the fire without endangering the lives of the women and children. The rebels also placed women in front of their lines as they moved on the fort, or were proceeding to take positions, while the flag of truce was at the fort in order to compel our men to withhold their fire, out of regard for the lives of the women, who were made use of in this most cowardly manner. For more full details of the attack, and the treacherous and cowardly practices of the rebels there, your committee refer to the testimony herewith submitted.

On the 13th of April, the day after the capture of Fort Pillow, the rebel General Buford appeared before Columbus, Kentucky, and demanded its unconditional surrender. He coupled with that demand a threat that if the place was not surrendered, and he should be compelled to attack it, "no quarter whatever should be shown to negro troops." To this Colonel Lawrence, in command of the fort, replied that "surrender was out of the question, as he had been placed there by his Government to hold and defend the place, and should do so." No attack was made, but the enemy retired, having taken advantage of the flag of truce to take some horses of Union citizens, which had been brought in there for security.

It was at Fort Pillow, however, that the brutality and cruelty of the rebels were most fearfully exhibited. The garrison there, according to the last returns received at head-quarters, amounted to nineteen officers and five

hundred and thirty-eight enlisted men, of whom two
hundred and sixty-two men were colored troops, comprising one battalion of the Sixth United States Heavy
Artillery (formerly the First Alabama Artillery) of
colored troops, under command of Major W. J. Booth;
one section of the Second United States Light Artillery,
colored, and one battalion of the Thirteenth Tennessee
Cavalry, white, commanded by Major W. F. Bradford.
Major Booth was the ranking officer, and was in command of the fort.

On Monday, the 12th of April, the anniversary of the
attack on Fort Sumter, in April, 1861, the pickets of the
garrison were driven in just before sunrise, that being
the first intimation our forces then had of any intention
on the part of the enemy to attack that place. Fighting
soon became general, and, about nine o'clock, Major
Booth was killed. Major Bradford succeeded to the
command, and withdrew all the forces within the fort.
They had previously occupied some intrenchments at
some distance from the fort, and further from the river.

This fort was situated on a high bluff, which descended
precipitately to the river's edge, the ridge of the bluff on
the river side being covered with trees, bushes, and
fallen timber. Extending back from the river on either
side of the fort was a ravine or hollow, the one below
the fort containing several private stores and some dwellings, constituting what was called the town. At the
mouth of that ravine, and on the river bank, were some
Government buildings containing commissary stores.
The ravine above the fort was known as Cold Creek
Ravine, the ridge being covered with trees and bushes.
To the right, or below, and a little to the front of the
fort was a level piece of ground, not quite so elevated as
the fort itself, on which had been erected some log huts,

or shanties, which were occupied by the white troops, and also used for hospital and other purposes. Within the fort tents had been erected with board floors, for the use of the colored troops. There were six pieces of artillery in the fort, consisting of two six-pounders, two twelve-pounder howitzers, and two ten-pounder Parrots.

The rebels continued their attack, but up to two or three o'clock in the afternoon they had not gained any decisive success. Our troops, both white and black, fought most bravely, and were in good spirits. The gunboat No. 7, New Era, Captain Marshall, took part in the conflict, shelling the enemy as opportunity offered. Signals had been agreed upon, by which the officers in the fort could indicate where the guns of the fort could be most effective. There being but one gunboat there, no permanent impression appears to have been produced upon the enemy; for as they were shelled out of one ravine they would make their appearance in the other. They would thus appear and retire as the gunboat moved from one point to the other. About one o'clock the fire on both sides slackened somewhat, and the gunboat moved out in the river to clean and cool the guns, having fired two hundred and eighty-two rounds of shell, shrapnel, and cannister, which nearly exhausted the supply of ammunition.

The rebels, having thus far failed in their attack, now resorted to their customary flags of truce. The first flag of truce conveyed a demand from Forrest for the unconditional surrender of the fort. To this Major Bradford replied, asking to be allowed one hour to consult with his officers and the officers of the gunboat. In a short time a second flag of truce appeared, with a communication from Forrest, that he would allow Major Bradford twenty minutes in which to move his troops out of the fort; and if it was not done within that time an assault would be ordered. To this, Major Bradford returned the reply, that he would not surrender.

During the time these flags of truce were flying, the rebels were moving down the ravines and taking positions from which the more readily to charge upon the fort. Parties of them were also engaged in plundering the government buildings, and commissary and quartermaster's stores, in full view of the gunboat. Captain Marshall states that he refrained from firing upon the rebels, although they were thus violating the flag of truce, for fear that should they finally succeed in capturing the fort, they would justify any atrocities they might commit, by saying that they were in retaliation for his firing while the flag of truce was flying. He says, however, that when he saw the rebels coming down the ravine, above the fort, and taking positions there, he got under weigh and stood for the fort—"I determined to use what little ammunition we had left in shelling them out of the ravine." But he did not get up within effective range before the final assault was made.

Immediately after the second flag of truce retired, the rebels made a rush from the positions they had so treacherously gained, and obtained possession of the fort, raising the cry of "No quarter!" But little opportunity was allowed for resistance. Our troops, black and white, threw down their arms, and sought to escape by running down the steep bluff near the fort, and secreting themselves behind trees and logs, in the bushes, and under the brush—some even jumping into the river, leaving only their heads above the water, as they crouched down under the bank.

Then followed a scene of cruelty and murder without parallel in civilized warfare, which needed but the toma-

hawk and scalping-knife to exceed the worst atrocities
ever committed by savages. The rebels commenced an
indiscriminate slaughter, sparing neither age nor sex,
white or black, soldier or civilian. The officers and men
seemed to vie with each other in the devilish work. Men
and women, and even children, wherever found, were
deliberately shot down, beaten, and hacked with sabres.
Some of the children, not more than ten years old, were
forced to stand up and face their murderers while being
shot. The sick and wounded were butchered without
mercy, the rebels even entering the hospital-building
and dragging them out to be shot, or killing them as
they lay there unable to offer the least resistance. All
over the hillside the work of murder was going on.
Numbers of our men were collected together in lines or
groups and deliberately shot. Some were shot while in
the river, while others on the bank were shot and their
bodies kicked into the water, many of them still living,
but unable to make any exertions to save themselves
from drowning. Some of the rebels stood upon the top
of the hill, or a short distance down its side, and called
to our soldiers to come up to them—and as they approached, shot them down in cold blood: if their guns
or pistols missed fire, forcing them to stand there until
they were again prepared to fire. All around were heard
cries of "No quarter! no quarter! kill the d—d niggers,
shoot them down!" All who asked for mercy were
answered by the most cruel taunts and sneers. Some
were spared for a time, only to be murdered under circumstances of greater cruelty.

No cruelty which the most fiendish malignity could
devise was omitted by these murderers. One white
soldier, who was wounded in one leg so as to be unable
to walk, was made to stand up while his tormentors shot

him. Others who were wounded and unable to stand
up, were held up and again shot. One negro, who had
been ordered by a rebel officer to hold his horse, was
killed by him when he remonstrated. Another, a mere
child, whom an officer had taken up behind him on his
horse, was seen by Chalmers, who at once ordered the
officer to put him down and shoot him—which was done.
The huts and tents in which many of the wounded had
sought shelter were set on fire, both that night and the
next morning, while the wounded were still in them—
those only escaping who were able to get themselves out,
or who could prevail on others less injured than themselves to help them out; and even some of these, thus
seeking to escape the flames, were met by these ruffians
and brutally shot down, or had their brains beaten out.

One man was deliberately fastened down to the floor
of a tent, face upwards, by means of nails driven through
his clothing and into the boards under him, so that he
could not possibly escape, and then the tent set on fire.
Another was nailed to the side of a building outside of
the fort, and then the building set on fire and burned.
The charred remains of five or six bodies were afterwards found, all but one so much disfigured and consumed by the flames that they could not be identified;
and the identification of that one is not absolutely certain,
although there can hardly be a doubt that it was the body
of Lieutenant Akerstoom, Quartermaster of the Thirteenth
Virginia Cavalry, and a native Tennesseean. Several
witnesses who saw the remains, and who were personally
acquainted with him while living, have testified that it
is their firm belief that it was his body that was thus
treated.

These deeds of murder and cruelty closed when night
came on only to be renewed the next morning, when the

demons carefully sought among the dead, lying about in all directions, for any other wounded yet alive, and those they found were deliberately shot. Scores of the dead and wounded were found there the day of the massacre, by the men from some of our gunboats, who were permitted to go on shore and collect the wounded and bury the dead. The rebels themselves had made a pretence of burying a great many of their victims, but they had merely thrown them, without the least regard to care or decency, into the trenches and ditches about the fort, or the little hollows and ravines on the hillside, covering them but partially with earth. Portions of heads and faces, hands and feet, were found protruding through the earth in every direction; and even when your committee visited the spot, two weeks afterwards, although parties of men had been sent on shore from time to time to bury the bodies unburied, and rebury the others, and were then engaged in the same work, we found the evidences of this murder and cruelty still most painfully.

We saw bodies still unburied (at some distance from the fort) of some sick men who had been met fleeing from the hospital, and beaten down and brutally murdered, and their bodies left where they had fallen. We could still see the faces, and hands, and feet, of men, white and black, protruding out of the ground, whose graves had not been reached by those engaged in reinterring the victims of the massacre; and although a great deal of rain had fallen within the preceding two weeks, the ground, more especially on the side and at the foot of the bluff where most of the murders had been committed, was still discolored by the blood of our brave but unfortunate men, and the logs and trees showed but too plainly the evidences of the atrocities perpetrated there.

7

Many other instances of equally atrocious cruelty might be enumerated, but your committee feel compelled to refrain from giving here more of the heart-sickening details, and refer to the statements contained in the voluminous testimony herewith submitted.

Those statements were obtained by them from eye-witnesses and sufferers. Many of them, as they were examined by your committee, were lying upon beds of pain and suffering, some so feeble that their lips could with difficulty frame the words by which they endeavored to convey some idea of the cruelties which had been inflicted on them, and which they had seen inflicted on others.

In reference to the fate of Major Bradford, who was in command of the fort when it was captured, and who had up to that time received no injury, there seems to be no doubt. The general understanding seems to be that he had been brutally murdered the day after he was taken prisoner.

How many of our troops thus fell victims to the malignity and barbarity of Forrest and his followers cannot yet be definitely ascertained. Two officers belonging to the garrison were absent at the time of the capture and massacre. Of the remaining officers but two are known to be living, and they are wounded now in the hospital at Mound City; one of them, Captain Porter, may even now be dead, as the surgeons, when your committee were there, expressed no hope of his recovery. Of the men, from three hundred to four hundred are known to have been killed at Fort Pillow, of whom at least three hundred were murdered in cold blood after the fort was in possession of the rebels, and our men had thrown down their arms, and ceased to offer resistance. Of the survivors, except the wounded in the hospital at Mound

City and the few who succeeded in making their escape unhurt, nothing definite is known, and it is to be feared that many have been murdered after being taken away from the fort.

When your committee arrived at Memphis, Tennessee, they found and examined a man, Mr. McLagan, who had been conscripted by some of Forrest's forces, but who, with other conscripts, had succeeded in making his escape.

He testifies that while two companies of rebel troops, with Major Bradford and many other prisoners, were on the march from Brownsville to Jackson, Tennessee, Major Bradford was taken by five rebels, one an officer, led about fifty yards from the line of march, and deliberately murdered, in view of all there assembled. He fell, killed instantly by three musket-balls, even while asking that his life might be spared, as he had fought them manfully, and was deserving of a better fate. The motive for the murder of Major Bradford seems to have been the simple fact that, although a native of the South, he remained loyal to his Government. The testimony herewith submitted contains many statements made by the rebels that they did not intend to treat "home-made Yankees," as they termed loyal Southerners, "any better than negro troops."

There is one circumstance connected with the events herein narrated which your committee cannot permit to pass unnoticed. The testimony herewith submitted discloses this most astounding and shameful fact: On the morning of the day succeeding the capture of Fort Pillow, the gunboat Silver Cloud (No. 28), the transport Platte Valley, and the gunboat New Era (No. 7), landed at Fort Pillow under flag of truce, for the purpose of receiving the few wounded there, and burying the dead.

While they were lying there, the rebel General Chalmers, and other rebel officers, came down to the landing, and some of them went on the boats. Notwithstanding the evidences of rebel atrocity and barbarity with which the ground was covered, there were some of our army officers on board the Platte Valley so lost to every feeling of decency, honor, and self-respect, as to make themselves disgracefully conspicuous in bestowing civilities and attention upon the rebel officers, even while they were boasting of the murders they had there committed.

Your committee were unable to ascertain the names of the officers who have thus inflicted so foul a stain upon the honor of our army. They are assured, however, by the military authorities that every effort will be made to ascertain their names, and bring them to the punishment they so richly merit.

In relation to the reinforcement or evacuation of Fort Pillow, it would appear that the troops there stationed were withdrawn on the 25th of January last, in order to accompany the Meridian Expedition, under General Sherman. General Hurlbut testifies that he never received any instructions to permanently vacate the post, and deeming it important to occupy it so that the rebels should not interrupt the navigation of the Mississippi by planting artillery there, he sent some troops there about the middle of February, increasing their number afterwards until the garrison amounted to nearly six hundred men. He also states that as soon as he learned that the place was attacked, he immediately took measures to send up reinforcements from Memphis, and they were actually embarking when he received information of the capture of the fort.

Your committee cannot close this report without expressing their obligations to the officers of the army, and many with whom they were brought in contact, for the assistance they rendered. It is true, your committee were furnished by the Secretary of War with the fullest authority to call upon any one in the army for such services as they might require to enable them to make the investigation devolved upon them by Congress. But they found that no such authority was needed. The army and navy officers at every point they visited, evinced a desire to aid the committee in every way in their power, and all expressed the highest satisfaction that Congress had so promptly taken steps to ascertain the facts connected with this fearful and bloody transaction, and the hope that the investigation would lead to prompt and decisive measures on the part of the Government. Your committee would mention more particularly the names of General Mason Brayman, military commandant at Cairo; Captain J. H. Odlin, his chief of staff; Captain A. M. Pennock, United States Navy, Fleet Captain of Mississippi Squadron; Captain James W. Shirk, United States Navy, commanding Seventh District Mississippi Squadron; Surgeon Horace Wardner, in charge of Mound City General Hospital; Captain Thomas M. Farrell, United States Navy, in command of gunboat Hastings (furnished by Captain Pennock, to convey the committee to Fort Pillow and Memphis); Captain Thomas Pattison, naval commandant at Memphis; General C. C. Washburne; and the officers of their commands, as among those to whom they are indebted for assistance and attention.

All of which is respectfully submitted.

B. F. WADE.

D. W. GOOCH.

Adopted by the committee as their report.

B. F. WADE, Chairman.

7 *

PART II.

PERSECUTION OF UNIONISTS IN THE REVOLTED STATES;

OFFICIAL DOCUMENTS, ETC.

PERSECUTION OF UNIONISTS

IN THE

REVOLTED STATES;

OFFICIAL DOCUMENTS, ETC.

PRELIMINARY.

THE volumes of history scarcely furnish a chapter more replete with fiendish cruelty and atrocity, than do authentic accounts of the treatment of Unionists in the revolted States; while at the North, Secession sympathizers have generally been unmolested, have been allowed freely to express their opinions, and to discuss and condemn all measures employed for the suppression of the revolt, Unionists in the revolted states have been persecuted in every way, and subjected to every outrage; have been shot down without ceremony, hung without trial, hunted with blood-hounds, and tortured without mercy. Indeed, violence and savage ferocity have characterized the rebellion from the beginning, and by these means mainly have the masses of the Southern people been overawed, and made to acquiesce in the revolt.

This is so forcibly set forth in the following communication from Captain D. H. Bingham, of Alabama, that we insert it in this place.

INAUGURATION OF THE REIGN OF TERROR.

WHEN the rebellious states seceded in the fall and winter of 1860–1, the masses of the people were violently opposed to the measure, and in their primary meetings and social gatherings, expressed their opposition in no equivocal terms. Hence it was determined to inaugurate a reign of terror, in order to stifle the voice of opposition, and secure uniformity of sentiment and action.

As South Carolina was the first state to secede, so it was the first theatre of those barbarous cruelties which were designed to overawe the non-slaveholding population, who, however numerous, had few political rights, and no social position, and had been accustomed to be as submissive to the behest of the slaveholders as the negroes themselves. The reign of terror was introduced by putting forward that class of reckless and brutalized men, known as overseers and negro-drivers, who have ever been found ready, at the bidding of their employers, the slaveholders, to engage in the most atrocious acts. This class of menials were organized into squads of half a dozen, more or less according to exigency or design of the service they were expected to perform, and their business was to ride through the different neighborhoods, and inquire into the sentiments of every poor man, and wherever they found one who expressed himself as willing to give the administration of Mr. Lincoln a fair trial, he was forthwith taken out and "Lynched," until he professed to renounce his sentiments. In this way was South Carolina revolutionized within twenty days.

In other states, in which the non-slaveholding white population was proportionally larger, a somewhat different mode of operation was adopted to secure the same object. In Alabama, particularly the northern portion of the state, vigilance committees were organized, self-constituted in many cases, under the pretence that the country was full of abolitionists, and that the officers of the law were inadequate to the protection of the people against these emissaries of the Lincoln Government. These vigilance committees had their secret conclaves, in which measures were discussed, plans laid, plots devised, charges manufactured. At first the free negroes particularly were assailed. They were unceremoniously dragged before the committees, tried in secret, condemned, and led forth to execution without the public knowing for what, beyond the statement of the members that the evidence was sufficient. Among those who were thus condemned and executed, was an aged negro preacher, who had lived about Mooresville, Limestone county, Alabama. He was hung in February or March of 1861, his heart cut out and carried upon the point of a knife through the streets by a semi-barbarian drunkard; and the public do not know, to this day, the evidence on which that negro was executed, beyond the mere assertion of the committee that they had evidence enough to hang him.

The country, at the time, abounded with travelling foot-pedlars, mostly Germans and Italians, who imperfectly spoke our language. They were inhumanly set upon by these human blood-hounds; some were shot and found dead in the roads; others were unceremoniously dragged before these committees, and ordered to leave the country.

But these committees did not stop here; they proceeded to assail the native white population when suspected of Unionism, robbing, torturing, shooting, hanging them without ceremony or form of trial.

At the firing on Fort Sumter, the sentiment of the non-slaveholding population was decidedly Union. But in one month's time, by such appliances of violence and cruelty, this sentiment was extensively suppressed; the more easily, as the few had been wont to control the many, and the many were dependent on, and wont to cringe to the few.

Such were the means first employed to secure uniformity of opinion and action, and bring the entire people under the domination of those who had contemplated and been devising, during thirty years, the dismemberment of the Republic.

The next step was the organization, by the Rebel Congress, of "Partisan Rangers," or legalized guerrillas. Every cut-throat scoundrel at once became emulous of the distinction and power and plunder which the command of a guerrilla band would afford, and set to work to raise a company, battalion, or regiment, according to his means and capacity. Thus originated the military career of such monsters of cruelty and crime as Forrest, a notorious gambler and negro-trader of Memphis, Tennessee; of John Morgan, another gambler, and a robber and libertine, of Louisville, Kentucky; of Roddy, Biffles, Champ Ferguson, Frank Gurley, Quantrell, and a host of others of like character. The primitive object of the organization of the "Partisan Rangers" was the suppression of the Union sentiment of the southern portion of the country; and the narrative contained in the following pages of their bloody atrocities upon Union men, women, and children, in East Tennessee, Northern Alabama, Kentucky, and other states, shows how fully this design has been carried into execution.

MURDER OF MR. TURNER.

A MOST brutal murder was committed upon a young man, named Turner, belonging to the Twenty-ninth Regiment Ohio Volunteers, on or about the 18th of July, 1863, near Port Republic, Virginia, by a rebel cavalry officer. As young Turner was passing, he was ordered by the officer to halt, and did so, when the ruffian deliberately drew out his revolver and shot him through the heart, cursing him for being a d—d Yankee. When asked by one of his own party why he had killed the young man, he said that too many of the d—d rascals are getting away, and he was determined that none he had anything to do, with should escape. The above comes from a prisoner, who saw the deed committed.*

MURDER OF MARSHALL GLAZE, JR, AND OTHERS.

ON Monday evening, September 18th, 1863, from twenty to thirty Rebels went to the house of an old gentleman by the name of Marshall Glaze, on Spring Creek, Virginia, and brutally murdered John McMullen, Marshall Glaze, Jr., and a Union soldier who had been stopping at the house for some days, waiting for his discharge, being so infirm that he could not proceed further.

Marshall Glaze, Jr., and two or three soldiers from the Ninth Virginia Regiment, who were on their way home, had been invited to stop for the night at the house. They

---

* From Captain J. E. Johnson, of New York.

8

went to bed in some out-buildings. During the night, a party of rebels came to the dwelling and demanded to be informed where the soldiers were. Not being answered, the rebels by some other means discovered the place where they were asleep, and immediately rushed upon them, killing McMullen, the discharged soldier, and young Glaze, at the first fire. The other three were fortunate enough to break through the ranks of the murderers, and succeeded in making their escape.

The rebels then went to the house of Mr. W. Noyes in the neighborhood, and attempted to persuade, and finally to force, a young girl (no doubt for an evil purpose) to go with them. On her refusal, they deliberately shot her, and she instantly expired.*

MURDER OF REV. JAMES WEBSTER.

REV. JAMES WEBSTER, who owned and lived on a farm in Virginia, a thorough Union man, but very cautious in expressing his views in regard to secession, was one day, while in his barn alone thrashing wheat, surprised by seeing a gang of armed guerrillas enter. He asked them what they had come for? They answered, for him; that he was a Union man, and they knew it, and they were going to carry him to Richmond. He protested against this, and tried to reason the case with them; but without avail. They laid hands upon him, and forced him to go with them, not allowing him a change of clothing, although he begged that privilege. They drove him three days without giving him a morsel of food, so that he actually died of hunger and exhaustion.†

* From Mr. McWhorter, member of the House of Delegates of West Virginia, in 1863.

† From A. B. Hough, of Virginia.

OUTRAGES ON UNION PEOPLE IN NORTH CAROLINA.

In January, 1863, all the salt at Laurel Hill, North Carolina, near the Tennessee line, was taken possession of by the rebel authorities, and, in consequence, the salt in the region around of which they had not possession was selling at from seventy-five to one hundred dollars per sack. The commissioned officers of the rebel government declared that the Tories, a name they give to the Unionists in that portion of the country, should have none. They positively refused to give them the portion to which they were justly entitled when it was distributed. This outrage aroused the long-suppressed anger of the Union men, and they collected together and determined to take their portion of the salt by force if necessary. They proceeded to the place where it was kept (Marshall, North Carolina), and took what they considered their share.

Shortly after, the Sixty-fifth North Carolina Regiment, under command of one Lieutenant-Colonel James Keith, was ordered to Laurel Hill to arrest the offenders. Samuel M. Allen was Colonel of the Sixty-fifth, but had been suspended for drunkenness, and therefore the command fell upon this Keith.

Before the regiment arrived at Laurel Hill, those engaged in the salt seizure fled and were not to be found, and the innocent had to suffer in their stead. The following persons were arrested:—Joseph Wood, about sixty years of age; David Shelton, forty-five; E. King, forty; H. Moore, forty; Wade Moore, thirty-five; Isaiah Shelton, fifteen; Willie Shelton, twelve; James Metcalf, ten; Jasper Channel, fourteen; Samuel Shelton, nineteen, and his brother, aged seven; in all, thirteen. All of them protested against being arrested, and declared that they were innocent, and begged for a trial, that they might prove their innocence.

Colonel Allen, who was with the regiment, said they should have a trial, and they were going to take them to Tennessee for that purpose.

They all started off, thinking that everything would soon be right, but had proceeded only a few miles when they were marched from the road to a gorge in the mountains. Halting here, five of them were ordered to kneel down. A file of soldiers was then placed in front of them with loaded muskets.

The terrible reality now flashed upon their minds that they were about to be murdered. Old Mr. Wood exclaimed, "For God's sake, men, you are not going to shoot us? If you are, give us at least time to pray.' Colonel Allen was reminded of his promise. They were told that he was not in command, had no authority to make such promises, and that there was no time to be lost in praying. The word was given to fire. The old man and boys put their hands to their faces, and rent the air with their agonizing cries of despair. The soldiers hesitated to obey the command. Keith told them if they did not fire he would make them change places with the prisoners. Again the order was given, and the five men fell pierced with bullets.

Wood and Shelton were both shot through the head, and their brains scattered upon the ground. They died without a struggle. The others lived a few minutes. Five others were ordered to kneel down—with them little Willie Shelton, who said, "You shot my father in the face; please do not shoot me in the face!" He covered his face with his hands, and the order of "Fire!" was again given. Five more fell. Poor little Willie was wounded in both arms. He ran to the officer, and clasping him around the legs, implored him to spare his life, saying, "You have killed my poor old father and my three brothers! you have shot me in both arms! I forgive you for all—I can get well again; do let me go home to my mother and sisters!" What man, with a heart, could resist such an appeal? But little Willie pleaded in vain. He was again dragged back to the place of execution, and again that terrible word "Fire!" was given. He fell dead, eight balls having penetrated his body. The remaining three were ordered to kneel down, and again the word "Fire!" was given, and they fell. Those in whom life was not entirely extinct were despatched with pistols.

The miscreants then dug a hole in the ground, and tossed the whole thirteen into it. Its depth was not sufficient, and some of the bodies of the murdered men lay above the ground. Sergeant N. B. Jay, a Virginian, but attached to this command, got up on the bleeding bodies and commencing to dance, cried out, "Some one pat Juba* for me, and I'll dance the d—d scoundrels down to and through hell." The grave was covered very lightly with earth. The next day the families of the murdered men heard of their fate, and search was made for their bodies. When the grave was found, the swine had rooted up one of the corpses, and partly devoured it.

A portion of Keith's men went to Tennessee, and the others returned with Keith to Laurel Hill, and told the inhabitants that the murdered men were taken to Tennessee, to be tried in accordance with the pledge of Colonel Allen.

By those who went to Tennessee many Union men

* A negro song.

were killed along the way. Those who returned with
Keith to Laurel Hill began to torture the wives of loyal
men, to force them to tell where their husbands had hid
the salt. The women refused to disclose anything. Then
the inhuman wretches gathered together some hickory
switches, and commenced whipping them until the blood
was seen to run down their persons upon the ground.
Mrs. Sarah Shelton, wife of E. Shelton, who escaped
from the town, and Mrs. Mary Shelton, wife of L. Shelton, were whipped and then hung by the neck until life
was nearly extinct. When let down, and consciousness
had returned, they still positively refused to give any
information. Martha White, an idiotic girl, was taken
out and whipped, and then tied to a tree by the neck,
and left there all day.

Old Mrs. Eunice Riddle, aged eighty-five years, was
inhumanly whipped, hung, and then robbed of a considerable amount of money. A great many others were
threatened with torture. The daughters of William Shelton were requested to sing and play for them. They
sang and played the national airs of the Union. Keith,
learning this, ordered the ladies to be arrested, and sent
a guard to the house, where they remained all night.

Mrs. Sallie Moore, aged seventy years, was whipped
with hickory switches until the blood ran down from her
back to the ground.

One woman, name forgotten, who had a child five or
six weeks old, was tied to a tree in the snow, and her
child placed in the door in her sight, the villains telling
her that, if she did not tell where the salt was hid, she
and her child would be kept in that position until they
both perished. Sergeant N. B. D. Jay, of Captain Rey-
nolds's company, and Lieutenant R. M. Deever, assisted
their men in the perpetration of these outrages. Houses

were burned over the heads of the Union people, and
everything of value was stolen by these men.

The perpetrators of these outrages were soldiers belonging to the army of the Confederate States, and the
men who commanded them were commissioned by the
same government, and therefore the Confederate Government had them in their control, and could have punished them, if they did not sanction their acts; but the
villains were looked upon as brave men for these acts of
cruelty.*

MURDER OF A ONE-ARMED MAN IN NORTH CAROLINA.

By the battle of Gettysburg, Pennsylvania, the rebels
suffered such a defeat that the Unionists of the South,
growing bold, began to speak their sentiments aloud, in
opposition to the rebel government. Particularly was
this the case in Central North Carolina, so that three
regiments were sent from the rebel army to overawe the
people and quell the disturbance. Many acts of cruelty
were perpetrated by these soldiers, causing serious skir-
mishes between them and those Unionists who were lucky
enough to have arms, and several lives were lost on both
sides.

Among the most atrocious acts committed by these
soldiers was that practised upon a young man in Randolph county, who, by some accident, had lost one arm,
and was therefore not subject to conscription. They
went to his house, and, under the pretence of getting him
to show them the way to a neighbor's, decoyed him into
a piece of woodland, where they brutally shot him.

---

* Colonel Crawford, Vice-President of the State Convention, held at
Nashville, Tenn., 1863.

He was heard begging and imploring for his life at a great distance. His body was found three or four days afterwards, having from appearance received some seven or eight pistol-shots.

From the marks of blood and the foot-prints, it appeared that they compelled him to run around them in a circle, shooting at him as he ran, trying to see how many times they could hit him without killing him. All this was done because he loved the Union.*

BARBAROUS TREATMENT OF UNION SYMPA-
THIZERS IN THE REBEL ARMY.

In the month of October, 1863, at Rapidan Station, four miles above Orange Court-House, Virginia, a young man belonging to Company B, Forty-fourth North Caro-Carolina Regiment (rebel), a Unionist, who had been conscripted, was inhumanly shot under the following circumstances :—

Many of his regiment had deserted, and entered the lines of the Union army. Certain soldiers of other regiments, suspecting him to be a Union man at heart, to draw out his sentiments, told him that they would not belong to such a regiment, &c. At last, being irritated, he said "I don't care if the whole regiment deserts." This was all they wished. They immediately reported his words to their officers, and he was arrested as a deserter, tried by a court-martial, and sentenced to be shot. He endeavored to explain in what manner he was constrained to use this language, and declared he had no thought of desertion. But they declined to listen to his

---

* Bryan Tyson, author of the "Ray of Light."

explanation, and ordered him to be put into confinement. The guard hurried him away, and in the course of a few days he was carried out and shot. He met his fate like a brave man.

Another soldier, belonging to a North Carolina brigade, was sentenced to death under similar circumstances, and the authorities went so far as to tie him to a stake before they shot him.*

MURDER OF THREE BROTHERS.

In the summer of 1862, three young men, brothers, by the name of Anderson, not liking the way in which the Union men were treated in their vicinity, left their home, which was in Hawkins county, Tennessee, and attempted to make their way to the Union lines in Kentucky. They had reached Clinch river, about seventy-five miles above Knoxville, Tennessee, when they were surprised and captured by a band of Confederate cavalry, and inhumanly shot without mercy by their captors, who had been sent in pursuit of them. After killing them, they threw their bodies into the river, where, not long after, they were found, only fifteen miles from their desolate and forsaken home. The only reason assigned for this brutal murder was, that they were Union men, and were leaving the country.†

---

* R. D Talley, Chatham Co., North Carolina.

. † Colonel R. Crawford, of Tennessee, one of the Vice Presidents of the State Convention, held in Nashville in 1863.

ASSAULT ON MR. GRIER, A KENTUCKY STATE SENATOR.

CINCINNATI, October 8th, 1862.

L. W. HALL, Ravenna, Portage Co., Ohio.

Dear Sir: In great distress of mind, I will attempt to recount to you the misfortunes and troubles I have recently had to encounter in Kentucky. I am now a refugee. The torch of the incendiary rebels has been put to my mills, my store, and my dwelling. All is consumed; the labor of nearly twenty years is destroyed. On last Wednesday night the rebel cavalry of John Morgan, to the number of eight hundred, encamped within two miles of my place. Through the whole night they were momentarily expected to come upon us; every person left the road and hid in the woods; I could not do so, my wife was so near her confinement; my anxiety for her kept me near my dwelling. To allay her fears for my safety, I had to appear to be absent. Nothing occurred during the night. As the morning dawned, I went further from my house, and took a view of the premises and the roads leading to them. I could see no rebels; and I determined to see my wife, let the consequences be what they might. As I was near my door, eight rebels suddenly appeared before me, with their guns presented to my breast, and took me a prisoner. Soon the whole rebel band was upon me. Morgan cursed the men for taking me a prisoner, saying "that he had ordered them to shoot me down upon sight." He then opened my store door, and told his men to rifle and fire it. I implored him not to do it, as it was so near my dwelling that it would also be consumed. I informed him of the condition of my wife; for myself I asked nothing; but I begged him in common humanity not to, destroy my wife and little children. He answered with a horrid oath that he intended to burn everything I had; he would put fire to my house, and burn my wife and children up in it; he would wipe out the whole Abolition concern. This threat was applauded by many of his men, who said they went for killing men, women, and children. I was then placed upon a horse without a saddle, and conducted to the front of their column, and orders were again given to shoot me down if they were fired upon by bushwhackers, as they styled the Union men. I assured them that they would be fired upon if the people had any spirit, and I believed they had; that when they saw the conflagration of their homes, they would way-lay and fire upon them, even if their number was ten times greater. After firing my property, he (Morgan) rode past me and said, pointing to the flames, "You find your loyalty to your Abolition Government pretty expensive, don't you?"

Before we reached the woods, the captain of the men that took me prisoner, removed me from my position in the front, and placed me in his company near the rear. Immediately upon entering the woods they were fired upon. I was surprised that I was not shot. Morgan rode past and demanded the reason I was not shot, as he had ordered. They said they had not heard the order. He told them, if fired upon again, to shoot the prisoner. They then amused themselves by pointing their guns at me, and saying that they wished they might have the pleasure of shooting me. After some time we were ordered to advance, and were soon again fired upon. I heard the guns click behind me, and felt sure that my end was right then at hand. Their captain, John T. Williams, ordered them not to fire; he said that it was cold-blooded murder; that his men had taken me prisoner, that he was not yet mustered into the service, did not belong to General Morgan's command, and would not obey him in this, but would take me to West Liberty and put me in jail till further orders. This was some relief to me, you may be assured. Thus we proceeded for nearly twelve miles, my friends, the Unionists, emptying a saddle every five minutes, and my captors setting fire to every Union man's house as they went along.

At last they commenced falling close around me, and my guardian friend, the captain, said he could not save me any longer. I soon took advantage of the excitement prevailing, jumped from my horse and fled to the woods, unobserved, and thus made my escape. I reached where had been my home at dark, and found my wife had been carried by some kind ladies to an unoccupied house, and a physician present who said he would stay with her. It was not more than twenty minutes till Morgan's guerrillas were again upon me. I escaped through the fields to the woods, making my way for Portsmouth, thirty-five miles distant, my nearest point of complete safety, where I arrived next morning without food, sleep, or rest. I immediately came to this city, where there was owing me seventy-five dollars, with which I will purchase a Ballard rifle, and return to the vicinity of my family; hide in the woods and caves, and pick off every "Butternut" I see until I can get my family away to some place of security.

Why is all this persecution of me? It is because I condemned this wicked rebellion; urged a vigorous prosecution of this war, and in my place in the Senate of Kentucky, opposed the temporizing policy of my own party. For this I am burned and hunted out of Kentucky.

I am now unequivocally for confiscation, subjugation, extermination, hell and damnation.

Yours respectfully,
W. C. GRIER.

OUTRAGES ON THE PEOPLE IN THE MOUNTAIN DISTRICTS OF KENTUCKY.

On the 12th of May, 1863, Colonel Gilbert started out with a detachment of the Forty-fourth Ohio Regiment, on an extensive reconnoissance from London, Kentucky, to ascertain the strength and situation of the numerous bands of guerrillas who were then prowling about that section of the country. He found them very numerous. They fled at the approach of the Forty-fourth, which followed in hot pursuit, but were unable to overtake them.

His forces searched the country from London to Barboursville; thence to Cumberland Ford, and along the Cumberland River from Williamsburg, south to Big Creek Gap. Detachments of Colonel Gilbert's men drove the rebel bands up Poor Fork to Yellow Creek, and also into the mountain wilds from Winchester up to the forks of Goose Creek.

Colonel Gilbert's command cleared that portion of the country. The guerrillas seemed to have no taste for fighting, and fled in disorder whenever the Union soldiers approached them. In the chase four or five were killed, and some sixteen taken prisoners. Colonel Gilbert's command sustained no loss. The people were found to be very loyal.

It was ascertained that the rebels were in the practice of inflicting all sorts of tortures to compel the women

9

and children to tell them where they had hidden their corn, &c. They forced the men into their ranks, divested the women and children of all their clothing, even taking their shoes from off their feet.

Major Moore found near Red River two men, divested of everything but their pantaloons, and almost starved. Lieutenant Shaw and others saw similar instances of barbarous treatment.

These Unionists were first reduced to want by Morgan and his men, and afterwards pillaged by the rebel hordes who were driven out by Colonel Gilbert, until starvation or flight seemed to be the only alternative left them.

DEPREDATIONS IN KENTUCKY BY HUMPHREY MARSHALL'S AND CLUKE'S MEN.

GRAY HAWK, Jackson County, Ky.,
April 13th, 1863

Dear Sir: This leaves me lower in spirits than I have been since I have had a family. Some ten days ago, Cluke, with some five hundred men, came in through Proctor, in Owsley county, taking all the horses they could lay hands on. They came to my house, took a mule from me, and destroyed all the corn I had; pastured on my wheat, and committed other depredations.

On Tuesday, the 7th of this month, Humphrey Marshall's men, with the guerrilla band from Breathitt county, commenced coming into our county by Proctor, taking horses, cattle, and everything they could get hold of. They came on to Booneville; burned the jail; destroyed the records in the clerk's office; cut up the books and scattered them through the streets; came to my house, took every horse and mule I had, numbering thirteen. Among those aiding this work were Jack May, Jerry South's son, Wm. P. Lacey, James Hurd, and Robert Allen. They pursued my two oldest sons up the branch stream from my house, shooting at them until their ammunition was nearly expended. Lacy then charged upon my oldest son with his musket in hand, cursing him, and swearing he would hang him. My son drew his pistol, shot Lacy through the arm, and into his canteen. Lacy threw up his hand and halloed "Don't." My son fired again, hit Lacy under the ear, and dropped him from his horse, dead. The boys then, the musket-balls still flying around them, ran down a steep cliff, which the horses of the marauders could not descend, and made their escape into the woods. The rebels, setting fire to my buildings, burned up everything I had, leaving my wife and children with nothing but the clothes they had on. My wife got down on her knees to them, and offered them one thousand dollars in cash if they would not burn the dwelling. They would not hear her. She then tried to get the things out of the house, but they kept her off with their muskets. Some few things, which she did get out, were taken from her, consisting principally of thirty-three bed-blankets. The balance all went to the flames. I was in Jackson county at the time, and am still here.

My wife is in a school-house below where my house stood, with my three youngest children. My two boys are hid in the mountains, with nothing to eat, wear, or sleep on, except what the neighbors furnish them. My wife is also dependent on the charity of the neighbors. Neither of us can get to see the other, as the rebels are still passing. Mine, I understand, was the seventeenth house they have burned on the route up as far as my place. I understand they have burned Clark's salt-works. How true this is, I do not know. The damage reported to have been done so far up as my house is certainly true. My son came to me last night, and gave me all the particulars.

I have begged and plead hard with the authorities below for help. One thing you know, and that is, the people here generally are so poor that they cannot get away, and if they could, how are they to subsist?

These counties that are suffering so much are the most loyal portion of the state. Clay, Owesley, and Jackson, which have furnished on an average five hundred volunteers to the country, not one of whom is near enough to come to the rescue of their friends; they are all at Vicksburg, Murfreesboro, and other points out of the State.

I have not seen my wife for some three weeks, and don't know what to do. We have no meat or grain to live on here, and no horses or mules to take us away; no means to buy with. All my papers, notes, accounts, deeds, and everything I had, are burned up, and I have not clothing even for a change. I am going to try to get through to my family to-night, if I can, and will in a few days decide what we will do. A number of families must starve, if not soon rescued.

Yours, truly,

ABIJAH GILBERT.

MURDER OF JAMES McCULLUM.

ON the 13th of February, 1863, a party of Confederate soldiers were sent with orders to conscript Mr. James McCullum, an honest, industrious, hard-working Union man, residing in Greene county, Tennessee. When they

arrived in sight of his house he was engaged in feeding cattle. Seeing their approach, and knowing their purpose, he thought to evade them, and ran towards the barn. One of the party, without hailing or stopping him, which could easily have been done, brutally shot him through the neck, killing him instantly. His three little children, who were standing near, seeing their father had been murdered, ran to their mother, who was in the house, and told her. She ran out, shrieking, and wringing her hands in anguish. Approaching the monsters, who were sitting on the fence laughing at her agony, she asked them why they had killed her husband? They answered, "Because he was a d—d Tory!"*

ATROCITIES OF CHAMP FURGUSON.

THE annals of no civilized, nor even savage warfare, could furnish, perhaps, a parallel to the crimes and barbarities of Champ Furguson. He boasted of having killed fourteen men; and there is no question of the truth of his assertion. Having by some means managed to get command of a party of ruffians in their raids upon the Union citizens of Tennessee, which were very frequent, he and his gang captured John Williams, William Delk, John Crabtree, and a negro man, at Mrs. Alexander Hough's, in Fentress county. Tying them together, they drove them to the house of William Piles, on Wolf Run. On the way, the murderers gratified their savage propensities by cutting splinters of wood and thrusting them into the unfortunate men's flesh, and cutting them off

---

* From Colonel Crawford, one of the Vice-Presidents of the State Convention held in Nashville, Tennessee, in 1863.

9 *

close to their bodies. And to cause the poor fellows to travel faster, they pitched their bowie-knives into them.

After arriving at Piles's, the villains tortured them by piercing them with their bayonets, and cutting off pieces of flesh until life was nearly extinct. When they tired of this, Champ Furguson despatched William Delk by actually hacking him to pieces with his bowie-knife; and his comrades killed the others with their guns and pistols. They had stripped them after having arrived at Piles's house, and all these tortures were inflicted upon them in a state of nudity, in the presence of Piles's family. The posts and fence around the yard were smeared with blood, which was seen for weeks after, showing that they compelled their unfortunate victims to run around the yard while they prosecuted their murderous work.

Thence Furguson went to Elam Huddleston's, a well-known Union man, who, seeing him coming, fled into his house and fastened the door; but, after exchanging some twenty shots with Furguson and his bandits, was at last wounded and captured.

Furguson immediately, with fiendish malignity, ripped Huddleston open, and then the savage brute cut his heart out, alleging as an excuse for his brutality that Huddleston was acting the 'possum.

From this he went to the dwelling of a man named Rodgers, whom he found sick in bed. He told Rodgers that he had come to kill him. His little son hearing this, dropped on his knees, and begged in the most piteous manner that he would not kill his father.

His petition, which, one would think, might have moved the heart of any man, made no impression on such a brute as Furguson, and he levelled his gun and shot the sick man in his bed.

The boy then began to cry aloud, when Furguson turned toward him with a pistol and shot him through the head, in the presence of the family. This child was but ten years of age.

He then robbed them of an amount of money, took some horses, and left them to weep over their dead husband and father, son, and brother.*

ASSAULT ON TWO AGED UNION MEN IN EAST TENNESSEE.

WASHINGTON, May 23d, 1864.

Dear Sir: * * * * In the early part of March of this year, as our corps (the Ninth) was resting at Moose Creek, in East Tennessee, I stopped over night at a farm-house. In the evening the old man, speaking of the rebels and their cruelties, said to me, that they had burned one of his barns, driven off his cattle, burned his fences, and told him that if he made any fuss about it they would shoot him. One of the officers told his daughter, a young woman of eighteen, when she tried to save the barn, that if she did not keep quiet he would turn her over to his men.

The old man told me that when our army retreated from Moose Creek, a few weeks before, the rebels tried to kill an aged neighbor of his, residing a short distance from his place. The next day I called on the neighbor, and found him in bed with his head bound up. With great difficulty could he speak. In the course of our conversation, he told me that when our army retreated from Moose Creek, a few weeks previous, the rebels

* General J. B. Rodgers.

came down from Morristown to his house, and dismounting, called him out of his house, and asked him several questions about the way our army had retreated; the number of men in our command; and if we had any artillery, &c. The old man endeavored to evade the questions. The officer seeing this, became excited, and insisted upon an answer. The old man becoming irritated, plainly told them that he would not give them any information. Hearing this, the officer drew his revolver and deliberately shot him in the mouth, evidently with the intention to kill him. The old man stated that for some days he was not expected to live. I have heard of a great many cases of rebel cruelties from my regimental commanders, but not having been able, through sickness, to join my regiment until the latter part of December, 1863, and not seeing them myself, I will not mention them.   Your friend, &c.

ALFRED O. BROOKS,

Late Captain Twenty-ninth Massachusetts Volunteers, Ninth Army Corps, U. S. A.

ASSAULT UPON MR. JOHNSON, OF CLINTON COUNTY, TENNESSEE.

MR. JOHNSON, living in Clinton county, Tennessee, was brutally assailed by that blood-hound, Champ Furguson, on the day of the murder of Mr. Lewis Pierce. After Pierce had been killed, Champ and gang entered Mr. Johnson's house, cursing and yelling. Surrounding Mr. Johnson, they drew their pistols and knives to kill him, but his wife and daughter clung around him and pushed the villains off: when they made an attempt to kill him, they kept them off until one of the gang, or some friend of Mr. Johnson, cried out that Captain Beckett's forces (United States) were coming. The cowardly miscreants hearing this, ran to their horses, and mounting them, galloped away as fast as their horses could carry them. The life of Mr. Johnson was saved. In a short time, however, the cowards sent word to Mr. Johnson, that they intended to visit him again, and kill him and his family, for no d—d Yankee should live in the country. The cause of the would-be murder was, that Mr. Johnson was born in Connecticut. He was a quiet and good man, and was respected as such by all who knew him. He had lived in Clinton county many years. We mention this case, because it is the only one in the long catalogue that has escaped speedy death, when once caught by Furguson. We believe Mr. Johnson has since moved his family North, and thus saved his life.*

MURDER OF JESSE BRIGHT AND OTHERS.

IN the month of April, 1862, an old man named Jesse Bright, aged sixty years, with two sons and two nephews, living in Johnson county, Tennessee, were arrested by a company of Colonel Foulke's Cavalry, composed of Tennesseeans and North Carolinians, and carried off to be tried for disloyalty to the Confederacy. The old man had been arrested once before, taken to Knoxville, Tennessee, and tried, but no evidence being produced against him, they were compelled to release him. When the

---

* Dr. J. D. Hall, of Tennessee.

cavalry men arrived in Ash county with their prisoners, a groggery-keeper, no doubt a brother murderer, proposed to treat them to eight gallons of brandy if they would hang the old man, his sons and nephews, without a chance of a trial. They eagerly accepted the offer, and the five unfortunate men were hung to the first tree without further ceremony.*

SUFFERINGS OF UNION MEN IN EAST TENNESSEE.

DURING the early part of the year 1862, the rebel authorities of Knoxville, Tennessee, issued an order prohibiting all the Unionists from leaving that section of the State under penalty of death, shooting, bayoneting, and sabring all those who attempted to do so; but promised a pardon to all those who had escaped, if they would return.

Yet they sent to Mrs. Maynard, wife of the Hon. Horace Maynard, ex-member of Congress, a notice to leave her property and home in Knoxville within thirty-six hours, and not to return under severe penalty. The wife of the Hon. Andrew Johnson, then Military Governor of that State, very ill with consumption, received a similar notice. Mrs. Johnson had not seen her husband for nearly two years, and it was thought that she could not survive the execution of the order.

* Colonel R. T. Crawford.

MURDER OF DR. RICE AND OTHERS.

ON the night of July 15th, 1862, Dr. Rice, Benjamin Daniels, and John Barnes, Union men, were brutally hung by a gang of guerrillas near Tennessee Ridge twenty-five miles from Nashville, for no other cause than that they had, a day or two before, allowed the men employed in erecting a telegraph line for the use of the United States army, to stay at their houses.

HANGING OF MR. STEWART.

THE father of a family, named Stewart, residing near Robinson's Springs, Tennessee, among the Cumberland Mountains, was brutally murdered by a party of Confederate soldiers. He had served in the army of the United States under General Jackson, at New Orleans, in 1814-15.

On all occasions he was true to the Union—and to secession decidedly opposed.

At the breaking out of the rebellion, he became a conspicuous object for the vengeance of the rebel leaders, although seventy-five years of age. He was soon waited upon by a deputation of these miscreants, and informed, that he must aid the rebellion. He frankly declared his unwillingness to break up a government under which he had so long and so happily lived; but he would remain at home and not molest any one in the enjoyment of his opinions.

This declaration would not satisfy them, yet he was allowed to remain in quietness for a few days. One day, however, as he was tottering through his yard, a squad of Confederate soldiers rode up, and one of them, Lawson Hill, told him "That he was a dangerous man, and had harbored Union men."

He declared that no one had been about his house for months, but his own family and their connections; they maintained that they knew better, and required him to go some twenty miles to a place for trial. The old man told them, he was not able to do it, if it were to save his life. "Well," said one of them, Lawson Hill, "if you will not go to trial, we must try you ourselves, and, be sure, hang you, guilty or not guilty." After some further discussions, they told him "that it was the policy of the Confederates, to destroy the last Union man in the country." They then took this poor old man to an apple tree in his own yard, and hung him till he was dead, in the presence of his horror-stricken family. This man Hill was formerly a member of Congress from Tennessee, and glorified in the murder of a man of seventy-five years of age simply because he was a Union man.*

MURDER OF A DERANGED WOMAN.

In April, 1862, two rebel murderers in the garb of soldiers, named Wood and Ingersoll, went to the house of Mrs. Ruth A. Rhea, on Lick Creek, in Greene county, Tennessee, with the determination to conscript her son, her only support, she being partly deranged. As she saw them approaching the house, she seized a stick, and commanded them to leave the premises, and raised her stick to strike. One of them, well aware that she was

---

* General J. B. Rodgers.

deranged, said he would run her through with his bayonet. His threats were of no avail, for she instantly
brought down the stick with all her force on his cowardly person.   He proved his bravery by shooting her
through the breast, killing her almost immediately, and
then went off, rejoicing at having murdered a deranged
woman, old enough to be his mother, leaving her body
upon the ground, to be buried by her distressed son,
when he might venture forth from his hiding-place. *

ATTACK ON GENERAL J. B. RODGERS'S HOUSE.

On the night of the 20th of September, 1863, three
guerrillas came to the house of General John B. Rodgers,
in Van Buren county, Tennessee.

Their names were French (raised in Warren county,
son of Mason French), Lamb, and Hembree. They
rushed into the house, and, with cocked pistols in their
hands, demanded to know where General Rodgers was,
for they had come, they said, to kill him that night.

Mrs. Rodgers informed them that the general had been
at home, but had remained there only four hours, and
was then in Memphis.

One of these abominable murderers swore that it was
a lie; that the general was concealed about the premises,
and they intended to have him. They then searched the
house, destroying everything in their way, like madmen,
and causing consternation and terror to the family.

The youngest son of the general, named William, took
the hint, and concluded it was time for him to leave.
Willie is only about twelve years of age; but thinking

---

* Colonel R. T. Crawford, of Tennessee.

that the boy would be a man some day, and a Union man, one of them tried to shoot him.

The child bounded out of the house, and fled in the darkness. One of the guerrillas followed in hot pursuit, still endeavoring to shoot him (a child twelve years of age). But little Willie knew the ground too well for the guerrilla. He made good his escape, and secreted himself in a clump of briars. His pursuer still pushed on, but finding his efforts vain, abandoned the chase as fruitless. As soon as the child found the way clear, he left his hiding-place and made for the woods, where he lay out in the wet and cold all night. The result was a serious cold.

After these efforts, the bandits robbed the general's farm of the last horse and mule, and then betook themselves to Mr. Isaiah Hatson's, whom they shot three times, killing him almost instantly. Thence they went to the house of Mr. Hunter, whom calling out on the piazza, they shot and instantly killed. They also shot his son at the same time, all for being Union men.*

MURDER OF OLD MR. WOOD.

On or about the 15th of January, 1862, Champ Furguson, for some reason greatly exasperated, came to Albany, Kentucky, cursing all the Unionists in the place. He swore that he would kill some d—m Lincolnite before he left that night, and a horse he must have, he said, as the one he was riding was not good enough. Mr. D. Kozier, a citizen of Clifton county, having ridden a very fine one to Albany that day, left it standing fast-

---

* S. C. Wilson, of Tennessee.

ened in the road while he went into a friend's house to
attend to some business. Champ seeing it, rode up and
immediately appropriated it for his own use, at the same
time asking to be shown the owner, as he wanted to put
a ball through him, as a compensation, we suppose, for
the horse. But Mr. Kozier, not wishing to receive such
pay, and being unarmed, fled.

Toward evening Champ left Albany, still swearing
that he would kill some one that evening. On his way
he passed the dwelling of Mr. Wood, who was standing
in the door-way as the fiend came up; drawing his pistol, he told Mr. Wood that he had come to kill him.
"No, you won't," said Mr. Wood, "for I have trotted you
on my knee many a time when you was a baby; we
have lived together since you were a child, and have
always been good neighbors, and I never harmed you."
"You are a d—d Lincolnite," cried Champ; "you ran off
your mules, and besides you packed the d—d Union
flag at Camp Dick Robinson" (Mr. Wood was a color-
bearer in the Union army, but being too old he left the
army). "I will kill you anyhow;" suiting the action to
the word, he fired, shooting the old man in the abdomen,
who immediately fled into the house. Champ jumped
from his horse, and followed the old man, still firing at
him. Mr. Wood seeing this, seized a small hatchet,
turned round, and struck Furguson a severe blow on the
head, nearly stunning him, and would have killed him,
had not one Philipot, who had come from Albany with
Champ, interfered, threatening Mr. Wood with instant
death if he struck another blow. The old man, seeing
that he was deprived of the liberty of defending his life,
ran up stairs. Mrs. Wood and her daughter, hearing the
fracas, came to the rescue. Champ and his companion

seeing them coming, ran out of the house, and mounting their horses they made off. Mr. Wood's wound was so severe that he died next day.*

MURDER OF AN OLD MAN AND HIS THREE SONS.

In the latter part of September, 1863, a party of rebel bandits were prowling about the State of North Carolina, committing all sorts of depredations upon the Union people of the State. It was hinted by some one of the rebel sympathizers, that an old man and his three sons (name forgotten), living in Wilks county, were Unionists, and that it would be an act of patriotism to put them out of the way. Upon hearing this, the fiends started for the old man's house. Rushing into it, they seized the father and his three sons, before they could offer any resistance. The old man asked his captors why they had arrested them? The reply was, "You are d—d Union traitors, and it is our business to see that such as you are put out of the way." They then hurried them off to the woods, a short distance from the house, and, without even the form of a trial, hung them to the trees bordering the woods in sight of their home. While this work of murder was going on, the fiends kept yelling like savages. After they were satisfied that life was extinct, they went off, leaving the bodies of the four unfortunate men hanging, to be buried by whomsoever it might concern.†

----

* Dr. J. D. Hale, of Tennessee.
† B. K. Tulley, North Carolina.

MURDER OF PHILENEAS PLUMLEY.

PHILENEAS PLUMLEY, living in Van Buren county, Tennessee, eight miles south of ——, was inhumanly robbed, and then murdered, by a gang of Confederate soldiers in the early part of 1863. Mr. Plumley was ex-sheriff of Van Buren county, was an honest and respectable man, and had amassed a snug little fortune in property. He had just sold a large quantity of cotton, worth from six to eight thousand dollars, to Mr. Asa Faulkner. The rebels by some means learned this, and supposing he had received all the money, concluded to rob him. They went to his house, and not finding him there, they went to his father-in-law's, and arresting him, brought him back to his own house. They then demanded his money. He gave them one thousand dollars, telling them that was all he had received for the cotton, and expected to get the balance in a few days.

The disappointment so enraged the fiends that they drew out their pistols and fired, wounding him severely. Falling upon his knees, he begged them not to kill him. Dragging him into the yard, they finished their bloody work by firing five or six more balls into his body. Mr. Plumley was a quiet, inoffensive Union man, aged forty-five. He left a wife and seven little children (who all witnessed his murder) to mourn the loss of a good husband and father. Mr. Faulkner, hearing of the distressed condition of Mr. Plumley's family, went and paid Mrs. Plumley the balance due on the cotton.*

---

* General J. B. Rodgers.

10*

ATTACKS UPON J. J. PALMER'S HOUSE.

HEADQUARTERS, SEVENTH TENNESSEE REGIMENT,
Fort Cliff, Scott County, Tennessee, July 28th, 1862.

LIEUT.-COLONEL HOAGLAND: Dear Sir—Agreeably to your request, I hereby make a statement of three several attacks made upon me and my house. I have been residing during the past two and a half years in Rhea county, Tennessee, on the stock-road leading from Kentucky to the Tennessee river. My native State is New York; and the city of New York had been my place of residence for some twenty years previous to my coming to Tennessee.

I was at my residence on the night of the 13th instant, when I was attacked by thirteen rebels, who shot at me three times, and hit me in the left arm with three balls. I then fired upon them with my Enfield, and ran them off. The following day, in my absence, nearly one hundred of the same gang came to my house, and commenced an indiscriminate plunder of my house and store, taking from three to four hundred dollars' worth of property from me.

I was attacked again on the following Friday, by eighteen of the rebels. They were within twenty steps of the house when I discovered them. My wife was outside, and running in, closed the door after her. She was then ordered by them to open the door, or they would shoot her. I seized my gun, and rushed to the door and threw it open, when one of them fired upon me, at a distance not exceeding twelve feet, and I delivered my fire upon them, there being three of them in the yard. I then drew my navy-revolver, and ran into the yard and out to the gate, driving them all out of the yard. They fired four or five times while I stood at the gate. I now had time to make good my retreat to the upper part of the house, where I had a fine opportunity to fire upon them and be safe myself. They retired, as they supposed, to a safe distance, where they seemed disposed to remain, like a pack of hungry wolves; but a few discharges from my Enfield at any of them that showed themselves, persuaded them to leave for parts unknown.

I received one shot in the left breast, and another in the right side; one through the right arm, and another grazing it; and one in the right foot. My wife received one shot in her left hip, which glanced upon a reed of her hoop-skirt and did but little damage; another struck her right arm, doing little injury. I remained in the house and kept up a constant watch until night, when I made my escape to this camp. My family are now fugitives from home, and my property will be destroyed. They burst a cap at my wife on the 14th, when at their plunder, and struck her on the breast with the breech of a gun; and burst one also at one of the girls living in my family on the day of the last attack.

The rebels have reported three of their number dead, and I am credibly informed three others are wounded.

Respectfully submitted,

J. J. PALMER.

HORRIBLE OUTRAGES COMMITTED IN ALABAMA AND MISSISSIPPI.

THE greatest outrages imaginable were endured by the Unionists in North Alabama and Mississippi, in the latter part of 1862, and the early part of 1863.

In Mississippi the rebels conscripted all the men that

they could find between the ages of eighteen and sixty. The arch-traitor, Jeff Davis, sent to the above-named State no less than one thousand commissioned officers to enforce the conscription. The Unionists, to avoid this, fled to the woods, and the fiends set blood-hounds upon their tracks, and by this inhuman mode captured a great many, some of whom were nearly torn to pieces by these dogs before their pursuers came up.

In Alabama the conscription was prosecuted with still greater severity. During the latter part of 1862, a young girl, name forgotten, as she was passing through the woods in North Alabama, carrying food to her father, who had hid in a cave to escape conscription, was attacked by one of these blood-hounds, and literally torn to pieces. About the same time, two women who were making their way to Corinth, were overtaken by these dogs, near Tuscumbia, Franklin county, Alabama, and torn to pieces.

Nearly one thousand of these down-trodden Union men escaped to Corinth, Mississippi, and were treated with great kindness by the commander of the post, General Dodge, who sent out detachments of men to assist those who were endeavoring to escape. Some of the families, which came in at the above-named place, were without food, and had scarcely enough clothing to hide their nakedness; some of the men were cripples, and others of them over eighty years of-age.

General Dodge established an encampment for these refugees at Purdy, where they were free from such persecutions. Immediately after these refugees arrived, they set about forming a regiment, and it was not many weeks before it was full, ready and anxious for a fight. It was made up entirely of those who had suffered persecutions. They appointed Captain T. C. Cameron, then Provost-Marshal of Corinth, to be their Colonel.

The following is a copy of a letter from General Dodge to Captain Sawyer :—

HEAD-QUARTERS, DISTRICT OF CORINTH, MISS.,
January 24th, 1863.

Captain: I have the honor to submit a few of the outrages committed upon citizens of Alabama by the Confederate troops. While all their leaders, from the President down, are boasting of their carrying on this war in accordance with the laws that govern nations in such cases, I think a few simple facts might put them to the blush. I will state merely what I know to be true.

Abe Canadi and Mr. Mitchell were hung, two weeks ago, for being Union men. They were on the Hackleboro Settlement, Marion county, Alabama.

Mr. Halwork and his daughter, of the same county, were both shot for the same cause. The latter was instantly killed; the former is still alive, but will probably die. Peter Lewis and three of his neighbors were hunted down by one hundred blood-hounds and captured.

The houses of Messrs. Palmer, Welsby, Williams, and the three Weitmaus, were burned over their heads. The women and children were turned out of doors; and the community was notified that if they allowed them to go into other houses, or fed or harbored them in any manner, they would be served the same.

Mr. Peterson, living at the head of Bull Mountain, was shot.

I am now feeding some one hundred of these families, who, with their women and children, some gray-haired men, and even cripples on crutches, were driven out, and found their way here through the woods, by byways, without food or shelter. All this was done for the simple reason that they were Union men, or that they had brothers or relatives in our army. The statements of these people are almost beyond belief, did we not have the evidence before us. I am informed by them that there are hundreds of loyal men and women in the woods of Alabama, waiting an opportunity to escape.

I am, very respectfully, your obedient servant,
                              G. M. DODGE,
                                   Brigadier-General.
To Captain R. M. SAWYER,
        A. A. Gen., Memphis, Tennessee.

HANGING OF JOHN W. BUCK.

MR. JOHN W. BUCK, of Holmes county, Mississippi, an honest and upright man, was inhumanly murdered by a party of men calling themselves guerrillas, in the early part of the year 1863.

They were on his track several days, but by some means he managed to evade their vigilance. They were, however, determined to have him; so they lay in ambush, and when all was ready, rushed upon and captured him, and carrying him off to a safe distance, told him that they were going to hang him. He asked them to allow him a few moments to pray; but they told him that they had not the time to wait for him, as they were in a hurry to finish the job; and without further notice they deliberately hung him to a tree.

This murder was committed for no other reasons than that Mr. Buck was a Union man, and had rendered his Government some important services in suppressing this wicked rebellion.*

---

* Colonel Winslow and others.

MURDER OF DR. ALYWARD.

STILES, IOWA, July 15th, 1862.

DEAR SIR: I hasten to give you the news of the death of Dr. William Aylward, who was hung on the 14th instant, some eight miles west of Memphis, in Scotland county, Missouri. A party of guerrillas under one Colonel Porter, surrounded the town on Sunday evening, the 14th instant, and, among the Union citizens taken, were Dr. Aylward and Captain William Dawson. After pillaging the town, they forced Dr. Aylward and Captain Dawson into a two-horse wagon and left town. When they had proceeded about eight miles, they hung Dr. Aylward from a limb of a tree and left him hanging. The fate of Captain Dawson is not yet known to his friends, but we suppose he has suffered the same fate.

Yours, &c.,

R. C. DOUGHERTY.

BUSHWHACKING IN MISSOURI.

THE following is an extract from a letter of a Baptist minister, of Green county, Missouri. His name is withheld, because we have no authority to give it. But the statement may be relied on as being correct in every particular.

"The bushwhackers are at work again, as I expected they would be, as soon as the spring (1862) opened, and the leaves would hide them, and they could find grass sufficient to feed their horses. Every few days we hear of some one being shot by these men from the bush. They made a raid in Cedar county, not long since, and killed some ten men, with most of whom I was acquainted. Seven of them were soldiers. They first stripped them of everything except their shirts, then placed them together, and shot them from behind, leaving their dead bodies on the ground. They then passed on to the north of Stockton, and brutally murdered two citizens. They then went to the house of Mr. O. Smith, an old Baptist preacher, that I have known for nearly twenty years, and shot him, eighteen balls penetrating his body. They then robbed his dead body of three hundred dollars in money, and threw the empty purse in his wife's face. A party of them passed my house, not long since, going north, about fifty in all; twenty taking one road and the rest another. This is the way they scatter about, seizing horses, robbing stores, &c., and coming together at appointed places. As they passed here they took horses from the place. They also stole the mail-carrier's horses in this raid."

OUTRAGES COMMITTED BY MOSEBY.

As a portion of the wounded men and officers of the army of the Potomac, after the battle of the Wilderness, in Virginia, were being conveyed to Washington from Belle Plain by the way of Culpepper, they were attacked by Moseby and his marauding bands, on the night of the 11th of May, 1864. The train was composed of eighteen ambulances, our informant being in one of the foremost. Part of the train by some means got considerably in advance of the other, and stopped to wait for those in the rear to close up. It was at this time that the cowardly villains rushed upon the hindmost train as it was passing a piece of woodland, yelling and firing at the sick and wounded, and then in obedience to peremptory orders, the train immediately stopped. They then turned it into the woods, and robbed the wounded men and the drivers of all the valuables they had upon their persons. This done, they unhitched the horses from the ambulances, making the drivers prisoners. They went off, leaving the wounded men without help, and in a condition to starve or again be attacked by the straggling bands of guerrillas, who infested the country at that time.

In a few moments they came down with a rush upon the foremost train, ordering it to halt, firing at them all the time, the balls riddling the ambulances. One of Moseby's officers rode up to where the Adjutant of the Twentieth Massachusetts Regiment was, and ordered one of the drivers down from his seat on the ambulance. The Adjutant told the man to sit still. The fiend then fired upon the Adjutant, mortally wounding him. He has since died. The wounded were ordered to deliver up all their watches, money, and other valuables immediately, and if they did not do it, he would order his men to fire into them. Of course the devilish order was complied with. One of the drivers was inhumanly shot, and died instantly. Some of the wounded were shot as they were lying in the ambulance, causing them to suffer more intensely, for serving the country they loved.

This is only one of the many thousand of the damnable outrages, that have been committed by this rebel fiend within a few miles of the capital of our nation.*

---

* From Major W. F. Draper, Thirty-sixth Regiment, Massachusetts Volunteers.

11

FIENDISH ATROCITIES IN TEXAS.—MURDER OF MR. McKEES.

WE give below the particulars of some of the horrid barbarities that have been inflicted upon innocent Union people by the desperadoes of Texas, as related by G. Wilson Plummer, a refugee from Orange, Texas, who was robbed of all he possessed.

During the month of June, 1861, Jim Worsham, Ben Saxton, Charles Saxton, and Joe Jordan, all having been for years notorious thieves and murderers, were engaged by a chivalric party of Secessionists to murder a Mr. McKees, a native of Canada, on account of his anti-slavery views. Mr. McKees was an educated man, and his parents having been people of means, sent him to a military academy in Canada, where he acquired a thorough knowledge of military tactics.

Being of a roving disposition, he left home, and after taking a trip to China and Australia, he came to Texas in reduced circumstances. He was soon employed by John Livingston, a shipbuilder in the lower part of the town of Orange, upon the west bank of the Sabine river.

The rebels of Orange, having learned accidentally, one day, that McKees understood military movements, applied to him in a body, and demanded that he should instruct them in the school of the soldier; when McKees said that he could not spare the time, they insisted upon his teaching them, making use of threatening language.

Finding resistance impossible, he yielded to their demands; but after drilling them six weeks, growing tired of the business, he was advised by his employer, Mr. John Livingston, to give it up, and devote his time to his trade, which was that of a ship-carpenter.

He feigned sickness, and was relieved from duty by the rebels. Wishing to escape the fate which he saw awaited him (the rebels talking of appointing him their Captain), he soon recovered from his illness, and pretended to be a rabid Secessionist; and in order to carry out his plans for an escape, said he was anxious to see some active service in the field, and intended to go to New Orleans, and join the Confederate army.

In part remuneration for his past services as drillmaster, the rebels had given him a fine horse, and watching the most favorable opportunity, he mounted, one stormy night, and started for New Orleans.

He had been gone but a few hours when they missed him, and upon finding the horse gone, some of the rebels started off at daylight on the following day, and with fearful imprecations upon their lips, swore if they caught the d—d Abolitionist, they would hang him on the first tree. At Lafayette, a small town in the western part of Louisiana, the ruffians overtook him, and conveyed him back to Orange, Texas, where they carried him before a civil court, on the charge of horse-stealing, accusing him of having stolen the identical horse they themselves had given him, in part payment for his services.

The court returned a verdict of not guilty, and ordered McKees to be discharged, as the evidence of intent to steal was not sufficient to warrant his committal. The decision enraged the assassins, who were bent upon his destruction, and the mob seized him as he left the courtroom, and conveyed him to an old barn, half a mile distant, where, after taunting him with all manner of insults about his views upon slavery, they stripped him and administered a coat of tar and feathers.

Procuring a rail, they rode him into the town of Orange, followed by a brutal and insulting crowd, whom

they invited to shower insults of any kind upon the un-
happy McKees. The rowdies spat tobacco juice in his
eyes; and as they arrived in front of the bar-rooms,
threw him violently on the ground for the amusement
of the cruel and debased creatures who usually congregate about such places. After the mob had shouted
their approbation, he was taken up and conveyed to the
next shanty, where the same operation was performed.
McKees fainted several times from complete prostration,
and buckets of cold slops were thrown over him to
restore consciousness.

He begged them to kill him, rather than to torment
him in such a manner. Tiring of this, they took him to
an old shanty, and securing an old dirty negro, they
made McKees shake hands with him, and then, amid
the jeers of the crowd, told him "to take a drink with
his old Uncle," and compelled him to drink "Old Abe
Lincoln's health." After this, they seemed to be satisfied with demoniac sport of this kind, and two of the
ruffians prevailed upon the others to release him, on condition that if he was caught again attempting to escape,
he should be hung.   •

McKees was no sooner out of their clutches, than he
fell into the hands of others of the same party, who
heaped all sorts of indignities upon him in the street,
and hired boys to pelt him with rotten eggs, and call
him a negro-lover. Being hourly in fear of his life, he
resolved upon another attempt to escape from his persecutors, and started on foot for the mountains, hoping to
reach Mexico.

When six miles from Orange, the excited band overtook him and completely surrounded him, and with cow-
hides and pistols in hand, swore if he made any attempt

to escape, or offered any resistance, they would blow his brains out.

Jim Worsham grabbed him by the throat, and accused him of being a d—d miserable Abolitionist, while Joe Jordan applied the lash to his back, and whipped him till his strength was exhausted. McKees, who was now speechless, motioned to them to spare his life, as he saw Joe Jordan take from his coat-pocket a clothes-line, well knowing that they intended to hang him. The gang, which consisted of the two Saxton brothers, Jim Worsham, Joe Jordan, and three others, seized the defenceless man, and placing the rope around his neck, carried him across the road to a large tree, where they hung him.

The news was soon circulated throughout Orange that one d—d nigger-stealing Abolitionist was taken care of, and the citizens saw the fiend, Jim Worsham, parading in the bar-rooms, infuriated with liquor, swearing boastingly of what he and his confederates had accomplished for Texas by ridding her soil of an Abolitionist, while on his back they recognised poor McKees's clothing.

The next morning Mr. Hope Cooper, a farmer of Orange county, was driving to the town of Orange, when he was horrified at the sight of McKees's lifeless body suspended from a tree at the road-side. He drove back, and informed one of his neighbors, when they both returned and cut down the ghastly and terribly-mutilated form of the murdered man, and buried him in an adjoining field.

As soon as Jim Worsham, Joe Jordan, and their followers heard what Mr. Cooper had done, they swore with terrible oaths that they would cut the heart out of the Yankee sympathizer that had removed the body of an Abolitionist; but Mr. Cooper and his neighbors were

11 *

cautious, when questioned about the body, to plead entire ignorance of the whole affair.

MURDER OF MR. JAMES AND MR. MARSHALL.

In the month of August, 1861, a man by the name of James arrived in the town of Orange, from Galveston, and put up at King's Hotel. He reported, in the course of his conversation with a crowd in the bar-room of the house, that he had just arrived a few weeks previous at Galveston, from California. It is said that in the evening of the day of his arrival he was seen conversing with one or two negroes by Jim Worsham and his gang, who were lying in ambush for him.

In his interview with the negroes, it is asserted that he told them his mission was to liberate them, and that if they would prepare themselves the next night, he would secrete them on board a small schooner which belonged to him, and which was anchored in Sabine river, on the Louisiana side. One of the negroes to whom he revealed his plans, belonging to a Mr. Smith, a New-Yorker, who had been in Texas about a year and a half, went to his master and narrated the full particulars of the conversation that had taken place between Mr. James and himself, telling his master that James wanted to meet him (the slave) that night at twelve o'clock, and that he had promised to do so. Smith, upon learning this, determined to ferret out the matter, and accordingly dressed himself in his slave's suit of clothes, and, blackening his face, sallied out at the appointed time to meet Mr. James.

So complete was the disguise, that with the knowledge

obtained from the ignorant or treacherous negro, he succeeded in drawing from his unsuspecting confidant the whole of his plans. Making an agreement to meet again, the supposed negro vanished.

The next morning Smith reported to Charles Saxton, Jim Davis, and Jim Worsham what he had heard, and it was at once decided to take the life of Mr. James, who was expected to leave Orange that day. About nine o'clock Mr. James chartered a small boat, and hired a Mr. Marshall to row him across the Sabine river.

Both James and Marshall were in the boat, and Marshall was standing up pushing off from the shore, when Jim Davis, a notorious thief, and his companions, came rushing down the bank. The boat was not more than a dozen yards from the bank when Davis aimed a revolver at Mr. James, exclaiming, with an oath. " You are a d—d Yankee scoundrel, that tried last night to entice our negroes away, and I am going to shoot you on the spot, you miserable thief!" Mr. Marshall stood in front of Mr. James, expostulating with Davis, telling him he was mistaken in the man, and begging him to spare Mr. James's life. This intervention aroused all the beastly fury of Davis, who swore he would kill both of them, and suiting the action to the word, he fired upon Mr. Marshall, who fell in the bottom of the boat, exclaiming, " Great God, what have you done!" The ball entered the right breast, and passed nearly through the body.

They then put out a small boat, and brought both James and Marshall to the shore, and securing James, they laid Marshall under an old shingle-shed, where the hideous monster, Charles Saxton, took out his jack-knife and began to probe the wound for the bullet, cursing Marshall for groaning at the pain he was suffering.

Marshall besought him to let him alone, and in the

name of God to send for his wife and children, that he might see them before he breathed his last. At first this request was refused, but after earnest entreaties the wretches granted the dying man's only wish ; and Mrs. Marshall with her family of five small children, arrived just in time to witness his dying struggle.

Mrs. Marshall was so terribly stricken with grief at the loss of her husband that she survived his murder but ten days. Her babe of two years, and a bright little boy of six years, were laid at the side of their parents in two weeks after their death. Mr. Marshall was a native of the western part of Louisiana, a brickmaker by trade, and had always been respected as an honest and hard-working man.

After these desperadoes had got rid of Marshall, they turned their whole attention to Mr. James. They carried him before the civil authorities, on the charge of enticing negroes to desert their masters. Jim Davis produced several letters, which were known by loyal witnesses to have been forged, and affirmed under oath, that they found these letters in Mr. James's coat-pocket. The testimony was so strong and conclusive, that he was found guilty, and the sentence of death was passed upon him early in the forenoon by the judge. At night a mob broke into the jail, and dragging Mr. James to the nearest tree, hung him on the spot. After the body had been suspended fifteen or twenty minutes, it was cut down, and eight or ten blood-thirsty fellows removed the corpse to the interior of the jail. In a few minutes Dr. Hudson of Orange, and another doctor of the same town, assisted by the crew, whose malicious perjury on the witness-stand had been the cause of the sentence, began to mutilate the body, and while doing so, gave vent to the most horrible sentiments. Dr. Hudson cut out the

heart, and placed it in a glass pickle jar filled with
Louisiana whiskey, and this murdered man's heart has
been seen by various persons since his execution, and it
can be seen to-day in the drug and paint store of Dr.
Hudson in the town of Orange. After this, they
actually tried out all the fat from the flesh, and
divided it among each other for the oiling of their
fire-arms. One of the doctors secured the head and
carried it home, telling his wife to boil it till all the flesh
should drop off, but the wife refused to have anything to
do with it, and was horror-stricken at the barbarous
sight. Her husband, however, compelled her to place
the skull in a large copper-kettle, and boil it for several
hours, when he took charge of it, told his wife that he
had long desired an Abolitionist's skull for his study, and
now he had got one.

Charles Saxton, a notorious robber, gave a ball a week
or two after the murder, in honor of the Vigilance Committee, whose business was to clean out all anti-slavery
people from Texas. He invited all the Secessionists of
Orange, of both sexes, to the ball, and, as an inducement
to attend the assembly, told them he would exhibit a
genuine "Yankee skull." He had borrowed it from the
doctor; and fastening it to a shelf, placed a candle in
each eye-socket, and while most of the guests looked on
with satisfaction to behold the Yankee head, he made
the remark that "Yankee candlesticks were a decided
improvement over the old-fashioned ones." The next
morning Jim Davis and Saxton tied their pieces of
mutilated flesh in a meal-bag, and threw them into the
Sabine river, supposing that when the tide flowed they
would float off, but they kept floating to and fro for two
days, until Mr. George Kneeland, whose house was on
the river-bank, went to Saxton and Davis, and told them

if there was any law in the land, he would instantly
prosecute them, if they did not remove the remains from
the river and bury them properly. Fearing this threat
from Kneeland, who is an earnest rebel, the scoundrels
buried these portions of the body.

To corroborate the above, I relate the following
incident. Mrs. Freeland, a daughter of Robert Jackson
of Orange, one of the first Union families in Texas, was
anxious to borrow or purchase a large-sized copper-
kettle, for the purpose of making preserves. She was
well acquainted with Mrs. Dr. Hudson, and knowing nothing at that time of the dissecting of Mr. James's body
by the doctor), visited her for the purpose of securing the
kettle.

While there, the conversation ran from one point to
another, until the doctor's wife told how she was obliged
to boil a human skull in one of her kettles, for her husband. Mrs. Freeland was horrified, and left the house.

The following persons will vouch for the truth of the
statement in relation to the murder of Mr. McKees,
Mr. Marshall, and Mr. James, viz.: John Livingston,
David Livingston, Samuel Livingston, ship-carpenters in
Orange, Texas; Mrs. Nancy Jane Jackson, William
Jackson her son; Gowing Wilson Plummer, Mrs. Plum-
mer, and Albert Plummer her son. Mr. Plummer is a
New Englander, and was born in the town of Addison,
Washington county, Maine. He has been for four years
in the employ of the United States, as light-house
keeper at the "Texas Light," on the east bank of Sabine
Pass.   N. Y. Y.

MURDER OF CAPTAIN MONTGOMERY.

ON the evening of the 15th of March, 1863, Captain Montgomery was kidnapped and taken to Camp Bell, a rebel camp on the Rio river, in Texas, a short distance from the mouth of the river, where he was kept till the next day, during which time he was tantalized by those who had him in charge. He was told he was going to be hanged, and was asked, in a mocking manner, if he was not going to say his prayers.

Next morning, about ten o'clock, he was taken a short distance above the camp, to a retired place on the river. A rope was tied about his neck, and he was commanded to tell what he knew about the Federal forces. He refused to disclose anything. He was suspended to a branch of a tree for some time, and when taken down, again required to communicate information; he still refusing, and saying that, as they were going to hang him in any case, he should not make any disclosures. They repeated this operation four or five times, when he was hung up in earnest, and left by his murderers.

He remained in that condition five days, when he was taken down by a friendly old Mexican and buried a few feet in the ground. The murderers afterwards removed the earth, saying he should be left exposed. The notorious Captain Bruin, a Southern traitor of Northern birth, commanded the hanging party, and for his bravery and chivalry in thus hanging a helpless and defenceless man, was at once promoted, and now rejoices in the title of Major-Bruin.*

---

* Colonel Jesse Staneel, First Texas Cavalry.

HORRIBLE CRUELTIES OF THE REBELS TO THE GERMANS IN TEXAS.

In the month of May, 1861, a rebel command left the neighborhood of Austin, Texas, in order to break up and destroy a German settlement near El Paso, in Texas. It consisted of some two hundred and fifty souls. These Germans had sown and planted largely all kinds of grain. In addition, they had large flocks of sheep and herds of cattle; also horses, mules, and swine, in great numbers. It was one of the most prosperous settlements in the State. They were known to be Union men with no possibility of an exception.

Their fidelity to their adopted country enraged the rebels, and on the 20th of the month some eighty or a hundred of these ruffians attacked the Germans, without the slightest provocation.

An indiscriminate slaughter of men, women, and children was made. Out of the whole population it is not known that more than three persons ever escaped. Fathers, mothers, sisters, brothers, and loved ones, all constituted one heap of carnage. They actually murdered little innocent babes not one month old, and violated the chastity of women, and then pitilessly murdered them, both young and old. Many of the men they hung. After plundering the houses of all valuables, and taking whatever they wanted, they burned them. They drove off all the stock of every kind they could discover, and then returned with an air of triumph to their companions in guilt.

This band of miscreants is said to have been under the command of two men by the names of Dibrell and Jenkins, both of Tennessee. Dibrell has a brother commanding a guerilla regiment of Tennessee troops.*

BARBARITIES OF TEXAN RANGERS.

MONTEREY, MEXICO, November 4th, 1862.

DEAR FRIEND: * * * * You can hardly imagine how the Union men are treated in Texas. They are hung on the slightest suspicion, by bodies of irresponsible men, who, were they in a country where law was respected, would not be allowed outside of a prison-yard.

You have probably heard of the way that a small body of Union men were treated by a part of J. McDuff's company of Texas Rangers, at the head of the Nueces. I learn from a gentleman here who had a conversation with an officer who was present at the massacre, that twelve passports from provost-marshals of Western Texas were found on the bodies of the Union men killed, by which they were allowed to pass freely over any part of the Texan frontier.

After the affair on the Nueces, another party of twenty Germans were attacked on the Rio Grande, as they were preparing to cross it, by a large party of Rangers. They succeeded in killing a number of Rangers and driving them back, only having in the party one man slightly wounded. They immediately crossed the river, leaving their horses with the Texans, and throwing their guns into the water.

We have here upon the frontier about one thousand

---

* General Rodgers and General A. J. Hamilton's secretary.

12

Union men, who are only waiting for an invasion of Texas to get a chance to join the Union army.

> Yours truly,   M. McKinney,
> U. S. Vice-Consul.

MASSACRE AT BAXTER SPRINGS.

Baxter Springs, 63 miles below Fort Scott,
October 7th. 1863

Capts. Thalen and Loring: * * * * When I wrote to Major Blair, last night, it was supposed that Major Curtis was a prisoner, as we had searched the ground over near where his horse fell and could not find him. Moreover, Quantrell's Adjutant, or a person representing himself as such, who came into Lieutenant Pond's company with a flag of truce, said they had my Assistant Adjutant-General a prisoner.

To-day he was found, near where he was thrown from his horse, shot through the head, evidently having been murdered after becoming a prisoner. I shall start his body, with that of Lieutenant Parr, to Fort Scott this evening. You probably will have heard some of the particulars of the affair which occurred here yesterday, before you receive this.

The escort, Company I Third Wisconsin, and Company A Fourteenth Kansas, consisting of one hundred men, behaved disgracefully, and stampeded like a drove of frightened cattle. I did not anticipate any difficulty until we got below this point. We arrived near this camp about twelve o'clock, m., and halted on the hill, almost in sight of the camp, and not more than four hundred yards distant, to wait for the escort and wagons to close up. The escort came up and dismounted, to wait for the train, which was but a short distance behind. At this time my attention was called to a body of men, about one hundred in number, advancing in line from the timber of Spring river on the left, which you will recollect is not more than three or four hundred yards from the road.

The left of the line was not more than two hundred yards from Lieutenant Pond's camp at the spring. They being nearly all dressed in Federal uniforms, I supposed them to be Lieutenant Pond's Cavalry (two companies), on service. At the same time my suspicions were aroused by some of their movements. I ordered the wagons which had come up to the rear, and found the escort in line with their carbines unslung, while I advanced alone toward the party fronting us, to ascertain if they were rebels. I had advanced but a short distance when they opened fire. At the same time firing was heard down in Pond's camp. Turning around to give the order to the escort to fire, I discovered them all broken up, and going over the prairie to the west at full speed. They did not discharge the loaded carbines which they had in their hands, except in a few cases. Had the escort stood their ground as soldiers should have done, they could have driven the enemy in ten minutes. I endeavored in vain, with the assistance of Major Curtis, to halt and form a portion of them. When the escort stampeded, the enemy discovering it rushed on with a yell, followed by another line of about two hundred, that emerged from the edge of the timber. Being better mounted than our men, they soon closed in on them. The men of the escort were much scattered, and with them it was a run for life. After going a mile, I succeeded in halting fifteen men, including Lieutenant Pierce, Company

A, Fourteenth Kansas, who has done his duty well and nobly throughout.

As soon as I got them in line, and commenced advancing on the pursuing enemy, they fled and fell back to the wood, when their whole command (six hundred) formed in line of battle. The balance of the escort that had escaped were all out of sight in the advance. Major Curtis had been seen to fall from his horse, which had been wounded, and stumbled in crossing a ditch. About one o'clock I sent Lieutenant Tappan, who had kept with me all the time, with four men to Fort Scott, while with the other nine I determined to remain until the fate of those that had fallen could be ascertained, and whether the post at the Spring had been captured, which I much feared had been the case.

As they fell back to the road I followed them up over the ground we had passed, to look for the wounded, but all, with two or three exceptions, who had escaped accidentally, were killed, shot through the head. All the wounded had been murdered. I kept close to them, and witnessed their plundering the wagons. At one time they made a dash at me with about one hundred men, endeavoring to surround me, but failed in their purpose. As they moved off, on the road leading south, I went down to the Spring, and found our men all safe.

Lieutenant Pond, of the Third Wisconsin, and his command, are entitled to great credit for the manner in which they repulsed the enemy and defended the post. The colored soldiers fought with great gallantry. The band-wagon was captured, and all the boys shot in the same way after they were prisoners. The same was the case with the teamsters, and Mart, my driver. O'Niel (artist for Frank Leslie) was killed with the band boys. The office clerks were all killed except one, also my or-

.rly, Ely. Major Henning is with me. But few of the escort, who escaped, have come in. I suppose they have gone to Fort Scott. The dead are not all buried, but I suppose the number will not fall short of seventy-five.

The enemy numbered six hundred of Quantrell's and Coffey's commands. They are evidently intending to go south of the Arkansas. I have scouts on the trail. Two have just come in, and report coming up with them, at the crossing of the Neosho river.

Others are still following them up. Whether they will go directly south, on the Fort Gibson road, across Grand river to Cowskin Prairie, I cannot determine.

When they came in they crossed Spring river, close by Baxter. I have sent messengers to Arkansas river, and if they succeed in getting through safely, our forces there will be put on the alert, and may intercept them. I am now waiting the arrival of troops from Fort Scott. If I get them, which is doubtful, as the Fourteenth Kansas is not armed, I will follow the hounds through the entire Southern Confederacy as long as there is a prospect of overtaking them. And I will have it well understood that any man of this command, who again breaks from the line, and deserts his post, shall be shot on the spot; and there shall be no quarter to the motley bands of murderers.

I was fortunate in escaping, as in my efforts to halt and rally the men I frequently got in the rear, and became considerably mixed up with the rebels, who did not fail to pay me their compliments. Revolver-bullets flew around my head as thick as hail—but not a scratch!

I believe I am not to be killed by a rebel bullet.

Yours, truly,

JAMES G. BLUNT,
Major-General of Volunteers.

12 *

MURDER OF A LAD, FOUNT ZACKERY.

CHAMP FURGUSON and his ruffians had been roving over the country around Albany, Kentucky, shooting every person they saw who was suspected of being a Union man; but this license was speedily checked by the suspected approach of a party of United States soldiers, which caused Champ and gang to decamp faster than they had anticipated. As he was leaving, he told the inhabitants that he had killed four d—d Union men that day, and intended to kill more before he left the country. They searched over the town till night, and not finding any suspected Unionists, they left, taking the road toward Spring Creek. Upon their arrival, they met a lad named Fount Zackery. Champ riding up to him shot him, then jumping off his horse, drew out his famous knife, and cut the boy nearly in two, and taking the lad's horse started for Tennessee. This cruel murder was committed, because the boy had expressed himself in favor of the Union; besides, Champ wished the horse, and took this means of securing it. Young Zackery was an inoffensive boy, and was respected for his industry and perseverance.*

BARBARITY OF MISSOURI GUERRILLAS.

HEADQUARTERS, FIFTH CAVALRY, MISSOURI STATE MILITIA,
Independence, Missouri, January 11th, 1863.

GENERAL BEN LOGAN, Jefferson City: Sir—Private Johnson, of the artillery company, was brought in dead

---

* Doctor J. G. Hale, of Tennessee.

to-day; he is th fifth one murdered last week, four from the infantry and one from the artillery. (You would not wonder why it is, that I write you that guerrillas' wives should be forced out of the country.) They were all wounded, and were killed *afterwards* in the most horrible manner that fiends could devise. All were shot in the head, and several of their faces are terribly cut to pieces with boot-heels. Powder was exploded in one man's ear, and both ears cut off close to his head. Whether this inhuman act was committed while he was alive or not, I have no means of knowing. To see human beings treated as my men have been, is more than I can bear.

Ten of these men, armed as they are, with their wives and children to act as spies, are equal to twenty-five of mine. Guerrillas are threatening Union women in the country. I am arresting the wives and sisters of some of the most notorious ones, to prevent them from carrying their threats into execution. They have also levied an assessment upon the loyal men of the vicinity, and are collecting it very fast.   Yours, &c.

W. R. PENICK,
Colonel Fifth Cavalry,
Missouri State Militia.

OUTRAGES COMMITTED BY THE REBELS IN EAST TENNESSEE.

EAST TENNESSEE, a region about equal in area and population to New Hampshire or Vermont, having few slaves and no aristocracy, presented an unyielding resistance to the madness of Secession. Even after the first battle of Bull Run, the State gave 32,923 for the Union to 14,768 for Secession, a majority of 18,155. This region of unconquerable loyalty, the rebels determined to dragoon into subjection. They left no means untried, and hesitated not to perpetrate the most revolting barbarities. A reign of terror was established, which in point of ferocity, has scarcely a parallel in ancient or modern times among civilized nations. The Union people were driven from their homes, hunted with blood hounds like wild beasts, and shot down wherever found, without hesitancy or discrimination; their houses were burned down over the heads of their families, and even the chastity of the women was disregarded.

All this was done with the consent, if not by the direction of the rebel government. It grew naturally out of such atrocious orders as the following from J. P. Benjamin, rebel Secretary of War.

WAR DEPARTMENT, RICHMOND, November 25th 1861.

Sir: Your report of the 20th instant is received, and I now proceed to give you the desired instructions in relation to prisoners taken by you among the traitors of East Tennessee.

First. All such as can be identified in having been engaged in bridge burning, are to be tried summarily by drum-head court-martial, and if found guilty, executed on the spot by hanging. It would be well to leave their bodies hanging in the vicinity of the burnt bridges.

Second. All such as have not been so engaged are to be treated as prisoners of war, and sent with an armed guard to Tuscaloosa, Alabama, there to be kept imprisoned at the depot, selected by the government for prisoners of war.

Whenever you can discover that arms are concen-

trated by these traitors, you will send out detachments, search for, and seize the arms. In no case, is one of the men known to have been in arms against the government, to be released on any pledge or oath of allegiance. The time for such measures is past. They are to be held as prisoners of war; and held in jail till the end of the war. Such as come in voluntarily to take the oath of allegiance, and surrender their arms, are alone to be treated with leniency.

Your vigilant execution of these orders, is earnestly urged by the government.

Your obedient servant,
J. P. BENJAMIN,
Secretary of War.

Colonel W. B. WOOD,
  Knoxville, Tennessee.

P. S.—Judge Patterson, Colonel Pickins, and other ringleaders of the same class, must be sent at once to Tuscaloosa to jail, as prisoners of war. Yours, &c.

J. P. B.

By the violence and outrages arising from such unlimited orders as this, the Unionists of East Tennessee were placed in the most distressing circumstances, and forced to flee in every direction, seeking safety in the woods, caves, and mountain heights of that beautiful Switzerland of America.

To them it seemed as though the Union army would never come to their rescue; but although the night was long and dark, the day at last dawned, help and deliverance came, the old flag returned, and was hailed with acclamations of joy.

MURDER OF COLONEL McCOOK.

EXTRACT of a letter written by a gentleman who was in Huntsville, Alabama, at the time of the murder of Colonel McCook. We vouch for its truthfulness.

HUNTSVILLE, ALABAMA, August 8th, 1862.

Dear Sir: Colonel McCook was murdered by the notorious Frank Gurley, this morning. The facts of the case are these:—Colonel McCook was on his way with his brigade from Tuscumbia, Alabama, to Winchester, Tennessee, and being sick, was travelling in an ambulance, and was considerably in advance of his brigade, without a guard. When near Salem, Tennessee, he was surprised by a party of Gurley's men. The mules became frightened and started to run. Colonel McCook dropped on his knees, and seized the lines to help the driver hold them up, and was in this position when shot in the abdomen by Gurley, to whom he called out not to shoot, that he surrendered, and told him his name and rank; but his appeals were not heard or heeded by the blood-thirsty wretch. After killing Colonel McCook, the guerrillas took the mules out of the ambulance and burned it, and made off with at least two of his staff, before the brigade arrived. This Frank Gurley has been, since the rebellion commenced, at the head of a gang of thieves and scoundrels, numbering about eighty, who have depredated upon scattered soldiers, and the Unionists in the neighborhood of Madison and Jackson counties, Tennessee, inflicting upon them the most cruel barbarities imaginable, when they knew they had the advantage on their own side. If this war ever ends, and finds such scoundrels as Gurley alive, let him atone at the end of the halter for his fiendish cruelties.

The following order, issued by General Rousseau immediately after the death of Colonel McCook, explains itself:—

HEAD-QUARTERS, THIRD DIVISION,
Huntsville, Ala., August 8th, 1862.

Special Orders, No. 54.—Almost every day murders are committed by lawless bands of robbers and murderers, firing into railroad trains. To prevent this, or to let the guilty suffer with the innocent, it is ordered that the preachers and leading men of the churches (not exceeding twelve in number), in and about Huntsville, who have been active Secessionists, be arrested and kept in custody, and that one of them be detailed each day, and placed on board the train on the road running by way of Athens, and taken to Elk river and back, in charge of a trusty soldier, who shall be armed, and not allow him to communicate with any person.

When not on duty, these gentlemen shall be comfortably quartered in Huntsville, but not allowed to communicate with any one, without leave from these Head-quarters. The soldiers detailed for guard of this character will report to these Head-quarters for further instructions, upon the day preceding their tour of duty, at three o'clock P. M.

By command of
LOVELL H. ROUSSEAU,
Brigadier-Gen. Com'g.

F. J. JONES, A. A. A. G.

Who would ever have thought that it would have been necessary to issue such an order in this free and fair land of ours, and among those whom we supposed to be a civilized and intelligent people?

Yours, &c.   D. H. BINGHAM.

FIRING ON A HOSPITAL-BOAT.

In the early part of July, 1863, as the hospital-boats belonging to. General Curtis's command were passing down the Mississippi river, they were fired upon by a party of guerrillas upon the bank, who kept following it as they floated slowly down the river, discharging volley after volley upon the sick, wounded, and defenceless men who lay exposed to their murderous fire, expecting every minute to receive a fatal shot. The officer in charge of the boat shouted to them to stop, that it was a hospital-boat, and pointed to the yellow flag above him. They paid no attention to his appeal, but continued to fire, wounding a great many of the already sick and wounded. A captain on board was wounded seriously while pleading with them to stop. This outrage was continued until one of the Union gunboats came to their assistance. The gunboat fired a few well-directed shots at the cowardly miscreants, which caused them to de-camp faster than they had followed the boat. Thus ended the tragedy. The guerillas were commanded by a man who wore the uniform of a Confederate captain, but called himself a guerrilla, to vindicate the govern-ment whose orders he was carrying out.*

ASSAULT ON THE FAMILY OF MR. JOHN YOUNG, AND HEROIC CONDUCT OF HIS DAUGHTERS.

EARLY in the progress of the rebellion, it was seen to be the policy of the leaders to overrun Tennessee with

* From Dr. W. H. D. Williamson, of Southern Arkansas.

an armed force drawn from Texas, Mississippi, and Louisiana, under pretence of drilling the soldiers, and protecting the citizens from depredations. The real purpose of the treacherous crew was to consume and destroy the available resources of the country, and to disarm its inhabitants of every means of defence. Robbery was their great aim ; and cruelty and oppression were the means by which they proposed to torture the peaceful inhabitants into submission.

Every movement of the people was met with demonstrations calculated to excite terror and dismay ; every sentiment of attachment to the Union or the flag, was sought to be suppressed by the force of the bowie-knife and the bayonet. Violence was the order of the day, "Exterminate the Union men!" the watchword of the hour, with these marauding, murderous bands.

One of these ruffian bands was stationed in Fentress county, Tennessee, a short distance from the residence of Mr. John Young, who was known to be a Union man, and one of the best citizens of the country. His course had been such as to win the esteem of the virtuous in his vicinity. Retiring, industrious, unobtrusive, and correct in his deportment, he was just such an individual as those miscreants deemed it necessary to visit with their deepest vengeance. His influence and example, they thought, might damage the rebel cause, and rebel wickedness might labor under restraint extremely disagreeable to the rebel leaders in their deep guilt of treason and blood. Mr. Young was compelled to lie out in the woods and from his family, to avoid imminent danger of being arrested, and hung, or murdered in some other way.

One evening, at twilight, a large rough soldier came to the dwelling where Mr. Young's family still resided, with pistol in hand, and a bowie-knife in his bosom. He

13

told Mrs. Young that he wanted lodging for the night. The lady remarked, having two grown daughters with her, that she was not in the habit of entertaining soldiers in the absence of her husband.

The ruffian replied, that "By G–d he had come to stay, and he was going to stay, whether it suited her or not!"

Mrs. Young then said, "If you are determined to stay, why ask me anything about it?" And turning to one of her daughters, standing near, she directed her to go up-stairs and prepare a bed for the man. The daughter hastened up-stairs, and the soldier took his weapons in his hands and followed her. When he reached the room, he motioned the young lady to take one of the beds. She said "No." He said "He would see to that!" and advanced toward her. She, being a stout, vigorous woman, as he came to her, grasped him firmly by both his arms and screamed for help.

Her sister, Miss Mary Young, who was still below, seized an axe which happened to be near and ran up to the rescue. Here she found her sister struggling with the infamous wretch, and still holding him with a firm grasp.

This sister made one stroke at his head with the axe, and its keen edge fell just where the vertebræ join the neck. The blow was as fatal as it was fortunate. It nearly severed the head from the body. The villain fell instantly on the floor, weltering in blood.

Such was the recompense of brutal villany! Vengeance was swift and sure.*

---

* General J. B. Rodgers.

MURDER OF DOCTOR WILLIAM McGLASSEN.

IN the early part of November, 1862, a party of rebels under that notorious scoundrel, John Morgan, attacked a small body of United States soldiers near Burksville, Cumberland county, Kentucky. During the engagement three Union citizens were captured, among them Dr. Wm. McGlassen. After securing the doctor, they rode off five or six miles, when they met Champ Furguson and his gang, who proposed to kill the doctor. Morgan's men assented, and offered their assistance. As soon as they had concluded in what manner the prisoner should die, a large number of the marauders dismounted and commenced walking about until they had left him by himself. This done, one of them rushed upon him, levelling his gun at the doctor, and bursting a cap, ordering him at the same time to run for his life.

He started to run, but had hardly proceeded a dozen yards when the whole band fired about one hundred shots at him. The doctor kept running until he reached a deep gulley, into which, through weakness by loss of blood, he fell, when they rushed upon him, drawing their pistols, and discharged their contents at him, several of the shots taking effect in the body, and one or two hitting him in the head, killing him almost instantly. The fiends then commenced robbing the body. They took his watch, and what money he had. Not satisfied with this, lifting up his body, they took off his coat, pantaloons, and vest, and would have stripped his body of the last piece of clothing, had not some one of the murderers, who had a little humanity left, threatened to shoot them. Throwing the body down, they left it, to commit other depredations upon the Unionists in the surrounding country. This Champ Furguson, in a speech delivered to his admirers at Sparta, Tennessee, in August, 1863, said: "I have killed sixteen Lincolnites, and intend to kill enough more to make it number twenty-five; then I shall be ready to die."

What became of the other two prisoners we are unable to say, but hope they escaped. If not, they were, no doubt, treated in the same manner as Dr. McGlassen. None but the Almighty Ruler can number the many Unionists of the South who have fallen in this way; and their bones are now left bleaching beneath a Southern sun, without a mark to tell to whom they belong.*

FIRING ON UNITED STATES BOATS AFTER THE SURRENDER OF NATCHEZ.

United States Flag Ship Hartford,
Off Natchez, Mississippi, March 17th, 1863.

Sir: I trust that it is unnecessary to remind you of my desire to avoid the necessity of punishing the innocent for the guilty, and to express to you the hope that the scene of firing on the United States boats will not be repeated by either the lawless people of Natchez, or by the guerrilla forces; otherwise I shall be compelled to do the act most repugnant to my feelings, by firing on your town in defence of my people, and the honor of my flag.

I should be most happy to see his honor the Mayor on board.

Very respectfully,
D. G. Farragut, Rear Admiral.
His Honor, the Mayor of Natchez, Mississippi.

---

* Dr. J. D. Hale, of Tennessee.

WILLIAMSBURG BARBARITIES.

SHORTLY after the Eighth New York Regiment went into the battle of Williamsburg, Virginia, May 5th, 1862, Colonel Johnson, then commanding, was severely wounded, and taken off the field. The command then devolved on Major Reyson, who fell shortly after, pierced by three balls. The regiment was unable to carry him off the field. The next morning his body was found, stripped of all his clothing, and his head mutilated in a shocking manner, having been smashed with the butt of a musket, after death.

Captain H. B. Riley, Company G, First Regiment Excelsior Brigade, who wore a bullet-proof breastplate during the engagement, fell, badly wounded in the face, and before he could be removed, the regiment to which he belonged was forced back. When it regained its former position, the captain was found dead, with three bayonet thrusts through his breast, and the bullet-proof plate stolen. He had evidently been bayoneted while lying a wounded and helpless prisoner.

Orderly Sergeant Pease, Company E, First Regiment Excelsior Brigade, was slightly wounded, and taken prisoner. At the evacuation of the place the rebels tied his hands together, then fastened him to the rear of an army wagon, and started for Richmond. In the retreat he came up with Lieutenant Wilson, Company F, First Regiment Excelsior Brigade, who was a prisoner and badly wounded, and, through loss of blood and pain, unable to walk farther. The unfeeling wretches who had him in charge bayoneted him, and brutally left him by the road-side, hoping that it would either kill him or cripple him for life. The Union scouts found him shortly afterwards in a deplorable condition, and unable to speak.

13 *

FIRING ON WOMEN AND CHILDREN FOR CHEER-
ING FOR THE OLD FLAG.

UNITED STATES FLAG SHIP HARTFORD,
At anchor off the City of New Orleans, April 26th, 1862.

Sir: Upon my arrival before your city, I had the
honor to send to your honor Captain Bailey, United
States Navy, second in command of the expedition, to
demand of you the surrender of New Orleans to me, as
the representative of the Government of the United
States. Captain Bailey reported to me the result of an
interview with yourself and the military authorities. It
must occur to your honor that it is not within the pro-
vince of a naval officer to assume the duties of a military
commandant. I came here to reduce New Orleans to
obedience to the laws of, and to vindicate the offended
majesty of the Government of the United States. The
rights of persons and property shall be secure. I therefore demand of you, as its representative, the unqualified
surrender of the city, and that the emblem of sovereignty
of the United States be hoisted over the City Hall, Mint,
and Custom-House by meridian this day, and that all
flags and other emblems of sovereignty, other than those
of the United States, shall be removed from all the
public buildings by that hour. I particularly request
that you shall exercise your authority to quell disturb-
ances, restore order, and call upon all the good people of
New Orleans to return at once to their vocations; and I
particularly demand that no person shall be molested in
person or property for professing sentiments of loyalty
to their Government. I shall speedily and severely
punish any person or persons who shall commit such
outrages as were witnessed yesterday—armed men firing

upon helpless women and children for giving expression to their pleasure at witnessing the old flag.

I am, very respectfully, your obedient servant,

D. G. FARRAGUT,

Flag Officer, Western Gulf Squadron.

His Excellency,

The Mayor of the City of New Orleans.

MURDER OF A GERMAN

IN the month of August, 1860, whilst the steamship' McRay was in port at New Orleans, a most inhuman murder was perpetrated by a mob, on a German pedlar. The German was on the street, with a small lot of pictures, neckties, trinkets, &c. A small boy, who was looking at them, noticed a picture of Mr. Lincoln, then a candidate for the Presidency of the United States. Seizing it, he threw it on the pavement, and abused the German for having it in his possession.

A mob collected around the unfortunate man, and asked him what he was doing with the picture of Lincoln, the Black Republican. The German did not understand the English language well enough to know what the crowd meant by their inquiries; all he knew was that he had purchased the whole lot, with a little money he had with him, to sell again on a small profit. The mob could easily have inquired as to the truth of the matter, when the innocence of the German would have appeared. But this was too much trouble, or rather perhaps the truth was what they did not wish to know. It would have been an encumbrance on their consciences.

They became so incensed at the unfortunate German,

for no other cause than that he was found in possession
of a little photograph likeness of Mr. Lincoln, of whom,
at that time, he must have had very little if any knowledge, that they took his neckties out of his basket, and
of them made a sort of rope, which they fastened around
his neck, and attached to a lamp-post on the street.
Then two ruthless miscreants seized the unfortunate
man by the legs, and jerked him so hard that they broke
his neck, killing him instantly. His lifeless body was
left hanging, as if it were an every-day occurrence.*

VIOLATION OF A FLAG OF TRUCE.

ABOVE Sleepy-Hole, on the Nansemond river, April
21st, 1863, about 11 o'clock, A. M., a white handkerchief
was seen to be waved on the shore by a person in citizen's
dress. Captain Harris, of the United States steamer
Stepping-Stones, thinking the person to be Mr. Wilson,
and wishing to gain information as to the state of the
country, sent out a boat, containing five men, to bring
him off. As soon as the boat reached the beach it was
fired upon by a body of armed men concealed in the
undergrowth. All in the boat were killed or captured.
On the 22d, W. B. Cushing, Lieutenant, and senior
officer in the Nansemond, moved up from his anchorage,
and, in company with the Yankee, anchored near the
Stepping-Stones, and then proceeded at once to organize
a boat expedition from three vessels to punish the
rebels if they could be found. The boat sent the day

* This statement was given to the author by Mr. St. Clair, mate of
the steamship McRay.

before was found, together with four muskets, and the dead body of Richard Richchurch, seaman of the Minnesota.*

FIRING UPON A BOAT'S CREW WITHOUT PREVIOUS SUMMONS TO SURRENDER.

U. S. Steamer Pocahontas,
Brunswick River, March 12th, 1864.

Sir: I have to report that yesterday afternoon, having received permission to land near Brunswick, Georgia, and procure fresh beef for our crew, I took the second cutter, with ten men and a coxswain, and, with Acting-Paymaster Kitchen, landed at half-past three o'clock. Having accomplished our object, we left the shore about five o'clock P. M. on our return to the Pocahontas. As the men commenced to pull, and when we were about twenty yards from the beach, one musket was fired from a thicket, in the direction of the town. This appeared to be a signal, for almost simultaneously with the report a force of forty or fifty men showed themselves within the thicket, and fired a volley at our boat, killing two men, and wounding one seriously.

In the confusion following this first fire, several of the men jumped overboard and clung to the gunwale of the boat. This, with the loss of the men first wounded, and two others seriously wounded by the fire of a second volley, diminished very materially the effective force for pulling, so that it was some time before we could increase our distance from the shore. However, as Pay-

---

* See letter of W. B. Cushing, senior officer in the Nansemond river, to Rear-Admiral S. P. Lee, dated April 23d, 1863.

master Kitchen steered, and I pulled the stroke-oar, by great effort we were enabled gradually to work our way out into the stream, *being all the time exposed to a galling fire.* * * * *

I would add, that their first volley was fired without hailing the boat; but when they saw us still trying to pull from shore, one of them called out, "Surrender, you d—d sons of b—s!" But as they had already killed two men, and wounded others, I replied, "No, I won't surrender."

While we were still within their range, you came up in the gig and took us in tow. On examining the men, I found two killed, three seriously wounded, and four slightly.

A. C. RHODES,

Assistant-Surgeon.

To J. B. BALCH,

Lieut. Com. U. S. Steamer Pocahontas.*

REBEL FEMALE DUPLICITY ENDING IN MURDER.

THERE resided, some eight miles from Tullahoma in Tennessee, a fine-looking and rather preposessing woman, by the name of Cobb, who very frequently visited Tullahoma, for the purpose apparently of selling fruit. With her Jezebel jokes, and Judas-like smiles, she soon formed an intimacy with two young men, belonging to the Eighth Ohio Battery. She told them, if they would pay a visit to where she lived, "she would treat them (it was in the month of September) to some delicious peaches and apples." The unsuspecting young "battery men" started from Tullahoma on the 17th, to visit Miss

---

* Report of the Secretary of the Navy, 1862, page 212.

Cobb, and have never since been heard of. A few days after, an officer and soldier, believing they could obtain some intelligence of their friends, went in that direction in search of them, but could learn nothing of them, after visiting the place. The news soon got out from the Cobbs, of the two being in the neighborhood; and some eight or ten men of the vicinage assembled, and captured the officer and soldier. After robbing them of their horses, guns, and money, they determined to kill them by shooting, and for this purpose placed the two against a tree at a short distance, to be fired at by the marksmen. They fired chiefly at the officer, killing him outright; but only slightly wounded the soldier, so that he made his escape, and, after rambling through the woods several days, found his way back to Tullahoma, and informed Colonel Collum, who at once sent out a sufficient scout, and picked up some eight or ten men of the vicinage, together with Miss Cobb and her mother, taking them all to Tullahoma. When they came into the presence of the wounded soldier, he readily identified five of them as being of the party. The mother and daughter denied all knowledge of the transaction. The daughter, however, was heard to say to her mother in an under tone, we had better tell all about it; but the mother instantly ordered the daughter to be silent, and not speak one word. Colonel Collum ordered them to be sent to the Penitentiary at Nashville. On the night of the 19th of October, Company H, First Middle Tennessee Cavalry, caught Miss Cobb's two brothers, about one half mile from where she lived. From letters found on their persons, it appears they had been recently connected with Bragg's army. In all probability they were spies, doing all they could for the rebel cause.

The Union men who had been compelled to fly from

and abandon their homes last summer by these same Cobbs, and others, and who now reside in Shelbyville, inform me, that this Miss Cobb pursued the practice of enticing Union soldiers all last summer.

The scouts brought in the remains of the murdered officer, and he was interred at Tullahoma; but not one vestige of the two first soldiers could be found.[*]

MURDER OF JOSEPH STOVER.

IMMEDIATELY after the disbandment of the Home Guards of Fentress and Clifton counties, Tennessee, in 1863, through the influence of the rebel citizens of the said counties (it is said that they were disbanded for the purpose of letting that notorious villain, Champ Furguson, commit his depredations upon the inoffensive citizens of that country), Joseph Stover, a private of the First Kentucky Cavalry, visited Wolf river on business. He had been there but a short time when he saw Champ Furguson and his gang of bandits, crossing at Rome's old mill. Mounting his horse, he endeavored to make his escape without being discovered, but the ever-watchful eye of that fiend saw him riding off, and he ordered his men to charge after and capture him. He made good his escape as far as Henry Johnson's residence, where he was overtaken and captured. Surrounding him, they shot at him several times, mortally wounding him, but this did not satisfy Champ's fiendish thirst for blood. Death did not come soon enough for him. Jumping from his horse, and drawing his knife, he ran it through

---

* General J. B. Rodgers.

Stover's body, killing him instantly; after which his companions in guilt kicked the lifeless body, and even went so far as to stamp on the head, and grind the face with their boot-heels.*

SI GORDON.

THE Union citizens of Leavenworth county, Kansas, (the adjoining county to Platte county, Missouri, the only dividing line being the Missouri river), had been subjected to all sorts of inhuman outrages; murders and robberies being committed every day by a gang of miscreants under one Si Gordon. General D. Hunter, in view of Gordon's success in evading the vigilance of the United States forces, which were sent out after him time and again, was led to inquire into the cause of it. He ascertained that the rebel sympathizers of Platte county were extending to Gordon all the aid in their power, by giving him information of the approach of the United States forces, and secreting him and his gang, whenever there was a chance of their being captured; and knowing that it would require a double force before he could capture him—one to guard the sympathizers, and one to hunt up the marauders—he was compelled to issue the following retaliatory order, to effect the delivery of the said Si Gordon into his hands, before he committed any more of the fiendish murders of innocent people of Lawrence and the adjoining counties:—

---

* Dr. J. D. Hale, of Tennessee.

To the Trustees of Platte City, Platte County, Mo.

GENTLEMEN: Having received reliable information of depredations, and outrages of every kind, committed by a man named Si Gordon, a leader of rebel marauding bands, I give you notice, that unless you seize and deliver the said Gordon to me, at these Headquarters, within ten days from this date, or drive him out of the country, I shall send a force to your city, with orders to reduce it to ashes, and to burn the house of every Secessionist in your county, and to carry away every slave.

Colonel Jennison's regiment will be intrusted with the execution of this order.

The attention of the following persons is particularly directed to this notice. * * * *

D. HUNTER,
Major-General Commanding.

MURDER OF MR. TABOR.

MR. TABOR, living in Clinton county, Kentucky, about three miles above Albany, was brutally murdered by that notorious murderer, Champ Furguson, and his band of marauders. Mr. Tabor was a farmer, highly respected, and very frank, never attempting to conceal his sentiments, and, in consequence, became obnoxious to his rebel neighbors. They frequently robbed him of whatever they wished. On one occasion they stole from him a family of ten negroes, and running them off, sold them and appropriated the avails.

In conversation one day, he expressed his willingness to shoulder a musket, if necessary, in defence of the Union. This getting to the ears of the rebels, he was compelled, like many others, to leave home, and hide in the woods and caves to avoid being murdered. After being a fugitive from home several months, he learned that the Union troops had taken possession of Albany, and thought that he would venture to return home to see his family. Upon his arrival, one of his rebel neighbors, Durham Graham, notified Champ and his gang of Mr. Tabor's return. Mustering up courage, they started immediately upon their bloody mission, Graham accompanying them.

Like a pack of thieves, they quietly stole up to his house, and rushing upon the old man, took him prisoner. His wife begged and pleaded with them not to kill her husband, but, if they were determined to kill him, she begged them to kill him at home, and not take him away and do it. The lying fiends assured her that they did not intend to kill him. They ordered the old man to get up behind Graham, the villain who had betrayed him. (This Graham had taken the oath of allegiance to the United States Government.) All being ready, they started down the lane leading from his house to the main road. They had not proceeded far, when Mr. Tabor was pushed violently from the horse. This was the signal for them to commence their bloody work. Champ and his gang, as soon as the old man's feet struck the ground, fired at him, until he fell pierced with bullets. The old man still surviving, Champ jumped from his horse, and drawing his knife, cut him until he was satisfied that life was entirely extinct.

Mounting his horse, he rode off with an air of triumph, leaving the body in the road, to be buried by his distressed family.

Mr. Tabor had four sons in the Union army, and that was the cause, with his being a Union man, the fiends had for murdering him.*

FIRING ON DROWNING MEN.

DURING the spirited engagement between the gun-boats Mound City, St. Louis, Lexington, and Conestoga, and the rebel batteries, at St. Charles, on the White river, a shot from one of the batteries penetrated the port casement of the Mound City, a little above and forward of the gunport, killing three men in its flight, and exploding her steam-drum. As a consequence, many of the crew leaped overboard, for whose rescue boats were immediately sent. But the rebels, instead of compassionating, and seeking to deliver, actually fired upon these scalded and drowning men, and those sent to their rescue, wounding many and killing others.

Says Rear-Admiral C. H. Davis, then commanding the Western Flotilla, in his report of June 19th, 1862, to the Hon. Secretary of the Navy:

"The victory at St. Charles, which has probably given us command of White river, and secured our connection with General Curtis, would be unalloyed with regret but for the fatal accident to the steam-drum and heater of the Mound City.

"Of the crew, consisting of one hundred and seventy-five, officers and men, eighty-two have already died, forty-three were killed in the water or drowned, and twenty-five are severely wounded.

---

* Dr. J. D. Hale, of Tennessee.

FIRING ON DROWNING MEN.

179

"After the explosion took place the wounded men were shot by the enemy, while in the water, and the boats of the Conestoga, Lexington, and St. Louis, which which went to the assistance of the scalded and drowning men of the Mound City, were fired into both with great guns and muskets, and were disabled, and one of them forced on shore to prevent sinking.

"The department and the country will contrast these barbarities of a savage enemy with the humane efforts made by our own people to rescue the wounded and disabled, under similar circumstances, in the engagement of the 6th instant."

In his report of June 18th he says: "Many must have been killed by the enemy while they were struggling in the water. I was close to the spot, and distinctly saw and remarked on the cowardly act, at the moment they were perpetrating it."

MASSACRE OF AMERICANS AND GERMANS IN TEXAS.

IN the latter part of 1862, a party of rebel murderers, commanded by that prince of fiends, Captain J. M. Duff, visited the counties of Keer, Gillespie, and Kendall, in Texas, having been ordered there by the rebel government to crush the Union sentiment that was known to exist there. As soon as he arrived with his command, which consisted of five hundred of the worst desperadoes that ever polluted the soil of Texas, he issued an order to confiscate all the property of every Union man in the above-named counties, who refused to take an oath to support the Confederate Government within ten days. He also ordered his men to take no Union man prisoner

14* .

who was found away from his home, but shoot him down on the spot. A few days after the above order was issued, some twelve or sixteen Unionists were hung. They begged for a trial, but he refused to hear their defence; so they had to die without it. ⸢

In a creek near the town of Fredericksburg, some Unionists found the bodies of four men who had been drowned, each one having a large stone tied to his neck. It was believed that these men were drowned by order of Duff. After committing enough murders to satisfy his savage propensities, he started to break up a settlement of Americans and Germans, near Grand Cape, on Johnson's Creek, in the same State, which was known to the Confederate authorities to be strictly loyal. The settlers being informed that Duff was coming, gathered together a small force to stop his progress, and protect their families from such a vile scoundrel. For a while the settlers held them in check, but they were soon overpowered and forced to fly to the mountains for protection. After having arrested all the men he could find, Duff started away with his command, pretending to go to Fredericksburg, but soon returned, expecting to find that the Unionists had come out of their hiding-places in the mountains and returned home. In this he was mistaken, for they were used to such tricks, and stayed away from the settlement. Duff finding this to be the case, commenced an indiscriminate plunder of every farm, running off the stock, destroying crops, and the like. He also burned a great many of the Unionists' houses, and arresting the families, sent them away as prisoners. The refugees learning this, concluded to fly to Mexico, as they knew it was the determination of Duff to hunt them up and murder them. As the fugitives were making their escape, they were joined by a great many others who were on the same errand, until their numbers were swollen to seventy. In consequence of the bad roads, their progress was slow, and before they reached the Rio Grande, they were overtaken by a party of two hundred rebel fiends, who were sent after them. The refugees made a desperate resistance, but the rebels were soon reinforced, and all excepting twelve were killed or captured. They who were captured were shot or murdered in some other way. Of the twelve who made their escape, only three ever reached Mexico. The other nine, covered with wounds, wandered about until they were captured, when they were immediately shot or hung.

When Dr. Adolph Deval, the celebrated German traveller, heard of the above affair, he stated as follows: —"I know personally the most of these unfortunate victims who have been murdered so mercilessly, not because they rebelled against the Government, but because they would not act against the Union, and would rather fly to Mexico. These murdered Union men were some of the greatest benefactors of the State. • They had done the hardest pioneer work in it; cleared it from the wild beasts and Indians; they had saved it to civilization through more than one period of pestilence and famine, and had secured their present persecutors against the incursions of the Indians, and had done the best service as volunteers in the Mexican war, and the wars on the frontier. They placed the arts and sciences in Texas as well as they could be found anywhere among the American Germans. They furnished proof that they could cultivate sugar and cotton without the least damage to health, and increase the riches of the country many millions of dollars, and the foregoing sufferings are their reward."*

---

* Colonel William McNair, of California.

SACKING OF LAWRENCE.

FROM AN EYE-WITNESS.

ANOTHER chapter of the history of Lawrence has been written in blood. The world knows, before these lines are traced, that the desperate guerrillas of our border have destroyed the far-famed and historic town of Lawrence. They accompanied the act with deeds of ferocity unexampled in the annals of human warfare. Sad is the thought to contemplate so dread a calamity as has befallen us; but it is due to Kansas and the world that the history of this deep guilt should be told, and a record be made of these sad, sickening sufferings, which shall be engraven in the hearts of men for ever.

It is further deemed important that this record should be detailed by some one whose fortune or misfortune it was to be a witness of this fearful tragedy; and, lest no one else should undertake the task, I propose to make this record; and I do not know in what shape I can better put it than in the form of a personal narrative of what I saw and heard.

The narrative must commence with the attack itself; as the blow fell like a thunderbolt in a clear sky, without the least anticipation or warning. Fears had been previously entertained, but it was not considered possible that a hostile force could pierce the lines of General Ewing, avoid his scouts, and penetrate fifty miles into a populous region, and attack the third town in the State, without notice of the raid being given in season to prepare for defence. Hence, after attending public meeting on Thursday, the 20th of August, 1863, the citizens had retired to rest, undisturbed by presentiments or fears of the impending catastrophe.

My own presence in the town at this precise juncture was an accident, and intended but for a day. Early on Friday, the morning after my arrival, I was awakened by a rapid and continuous discharge of fire-arms in the street.

At first I failed entirely to realize the nature of this occurrence, and it was not till the sound of the shots, intermingled with shouts and yells, and the cry of "Hurrah for Quantrell!" swept through the air, that the drowsiness left my eyes, and I became aware that the guerrillas were upon us.

The Kansas river here flows on the east and north side of the city, and the principal street (Massachusetts) runs at right angles with it, north and south.

Upon this street, some forty rods from the river, stood the Eldridge House, a large and fine brick building, located on a corner, and facing the east and north. My room was on the third floor, looking toward the river, and on account of the heat of the weather both windows and curtains were open.

I sprang from my bed on hearing the cries of "Quantrell," and approached a window. The streets were filled with horsemen, dressed in the wildest fashion of the border, and armed to the teeth with carbines and revolvers. They were riding to and fro, in all directions, yelling and whooping like so many demons, and apparently shooting down every man who appeared in sight.

At the moment when I went to the window, one of these men, who seemed apparently to be scrutinizing the hotel, evidently espied me, for I heard him shout: "There's a man, G—d d—n him! shoot him, G—d d—n him! shoot him!" I gave him no time for the execution of his kind purpose; but that moment furnished me with a foretaste of the dreadful fate in store for the devoted town.

At first I thought it a mere dash of a party of horse-thieves, and waited awhile, expecting to hear the sound recede, and to see the raiders disappear. I could not suppose the citizens so utterly unprepared for defence as to make the destruction of the town at all possible. After a few moments had passed without signs of a retreat, I listened for sounds of resistance, but was rewarded only by the warning of the hotel gong, which was now rung loudly through all the halls of the building.

I proceeded then to dress, stealing occasional glances into the street. These showed me men flying in terror, and pleading for mercy, but in every instance unhesitatingly shot down. One man rushed out upon the sidewalk, on the east side of the street, apparently designing to cross, but a trooper riding past, wheeled his horse, and discharged his revolver full at his breast. The man threw up his arms and apparently implored quarter, but the only response made was curses and shots, repeated again and again; under these he sunk to the ground, and probably died on the spot.

My own course was soon determined on. It was apparent that no resistance was being made to the attack, and I had no weapon whatever in my possession. To attempt to escape into the street, would clearly be madness; the nearest approach to safety was to watch and wait. My pocket-book and watch I placed in my travelling-bag, and concealed the latter in my wash-stand, hoping that good fortune might enable me to carry it away, but satisfied that all valuables about the person must inevitably be lost.

This done, I was prepared for any movement that might seem safest. Till I became satisfied that no effort was to be made for the defence of the house, I chose to remain in my room.

This last hope was soon dissipated by the voice of the guerrillas in the halls. They were in possession of the building, and making an examination of the rooms. Twice the robbers passed my door and dealt upon it heavy blows, intending to break it in; but, hoping that they would speedily abandon the building and fly, I made no movement to admit them.

The third time, the door yielded, and I found myself face to face with a couple of the ruffians, one of whom presented his revolver, and demanded my surrender. This I unhesitatingly made, and stated that I was not a citizen of Lawrence, but simply there for a day, and hoped to be allowed to depart unmolested. My name and residence were demanded, as also whether I was not an officer of the Government. In regard to my money, I made an answer previously designated, and which I was sure would possess so much more plausibility than it did truth (I hoped to be pardoned for the immorality), as to defy disbelief. A moral lesson was inculcated, in which I was sincerely assured of protection in case of speaking the truth, but instant death, as a penalty for its infraction.

One other instance of danger occurred, where a citizen, standing by, with the intention of doing me a service, vouched for my statement, by saying that he knew me, and that I was a "railroad man." "A railroad man!" exclaimed my captor, in a tone of menace; "that is a damned sight worse than being an officer!" I ventured to differ from the flattering conclusion, and, after a moment's hesitation on his part, was ordered to take my place with the prisoners, in the main hall, and wait orders.

Here I found assembled nearly all the inmates of the hotel; a promiscuous assemblage of men, women, and children, all waiting orders. All had dressed hurriedly, and with various degrees of success; among the deficiencies being the boots of a Judge of the Supreme Court, who, like myself, had not been able as yet to recover them from the possession of the porter, to whom they had been delivered the evening before. Although we had with us some officers in the military service, none had the ill-fortune to be in uniform. The whole number congregated (it is only guesswork) might have been fifty; quite possibly larger.

On the broad landing of the stairs leading to the lower hall, stood a guard, whose business was, it seems. to prevent any of our party from going down. This man had not a bad countenance, and civilly answered such questions as the bolder of our company ventured to make. He informed us that Quantrell himself was in command of the expedition.

The search of the house was soon over, and one by one, all the inmates who had lingered in their rooms were brought out and added to our company.

We could hear a process of investigation and plunder going on, intermingled with oaths and threats, which are always so freely used in the discourse of rebel bushwhackers. No absolute violence, however, so far as I am aware, was offered in the hotel, excepting to a half-witted man, Joseph Eldridge, brother of the owner, who was brutally shot, after his mental condition was made known to his murderers.

Presently a bushwhacker came up the stairs, paused upon the landing, and looked us over. It was Quantrell, *the terror of the border, and a former citizen of the town.* To some old acquaintances he spoke civilly enough, and with two or three of them shook hands, assuring us that we were entirely safe, and should receive complete protection from personal violence.

Quantrell would pass anywhere for a well-looking man, and exhibits in his countenance no traces of native ferocity. He is of medium height, well built, and very quiet and very deliberate in speech and motion. His hair is brown, his complexion fresh; and his cunning and pleasant blue eyes, and aquiline nose, gave to his countenance its chief expression. During the few moments which he spent with us at this time, he conversed freely about himself and the present expedition, receiving with marked complacency some compliments on the completeness of his present success, and not hesitating to express his consciousness, that it was by far the greatest of his exploits.

He desired to know whether Governor Carney was in the city, and finally left us, taking with him one of our party, to quiet some of his men whom he was about to send in search of "Jim Lane."

Quantrell is a native of Ohio, and lived in Lawrence a few years since, under the assumed name of Charley Hart. He is said to have been, or pretended to be, a Free States man; but after removing to the border country, became noted as a thief, and finally emigrated to Missouri, to escape the consequences of numerous indictments found against him, in the different counties in which he had plied his lawless vocation.

When the war broke out, his restless spirit and unscrupulous disposition, forbade his remaining quiet, and as his reputation in Kansas made it impossible for him safely to join the United States service, whereby his propensities to steal would be limited, he at once, in the true mercenary style, took service with the less critical

15

rebels ; only preferring to operate independently, rather than subject himself to the control of the Confederate organization. That he is naturally a great rascal, I do not doubt ; but that he is naturally cruel, I do not believe.

The departure of **Quantrell** was succeeded by a brief period of suspense. He had given us reason to believe that he would not destroy the hotel, and we cherished the hope that a short time would witness the departure of the outlaws, without the perpetration of other serious damage. The interval of uncertainty, however, was employed by most, in making any necessary preparations for possible departure. Some had succeeded in secreting money or valuables under the carpets, or in other places not likely to be examined ; and such now transferred them to their persons ; or committed them to safer custody of female friends.

We were not long left in doubt, however, as to the intention of our captors. Quantrell soon reappeared ; and it became evident that he had resolved to destroy the town. He reassured us of personal protection, and directed us to leave the house and proceed under guard to some safe suburb.

In contemplation of this, I had secured my boots, and placed my travelling-bag in a convenient spot, determined to make an effort to save it. Believing that no further personal examination would occur, however, and knowing that my bag might be taken from me, I took out my money and watch and placed them in the pockets of a linen travelling-coat which I wore over my other. Thus prepared for the inevitable hegira, I joined the melancholy procession which filed down the stairs and into the street, and for the last time departed from the stately and historic Eldridge House, where I had so often found refuge from the discomforts of pioneer life, and shared the excitements of Kansas events.

We descended the stone steps of the hotel, and crossed Massachusetts street diagonally into Winthrop toward the east. The shooting had pretty much ceased, for the reason that all straggling citizens were already killed or had fled; and the bushwhackers were now intent on plunder, setting fire to each building successively as soon as it had been rifled of its contents.

The first sight which greeted us was the blazing livery-stable of the brothers Willis, from which their horses had already been taken by the thieves, and which insured the destruction of the office of the Lawrence Republican, to which it was contiguous.

As our party moved along Winthrop street, shouting desperadoes crowded upon us, filling the air with curses and threats. When we arrived about opposite the office of the State Journal, one of them rode up on the right to the head of our column, and ordered out of the ranks a young man walking just in front of me, who carried in his hand a travelling-bag, and was evidently a stranger.

"Here, step out here, you!" And when the young man obeyed: "G—d d—n you! you are a red-leg!" And two successive shots from his revolver demonstrated the sincerity of his blood-thirsty design. A burst of horror and remonstrance rose from our whole party, and several of us rushed toward the infuriated wretch, beseeching him not to murder in cold blood an inoffensive stranger.

Fortunately, almost miraculously, neither bullet had taken effect, except, as I afterwards saw, to cut slightly one leg of the victim's pantaloons.

One of our guard, David Porter, whose name I desire to record, peremptorily commanded the desperado to stop

firing, and to molest no one in this party, as they were
promised protection by Quantrell.

"D—n you," was the reply, "I shan't obey you, and
I will shoot Quantrell himself!"

"G-d d—n you," replied Porter, "I am placed here to
protect these prisoners, and I will do it!" And he added,
presenting his revolver, "If you shoot a man of them I
will kill you!"

All this, which occupied but a minute of time, occurred close behind one of the old circular earthworks of
1855, built for the defence of the town, and now nearly
level with the ground, being scarcely more than a ring
of raised earth with a depression in the centre.

The guard now ordered us into this place to remain,
but Quantrell, whom we espied in front of the City Ho.el
(formerly Whitney House), between us and the river, was
sent for, and speedily rode up. He said to us, briefly:
"One man, Stone (landlord of the City Hotel), was kind
to me years ago, when I lived here, and I have promised
to protect him and his family, and house. All of you
go over to the City Hotel, and go into it, and *stay in it*,
and you will be safe. But don't attempt to go into the
street."

These few words brought us relief, hard to describe.
We lost no time in following the direction given us, and
were made welcome by the landlord to the shelter and
protection of his house of refuge, where a number of
fugitives were already congregated.

An incident here occurred. When the flames burst
from the windows of the Eldridge House, and the block
of buildings of which it formed a part, an imperative
duty now seemed to present itself to my mind. We had
been told that Joseph Eldridge, before mentioned, was
lying wounded in the cellar of the house. Now that the

building was on fire, an effort must be made to save him. Mr. J. C. Horton and myself agreed to go over, if we could obtain a guard, and search for and bring him away. We stated the fact to one of our escort, named Ladd, who was sporting a captain's coat belonging to Captain Banks, Provost-Marshal of the State, and a prisoner with us; and Ladd seemed not altogether unmoved by our representations. Mrs. Norton, wife of the landlord, also besought an effort for a babe in one of the chambers; to which Ladd assented, till she thoughtlessly added, "It is a black babe;" when he exclaimed brutally, "O, it is a black baby! d—n it, let it burn!"

But he consented to aid us in finding Eldridge, and we proceeded under his protection toward the burning building. Having arrived near it, however, a glance showed us the utter impossibility of effecting our object. The flames had already made such progress as to render any attempt to approach the house an act of madness, and we sadly turned back and regained the protection of the City Hotel. I was glad to learn, later in the day, that Eldridge had in some way escaped from the building, and lived to receive attentions from his friends—which, however, were insufficient to preserve his life.

Another incident, at that time somewhat serious, but now amusing, occurred. On passing into the City Hotel, I was followed by one of the guard left by Quantrell to protect the building, who, after a very slight examination of the coat worn under my linen duster, communicated the fact to me, in confidence, that he must have it! The information caused me considerable surprise, as I had flattered myself that we henceforth were to be free from personal molestation. I saw, too, with regret, that my interlocutor had a *decided distaste* for argument, and was utterly insensible to the reasons I gave for objecting to

15 *

comply with his summary demands: in fact, logic seemed to chafe his not pleasant spirit, and I finally resorted to a Yankee feat of a trade, and by a judicious practice of the best arts at my command, and an exercise of some good strategy in not revealing the fact that I had still about me some money for current expenses, I finally succeeded in compromising the case, by the payment of a greenback, representing ten dollars, current money; and thus saved myself from all further annoyance of this description.

This incident, however, greatly shocked a confidence which I was becoming ready to misplace in the abstract honor of rebel bushwackers, and I lost no time in transferring my remaining funds to the possession of a lady friend, who kindly consented to hold it as a special deposit, payable on demand.

Nothing was stipulated in regard to interest, though I should have been poorly satisfied with myself had I failed, in recovering my loan, to pay (when it is customary to receive) at a rate that would disturb the financial equipoise of any invested in Wall street.

The City Hotel is a wooden parallelogram building, painted brown, and two stories in height, standing broadside to the river, which runs in its rear.

It is just opposite the ferry on the Leavenworth road, and in plain view of a squad of soldiers, about a dozen in number, stationed there to protect the timber on the railroad lands, and whose minie rifles effectually covered the whole south bank of the stream and the houses standing upon it. Early in the day, these minie bullets had picked off two or three incautious bushwackers, and inspired a remarkable amount of subsequent caution.

Now, as our guard occasionally passed out from the protection of the hotel, the whistling of a minie would be distinctly heard, till, at last yielding to the demands of our protectors, and fearing that a successful shot might so inflame the gang as to invite them to indiscriminate butchery, it was agreed to procure a cessation of the firing.

Mr. Stone, the landlord, was asked to raise a flag of truce on his house, but the brave old man refused, saying he never had done such a thing, and he would not now begin.

Finally his daughter, Miss Lydia Stone, not less brave, seized a white handkerchief, and ran down to the ferry, waving it as she went, and succeeded in making our friends on the other side understand that it was our safety that they should intermit their firing.

Nothing remarkable whatever transpired till the departure of the gang. The whole length of Massachusetts street was a mass of ruins, and numbers of our party were witnesses to the destruction of their stores and offices, while occasional explosions warned us that the flames had penetrated the deposits of powder kept for sale. The best dwellings, too, in various directions, were in flames, and it became evident that the terrible work of the raiders was about done.

At length Quantrell appeared, and announced his departure at hand, promising to leave us our guard till his forces were all away. He then politely raised his hat to the ladies, and hoping that their next meeting might be under pleasant circumstances, bade them good-day, and rode off. Presently the whole party was seen filing out of the city, upon the road by which they entered.

I saw them well advanced in the direction of Franklin, visible for the last time upon an elevation of ground about two miles from the place where we were. This must have been a ruse to deceive us as to his real course, for

it is known that he went due south, striking across the
Wakarusa bottom, crossing Benton's bridge, and making
for the Santa Fe road.

We had yet to learn, notwithstanding the departure
of the outlaw and his gang, that we had yet another
chapter of terror to endure. Our guerrilla guards, one
by one, left us, and we began to regard this latter movement as putting an end to our captivity and alarm. Pru-
dence, however, dictated we should not scatter, but
remain concentrated till every appearance of danger had
vanished; stragglers might yet be around; and so it
turned out.

It was not long after the departure of the guard, when
two of the infuriate ruffians returned, maddened by
liquor, and rode up to the house, clearly intent upon the
most fiendish mischief. None of us knew how many
men might be behind, and there seemed to be no pru-
dence in departing from the quiet course we had previously pursued. We did not know then what afterwards
became apparent, that they were especially exasperated
at Mr. Stone and his family, for marks of favor bestowed
by their chief, and held him responsible for cheating
them of the wholesale vengeance they had intended to
visit on every person in the place.

One of them, too, was infuriated at Lydia Stone, because Quantrell had obliged him to restore to her a ring,
which she claimed as her property. After some brutal
threats, an order was given that all the men and all the
women should come out of the house and take position
in separate rows; the object being, as I now believe, to
single out and shoot all the members of the Stone family
first, and afterwards such others as fancy or chance
should destine to death. Some were unwise enough to
obey this order. Others of us judged it better to remain

in the house, which afforded a partial shelter, and a plan
was formed for seizing and detaining the ruffians, in case
they dismounted and endeavored to enter, though not a
man of us had any weapon; still this would have been
the safer course, had they given us the opportunity.
But seeing that only a few were likely to leave the building at their command, they commenced questioning those
who were out as to name and residence. One, a stranger,
replied that he was from Ohio. That was worse than
Kansas, said one of the wretches, and immediately fired.
The man shot had been wounded early in the day; but
I understand that neither wound proved dangerous.

In the confusion that followed, several more shots
were fired, two persons, I believe, being killed. Mr.
Stone went boldly out to remonstrate on the shooting of
the Ohio man, and was immediately shot in the abdomen,
dying of the wound in two or three hours. A complete
panic followed.

It was believed, and I think correctly, that more of
the gang were in the city, and it was expected that every
moment would bring them up to join in an indiscriminate
massacre of the men. No woman had yet been shot,
though a pistol was aimed at Lydia Stone; and the safest
course by many was deemed to be, for the men to leave
the house by the rear, which side the bushwhackers
avoided from fear of the minie balls of our friends
across the river.

I was now satisfied that the main body of the gang
had left town, and that the number remaining was not
formidable, if we could obtain any arms. Seeing that
all self-possession was gone (for the first time), I determined, for myself, to seek the river bank, and get some
sort of aid. I left the house, and ran to the bank above

the ferry, where, to my surprise, I found General Deitzler, apparently on the same errand.

He had made his home with Governor Robinson, and
was very weak from disease, but he seemed anxious to
be of some service in the terrible ordeal through which
we were passing. I stated the facts to him, and as the
ferry-boat was now, for the first time, coming over the
river, he shouted to the ferry-man to go back and get the
soldiers on the north bank to come over and drive out
the stragglers. The boat once started to turn back, but
finally kept on its course. On learning that there were
at the hotel but two of the ruffians, he said to me: "I
have two revolvers at the house: if you will go with me
and get them, we will each take one and try our chances."
To this I agreed, and we started to go; but on inquiring
what house he meant, I understood it to be the residence
of Governor Robinson, on Mount Arrad, a mile distant,
and assured him that we could not go and return in time
to be of the least service.

I afterwards learned that Governor Robinson had
removed to the city, and was occupying a house near
the river, from which we might have procured the
weapons, and probably reached the rear of the hotel
unnoticed, and picked off the bushwhackers easily from
the windows.

It was not long till aid reached us. Seeing that the
ferry-boat had reached the south bank, and was receiving
on board such stragglers as had sought the landing, I
conceived the idea of going over and procuring the
soldiers to come across and drive the stragglers away.
Arriving at the boat as it was putting off, I communicated my desire to such persons as I found there, and
immediately on its landing, we represented the facts to
the soldiers, freely using the name of General Deitzler

and imparting his wish to the same effect, in order to justify their going over.

The officer in command was not present, and the brave boys were burning to go; yet they feared to act without orders. But chivalry overcame discipline, and when the ferry-boat went back, it carried not only the soldiers (who, by the way, belonged to the Kansas Twelfth Regiment), but also several Delaware Indian warriors, who had mustered with guns and bows and arrows, and a number of settlers on the Indian territory, in all perhaps twenty-five men.

On gaining the south bank, the party moved in good order up the hill, and reached the scene of disaster, to give a parting shot at the flying scoundrels, perhaps a dozen, who ran at the appearance of armed men.

No damage was done by the fire, but it is certain that of the two wretches who had paid the last visit to the City Hotel, one was caught by citizens, as he fled, and killed on the spot, and the other is reported to have been slain by the arrows of our Delaware warriors.

I must briefly pass over the harrowing scenes that every part of Lawrence presented, as I commenced a tour of inspection, in company with Captain Shannon, in order to assist, if necessary, in the care of the wounded.

With the frantic cries of new-made widows and orphans still ringing in my ears, and the remembrance of stark corpses, some naked, and some half consumed by fire, pictured eternally upon my brain, I have no heart to dwell on the horrible visions which that visit revealed. Of the wounded, we saw barely three; of corpses, great numbers.

The shots were mostly in the head or abdomen, all aimed to kill. In most instances, the fiends had made sure of their work, repeating the discharges if a doubt remained.

Dead bodies were everywhere—some had been shot down as they left their houses, some as they fled along the street, some were followed into buildings and there dispatched.

Several new recruits, sleeping on the plank side-walk, in front of their quarters, on account of the heat of the weather, were shot as they lay, when the gang first entered, and their half-consumed bodies still rested precisely as they died. In some cases, the fires had simply burned off the clothing; in some, it had scorched the muscles into horrible distortions of the limbs; in some, arms and legs were burned off, and only the ghastly trunk remained.

We first entered a Methodist church, and found there two men wounded, Mr. Holks, with a fearful bullet-hole in the face, which Drs. Fuller and Cariff were endeavoring to probe, and Joseph Eldridge, before mentioned, also wounded in the face, and lying utterly insensible.

Near by lay the corpses of James Eldridge and James Perrine, two mere boys, clerks in the store of Eldridge & Ford. Other bodies were being continually brought in. Women, angels of mercy, were already here, ministering to any want which appeared, and the few physicians in town were doing their utmost for the equally few wounded. Seeing that our services were not needed, we again sought the street.

Such a sight, too horrid for language to describe, soon produced its natural effect; vengeance began to be breathed.

Men on horseback, armed with guns and revolvers, had for some time been arriving from the country, ready for the infliction of punishment on the savage miscreants.

Vengeance, blood, death, were the dooms breathed on the infamous traitors. A large number were assembled in Massachusetts street, in the south part of the town, busied in supplying themselves with ammunition, and waiting for some leader to whom to intrust the command. All the good horses in the stables the bushwhackers had taken, and all the good arms they could find; generally turning loose their own jaded steeds on getting fresh ones.

Hence many men, burning for action, had only guns but no horses; and some had come in on horses, but were destitute of arms. In many cases, one of the men would take both horse and gun and assume his place, ready for a start. It was plain, that the great want was a leader.

Just then, a man on a sorrel horse dashed up, and rode to the front almost before he was recognised. But a glance was sufficient, for all were familiar with the sinewy form and swarthy lineaments of the "grim chieftain," and notwithstanding the bitter political animosity cherished against him in Lawrence by a large party, the instantaneous shout of "Jim Lane!" reminded me of the old times, when he was the recognised chief of every enterprise of daring and audacity.

Lane had been awakened very early, and as his house is in the western suburbs of the city, he had little difficulty in escaping to a convenient cornfield, before the raiders reached his house.

So exasperated were they at losing so desirable a prize, that the miscreants at first proposed to shoot Mrs. Lane, instead of her husband. They then determined to kill his son, a boy of perhaps a dozen years. But even their ferocity was not quite sufficient for the cold-blooded

16

slaughter of women and children, and they finally plundered the house, applied the torch and rode off.

I should judge that the bushwhackers had a start of about an hour and a half. As they killed, plundered, and burned as they went, their progress was slower than that of their pursuers. The chief want of the latter was ammunition, of which none was believed to have escaped destruction, though this belief, as it afterwards appeared, was erroneous. Some time would be lost on the road in endeavoring to get a supply.

Lane's decisions were very prompt. Charging some of us with a few commissions to execute, the chief among which was the injunction to send after him every possible man, he gave the order to pursue, and dashed away, followed by perhaps a hundred and fifty of his hastily mustered forces.

This number, of course, increased as he went. For the next hour, Captain Shannon and myself made it our business, to send after Lane every armed and mounted man, as fast as they appeared.

For ourselves, being destitute of both arms and horses, this was the only service we found it possible to render. My next course was to get a means of conveyance back to Leavenworth, where I had intended to return on that day. Horses there were none in the place, and hours were consumed in vain, in endeavors to find some conveyance to enable me to reach the above-mentioned locality. Finally, it was ascertained that all the horses of the stage company had escaped capture, the hostlers having, with commendable self-possession, turned them loose early in the morning. The astonished brutes had fled to the river bottom, and after the guerrillas had gone were easily captured and returned to their stalls. So finding a load in readiness, the driver, in the absence of the agent, agreed to take us over.

We got some dinner at the City Hotel, the only one not burned, and in which lay the corpse of the brave landlord, whose previous kindness to Quantrell had been so serviceable to us, but had resulted so fatally to himself.

His family should be the especial care of the people of Lawrence, and his daughter, Lydia, possess the admiration of all who esteem feminine graces joined to heroic courage.

About four o'clock, we turned our backs again upon the ill-starred citadel of Kansas liberty, and bade adieu to its smouldering ruins, its unfortunate dead, and its scarcely less fortunate living.

Early in the day, I estimated the number of dead at fifty, but later, I was satisfied that it must reach a hundred. At the time of my writing, it is said that even this number is too small. Scarcely a man of these was able to offer the least resistance; so that the slaughter was simply premeditated and cold-blooded butchery.

The negroes were marked as special victims, but their old schooling stood them in good stead. They are accustomed to being hunted down; and on the first alarm they fled to the cover of bushes, holes, and cornfields, and generally escaped.

Even the servants of the Eldridge House found some means of egress and escape, and I think were nearly, if not quite all saved. A camp of colored recruits, I am told, located in the southern suburb, was early warned by the lieutenant in charge, and, with one exception, escaped to the woods in safety.

Later in the day, the mourners went about the streets

hunting and bewailing their dead, and inquiring for some new city of refuge.

Ex-Governor Robinson, had risen early, as is his habit, and gone to his farm on Mount Arrad. He there saw the entrance of the bushwackers, and was enabled to remain concealed. General Deitzler was a guest at his house near the river; but the fact was unknown to the bandits. It is probable that his house owes its safety to the minie rifles of the soldiers on the north bank, which covered it completely. General Deitzler would certainly have been shot, if taken, as would any man known to be a Federal officer.

Quantrell stated to the Hon. R. S. Stevens, one of the Eldridge House prisoners, that his force was four hundred and fifty-three men.

That this was false, I have no doubt, and I am satisfied that the whole number could not have exceeded two hundred. He also stated to different parties that his rendezvous on Wednesday night, was five miles from the State line in Kansas, and that his force then scattered, and came within fifteen miles of Lawrence, where they again rendezvoused, and rested till Monday morning. From that point, he stated that he came to Lawrence, and entered the place in four columns, by as many different streets. Partly corroborative of this, I learn that parties coming to Lawrence from the Missouri line, on Thursday, report that they saw numerous horsemen, singly, and in parties of two or three, travelling in the same direction. They had no suspicion of a hostile movement. Quantrell boasted of having completely outwitted General Ewing, and seemed greatly pleased at his own strategy.

That it was previously resolved to show no quarter, seems hardly probable from the facts, though it is certain that it was determined to shoot down every man who was seen, previous to obtaining complete possession of the town. Had the gang entered the Eldridge House at once, making no conditions, it is my opinion that every man in it would have been shot, as soon as seen.

But Quantrell could not believe that the building was entirely defenceless, and having no time nor artillery for a siege, and no wish to be shot from a window, he demanded the surrender of the house.

This was made by Provost-Marshal Banks, and the prisoners were promised protection.

This promise, I think, Quantrell did all in his power to redeem. Individual instances of atrocity or clemency grew immediately out of the temper of each ruffian respectively.

Messrs. Griswold, Trask, Thorpe, and Baker were called out of their houses, and promised protection, and then shot down in the street in the presence of their families. On the other hand, the Rev. Mr. —— was not only spared, but was asked if he was not a Baptist missionary preacher; and on answering in the affirmative, was allowed to keep his money and one or two watches.

This case differed widely from that of the Rev. Mr. Snyder, a Methodist preacher, who was murdered by the gang at his house as they first entered the town.

Elias Loomis, a stage-driver, in compliance with the entreaties of his wife, was promised protection, and was told to bring from his house anything he chose before it was burned. As he turned to enter, he was shot twice, and falling into the cellar, was consumed by the fire.

I was told by the wife of a prominent citizen, that she saw three men near her house attempt severally to escape, each having in his arms a child. All three were shot down, but the children escaped.

16 *

The wife of one of the victims threw herself before
him, and clasped him in her arms, but the fiends coolly
fired over her head, and instantly killed him.

Judge Carpenter, attempting to fly, was pursued and
shot. His wife and sister strove to protect his body with
their own, but the assassins placed the muzzles of their
revolvers between the persons of the women and discharged the contents into Carpenter's head.

Women were torn from their husbands, and the latter
shot in their presence. The instances of utter inhumanity and atrocity are sufficient to swell this narrative
into a volume.

The loss of life, contrary to the usual experiences in
similar cases, was at first greatly under-estimated. As
I close the narrative, I am informed by the Hon. M. J.
Parrott, who went over as chairman of the relief committee, on Friday night, and returned early on Sunday
morning, that the number of corpses buried before he
left was one hundred and eighteen.

Undoubtedly, bodies will continue to be discovered,
and I think it not unlikely, now, that the number will be
swelled to one hundred and fifty. The loss in money and
property has been estimated at two millions of dollars.

Should that calculation at all follow the course of
the loss of life, the sum will prove to be immensely
greater. So far as its present business is concerned,
Lawrence is as much destroyed as though an earthquake
had buried it in ruins. It has left but a single small
hotel, and one store, minus its entire stock of goods.

All its mechanics' shops are gone, and the best of its
dwellings. Not a newspaper office remains. Most of
the leading citizens may be said to be financially ruined.

Sympathy has been prompt and abundant. Immediately on the news reaching Leavenworth, every citizen

seemed to vie with his neighbor in giving substantial aid. Committees were appointed to proceed to the scene of disaster, and others to raise money in aid of the wounded.

It is stated that ten thousand dollars have already been procured to supply the necessaries of life; and teams have immediately started over with food, medicines, clothing, and coffins. The chief Quartermaster at the Fort gave government transportation.

Governor Carney issued a proclamation, and himself gave one thousand dollars in money. Mayor Anthony exerted himself to the utmost, officially and privately, in behalf of the sufferers. And the Hon. M. J. Parrott and A. C. Wilder went in person to render service. Sympathy and vengeance divided the public sentiment.

Such was the catastrophe—such the wickedness— which was suddenly let loose upon the inhabitants of this defenceless and unprotected town. Man, when unrestrained by the ties of law or morality, is a monster of cruelty and injustice.

MURDER OF MR. LEWIS PIERCE.

MR. LEWIS PIERCE, being sick, was stopping at Mr. Johnson's house, in Clinton county, Tennessee. He was so ill as to be scarcely able to leave his bed. One day, shortly after the Home Guards had been disbanded, hearing the tramp of horses, and the voices of men in the road, and suspecting that it was Champ Furguson—that cold-blooded murderer, and his band of assassins, who had come to take his life—as was natural, he endeavored to escape by getting out of bed and running from the house; but being weak from sickness, he was soon over-

taken by Furguson, who ran him through with the knife
presented to him by General Braxton Bragg (then commanding that department), cutting him in a shocking
manner. This not killing him instantly, two of Champ's
imps of crime seized the poor man's legs, while a third,
stepping up, drew his knife and commenced disembowel-
ling their already dying victim. His entrails were then
laid on a log, and the body thrown violently on the
ground.

While these fiends were carrying on this work of
blood, Champ and his band applauded them for their
bravery. Such is the manner in which the Union men
of Tennessee were treated. It was worth the life of a
man in many localities even to be suspected of being a
Union man.*

VIOLATION OF A FLAG OF TRUCE.

On the 27th of March, 1863, as the United States
bark Pursuit was lying off Gladsdin's Point, in Tampa
Bay, Florida, on blockading duty, a smoke was discovered on the shore, and shortly afterwards three persons
appeared on the beach waving a white flag. The commander of the Pursuit, Act. Vol. Lieutenant Randall,
supposing they wished to communicate with the Fleet,
sent out a boat, in charge of Acting-Master H. K. Lapham, with a flag of truce flying.

On the boat nearing the shore, two of the party were
seen to be dressed in women's clothes, with their hands
and faces blackened so as to represent negroes. One of

---

* Dr. J. D. Hale, of Tennessee.

them appeared to be overcome with joy, and exclaimed, "Thank God! thank God! I am free!"

On the boat touching the shore, the female dresses were thrown off, and it became evident that their late wearers were white men, disguised for the purpose of decoying the boat on shore. Immediately after, about one hundred armed rebels rose from the bushes and demanded the surrender of the boat; which of course was refused, as they had come in answer to the flag. A volley of musketry was then fired into her, wounding the officer in charge, Acting-Master H. K. Lapham. As soon as those in the boat recovered from their surprise, they fired upon the miscreants, until the boat was out of range.*

PERSECUTION OF UNION MEN IN THE SOUTH-WEST.

AT a meeting in the Cooper Institute, New York City, Saturday, October 25th, 1862, Rev. Mr. Aughey, of Mississippi, delivered an address, condemning the course that the South had taken in the rebellion. He stated that the Union men were treated in the most cruel manner. Speaking of the sufferings that he had endured, he said: "I was seized by the rebels, heavily ironed, and placed with eighty others in a southern dungeon. My crime was that I had used seditious language, or, as they term it, had talked Union talk. While I was in that prison numbers were led out and shot.

"At first they provided coffins for those that were shot,

---

* See Letters of T. Bailey, Act. Rear-Admiral, to Secretary of the Navy; also Letters of H. K. Wheeler, Act. Surgeon, to W. Randall, Act. Vol. Lieut. commanding Pursuit.

but the great number of executions exceeding the supply, they dug a trench, and made the men sit down on the brink, and a certain number of soldiers advanced and fired three balls into the head and three into the heart. This was the mode of execution.

"They sent after me with bloodhounds; yes, with bloodhounds. They hunt the Union men now with these ferocious animals."

REASONS FOR DESERTING THE REBEL SERVICE— REIGN OF TERROR IN TEXAS.

LETTER OF CAPTAIN W. H. HENDERSON.

WHEN men once espouse a cause, I know it is generally considered weak-minded to desert or abandon it. But men of sense, when convinced of an error, will always repent, and make amends so far as in them lies. I espoused the cause of the rebellion in May, 1861, served as an officer in the Confederate army to the best of my ability until September, 1862, when I was put under arrest, by order of General Van Dorn, and held as a prisoner until the second of the month of November, 1863. Notwithstanding I demanded an investigation of the charges time and again, it was refused. I urged a trial last month through the medium of influential friends, and the charges were investigated on the second of last month. I was exonerated and reinstated, sent to Avery's Island, on Vermillion Bay, to picket the roads and bay, and I deserted the command on the 11th, and reached the lines of the United States forces on the 22d or 23d, or thereabouts; I cannot state precisely. I know that I shall be looked upon and treated with contempt by those whose sympathies are still with the rebels. Let it be so. I am prepared to meet their cold looks, and treat them with as much respect as I consider the cause to which they cling entitles them. I have done what I did after mature deliberation. I became convinced that I had embarked in a bad cause, and, after I was exculpated from the charges against me, I considered I had a right to act for myself. I enlisted in the rebellion against the earnest entreaties of my parents, and left my dear mother in tears when I started for the rebel army. Oh! that I had taken her counsel, and not proceeded, in spite of her tears, to the execution of a deed which I shall ever repent. But I think the adage is exemplified in this case, that experience is a dear school, but fools will learn in no other.   *   *   *   *   *   *

There is much disaffection toward the rebel government among the trans-Mississippi people. Many, who previous to the Emancipation Proclamation of the President of the United States were good Secessionists, are now as good Union men as they were rebels. They saw plainly that by complying with the Proclamation the war could be brought to a speedy close, and the further effusion of blood be avoided.

But why have not the people in the rebel states more generally complied? Gladly would seven-eighths of the non-slaveholding population have done so, but a proposition or hint of such a thing from any person would have been the signal of death to him or her without ceremony. It would have frustrated the designs of Generals Lee, Joe Johnson, Bragg, Beauregard, Smith, Holmes, Magruder, Bill Yancey, &c.

They all aspire to the presidency of the Confederate States, and before they would consent to the restoration of the Union, thereby blasting for ever their political aspirations, they would see the soil of Texas crimsoned with the blood of her partly deluded and down-trodden people.

I assert, positively, that it is not the fault of the citizens of the States in rebellion that this war has not ended, and the Union been reconstructed. Twelve months ago, if the legal voters could have given expression to their sentiments perfectly untrammelled, they would have voted reconstruction by a two-thirds majority. The United States Government should wage a war of extermination against (the leaders) of the rebellion, and never lay down the sword till Jeff Davis, with every other leading conspirator, is seen dangling from the limbs of trees at the end of a rope. I have witnessed scenes in the Confederate army perpetrated upon the helpless and unoffending, by Confederate soldiers, that would make inhumanity itself blush. When General Taylor retreated from the Teche last summer, or the latter part of last spring, there was scarcely a farm-house on the line of march but bore ocular proof of the depredations of Sibley's men, and the only excuse they gave for robbing the citizens was, that they did not want to leave it to the Yankees.

They even went so far as to shoot cattle down on the prairie, and leave them lying to be eaten by the buzzards. I saw a Texas soldier shoot a soldier's wife's cow in her yard, and it the only one she had; and because she remonstrated, set her house on fire, and turned her and her little ones out of doors.

Who, I ask, is responsible for all this? Echo answers —Jeff Davis & Co.; and the ghosts of thousands of helpless women and children and poor deluded soldiers will witness against them in the day of judgment.

I am aware that I may be stigmatized as a deserter. Let it be so; I am prepared to breast the storm of sneers and reproaches from those who were once my friends. I am here without money and without good clothes, but let come what will I am determined to lend all the aid in my power to crush the rebellion, and restore the Union as it was, save the institution of slavery. I know, if I should be so unfortunate as to fall into the hands of the rebels, they will show me no quarter, consequently when they get me they will only get my dead body.

I am ready and willing to go wherever I may in the judgment of the general commanding be most useful; and I am determined, let others do as they may, to serve the United States Government to the best of my ability, and when I shall fall, I hope it may not be till I have wiped the stain from the stars and stripes which I have put upon them, by having been so silly as to have been blinded by what the southern demagogues say about our wrongs. If slavery is the cause of our family quarrels and dissensions, do away with it, for God's sake—the sooner the better.

I give you these few reasons for deserting the rebel army. There are those who may discard me from our former friendship on account of the course I have pursued. If so, I say go to the rebel army and meet me on the prairies of Texas, and we will settle all.

W. H. HENDERSON,
Formerly Captain C. S. A.

17

MURDER OF WILLIAM JOHNSON.

WILLIAM JOHNSON, an inoffensive Union man living in Fentress county, Tennessee, was brutally murdered by that fiend, Champ Furguson, and a band of rebel villains made up from his own and a part of Bledsoe's company of murderers. Mr. Johnson was at work in a field a short distance from his residence, when he heard the click of some guns. He raised his head, and saw these marauders standing with their guns pointing at him. Knowing his chance for escape was small, he stood still, when the fiends fired at him, without any order or offer of surrender. After the first volley, he started to run, and was pursued, the fiends firing at him and wounding him severely. He ran toward the river, thinking that if he gained it he might escape; but before he reached the river the murderers had wounded him so severely that he could not keep his balance, and fell over the cliff just as the gang came up. In a short time the neighbors came out and looked for the body, and found it mangled in a most shocking manner. It was taken up and buried secretly, his friends being convinced that if Champ should be informed that they had buried the body of this inoffensive man, they would share the same fate.*

ASSASSINATION OF MR. HOUGH.

MR. ALEXANDER HOUGH, of Fentress county, Tennessee, a poor, inoffensive, but strong Union man, had by his frequent remarks against secession become a very

---

* Dr. J. D. Hale, of Tennessee.

dangerous man in the estimation of the rebels, and they determined to put him out of the way. Some of the men belonging to one Bledsoe's company, called on that ever-ready assassinator, Champ Furguson, and requested him to lead an expedition against the life of Mr. Alexander Hough. Champ and his murderous associates immediately started for the victim's house.

Arriving there, they instantly surrounded it, so that escape was impossible. The bandit and a few of his picked men then entered the house, and found Mr. Hough mending his shoes. They arrested him. His family were terror-stricken, knowing what his fate was likely to be. They plead for his life. The villains assured them that they intended him no harm—they would keep him a prisoner a few days and then send him home.

After securing him, they started off, and had proceeded but a short distance, when the cry of "Shoot him!" "Shoot him!" was raised, and several made an attempt to do so, but their gallant leader stopped them, saying that they were still in sight of Hough's family. After travelling some distance further, they halted at old Piles's place, on Wolf Run, for water. Mr. Hough was left standing alone in the yard, when one of the fiends, seizing the opportunity, shot him in the arm, tearing it nearly off. The old man then sunk down and begged for water. They told him he could not have it. Rallying himself, he then got up and started for the spring. The whole band fired at him, two shots taking effect in his body. He fell, but struggling, gained his knees, and plead with them to send for his family, that he might see them before he died. This was refused the dying man. He besought them to give him a few moments for prayer. Champ cried out, "No, d—n you, this is no time to pray!" and turning to his men, he commanded them to kill him.

Two of Mrs. Piles's daughters ran up to the dying man and raised his head, regardless of the balls that were flying about them. Champ, seeing that they were rescuing him, rushed forward, and pointing his pistol at the head of the dying man, fired, saying—"Now you can have him!"*

SHOOTING PRISONERS.

ON Saturday, April 2d, 1863, as three Union soldiers were stopping on the farm of a loyal citizen in Louisiana, within three miles of the Union lines, they were attacked by a party of guerrillas, and forced to surrender. They were then tied together, and marched a few miles off, when the guerrillas held a consultation, and decided to murder them by shooting.

The soldiers, upon being informed of their doom, attempted to escape, when they were fired upon by the guerrillas, and one of them was instantly killed, three balls having penetrated his body. The other two succeeded in making their escape. The murdered man's name was Cyrus McKey. A squad of cavalry were sent out to rescue the body of the murdered man, and when they found it it had been horribly mutilated after death.

Brigadier-General Ransom, hearing of this abominable outrage, issued the following order:

HEADQUARTERS, DEPARTMENT THIRTEENTH ARMY CORPS,
Natchitoches, Louisiana, April 2d, 1864.

GENERAL ORDERS, No. 11.—Charles Diggs, and —— Lane, citizens residing near the camp, having to-day

---

* Dr. J. D. Hale, of Tennessee.

murdered, in cold blood, Private Cyrus McKey, Company I Twenty-fourth Iowa Infantry Volunteers, and escaped by flight, it is therefore ordered that the dwellings of said Diggs and Lane be burned, and that all property on their respective plantations, which may be of use to the army, be seized and turned over to the Quartermaster or Subsistence Department, for the use of this army.

Captain Bacon, commanding detachment Eighteenth New York Cavalry, will detail a company to report to Captain J. W. Martin, Company I Twenty-fourth Iowa Infantry, to-morrow morning at 8 o'clock, who will execute this order.

The commanding officer of the Forty-eighth Ohio Infantry Volunteers will cause the men of his regiment, who were with private McKey, to be punished severely for violation of orders in leaving camp without authority.

By order of

Brigadier-General T. E. G. RANSOM.

C. E. DICKEY,

Captain, and A. A. G.

MURDER OF MR. WILLIAM FROGG.

A SHORT time after the rebel forces were driven from Kentucky, in 1863, Mr. William Frogg, who had been from his family some time waiting upon his sick brother, at Summersett, started for his home. Upon his arrival some of his friends told him that it was dangerous for him to stay at home, and advised him to leave, as that notorious cut-throat, Champ Furguson, was out on a hunt for Union men, and had threatened to kill him if

17 *

he was caught. One of Furguson's men, Harry Sublity, hearing that Frogg had been advised to leave home, called and told him to stay at home, and he would see that he was not injured. Frogg answered him that he should have to stay at home, as he was sick, and could not lie out in the wet and cold. After·the traitor was satisfied that Mr. Frogg would remain at home, he left the house, and hunting Champ up, informed him how he had succeeded in decoying Mr. Frogg into the trap he had set for him. The next day Champ, with Vest Gwinn and Sublity, visited the house, Champ entering and the other two standing outside. Champ asked Mrs. Frogg, in a friendly manner, where her husband was. She, not thinking he had come to murder him, pointed to the bed upon which Mr. Frogg and his little child were lying, saying that he was there; at the same time asking Champ to take a seat, and eat some fruit. "No," answered the bandit, turning toward the bed, "I have come to kill Frogg," at the same time ordering him to get up. "I can't," said Frogg; "don't kill me!" His wife, hearing the conversation, commenced begging and imploring the fiend not to kill her husband. Champ, hearing this appeal, turned and went to the door, when Gwinn motioned to him to return. He went back and deliberately shot Mr. Frogg, who sprang up in the bed. The blood-thirsty scoundrel then fired at him again, when Frogg fell back on the bed. This done, the fiend went out of the house, and joining his associates left the premises. Immediately after their departure, Mrs. Frogg started for assistance, and proceeded a short distance when she fell, fainting. The neighbors, hearing the shooting, soon gathered and found Mr. Frogg quite dead, and the little infant lying by his side covered with its father's blood.*

---

* Dr. J. D. Hale, of Tennessee.

FIRING ON DROWNING MEN.

FLAG STEAMER DINSMORE,
Off Morris Island, August 8, 1862.

SIR: On the night of the 5th, one of the launches designed to guard the right flank of our shore batteries, having been drawn out into the harbor in observation of a rebel steamer, was suddenly attacked by the latter.

Eight of the crew were picked up, and stated that the launch had been sunk. Yesterday a flag of truce came out from the enemy with a communication from General Gilmore.

Captain Green, the senior officer outside, reports to me that the officer informed our boat that the launch had not been sunk, but was captured with Acting-Master Haines and twelve men. This leaves only two men missing. The eight men who were received by our boat were all positive that they were all fired at from the steamer when they were in the water, and as this is in violation of the usages of war, I addressed a communication to General Beauregard on the subject, requiring that whoever should be convicted of the fact should be punished, otherwise I would not be able to prevent retaliation by our men. As yet I have received no answer.

Ensign B. H. Porter deserves mention from me for the energy, courage, and intelligence with which he performed the duty assigned him of observing the enemy, and also for picking up the eight men who in some way were lost out of the launch.

I have the honor to be, very respectfully, your obedient servant,   JOHN A. DAHLGREN,

Rear-Admiral, commanding S. A. B. Squadron.
Hon. GIDEON WELLES, Secretary of the Navy,
Washington, D. C.

MURDER OF CAPTIVES IN TENNESSEE, BY SHOOTING AND DROWNING.

HEADQUARTERS, DEPARTMENT OF THE CUMBERLAND,
Chattanooga, Tenn., Jan. 6, 1864.

GENERAL ORDERS, No. 6.—It having been reported to these headquarters that between seven and eight o'clock on the evening of the 23d ult., within one and one-half miles of the village of Mulberry, Lincoln county, Tennessee, a wagon, which had become detached from a foraging train belonging to the United States, was attacked by guerrillas, and the officer in command of the foraging party, First Lieutenant Porter, Company A, Twenty-Seventh Indiana Volunteers, the teamster, wagon-master, and two other soldiers, who had been sent to load the train (the latter four unarmed), were captured. They were immediately mounted and hurried off, the guerrillas avoiding the roads until their party was halted, about one o'clock in the morning, on the bank of Elk river, where the rebels stated they were going into camp for the night.

The hands of the prisoners were then tied behind them, and they were robbed of everything of value about their persons. They were next drawn up in line, about five paces in front of their captors. One of the latter, who acted as leader, commanded "Ready!" and the whole party immediately fired upon them. One of the prisoners was shot through the head, and killed instantly, and three were wounded. Lieutenant Porter was not hit. He immediately ran, was followed and fired upon three times by one of the party, and finding that he was about to be overtaken, threw himself over a precipice into the river, and, succeeding in getting his hands loose, swam to the opposite side, and although pursued to that side, and several times fired upon, he, after twenty-four hours of extraordinary exertions and great exposure, reached a house whence he was taken to Tullahoma, where he now lies in a critical situation. The others, after being shot, were immediately thrown into the river; thus the murder of three men, Newell E. Orcutt, Ninth Independent Battery, Ohio Volunteer Artillery, John W. Drought, Company H, Twenty-second Wisconsin Volunteers, and George W. Jacobs, Company D, Twenty-second Wisconsin Volunteers, was accomplished by shooting and drowning. The fourth, James W. Foley, Ninth Independent Battery, Ohio Volunteer Artillery, is now lying in hospital, having escaped by getting his hands free while in the water.

For these atrocities and cold-blooded murders, equalling in savage ferocity any ever committed by the most barbarous tribes on the continent, committed by rebel citizens of Tennessee, it is ordered that the property of all other rebel citizens, living within a circuit of ten miles of the place where these men were captured, be assessed, each in his due proportion, according to his wealth, to make up the sum of $30,000, to be divided among the families who were dependent upon the murdered men for support, as follows:—

Ten thousand dollars to be paid to the widow of John W. Drought, of North Cape, Racine county, Wisconsin, for the support of herself and two children.

Ten thousand dollars to be paid the widow of George Jacobs, of Delevan, Walworth county, Wisconsin, for the support of herself and one child.

Ten thousand dollars to be divided between the aged mother and sister of Newell E. Orcutt, of Burton, Grange county, Ohio.

Should the persons assessed fail within one week after notice shall have been served upon them, to pay in the amount of their tax, in money, sufficient of their personal property shall be seized, and sold at public auction to make up the amount.

Major-General H. W. Slocum, U. S. Volunteers, commanding Twelfth Army Corps, is charged with the execution of this order.

The men who committed these murders, if caught, will be summarily executed, and any persons executing them will be held guiltless, and will receive the protection of this army; and all persons who are suspected of having aided, abetted, or harbored these guerrillas, will be immediately arrested and tried by military commission.

By command of

Major-General THOMAS.

W. D. WHIPPLE,

Assistant Adjutant-General.

ATROCITIES COMMITTED BY INDIANS IN THE REBEL SERVICE.

HEADQUARTERS, ARMY OF THE SOUTH-WEST,
Forsyth, Missouri, April 12th, 1862.

SIR: In compliance with your request, conforming to the wish of the Joint Committee of Congress "to inquire into the fact whether Indian savages have been employed by the rebels in their military service, and how such warfare has been conducted by such savages against the Government of the United States,"

I hereby certify, upon honor, that I was present at the engagement near Leetown, Arkansas, on the 7th of

March ultimo, when the main charge of the enemy's cavalry was made upon our line; that there were Indians among the forces making said charge; and that from personal inspection of the bodies of the men of the Third Iowa Cavalry, who fell upon that part of the field, I discovered that eight of the men of that regiment had been scalped. I also saw bodies of the same men which had been wounded in parts not vital, by bullets, and also pierced through the heart and neck with knives, fully satisfying me that the men had first fallen from the gun-shot wounds received, and afterwards been brutally murdered.

The men of the Third Iowa Cavalry, who were taken prisoners by the enemy, and who have since returned, all state that there were great numbers of Indians with them on the retreat as far as Elm Springs.   *   *   *   *

Respectfully submitted,

JOHN W. NOBLE,

Regimental Adjutant Third Iowa Cavalry.

Major-General S. R. CURTIS, Commanding.

The following is an official letter from the commanding officer of the Third Iowa regiment in relation to the above :—

HEADQUARTERS, THIRD IOWA CAVALRY,
Jacksonport, Arkansas, May 11th, 1862.

General: On the morning of the 7th of March, I was on the battle field of Pea Ridge. While my command was engaging the enemy near Leetown, I saw in the rebel army a large number of Indians, estimated by me at one thousand.

After the battle I attended in person to the burial of the dead of my command. Of twenty-five men killed on the field of my regiment, eight were scalped, and the bodies of others were horribly mutilated, being fired into with musket balls, and pierced through the body and neck with long knives. These atrocities I believe have been committed by Indians belonging to the rebel army.

mm   Very respectfully, your obedient servant,
                    CYRUS BUSSEY, Colonel.
Major-General S. R. CURTIS,
            Commanding Army of the South-west.

The foregoing facts are also authenticated by the sworn testimony of Daniel Bradbury, John Lawson, and others.

FIENDISH CRUELTY OF GENERAL HINDMAN.

DURING the retreat of the rebel General Thomas C. Hindman from the State of Missouri to Arkansas, one of the most heart-rending barbarities was inflicted by him, upon one of his own men, that ever appeared in the annals of crime. The facts of the case are as follows : Upon arriving at a place called Prairie Grove, in Arkansas, a soldier whose name is forgotten, passing within a short distance of his own residence, left the ranks of the army without asking permission, and snatched a moment to run up and see his wife and children, having been away from his family over two years. Reaching his humble cot, he found his wife surrounded by her kind neighbors in the last agonies of death. A few gasps, and the last spark of life was extinguished, and his beloved wife was a corpse. Not unmindful of his duty as a soldier, the heart-stricken husband tore himself away from his distressed children, who clung to his knees and begged their father to stay with them—hastened back to his regiment, not having been absent more than an hour. Upon his arrival he sought his general, and told him of the death of his wife, asking permission to return home long enough to bury his wife, and provide for his little children, thus deprived of their mother, until the expiration of his term of service in the rebel army. What man, with a heart, could resist such an appeal! Besides this man was known to be one of the best soldiers in his regiment; always at his post, and always willing to do all he could to please his superior officers. When the soldier had finished his appeal, Hindman not only refused the poor man's request, but in his rage ordered him to be immediately shot, for leaving the ranks without permission from him. The poor man was dragged away, and, without a trial, was immediately shot, within a few miles of his sorrowful home. Such deliberate murders are common in the ranks of the Confederate army, and it is by such discipline that they keep the Union men in check, and make them fight for their worse than treasonable cause.*

LETTER FROM GENERAL RODGERS.

Sir: On the 7th of October, the rebels went to both of my homes; the one at Rock Island, and the one in McMinville, to which my family had, in part, removed, robbing me of everything about the place. They took my wife's and daughter's clothes (not leaving them a change), the shoes from off their feet, my wife's watch, and all the silverware, and five thousand dollars worth of

---

* Captain D. H. Bingham, of Alabama.

18

goods. They broke all my furniture to pieces, worth at least three thousand dollars; destroyed all my papers; and injured me in every way that their devilish minds could suggest. My loss cannot fall far short of thirty thousand dollars, and may be much more, in the way of papers. Upwards of eight thousand dollars in money was stolen from me. My wife says, "It is a clean sweep." I will go up home in a few days, and shall go to the commander of this department, General U. S. Grant, and get him to assess the rebels and their sympathizers, my neighbors, some of whom set them on. My family may, by this time, have gone to Illinois; as my daughter wrote on the 12th of October, that they would leave as soon as they could. I have not heard from them since. My office detains me (Tax Commissioner) at this moment, but will not longer than a few days. It is certainly a troubled state of things. My family shall not longer be subject to such trouble. I have authorized the purchase of a home at Brighton, Illinois, thirty-five miles above St. Louis; where I shall fix my family for the present. I am so unfixed in my mind, that I am not fit for any thing.   Yours truly,

J. B. RODGERS.

MURDEROUS · ASSAULT ON UNARMED NEGROES ON HUTCHINSON'S ISLAND, SOUTH CAROLINA.

UNITED STATES SHIP DALE,
St. Helena Sound, S. C., June 13th, 1862.

SIR: This morning, at four o'clock, it was reported to me that there was a large fire on Hutchinson's Island; and shortly after that, a preconcerted signal that the enemy were in the vicinity, had been made from the house of our pilots. I immediately started in the gig up Horn or Big River Creek, in the direction of the fire, accompanied by the tender Wildcat, Boatswain Downs; launch, Acting-Midshipman Terry; 1st cutter, Acting-Master Billings; 2d cutter, Acting-Master Hawkins; and 3d cutter, Coxswain Shurtleff. Soon after leaving the ship, a canoe, containing three negroes, was met, who stated that the rebels, three hundred strong, were at Mrs. March's plantation killing all the negroes.

As we advanced up the creek we were constantly met by canoes, with two or three negroes in them, panic-stricken, and making their way to the ship, while white flags were to be seen flying from every inhabited point, around which were clustered groups of frightened fugitives. When about two and a half miles from Mrs. March's I was obliged to anchor the Wildcat, from the want of sufficient water in the channel, with orders to be ready to cover our retreat if necessary.

On arriving at Mrs. March's, the scene was fearfully painful. Her dwelling and chapel were in ruins—the air heavy with smoke—while at the landing were assembled over one hundred souls, mostly women and children, in the utmost distress. * * * *

I there gathered the following particulars: The rebels, during the night, landed on the island from Fort Chapman, with a force of unknown numbers, guided by a negro who for a long time had been on Otter Island in the employ of the army—surrounded the house and chapel, in which a large proportion of the negroes were housed, posting a strong guard to oppose our landing.

At early dawn they fired a volley through the house. As the alarmed people sprang nearly naked from their beds, and rushed forth frantic with fear, they were shot, arrested, or knocked down. * * * *

It appears that the negro who guided the party had returned to them after the evacuation of the place, told them all the troops had been withdrawn, and that the islands were entirely unprotected except by this ship. I am therefore at a loss to account for their extreme barbarity to negroes, most of whom were living on the plantation where they had been born, peacefully tilling the land for their support, which their masters by deserting had denied them, and were not remotely connected with the hated Yankee.

Very respectfully, your obedient servant,
W. T. TRUXTUN,
Lieutenant Commanding.
Flag-Officer S. F. DUPONT,
Com. South Atlantic Blockading Squadron,
Port Royal, South Carolina.

Admiral Dupont, in transmitting (June 16, 1862) Lieut. Truxtun's graphic report of this murderous assault on unarmed men, women, and children, who had taken no part in the war—and were then scarcely expected to—who were quietly remaining and cultivating the soil where they were born and reared, describes the letter as "giving, in strong and earnest words, the condition of many of these sea-islands in consequence of the withdrawal of the army forces to Stono." He adds:

"The rebels surrounded the house with a ferocity characteristic, at all events, of this part of the South—murdered in cold blood the poor unfortunates, who were awakened from their slumbers to fall by the hands of the infuriated rebels.

"The contrabands have remained quietly here cultivating the plantations, under our protection, and it seems to me that the government is bound by every principle of justice and policy to shield them from these barbarous inroads."

Noble words! May they meet with a full response in every heart!

PROPOSED TREATMENT OF UNION PRISONERS.

THE following is from the Savannah (Georgia) Republican:—

"How shall we dispose of the [Federal] prisoners? Let the Quartermaster-General of the Confederate States issue his proclamation, stating that the prisoners will be hired out to the highest bidder, for some specified time, and in such number as the hirer may desire. I know of a gentleman of this city, a rice planter, who would gladly take two hundred of the Yankees on his plantation to build up and mend the dams of his fields. He is more desirous of doing this, he says, as the Northern gazettes have long asserted that we can do without negro labor, and he is anxious of testing the question. One good black driver to every forty Yankees, would insure good order and lively work among them."

HANGING OF JOHN BEMAN FOR UTTERING UNION SENTIMENTS.

THE following article, taken as it is from the Memphis Bulletin, a rabid Secession paper, affords the most convincing evidence of the atrocious treatment of Union men in the revolted States, simply for the utterance of Union sentiments. The coolness with which the tragedy

18*

is related is significant. It will be perceived that no apology is offered, no contradiction attempted, but the atrocious act is recorded with that silence which gives consent.

"John Beman is the name of the watchman on the steamer Morrison, who was hung near Mound City. He was a native of Norway, came to this country in 1811, and lived in Boston, where he has children. He was first examined by a committee, was proven to have said that he hoped Lincoln would come down the river and take everything; that he would die rather than live in the Southern States, and much more of the same sort that it is needless to repeat. The committee proposed to forgive him, if he would take an oath to support the Southern States. He indignantly repelled the proposition, and said that he would die first. Finding that he was determined and malignant, they threw a rope over the limb of a tree, and strung him up twenty-five feet, where he was hanging last night."

VIOLENCE TOWARDS NORTHERN PEOPLE.—OUTRAGE ON A LADY.

MR. COLLINS, son of Dr. Collins, a noted Methodist, who escaped from the South some time since, relates the following:—

Miss Gierstein, a young woman from Maine, who had been teaching near Memphis, became an object of suspicion, and left for Cairo on the cars. One of the firemen overheard her say to some Northern men, "Thank God! we shall soon be in a land where there is freedom of thought and speech." The fellow summoned the

Vigilance Committee, and the three Northern men were stripped, and whipped till their flesh hung in strips. Miss G. was stripped to her waist, and thirteen lashes given on her bare back.

Mr. Collins says the brave girl permitted no cry or tear to escape her, but bit her lips through and through. With head shaved, scarred and disfigured, she was at length permitted to resume her journey toward civilization.*

PERSECUTION OF UNION MEN, AND FACILITY OF GUERRILLAS IN TAKING THE OATH OF ALLEGIANCE.

EXTRACTS of a letter from Lieutenant Commander Le Roy Fitch, dated U. S. Gunboat Lexington, Paducah, Kentucky, April 2d, 1864:—

* * * * I would state that all men along the river, above Fort Henry, must be either disloyal in sentiment or actually engaged in the rebel cause; from what the numerous refugees tell me, none expressing sentiments the least loyal are permitted to remain at home or cultivate their farms.

Since so many of these guerrillas have been found dead on the battle-field, with the oath of allegiance in their pockets, I would believe no man of these guerrillas, though he had taken the oath forty times.

---

* New York Tribune, August 7th, 1864.

PROCLAMATION OF MARTIAL LAW IN MISSOURI,
BY MAJOR-GENERAL FREMONT, FOR THE SUP-
PRESSION OF REBEL DEPREDATIONS AND VIO-
LENCE.

HEADQUARTERS, WESTERN DEPARTMENT,
ST. LOUIS, Mo., Aug. 30, 1861.

CIRCUMSTANCES, in my judgment, are of sufficient
urgency to render it necessary that the commanding
general of this department should assume the adminis-
trative powers of the State. Its disorganized condition,
helplessness of civil authority, and the total insecurity
of life and devastation of property by bands of murderers and marauders who infest nearly every county in the
State, and avail themselves of public misfortunes in the
vicinity of a hostile force, to gratify private and neighborhood vengeance, and who find an enemy wherever
they find plunder, finally demand the severest measures
to repress the daily increasing crimes and outrages which
are driving off the inhabitants and ruining the State.

In this condition the public safety and success of our
arms require unity of purpose, without let or hindrance,
to the prompt administration of affairs. In order, therefore, to suppress disorders, maintain the public peace,
and give security to the persons and property of loyal
citizens, I do hereby extend and declare established martial law throughout the State of Missouri. The lines of
the army occupation in this State are for the present declared to extend from Leavenworth, by way of posts of
Jefferson City, Rolla, and Ironton, to Cape Girardeau on
the Mississippi river. All persons who shall be taken
with arms in their hands within these lines shall be tried
by court-martial, and if found guilty will be shot. Real
and personal property of those who shall take up arms

against the United States, or who shall be directly proven to have taken an active part with their enemies in the field, is declared confiscated to public use, and their slaves, if any they have, are hereby declared free men.

All persons who shall be proven to have destroyed, after the publication of this order, railroad tracks, bridges, or telegraph lines, shall suffer the extreme penalty of the law. All persons engaged in treasonable correspondence in giving or procuring aid to the enemy, in fomenting turmoil, and disturbing public tranquillity, by creating or circulating false reports or incendiary documents, are warned that they are exposing themselves.

All persons who have been led away from allegiance, are required to return to their homes forthwith. Any such absence, without sufficient cause, will be held presumptive evidence against them. The object of this declaration is to place in the hands of military authorities power to give instantaneous effect to the existing laws, and supply such deficiencies as the conditions of the war demand, but it is not intended to suspend the ordinary tribunals of the country where law will be administrated by civil officers in the usual manner, and with their customary authority, while the same can be peaceably administered.

The commanding general will labor vigilantly for the public welfare, and by his efforts for their safety hopes to obtain not only acquiescence, but active support of the people of the country.

J. C. FREMONT, Major-General,
Commanding Western Department.

TREATMENT OF SUSPECTED UNION MEN IN VIRGINIA.

TESTIMONY before the Committee on the Conduct of the War of S. A. Pancoast, a resident of Hampshire county, Virginia:

I was arrested November 10th, 1861, and carried to Winchester, on the charge of having carrier-pigeons with me. I had four little tumblers, and a pair of ruff-necked pigeons, which my little son had got in Baltimore. I was for a week kept there on parole. The Provost-Marshal was acquainted with me, and resigned his situation because Jackson demanded that I should be put in prison. I was put in the guardhouse, and remained there ten days, suffering every indignity that could be put upon me. I applied for a writ of habeas corpus, and was taken to Richmond the next night.

The lawyer whom I had employed, said that there was no charge against me—it was not what I had done, but what I might do; that it was in my power to injure them, and therefore I was sent to Richmond.

In Richmond I was kept in the Main Street Prison for three months, with the officers of the North. When they were released I was put in prison with the citizen-prisoners. There were from five to seven hundred citizens, with some soldiers. For a week or two we had no privy there, except by going down three flights of stairs. I have seen old men of seventy or eighty years of age stand from seven o'clock in the morning until twelve o'clock the next day, before they had an opportunity of going down stairs. Fifty cents and a dollar was frequently paid by those who had money, for the privilege of going down. That was the cause of our greatest suffering then.

While in Libby Prison, we had soup and beef once or twice a week. When the soup was brought into the room, I have seen them pick the maggots out of it before they ate it. If they did not eat that, they would have to go without. After the battle of Williamsburg, they picked out eight or ten of us, the firmest Union men there, and carried us to Salisbury, North Carolina, where we remained about ten months. When we got there, we were put into a small building, and kept there, without being allowed the privilege of going out for any purpose; and there, again, our greatest sufferings were caused by the difficulty of attending to the calls of nature. We had a box in the room, which we were compelled to use until the stench became awful.

We suffered very much during the warm weather. We were often compelled to lie so thick on the floor, that one could not turn over without all turning over. After a while, they allowed us a yard, containing five or six acres, where we were allowed to go in the day-time. At five o'clock we were compelled to return to the prison, which was then closed, and we remained in a close room until eight or nine o'clock the next morning. We could cook only in the yard—there was no chance to do so in the prison.

On our way from Richmond to Salisbury, we were seated on benches without backs (among us was an old man between seventy and eighty years of age), and compelled to sit there for fifty-three hours: for the guard had positive orders to shoot any of us who should stand up. I think that ride sent a great many old men to their graves. They never recovered from it. With the exception of the chills-and-fever of the country, we got along there a great deal better than we did in Richmond. The deaths were not so frequent. After Mr. Wood, Su-

perintendent of the Old Capitol Prison, Washington, D. C.,
returned from his visit to Salisbury, we were made to
suffer very much because we acknowledged that we were
Union men. We were kept in close confinement from
five o'clock in the evening until eight or nine o'clock the
next morning, without any fire all, through the cold
weather of the fall.

From that exposure I was taken with inflammatory
rheumatism, and suffered very much; and at last a surgeon, who was very kind to me, had me placed in a
building out in the yard. But this was not done until
they said that there was no hope of my living long. For
six or eight weeks I could not get up, or dress or un-
dress myself without assistance. At Richmond we had
a loaf of bread, and it was always good; but at Salisbury the bread was always sour—but with the exception
of the bread, our food at Salisbury was better than at
Richmond. We had a small allowance however—from
seven to fourteen ounces of food—for the twenty-four
hours. If we got fourteen ounces, we thought that we
were doing very well indeed.

While in prison in Richmond, a lot of "Louisiana Ti-
gers," sentenced to confinement with ball and chain, were
put in prison with us, and they abused us most shamefully. And at Salisbury, where we had a yard, the guard
around the fence would strike and punch at us with their
bayonets if we got near enough the fence for them to
reach us. This they would do every chance they could
get. And while in the prison, the guard below would,
at times, discharge their muskets up at the floor under
our feet, and the balls would pass up among us. This
was done several times. Since the 1st of August, a year
ago, until we came away, we buried one hundred and sixty-
seven of our Union prisoners. The death of these men

was caused mostly by want of suitable provisions. There was nothing for them, when they were sick, that was fitted for them. I think the most of them died from want of proper food. We had a surgeon there, but he had not much medicine to give us. And when a father was taken out to be buried, it was seldom that the son, if he had one there, was allowed to go to the funeral.

TESTIMONY OF JAMES M. SEEDS, OF CINCINNATI, OHIO.

I was arrested on the 6th of November, 1861, at Columbia, South Carolina. When I was first arrested, they took, of the money I had on my person, six hundred and thirty-five dollars. A few minutes after I was searched, we started on the cars for Richmond. I was arrested on suspicion of being General Rosecrans going through the country, and I was searched for important papers which it was supposed I had upon me. The next morning after we started, and had passed Salisbury, North Carolina, I jumped off the train and made my escape, and took what is called the Western Extension train, and went as far as that went, seventy-four miles, and then took the stage. I took the stage at Morgan-town, Buncombe county, North Carolina. An extra train followed right on after me, and I was again arrested just on the other side of the Blue Ridge. I was taken out of the stage by a mob, and it was with great difficulty that some men, who were friendly towards me, saved my life. I was then tied with my hands behind me, and made to walk seventeen miles to a town called Marion. There I again came very near being hung. I was there searched very closely and thoroughly, by the pulling off of my clothes and boots, and the searching of them all, and six hundred and twenty dollars more were taken from me, partly paper and partly gold. I was

19

then put into the county jail, in an iron cage, and locked up there that night with three thieves and two negroes. The next morning I was taken out, again tied with a rope, and put into a two-horse barouche and taken back to Morgantown. There three dollars of stage fare was paid back to me, and then they took that from me. That night I was made to walk six miles with my hands tied behind me, down to what is called the head of the road. I was treated very well there. The men working on the road there, took the rope off me and gave me a comfortable bed. I found them all Union men. My arrest and re-arrest had been made by Georgia men—some men of a Georgia regiment. I was then taken to Salisbury, North Carolina, where for the third time, I came near being hung. At Salisbury I was put in irons, and taken to Richmond. On the way above Raleigh, a mob wanted to take me out of the cars and hang me, but they did not do it. I arrived in Richmond on the night of the 12th of November, 1861, and was put into a building, called by them "No. 7," with some Federal prisoners of war. The next morning, still handcuffed, I was taken out of that building, and put into the Henrico county jail. A few days afterwards, I had an examination before James Lyons, and there they swore that, from all the evidence they could get, they believed me to be General Rosecrans. Lyons himself told me that I ought to have been hung; that they never ought to have brought me there. After that examination, I was taken back to the county jail. Lyons reported to their Secretary of War that they believed me to be a spy, and recommended the government to hold me as such, until he could get evidence enough to hang me. Some time in February, I sued out a writ of habeas corpus, employing as my lawyers, Messrs. Nance and Williams, a legal

firm there. The suit was brought before Judge Mere-
dith, I think. He said that, according to the evidence,
he would have to discharge me from prison. A man
named Patrick Henry Elliott was the lawyer for the
government, and put in the plea that the government
should hold me as a spy. When the judge made this
remark, and he found that I was about to be discharged,
Elliott said he thought the Secretary of War would discharge me, if my attorneys would go before him. My
attorneys were to meet Mr. Elliott, and did go before
the Secretary of War. Mr. Nance came to the county
jail afterwards, and told me that the Secretary of War
did make out my discharge for release from prison, and
that General Winder put in objections to my being discharged upon the ground of my being a Union man;
and stated that when I was arrested, there was a letter
found on me, written to a clergyman in Columbia, South
Carolina, recommending me as a good and reliable
Union man. That is what Mr. Nance told me was done
at the war office. The Secretary of War then said that
he would hold me three or four days longer, and give
General Winder a chance to produce that letter. Mr.
Nance came to see me about it, and I told him that there
was no such paper about me, and never had been. On
the 18th of March, I, with others, broke out of the
county jail and tried to make our escape. But I was
recaptured on the Pamunkey river, and taken back and
put into the county jail again, and there heavily ironed.
They did not iron me quite as heavily as they did some,
but more heavily than they did others. We were confined in the jail with negroes, thieves, and all kinds of
criminals. We were fed pretty well, but there were
from time to time eighteen or twenty negroes there, and
never less than four or five. On the morning of the

15th of May, we were hurried off to Salisbury, North
Carolina, on the cars, as Mr. Pancoast has described,
without the privilege of getting up from the seat, under
the penalty of being shot, and without anything to eat,
until along in the afternoon of the 16th of May. While
we were at Raleigh, I got a man named Kaschmier, one
of the police, to allow me to send out and get some cakes.
That evening, they gave each of us half a loaf of bread,
and a slice of meat, both raw and fat. That is all they
gave us from. the time we left Richmond, until we got
to Salisbury. And as near as I can recollect, we were
fifty-three hours on the road.

INHUMANITY TOWARDS NEGROES ON THE GOVERNMENT PLANTATIONS IN MISSISSIPPI.

REPORT OF BRIGADIER-GENERAL A. W. ELLET.

HEAD-QUARTERS, MISSISSIPPI, MARINE BRIGADE,
Flag Ship Autocrat, above Vicksburg, July 3d, 1863.

ADMIRAL: I have the honor to report that, in accordance with your instructions, I proceeded without delay,
on the evening of the 29th of June, to Goodrich's Landing, with my whole available command. I found the
troops at that point all under arms, and could plainly
see the evidence of the enemy's operations in the burning mansions, cotton-gins, and negro quarters, as far as
the eye could reach. It was two o'clock, on the morning
of the 30th of June, when I reached the scene of operations. I at once ordered the entire force to disembark,
infantry, artillery, and cavalry, and at daylight started
in search of the enemy, Colonel Wood, commanding the
negro troops, accompanying me with his whole force.

About five miles out, we reached Colonel Wood's outposts, where, the night before, two companies of negro troops with their officers had been surrounded and captured, after a spirited resistance and considerable loss to the enemy. From this point I started the cavalry in advance to push the retreating enemy, and, if possible, hold them until the main body could be brought forward. They overtook the enemy resting on the opposite side of the Bayou Tensas, and immediately engaged him, and held him in check till I arrived with the main body. The enemy had shown a large force of cavalry and several pieces of artillery. He endeavored to cross the bayou with one regiment of cavalry and turn my right flank, which movement was promptly met by our advance line of skirmishers, who repulsed the enemy handsomely. At the same time my artillery opened upon him with effect, and he retreated precipitately, having piled all the bridge flooring together, and burned it to prevent our crossing. I crossed three companies on the sleepers, who followed the line of retreat for near two miles. They found the road strewn with abandoned booty, stolen from the houses they had burned—among other articles a very fine piano.

Three of the enemy's dead were found on the field, and some thirty stand of small-arms were picked up. The enemy were undoubtedly, from information subsequently obtained, more than double our strength, and were provided with artillery and cavalry, but they were evidently not inclined to make a standing fight, their main object being to secure the negroes taken from the plantations along the river, some hundreds of whom they had captured. In passing by the negro quarters, on three of the burning plantations, we were shocked by the sight of the charred remains of human beings, who

19 *

had been burned in the general conflagration. No doubt they were the sick negroes whom the unscrupulous enemy were too indifferent to remove.

I witnessed five such spectacles myself, in passing the remains of those plantations that lay in our line of march, and do not doubt there were many others on the twenty or more plantations that I did not visit, which were burned in like manner. * * * *

Very respectfully, your obedient servant,
ALFRED W. ELLET,
Commanding Miss. Marine Brigade.
Acting Rear-Admiral D. D. PORTER,
Commanding Miss. Squadron.

TENNESSEE.

THE inhabitants of this State have been subjected to greater indignities and wrongs at the hands of the rebels than the people of any other portion of the country. At the commencement of the rebellion they gave a large majority for the Union. The rebel government, finding the Union sentiment so strong, to suppress it sent a large body of soldiers into the State, under the pretence of protecting the people from the depredations of the Lincolnites. Upon their arrival, Tennessee was declared to be part of the Confederacy. These soldiers traversed the State, committing indescribable cruelties upon those who were suspected of loyalty to the Union. Houses were burned, and their inmates compelled to fly for safety to the woods and mountains, or into the neighboring States; men were seized and forced into the rebel ranks, or subjected to every species of suffering, and in many cases to violent and excruciating death. Many were sent to. Richmond, where they were treated infinitely worse than the prisoners of war, and suffered a thousand deaths. Women were tortured to compel them to disclose the place of concealment of their fathers, husbands, brothers, and sons; refugees were pursued with bloodhounds, and often torn in pieces by these ferocious animals. Some, who had lain out in the woods for many months, suffering everything short of absolute starvation, were caught and hung without mercy, simply because they were Union men.

The time was when we were horrified by, and even discredited the statements of, the persecuted Union men who were fortunate enough to escape into the Union lines, but these statements are so well authenticated, and come to us from so many different and reliable sources, that no room for doubt is left.

As an illustration of the sufferings of the persecuted Union men of Tennessee, we give the following well-authenticated instances :—

In the early part of the rebellion, J. Staple, living in Scott county, Tennessee, for many years clerk of the county court, a man of great influence, thoroughly devoted to the Union cause, openly declared that the Southern people were madly rushing to ruin; that he was opposed to Secession, and warned his neighbors against the steps they were then taking, telling them that they never could conquer the Government, and would yet see the day that they would be sorry for what they were doing. "There could never be," he said, "two independent governments in this land, and the Northern people would never be satisfied until the rebellious States laid down their arms, and returned to their allegiance to the old Government." Mr. Staple was in his sixty-first year, and had lived in

Scott county nearly if not quite all his life, and a great many looked up to him as a father and guide. The rebels, finding that his influence was injuring their cause, concluded that the best thing they could do would be to rid the country of such a dangerous man, as they termed him, and thereby make others, who were more timid, acquiesce in and sanction their cause. They determined, therefore, to murder him on the first opportunity, and forthwith sent a squad of Confederate soldiers to the old man's house.

Upon their arrival they arrested the old and feeble man, telling him that they had come to kill him, as he had been injuring their cause by his d—d Union talk. The old man protested against his arrest; the fiends paid no attention to what he said, but hurried him off to a tree near by, and tying him to it, went off a few steps, and, turning around, deliberately shot him, killing him instantly, and went off, leaving the body still tied to the tree, to be taken down and buried by his distressed family, or some friendly neighbors. This is only one of their many fiendish murders, in which age and worth have been disregarded.

One would think, to hear the boastings of the chivalry, that it is their greatest desire to conduct themselves gallantly and honorably towards the fair sex. The following will show how far their conduct agrees with their professions. Mrs. Davenport, living in Greene county, Tennessee, a woman of respectability, associating with the best class of society, was visited by a party of fiends in the garb of Confederate soldiers. After threatening to burn everything about the place, they seized Mrs. Davenport. As soon as they laid hands on her, she knew it was for an evil purpose, and she screamed for help, and begged the ruffians to release her. But her entreaties were of no avail. They had come for a villanous purpose, and intended to carry it out. She was dragged off to a neighboring wood, and violated by the whole gang. They then let her loose, to seek her home and friends as best she could. An instance similar to the above, only of a more disgraceful character, was perpetrated upon a young lady named Walters, living in Haywood county, Tennessee. The fiends, after outraging, murdered her in cold blood, and then hung her old father.

In the month of April, 1863, a young woman, whose name is withheld for obvious reasons, was set upon by a pack of these fiends as she was quietly attending to the domestic affairs of her father's house, and dragged to a neighboring tree. The fiends stripped her of her clothing, piece by piece, until she was entirely naked. They then put a rope around her neck, in the mean time asking her to tell where her father and brothers were hid, as they were Union men, and they only wanted to catch them. Could they but do that, they said, they would not have occasion to hide out in the woods, as they were sent there to kill every d—d Union man in the country. She refused to disclose anything, and was immediately hung up to the tree, and after hanging a short time was let down by her tormentors, and allowed to dress herself. They then threatened her with tortures that none but fiends could devise, to compel her to tell where they could find her father and brothers, but she positively refused. After some more threatening they released her. Such conduct none but fiends could be guilty of.

A minister of the Gospel, in all Christian countries, is justly respected on account of the position he holds. Even the heathen treat the teachers of religion with reverence. The savage that roams the far western

forests, looks upon the ambassadors of Christ with senti
ments of respect. Even when the red man has been at
war with his white neighbors, he has seldom done violence to the minister and the missionary. The following
incidents will show into what depths of barbarism the
rebels have fallen in this respect. It matters not to them
what may be the position or character of the person who
adheres to the Union, they stop at nothing.

Rev. L. Carter, a Methodist minister, and his son,
living in Bradley county, East Tennessee, were dragged
from their homes, and inhumanly murdered by a party
of Confederate monsters, in the garb of soldiers. Their
crime was that they were d—m Union men.

Rev. Mr. Cavander, a Methodist minister, living in
Van Buren county, was brutally murdered, because he
was known to be a man of influence and a strong Union
man, and gave fearless utterance to his Union sentiments.
A party of rebel fiends, who were stationed in the neighborhood, rode up to his house, and calling him out,
immediately seized him, putting a rope around his neck,
then placing him upon a horse, they rode off to the
woods, telling him that he had been talking against the
Confederacy, and they wanted him to retract, and if he
refused, they would hang him. He replied, "God gave
me breath to bear witness to his truth, and when I must
turn it to the work of lies and crime, it is well enough
to yield it up to Him who gave it." They then, in a
tantalizing manner, told him to pray, for he had but
little time to do it, and he had better be quick about it. "I
am not one of those," he replied, "who have to wait until
a rope is around my neck, to pray." They then requested
him to swear that he would stand by the Confederate
Government, telling him if he refused, that they certainly would hang him. He positively refused, saying,

"Hang away, if you wish." One of them then climbed up a tree and tied the rope, which was fastened to his neck, to a limb of the tree, and another of the fiends gave the horse upon which Mr. Cavander was sitting a blow with a stick, which caused the horse to spring forward, and this inoffensive heroic man was added to the long catalogue of their country's martyrs. After his body had hung for some time, it was taken down, and the flesh actually torn from the bones by these worse than fiends, and thrown to the hogs. They then cut his heart out, and thrusting a stick through it, carried it to a neighboring village, and set it up in a public place, so that it could be seen by the passers-by, where it remained until it rotted. The fiends, when asked why they had done so, said it was to give warning to all the d—m Lincolnites, that they would be served the same way if caught.

Rev. Mr. Blair, of Hamilton county, East Tennessee, a Baptist minister, was arrested by a party of rebel soldiers, one of whom drew a knife across his throat, cutting it from ear to ear. The fiends did this in the presence of his distressed family, and then went off rejoicing that they had rid the soil of Tennessee of another d—m Abolition preacher.

They also murdered Rev. Mr. Douglass, a Presbyterian minister, for no other reason than that he was suspected of being a Union man.

In the early part of the rebellion, the rebels employed blood-hounds to hunt up the refugees, who, when caught, were either murdered or forced into the ranks of the Confederate army. But in the course of a year or two, the hunting of conscripts with these dogs became old. Besides, the fugitives learned how to elude the animals by putting pepper, onions, &c., into their shoes, and thus put them off the scent. The chivalry then tried a new method of hunting fugitives by employing Indians. Ar order was issued by the provost-marshal of Knoxville that he would give five dollars apiece to every Indian who brought in a conscript or his ears. The Indian naturally indolent, did not trouble himself with bringing in his prisoner, but would shoot him, and then cut of his ears and put them on a string, and bring them into Knoxville and receive his five dollars. There were a one time, in the mountains of Sevier county, some four or five hundred of these Indians, under the command o one Colonel Thomas, a prince of fiends, who allowed hi savage associates to commit all sorts of depredations and it is an established fact that they even killed inno cent women and children to satisfy the savage proper sities of their commander. They are fit associates fo their rebel brothers. The red man is the more human of the two.

In the month of March, 1862, Captain Cross and man named Davis, belonging to the Seventh East Ter nessee Union Regiment, were captured by a party c rebels, while they were away from their regiment. The were hurried off to a secure place, where they wer inhumanly murdered by their captors. The reaso assigned for this double murder was, that they wer Tennesseeans, and belonging to the Union army.

A party of rebels went to the house of old Mr. Smit in Blount county, and arresting him, took him into tl road, a short distance from his home, and informed hi that he must die; that no Lincolnite could live in Tei nessee. Mr. Smith plead for his life, reminding them o his age (he was over sixty); also telling them that l had a large fami y dependent upon him for support, ar that if they killed him, his family would starve. Plea ings were of no avail. They told him that they cou not stand there and hear such talk; that they wished to finish up the job and be off, as they had other business to attend to besides listening to him. They then drew their pistols and shot the old man, killing him instantly, and leaving his body lying in the road, to be buried by his wretched, horror-stricken family.

In November, 1862, two citizens of the city of Memphis, Tennessee, named H. Peers and T. Wolf, having some business of importance to transact in the country above Memphis, on their road stopped at the house of Judge Anderson, a strong Union man. After eating supper, they retired to bed; but had been there only a short time, when they heard a noise of voices outside of the house—then a thumping at the door—then a demand for the two men. Judge Anderson positively refused to let them in. They then set up a yell, and commenced battering down the door, which was soon accomplished, and the two unfortunate men were dragged from their beds. After robbing them of all their money, they informed them that it was their intention to kill them. The men plead for their lives; but it was of no avail. The cowardly miscreants, drawing their pistols, shot their helpless victims, killing Mr. Peers instantly, the ball entering his breast. Mr. Wolf was shot in the back two or three times, when he fell, and the ruffians left. Some time after they were gone, it was ascertained that Mr. Wolf was still alive. He was immediately carried to Memphis in a dying condition.

In the spring of 1862, an old man, named Neil, was murdered by a gang of Confederate soldiers in Middle Tennessee. Mr. Neil was a strong and earnest Union man, and was making his way to the Union lines after having all his property destroyed. A party of rebels dressed in Federal uniform were riding along the road, whom he

20

hailed, and expressed a desire to accompany them to the lines. After questioning the old man in regard to his sentiments, they said, "You are a d—d Lincolnite!" and shot him dead on the spot.*

INDIGNITIES TO ANDREW JOHNSON, LATE U. S. SENATOR, NOW MILITARY GOVERNOR OF TENNESSEE.

ANDREW JOHNSON, U. S. Senator from Tennessee, passed through Lynchburg, Virginia, on his way from Washington to Tennessee. A large crowd assembled and groaned at him. They offered him every indignity, and efforts were made to take him off the cars. Mr. Johnson was protected by the conductor and others. He denied sending a message asserting that Tennessee should furnish her quota of men.†

Our citizens heard yesterday, with every demonstration of delight, the indignity offered Governor Johnson on his way from Washington to Greenville. His presence in Virginia was regarded as exceedingly offensive to Virginians. He was insulted at almost every depot. At Lynchburg his nose was most handsomely pulled, while he was hooted and groaned at by a large crowd. The traitor is meeting his reward. We have heard since, from good authority, that at Liberty, Bedford county, Virginia, Johnson was taken from the cars, and a rope placed around his neck preliminary to a proposed hanging. Some old citizens of the county begged for him, saying that Tennessee would do for him what they proposed to do, and he was let off.‡

---

* The foregoing statements are abundantly confirmed by J. B. Neil L. S. Walters, T. E. Wister, J. H. Kennedy, and others.

† Commercial Advertiser, April 26th, 1861.

‡ Memphis Avalanche, April 25th, 1861.

ATTACK UPON MEMPHIS, TENNESSEE.

ABOUT four o'clock, Sunday morning (21st August last), the advance of the enemy, about four hundred strong, under Lieut.-Colonel Jesse Forrest, dashed into the lower end of Beal street; and while one-half of them scattered in squads of ten or fifteen in different directions, the others proceeded to the headquarters of General Washburn. A few minutes afterwards, the main body came thundering into town, and the whole city was at once in an uproar. Bodies of rebels, from ten to two hundred strong, filled the streets, pursuing and firing at almost every one they could see. The alarm-bells for rallying the militia were rung, signal-guns boomed from the fort, the bells on the steamers at the levee added their clamor to the general uproar, and the streets were crowded with rushing throngs of panic-stricken people, and squads of the enrolled militia hurrying to their respective armories. From the fact that nearly every avenue of communication between the different parts of the city was stopped by rebel cavalry, it was impossible to make any organized resistance. The militia in most instances were unable to reach their armories, and a great many of those who took part in the different fights were using their own or borrowed arms.

Lieut.-Colonel Forrest, with two hundred of the advance guard, pressed on up Beal street as soon as he entered the city, and made directly for General Washburn's quarters on Union street. A guard was thrown around the square in which the headquarters are situated, and Forrest with a part of his men entered and began to search for the General.

But a few minutes before this occurred, Colonel Starr

of the Sixth Illinois Cavalry, rode up to General Washburn's quarters and informed him of the state of affairs.
He directly went into the street, but seeing a body of
rebels coming rapidly toward him, he returned and went
out the back way, and almost simultaneously the building was assaulted in front. As he was leaving the premises, he was ordered to halt, and failing to comply, several
shots were fired at him, but without effect. His staff
with one exception (Lieut. Kinzy) escaped. Several
clerks employed in the Assistant Adjutant-General's
office were captured. The door being forced, search for
the General was at once commenced, and every room,
closet, and corner, was pried into. They even ascended
to the roof in their anxiety to find him. Finally, after
ransacking the building for about twenty minutes, the
search was abandoned, and the party left, taking with
them the General's overcoat and some papers, leaving the
following note (with others, of which I have heard but not
seen), which was picked up by one of the Seventh Illinois Cavalry.

HEADQUARTERS, MEMPHIS, August 21st, 1864.

To MAJOR-GENERAL WASHBURN: Any property belonging to you, that is missed, will be paid for six months
after the recognition of the Southern Confederacy.

By order of

Major-General N. B. FORREST, Commanding.

As thieves are not much given to paying for what they
steal, the writer of the above must feel confident that
the contingency under which he assumes to pay for what
was stolen from General Washburn, will never arise,
otherwise he would not assume the obligation so willingly. Two horses belonging to the General were also
taken.

From headquarters the rebels proceeded to the Gayoso House, on Front street, which is the general stopping-place of officers, and riding into the public hall, in which the office is situated, until it was crowded with horsemen, Colonel Forrest asked for General Hurlburt. The clerk replied that he was not in the house, when Forrest told him he was a d—n liar, and springing from his horse, asked the number of Hurlburt's room, which was readily given. He went up to General Hurlburt's room, but not finding him there, proceeded from room to room, forcing the doors and searching every possible hiding-place. The occupant of room number two hun- and sixty-one, says, that while they were in his room looking under and behind his bed for General Hurlburt, one of them peeped up the chimney, as if he thought the General had crawled up there, which was taken as a good joke, and the whole party laughed boisterously. While the search was going on, many of the guests were robbed of money, watches, &c., and the aggregate of their stolen accumulations must have amounted to several thousand dollars. Not being successful in finding General Hurl- burt, who happened to be spending the night with a friend in the city, Colonel Forrest registered the name of Major-General Forrest and staff, immediately under that of Major-General Hurlburt, and left the hotel.

While the rebels where at the Gayoso House, Lieu- tenant Harrington, of the Third United States Artillery, was captured and placed under guard behind the office counter. A few minutes after he was placed there, a rebel on the sidewalk fired through the window at him, the ball passing through his head, killing him instantly. The body was at once rifled of everything valuable, and left lying on the floor.

Captain Cook, of General Hurlburt's staff, had two

20*

thousand dollars taken from his room, and the cigar stand in the public hall was robbed of the same amount. The money belonging to the hotel was not touched, owing doubtless to the well-known principles of the proprietor.

The Gayoso Hospital was attacked by a force of one hundred and fifty rebels, who fired upon and wounded one of the guards, and afterward poured several heavy volleys into the windows, when they were ordered to cease firing. Proceeding to the rear of the building, they captured eight or ten convalescents, one of whom being unable to travel, was shot and severely wounded.

New items of barbarism committed by the rebels on Sunday are hourly coming to light. Besides the convalescent taken from the Gayoso Hospital, and shot because he could not walk fast enough to keep up on the retreat, three men in the hospital of the Thirty-seventh Illinois, who were too sick to get off their cots, were shot as they lay and then bayoneted. Two privates of the Seventh Wisconsin Battery, who were captured while they were asleep, were approached and shot without a moment's notice, as they were being taken to the rear. One of them was fifty years old.

The rebels captured about two hundred and fifty prisoners, mostly hundred days men. Many of these subsequently escaped, but others were murdered.

They fired on the patients in hospitals, shot several of the sick soldiers, and captured others.

The prisoners they took, who were unable to keep up with their cavalry, were killed.*

---

* New York Daily Tribune.

ATTACK UPON BRANDENBURG, KENTUCKY.

At daylight on the morning of, August 10th, 1864, the town of Brandenburg, Kentucky, was attacked by a body of rebels under one Capt. Dupaster. After entering the town and committing some depredations, they were driven from the town by the Home Guards, and after firing a few shots, they sent in the following insignificant demand for the surrender of the town :—

HEADQUARTERS OF THE SEVENTH KENTUCKY CAVALRY.

Home Guards: We demand an immediate surrender of the town, and if there is a shot fired at us from any person in the town, we will burn the place, and shoot every citizen who is caught bearing arms.

By order of
Captain Dupaster and Captain Bryant,
Commanding the Confederate forces,
in Meade County, Kentucky.

Of course the Home Guards refused to surrender the town, and after a slight skirmish the rebels were soundly thrashed and driven from the town. Next morning they were seen passing through Meade, and a body of Union troops pursuing them. (This article is authenticated by a man of high standing, whose name is withheld for fear of personal violence.)

GENERAL HUNTER'S CIRCULAR.

The depredations of the guerrillas became so numerous in the Valley of Virginia, murders and robberies so

frequent, and by the aid of the Secessionists the perpetrators so uniformly escaped justice, that General Hunter
was compelled to issue the following circular:—

HEADQUARTERS, DEPARTMENT OF WEST VIRGINIA,
In the Field, Valley of the Shenandoah, May 24, 1864.

Sir: Your name has been reported to me with evidence that you are one of the leading Secessionist sympathizers in this valley, and that you countenance and
abet the bushwhackers and guerrillas who infest the
woods and mountains of this region, swooping out on the
roads to plunder and outrage loyal residents, falling upon
and firing into defenceless wagon-trains, and assassinating
soldiers of this command, who may chance to be placed
in exposed positions. These practices are not recognised
by the laws of war of any civilized nation, nor are the
persons engaged therein entitled to any other treatment
than that due by the universal code of justice to pirates,
murderers, and other outlaws.

But from the difficulties of the country, the secret aid
and information given to these bushwhackers by persons
of your class, and the more important occupation of the
troops under my command, it is impossible to chase,
arrest, and punish these common marauders as they deserve. Without the courtenance and help given to them
by the rebel residents of the valley, they could not support themselves for a week. You are spies upon our
movements, abusing the clemency which has protected
your persons and property, while loyal citizens of the
United States, residing within the rebel lines, are invariably plundered of all they may possess, imprisoned,
and in some cases put to death. It is from you, and your
families and neighbors, that these bandits receive food,
clothing, ammunition, and information, and it is from
their secret hiding-places, in your houses, barns, and

woods, that they issue on their missions of pillage and murder.

You are therefore hereby notified, that for every train fired upon, or soldier of the Union wounded or assassinated by bushwhackers in any neighborhood within the reach of my cavalry, the houses and other property of every Secession sympathizer, residing within a circuit of five miles from the place of the outrage, shall be destroyed by fire, and that for all public property jay-hawked or destroyed by these marauders, an assessment of five times the value of such property will be made upon the Secession sympathizers residing within the circuit of ten miles around the point at which the offence was committed. The payment of this assessment will be enforced by the troops of the department, who will seize and hold in close military custody the persons assessed, until such payment shall have been made. This provision will also be applied to make good, from the Secessionists in every neighborhood, five times the amount of any loss suffered by loyal citizens of the United States, from the action of the bushwhackers whom you may encourage.

If you desire to avoid the consequences herein set forth, you will notify your guerrilla and bushwhacking friends to withdraw from that portion of the valley within my lines, and to join, if they desire to fight for the rebellion, the regular forces of the Secession army in my front, or elsewhere. You will have none but yourselves to blame for the consequences that will certainly ensue if these evils are permitted to continue. This circular is not sent to you for the reason that you have been singled out as peculiarly obnoxious, but because you are believed to furnish the readiest means of communication with the prominent Secession sympathizers of your neigh-

borhood. It will be for their benefit that you communicate to them the tenor of this circular.

D. HUNTER,

Major-General commanding.

Official copy.—P. G. BIER, A. A. G.

This circular had its desired effect, for the next day
after it was distributed the Secession sympathizers of the
valley immediately gathered together, and waited upon
the general, and offered their assistance and co-operation
in detecting and catching these guerrillas and bushwhackers. It would be well to state here that the guerrillas and bushwhackers are considered by the rebel
government as part of their army, which is thereby
responsible for their actions. It is a noted fact, when
any of them are caught by the Federal army, they always
claim to be a portion of the Confederate army, and they
persist in being considered as prisoners of war. Their
robberies, murders, and fiendish atrocities are all sanctioned by their government, and most probably ordered
by them.

APPROVAL OF THE BLACK FLAG.

FROM a Richmond correspondent of the Petersburg
(Va.) Express :—

The spring of hope must now, with the Yankees, die
upon the winter winds. Already has the *black flag* been
hoisted upon the soil of South Carolina, and war to the
knife, and the knife to the hilt, and thence to the shoulder, been proclaimed by her noble sons as the only booty
which Yankee hireling invaders shall receive at their
hands. This is right—it is the only way to conquer a

peace with a people so lost and degraded as those which compose the grand army of the Rump Government.

We look anxiously for news from the sunny South; hopefully, prayerfully; with no misgivings. Now that the rallying cry is "no quarter to the invaders of our soil," may we not believe that the course inaugurated by South Carolina will be followed up by our whole army, and thus end this war? So mote it be.

BARBARISM.

THE following correspondence between the Rebel General Sam Jones and General J. G. Foster, of the Union army, will plainly show how far into barbarism the rebels have fallen. By the laws of civilized warfare it is justly required that prisoners of war should be treated humanely; but the rebels, it will be seen from the following correspondence, have disregarded all the dictates of humanity, and placed fifty prisoners, who were unfortunate enough to have fallen into their hands, in a position exposing them to the murderous fire of the Union guns. Such conduct, one would think, belonged to the savage: but the high-toned chivalry of the South have not hesitated to adopt it, and even to proclaim it aloud.

HEADQUARTERS, DEPARTMENT SOUTH CAROLINA, GEORGIA and FLORIDA,
Charleston, S. C., June 13, 1864.

General: Five generals and forty-five field officers of the United States army, all of them prisoners of war, have been sent to this city for safe-keeping. They have been turned over to Brigadier-General Ripley, commanding the first military district of this department, who will see that they are provided with commodious quarters in a part of the city occupied by non-combatants, the majority of whom are women and children.

It is proper, however, that I should inform you that it is a part of the city which has been for many months exposed, day and night, to the fire of your guns.

Very respectfully, your obedient servant,

SAM JONES,

Major-General commanding.

Major-General J. G. FOSTER, commanding U. S. Forces on Coast of South Carolina, C. S.

REPLY OF GENERAL FOSTER.

HEADQUARTERS, DEPARTMENT OF THE SOUTH,
Hilton Head, S. C., June 16th, 1864.

Major-General SAM. JONES, Com. Confederate Forces

Department of South Carolina, Georgia, and Florida.

GENERAL: I have to acknowledge the receipt, this day, of your communication of the 13th instant, informing me that five generals and forty-five field officers of the United States army, prisoners of war, have been turned over by you to Brigadier-General Ripley, with instructions to see that they are provided with quarters in a part of the city occupied by non-combatants—the majority of which latter, you state, are women and children. You add, that you deem it proper to inform me that it is a part of the city which has been for many months exposed to the fire of our guns.

Many months since, Major-General Gillmore, U. S. A. notified Gen. Beauregard, then commanding at Charleston, that the city would be bombarded. This notice was given that non-combatants might be removed, and thus women and children be spared from harm. General Beauregard, in a communication to General Gillmore, dated August 22d, 1863, informed him that the noncombatant population of Charleston would be removed with all possible celerity.

That women and children have been since retained by you in a part of the city which has been for many months exposed to fire, is a matter to be decided by your own sense of humanity.

I must, however, protest against your action in thus placing defenceless prisoners of war in a position exposed to constant bombardment. It is an indefensible act of cruelty, and can be designed only to prevent the continuance of our fire upon Charleston.

The city is a depot of military supplies. It contains not merely arsenals, but foundries, and factories for the manufacture of munitions of war. In its ship-yards, several armed iron-clads have been already completed while others are still upon the stocks in the course of construction. Its wharves, and banks of the river, on both sides of the city, are lined with batteries. To destroy these means of continuing the war, is, therefore our object and duty.

You seek to defeat this effort, not by means known to honorable warfare, but by placing unarmed and helpless prisoners under fire.

I have forwarded your communication to the President, with the request that he will place in my custody an equal number of prisoners, of like grades, to be kept by me in positions exposed to the fire of your guns, so long as you continue the course stated in your communication.

I have the honor to be, very respectfully,

Your obedient servant,

J. G. FOSTER,

Major-General Commanding.

Official — D. J. MAYER, A. A. G.

Headquarters, June 21st, 1864.

21

BURNING OF CHAMBERSBURG, Pa.

MERE words are inadequate to depict the scene of
desolation that reigns on every side at this place; and
the visitor, as he carefully threads his way through the
main and cross streets, at many points, confronting the
heaped-up debris of scores of fallen buildings, cannot
fail to give the fullest expression of condemnation re-
garding the act of vandalism on the part of the rebels in
thus laying in ruins the beautiful village of Chambersburg, while his heart goes out in involuntary sympathy
with the hundreds of women and children, who have not
only been for the time rendered houseless and homeless,
but, in many instances, bereft of all their earthly possessions. To-night I grope my way through the smouldering ruins, and pause, in sad dismay, at the fearful
picture of destruction and desolation that surround me,
imagination summoning to my "mind's eye" the many
peaceful firesides, from whose home-altars the Lares and
Penates had so lately fled, affrighted by the rude glare
of those flaming brands suddenly and pitilessly assaulting their happy domains. In the centre of the town, on
the main street, is an open space called "The Diamond,"
on one side of which stand four marble columns, all that
remains of the bank building. Opposite, appear the
bare and blackened walls of the county court-house,
with its heavy white columns and portico. On every
side are the ruins of stores, warehouses, and elegant
mansions, the greater portion of their stone and brick
walls still standing, while heaps of ashes, with a few
charred timbers, alone mark the sites of less pretentious
dwellings. The rich and the poor suffered alike at the
hands of the filthy horde, led by that prince of modern

BURNING OF CHAMBERSBURG, PENNA.   263

freebooters, McCausland, and that aristocratic but degenerate scion of Maryland's soil, Harry Gilmore.

Much has already been said respecting the destruction of this picturesque valley-town, and much remains to be recorded. The people and press of the North generally, who have so freely condemned the citizens of Chambersburg, reflecting upon their non-resistance of the armed force which sacked and burned their very homes, would, I believe, modify this verdict, and, it may be, retract their insinuations, could they, in this quiet burgh—ten-fold more eloquent itself in the abomination of desolation which reigns around—hearken to the tales of the sufferers.

Dr. Richards, a prominent resident of the town, who, with his family, escaped as they "stood," saving nothing, stated to me the fact that the entire valley had been completely sifted as wheat, to give its best to the army of the republic, and that Chambersburg had not a score of able-bodied fighting men. The women, even, had been forced to work to till the fields. No military organization existed there—no leader to command—no men to rally around his standard, had a head been found. No arms were at hand, except those in private possession; we were ignorant of the forces to confront; all was confusion; we knew too well the ferocious character of the rebel band, and those who led them—and any show of resistance on our part, would have only resulted in our being slaughtered indiscriminately, thereby heightening the catastrophe. The few troops that were here, had been ordered away on Friday night, in search of the rebels. Two pieces of cannon were left. These were taken out at an early hour on Saturday morning, and fired at the advancing foe twice, and then removed to a place of safety. This firing was done more with a view of giving Averill, should he be in the vicinity, notice of the approach of the enemy, than with a view of repulsing them.

When McCausland and Gilmore, with their detachments, numbering altogether four or five hundred men, came into the town, we could plainly see their main column in line of battle on the hill beyond, with two pieces of cannon. We were powerless in their hands. I indignantly refused, he said, to comply with their demand for money, and told them they might sack and burn my property, but I would not give them a cent.

Dr. Richards told Gilmore, whom he knew by sight, that the money was a mere farce, and made only as an apparent pretext. Gilmore's reply was, "I tell you what it is, we came here out of our regular route with the sole purpose of burning your d—d town, in retaliation for Hunter's raid in the Shenandoah Valley."

From conversations with a few other prominent citizens, who still remained in the place, I learned that rumors had prevailed several days that the rebels were crossing the Potomac in force, but no one seemed to know where they were. About four o'clock, on Saturday morning, it was reported that they were approaching, when Lieutenant McLain, with one piece of artillery, took a position on New England Hill, and commenced shelling the enemy. As subsequently learned, the few shots that he fired were very effective, one officer being killed and five men wounded. Having no infantry support, he was obliged to retire. The rebels advanced, however, cautiously; their skirmishers entered the town by the side streets about six o'clock, and scattering in every direction.

McCausland and Gilmore presently rode in, and went to the Franklin House, where they ordered breakfast. The morning meal hastily disposed of, and a quantity

of the landlord's Bourbon freely discussed, they sallied
forth, and after riding through several of the streets,
drew rein in front of the County Court-House, McCausland ordering the bell to be rung for a town meeting.
There was no general response to the call, but to the few
persons who were gathered in knots near by, anxiously
watching the movements of the rebels. McCausland read
the following order:—

(No date or place)

A demand is hereby made upon the citizens of Chambersburg, Pennsylvania, for five hundred thousand dollars in United States Treasury notes, or one hundred
thousand dollars in coin. General McCausland is authorized, on behalf of the Southern Confederacy, to receive
the amount named. Should the demand not be complied
with the town will be destroyed.

JUBAL EARLY,
General Commanding.

One of the citizens asked McCausland if he had any
positive orders to burn the town, when he replied that
he had, and, at the same time, pulled from his pocket a
dirty slip of paper—part of which was subsequently
picked up in the street—and read as follows:—

In the Field (no date).

General Orders.—General McCausland is hereby ordered to burn the town of Chambersburg, Pennsylvania,
in retaliation for Hunter's raid in the Shenandoah Valley.
By order.   JUBAL EARLY,
General Commanding.

While this farce was being enacted, the men who
accompanied McCausland and Gilmore were sacking
private houses and stores, taking only money, jewelry,

21 *

and such valuables as they could carry in their pockets. Dr. Richards, and a few other citizens who had been arrested, were discharged upon peremptorily refusing to give the freebooters any money. Orders were then issued by McCausland and Gilmore to burn the d—m town. The torch was first applied to the Bank and County Court-House, and in a few minutes both buildings were enveloped in flames. The rebel soldiers, maddened by frequent potations of whiskey and other liquors, which they had found in the hotels and saloons, entered upon the work of destruction with evident delight. In some instances, women were driven out of their houses before the premises were fired, and in others, no notice whatever was given. Many persons lived over their stores, and were only made aware of their peril by the smoke and crackling flames beneath their feet. The prominent public buildings destroyed were the Court-House, Bank, German Reformed Church, where the German Reformed Messenger and another German paper were printed, office of The Franklin Repository, owned by McClure & Storer, the office of the Valley Spirit (Copperhead), Franklin House, and other hotels. Fires were kindled in over fifty different places, and the total number of houses laid in ruins is calculated at two hundred and sixty-three. Women were ordered by the drunken soldiers to throw away small packages of clothing.

The residence of Colonel Alexander K. McClure, half a mile from the town, was visited by a rebel guard, and fired in several places. His barn and out-houses were also destroyed, and the place left desolate. Mrs. McClure, though sick, was driven from the house, and not permitted to save any of her clothing. Gilmore, who was attired in citizen's dress, rode carelessly about the town, switching from side to side a long carriage-whip. He bore no mark to designate his so-called rank of Major. A gentleman· who knew him, said that he was much bloated, and, to use his own expression, "both Gilmore and McCausland looked as if they had been soaked in whiskey. I could not say they were drunk—only soaked."

Dr. J. L. Suesserot, a prominent and wealthy citizen of the place, succeeded by his individual exertions in saving not only his dwelling, office, and stable, but that portion of the town lying south and south-west of Main and Washington streets. Twice the rebels effected an entrance to his house, and were busying themselves breaking up a case of amputating instruments, when one of the officers with whom the Doctor had been talking, came up and drove them away. Money was demanded from the Doctor, but he refused to give a cent to the soldiers, and several times drove them away from his stable and fences, which they tried to scale. Each time his friend, whose name he did not know, and whom he had never before seen, came to the rescue and ordered them to leave.

I am credibly informed that, in addition to the work of pillaging and burning the houses, outrages of a worse nature were attempted by the rebel brutes.

No estimate has yet been made of the loss, though it is believed over a million of dollars will be required to replace the buildings. The loss on household property and the contents of stores will not fall short of a million and a half. As I passed through the town this morning, I saw several persons putting up temporary structures, and preparing to recommence business.

I give you here the statements of several gentlemen in regard to the sacking and burning of the town.

Soon after the rebels had entered the town, I was standing outside of my door, when a Mr. Douglas came up and said that he had just seen McCausland, and had told him to call some of the prominent citizens of the village together. He demanded five hundred thousand dollars in greenbacks, or one hundred thousand dollars in coin, and said if it was not paid, he would burn the place. I was perfectly indignant at such a demand, and said I would not give a cent if they sacked and burned my property. Douglas remarked: "They'll put the thumbscrews to us, doctor. McCausland's in earnest, for 1 saw it in his face." I paid no more attention to the matter, but set out to see my patients. Between seven and eight o'clock I met Mr. Thomas Kennedy, and while talking with him was arrested. They also arrested J. McDowell Sharp, William H. McDowell, William McClellan, and Mr. Kennedy.

At this moment Harry Gilmore rode up and said: "Gentlemen, you are my prisoners, and I shall take you to Libby Prison, as you have made no response to the call for five hundred thousand dollars levied by General Early." He then called for a guard to conduct us to the Court House. Knowing him by sight, I said, "Gilmore, I wish you to understand, that we are gentlemen, and that our word is as good as your guards. We will go with you without a guard." He said he supposed it was, but a guard was customary. We accompanied him to the Court House, and there he was joined by McCausland, who repeated the order of Early, demanding five hundred thousand dollars in greenbacks, or one hundred thousand dollars in coin. Some of the citizens had previously I understood, asked to see the order, when

McCausland read it, and also another order to burn the town. I did not see them or hear them read.

After a short parley between McCausland and Gilmore, the latter said: "Gentlemen, you are released." Walking up to him, I put my hand upon his horse's mane, and said, "Gilmore, you know that your demand for the money is ridiculous nonsense. The county alone could not pay it, let alone this village." Straightening himself up in his saddle, he said, with an ostentatious air: "I'll tell you what it is; we came out of our regular route, with the sole purpose of burning your d—d town in retaliation for what Hunter did in the Shenandoah Valley." He then galloped off, and superintended the firing of the Court House and Bank. My daughter escaped with only one change of clothing, and I saved only what I had on my back. Everybody in the place would have gladly joined in resisting the rebels, but we could have done nothing against such an armed band of cut-throats and thieves. The country has been so literally drained of young men, that women and children had to go into the fields. We had no arms, and even if we had, we would have been indiscriminately slaughtered, and our families left to the mercy of the brutal horde.

The town was fired in at least fifty places, and it is my belief, that they designed burning the village, whether or not the demand for money was complied with. I never before saw men act with such fiendishness, and gloat over the misfortunes of the women and children rendered houseless and homeless by their vandalism. The entire scene was the most horrible that I have ever witnessed. The screams of women and children, the yells of the drunken soldiers, and the roaring and crackling of the burning buildings, were terrible. In many instances, women were compelled to throw down small bundles

containing only clothing, and several of those packages
I saw the rebels toss into the flames, swearing that nothing should be taken away.

STATEMENT OF THE HON. JUDGE KIMMELL.

I reside in West Market street, nearly in the heart of
the town. It was known the day before (Friday), that
the rebels had crossed the river at Mercersburg, fifteen
miles south-west of the town. But we were all lulled
into a false security by the fact that, when Stuart and
Lee invaded the State before, strict orders were given
not to molest private property of citizens. As a consequence, we rested quite easy, not dreaming that they
would burn our houses, and drive us mercilessly from
our homes. The citizens generally, were prepared to
have their places of business pillaged. A little before
six o'clock on Saturday morning, having heard some
shells whizzing through the town, I went out on to my
front stoop, and was there joined by a neighbor. In
about half an hour thereafter, or less time, perhaps, two
men emerged from an alley next to my house, when Mrs.
Achenbach, another neighbor, who was standing by,
thinking them citizens, asked if they were fleeing.
Their answer was an oath and a coarse laugh. I remarked, "Those are rebels." At this moment, I heard
the clanking of arms, and looking eastward, saw a body
of mounted infantry and cavalry marching into the
town. As near as I can judge, there were between four
and five hundred men.

I then went to a upper chamber of my house, for
the purpose of securing some valuable papers, and,
while so engaged, I heard the rebels say as they passed,
that they were going to burn the town. At seven and
a half o'clock, I looked out, and saw a new three story

building opposite in flames. Several men approached, and I heard one tell Mrs. Achenbach, to get out of the way, as they were going to fire her house. Her prayers and entreaties for time to collect a few articles of clothing, were of no avail. With my daughter, who had got a change of apparel, I started out the back way, and conducted her to a place of safety, on a hill, from which position I distinctly saw the rebels dashing in a fiendish manner through the streets, and firing the houses. Women with children, each carrying little packages of clothing, were fleeing in every direction. The sight was fearful, and the horrible scene chilled my blood. The day was clear, and calm, but the burning houses created a draught, and the roar was prodigious. Pickets were stationed at the street corners, to prevent the people from even attempting to save their property. From intimations that we had of their approach the night previous, it was deemed prudent to remove all the records from the County Court House, and the books and money from the bank. I passed through the picket-line unmolested, though many citizens were driven back. Had no conversation with any of the crowd.

Finding that I could not save any of the burning property, I returned to the hill, and remained there until the rebels left. The citizens would willingly have joined in defending the place, but we had no arms and no leader, and moreover felt that it would, unless aided by some organized military body, have been uselessly sacrificing ourselves to have gone out against this band of cut-throats, thieves, and incendiaries. We were informed that the main force of rebels, two thousand five hundred strong, were drawn up in line of battle on one of the hills beyond the town ready for any emergency. In my opinion the demand for money was a mere pretext. I believe they intended destroying the town in the outset.

STATEMENT OF MR. CHARLES H. TAYLOR.

I reside on Main street, and am connected with the bank. About five o'clock on Saturday morning the rebels threw a skirmish-line about the town, and while advancing complimented us with a few shells, which happily did no damage. Upon entering, McCausland or Gilmore, who led the party, which was between four and five hundred strong, caused the town bell to be rung, but the citizens failed to respond. They then arrested Dr. Richards and several other prominent citizens, and read to them a requisition signed by Jubal Early, demanding five hundred thousand dollars in greenbacks, or one hundred thousand dollars in coin. They refused to comply; whereupon another order was produced to burn the town, both being signed by Early. I believe it was their intention to burn the town, whether the money was paid or not, as while they were reading the orders many of their men were gathering material to burn the buildings. Soon after this the town was fired in upwards of fifty different places. On the main street many families lived over their stores, but received no intimation whatever of the burning, except in finding fires kindled on the lower floor, and the upper part of their premises filled with smoke. Women, while escaping with their children, were ordered by the brutal soldiers to lay down little packages containing clothing. Men were robbed in the streets of watches, money, penknives, and other small articles. All were compelled to empty their pockets. I remained until nine o'clock, and assisted some ladies in removing their clothing. The scene was terrible.

STATEMENT OF SAMUEL SEIBERT.

Mr. Seibert says they first heard of the rebels at Clear Springs, and at another point on Friday. Next heard

of them at Shunkstown, and then at Mercersburg, whence
they came, as we subsequently learned, via Bridgeport
and St. Thomas. About two o'clock on Saturday morning we got word that they were advancing upon us.
Some of our men went out with two cannon on the hill,
and fired twice, killing one and wounding five of the
invaders. In two hours thereafter the rebels entered the
town, about five hundred strong. McCausland inquired .
for the town council, but none of them were to be found.
The bell was rung for a meeting, but the citizens made
no response. An order from Early was read to several
citizens, demanding five hundred thousand dollars in
United States notes, or one hundred thousand dollars
in coin, and in the event of its not being paid the town
was to be burned. They would not allow anybody, that
I could see, to put out the fire.

In my opinion it will take from a million to a million
and a half to replace the buildings that have been destroyed. There were, as near as can be calculated, two
hundred and sixty-three houses, stores, and dwellings
laid in ruins. While standing at the gate, between my
house and the carpenter's shop, a fellow rode up and demanded one hundred dollars. I told him I hadn't got
it; when he asked for fifty dollars, then ten dollars, and
five dollars, and compelled me to turn my pockets inside
out. He finally asked me for a box of matches, at the
same time looking toward my shop, and upon being refused rode off. There is no doubt but that they intended
burning the town, money or no money; for I knew several men whose houses were fired after they had paid from
fifty to one hundred dollars to have them saved harm-
less.

Many instances of individual bravery occurred during

22

the raging of the conflagration, a few of which I will narrate.

Miss Mary Black, daughter of Judge Black, a fine girl of eighteen summers, having packed up a bundle of clothing, threw it over her shoulder, and left the house. A few steps distant she was confronted by a fellow who presented a pistol, and told her to lay down her load, as it was too heavy for her to carry. Looking at the man an instant, she said, "What's that to you?" and quickly drawing a revolver from the folds of her dress, she knocked the pistol from his hand, and passed on without further molestation.

Mr. A. J. Miller, keeping a drug store on Main street, was engaged putting some valuable drugs into the vault of his cellar, and had just laid away his watch and money, when a rebel confronted him, and demanded his valuables. Seeing the property lying on the shelf, the fellow helped himself without further parley, and marched off. Mr. Miller then repaired to the garret with the intention of rescuing, if possible, a dog which he highly prized, the affrighted animal having fled thither. Being unsuccessful, he returned to his store, taking with him a double-barrelled shot-gun, heavily loaded. Upon entering he saw two fellows who had accidentally locked themselves in, and dropped the key. Without ado he fired upon one, who was groping about the floor for the key, killing him instantly; the other rebel ran for the back-door, and was about escaping, when Miller gave him the contents of the second barrel, and left him bleeding on the floor. The building was soon after fired, and the bodies of both rebels were consumed in the flames. Mr. Miller, in effecting his escape, came near being crushed by a falling wall.

A young lady, whose name I could not learn, wrapped

an American flag about her person and pistol in hand, defied any man to enter her house. By her determination she saved the building in which she resided, and the adjoining property.

Mrs. Watson, after extinguishing two fires which had been kindled in her house, drove the rebels out with a broomstick. Presently, however, they returned, and pursuing her to an upper room, secured her between a bedstead and the wall, then locking the door after them, they again fired the building. Some women, hearing Mrs. Watson's screams, broke open the door, and with great difficulty rescued her from her perilous position.

Shearer Howser, a returned soldier, and one who had been employed as a Union scout, ran up to one of the rebels, and with a "How are you?" grasped the fellow's hand, but before he responded to the salutation, Howser had secured his carbine, and ordered him to dismount. The fellow, not caring to have his head blown off so unceremoniously, exchanged places with Howser, and was driven off a prisoner to a neighboring village. Howser returned in the afternoon with horse, carbine, and the rebel's clothes, which were new, and a large roll of greenbacks, much elevated at his success.

Not the least active among the incendiaries was Captain Smith, son of Ex-Governor Smith, better known as Extra Billy Smith. He was observed by many people, going from house to house, applying the match, and scoffing at defenceless and homeless women, as they passed him in search of a retreat from the flames. It will be remembered that his father's property has always been protected by the Union troops.

After the departure of the main body of rebels in the afternoon, a major with seven men returned to the town, the officer swearing that not a house should be left, and that he would carry out General Early's order to the letter. He didn't care for McCausland or Gilmore, and should finish their incomplete work. The party was attacked by a number of citizens, and the men captured. The major, whose name, from some papers found in his pocket, is supposed to be Cook, was shot in twenty-five different places about the body before he fell. The prisoners were taken to Harrisburg under a strong guard.

One of the rebel soldiers was so incensed at the outrageous conduct of his companions, that he resolved to escape, and with the aid of a gentleman to whom he made known his desire, succeeded in getting away. He took no part with them in the burning of the buildings. Other honorable exceptions of like character I heard of —one man saying, "The Yanks had never committed so mean an act, and that it would damn the Confederacy."

From Dr. Trout I learn that the rebels, after leaving Chambersburg, visited McConnellsburg, arriving between four and five P. M., and remaining there until six the next day. Here they committed numerous outrages, stripping men naked in the streets, taking others out to hang them for not telling where their horses were, and robbing every one they met. There was evidently some trouble between McCausland and General Bradley, as they took different roads. Dr. Trout heard many expressions of indignation among the soldiers at the burning of Chambersburg, and one man said he'd never draw. trigger again for the Confederacy if they burned another town, &c. We are indebted to the New York Tribune Association for this well-authenticated statement.

AN APPEAL TO THE BENEVOLENT CITIZENS OF THE NORTH.

On the morning of the 30th of July, 1864, the rebels, under the command of General McCausland, with a force of about five hundred men, entered Chambersburg, Pennsylvania, and demanded five hundred thousand dollars from the citizens, under a threat of burning the town. This requisition was in writing, and signed by General Jubal Early.

It is now established by indisputable proof, that this demand was a mere pretext, on the part of the marauders, to cover up a purpose, formed before they reached the town, to burn it to the ground without giving any time to remove the private property, and scarcely time enough for the citizens to remove their families.

They fired the houses of our citizens in perhaps fifty places. Upwards of two hundred and fifty in the heart of the town were consumed, including all the public buildings, stores, and hotels, comprising about two-thirds of a town containing six thousand inhabitants. Thus a large body of citizens are reduced from comparative wealth to absolute poverty. These families have lost all their bedding, and all their clothing except what they had on their persons.

The loss will be largely over one million dollars. Without aid from abroad, there will be great suffering in our community.

The Rev. John R. Warner, of Gettysburg, providentially with us at this time, is the accredited agent of the citizens for receiving subscriptions and contributions for our relief.

F. M. KIMMELL,
BERNARD WOLFF, and many others.

22*

SUFFERINGS OF UNION MEN IN TEXAS.

ACCORDING to the uniform testimony of refugees, the outrages perpetrated by the rebels on the Union men of Texas, exceed description, and, if narrated, would seem incredible to such as have not been eye-witnesses.

Mr. Sumner said, in a speech delivered in New York City, that he was originally from Vermont, and emigrated to the South ten years ago; since which time he has lived in the town of Sherman, Grayson county, Texas. During the Presidential canvass, the supporters of Breckinridge, in that vicinity, claimed to be the only true Union men. But, after the election of President Lincoln, they threw off the mask and hoisted the lone-star flag. Mr. Sumner suggested to the people of his town to raise the stars and stripes in opposition. He met so much opposition that he thought he would give it up; but thinking the matter over, he bought the materials at a dry-goods store, and his wife made a flag. On the 1st of January, 1861, they hoisted it upon the square, and called upon the Union people to rally around it; and in less than half an hour it was flying over the court-house, and they took an oath that the first man who raised his hand against it they would blow his brains out. The rebels, seeing that they were determined, sought to compromise the matter, and promised to permit the flag to remain if the Union men would permit the lone-star to float beside it. Thinking that this would be the means of avoiding bloodshed, it was allowed on the part of the Unionists, and both flags flew undisturbed till the wind completely whipped them out.

Subsequently, the rebel mob at Austin called a Convention to pass a Secession ordinance; and were only prevented by Sam. Houston, who declared it should be submitted to a vote of the people. Grayson county gave a respectable majority for the Union, but in many parts of the State the Secessionists had the polls guarded with men armed with double-barrel shot guns, who swore they would shoot any man who voted the d—d Abolition ticket, as they called the Union ticket. Not satisfied with that, they marched men up to the polls and compelled them to vote the Secession ticket, although they did it under protest. Texas was declared to have gone out of the Union by some ten thousand majority. The rebels then hoisted the stars and bars.

Two papers were published in Sherman, one a Union and the other a Secession sheet. Discussion grew quite hot; and finally the Union office was broken into, and the main lever of the press stolen. This so enraged the Union people, that the next morning they went and tore down the Secesh flag, and stamped it into the ground. Two days after, one hundred rebels came marching into town, with double-barrel shot guns, to put up the flag. But being advised that if they attempted it, blood would be shed, they desisted; and as long as the speaker remained in Texas, no flag floated from that court-house. Mr. Sumner alluded to the fact that two Methodist preachers, Buly and Blunt, were hung as Abolitionists. Houses were burned by rebel incendiaries, for the purpose of exciting the people against the North by alleging that it was done by Abolitionists, leagued secretly together, to avenge the murder of the two Methodist ministers of Kansas.

James Bolan was appointed Provost-Marshal—a man who had often remarked that a poor white man had no more right to vote in the South than his slave. He waged war and robbery on the Union people. There was a family named Hillier, from the North. Mr. Hillier was waited upon by Bolan, and was allowed the choice to volunteer in the rebel army or prepare to be hung. He volunteered. Subsequently, his wife incautiously remarked, "She wished to God the Union army would advance and take possession of Texas, that her husband might return and provide for his family." Bolan sent six of his men, dressed in women's clothes, who informed her that they had heard she was an Abolitionist, and had come to wait upon her execution. They dragged her to the nearest tree, and, regardless of her pleadings for mercy, to spare her life for the sake of her innocent children, they put a rope around her neck, swung her up, and left her in her death-struggles, in the presence of her terrified little ones, till next morning, when some of the neighbors took down the body and buried it.

This act caused the citizens to feel alarmed, and three or four hundred leagued together for self-defence. About the 1st of October they were betrayed, and Jacob Lock, the President, was arrested. A courier came down to Sherman and stated that he (Lock) had been hung. Mr. Sumner could only rally eight men to go and release some men that Bolan had in custody. They rode all night, and were within eight miles of Bolan's place, in Cook county, the next morning. There they met a man hid in the woods, who informed them that Bolan had five hundred men under his command, who swore they would never rest till they had hung every Union man in Texas; that he had thirty or forty Union men, who would be hung that day.

Mr. Sumner returned home, and as soon as he could arrange his affairs started for the Union lines. Mr.

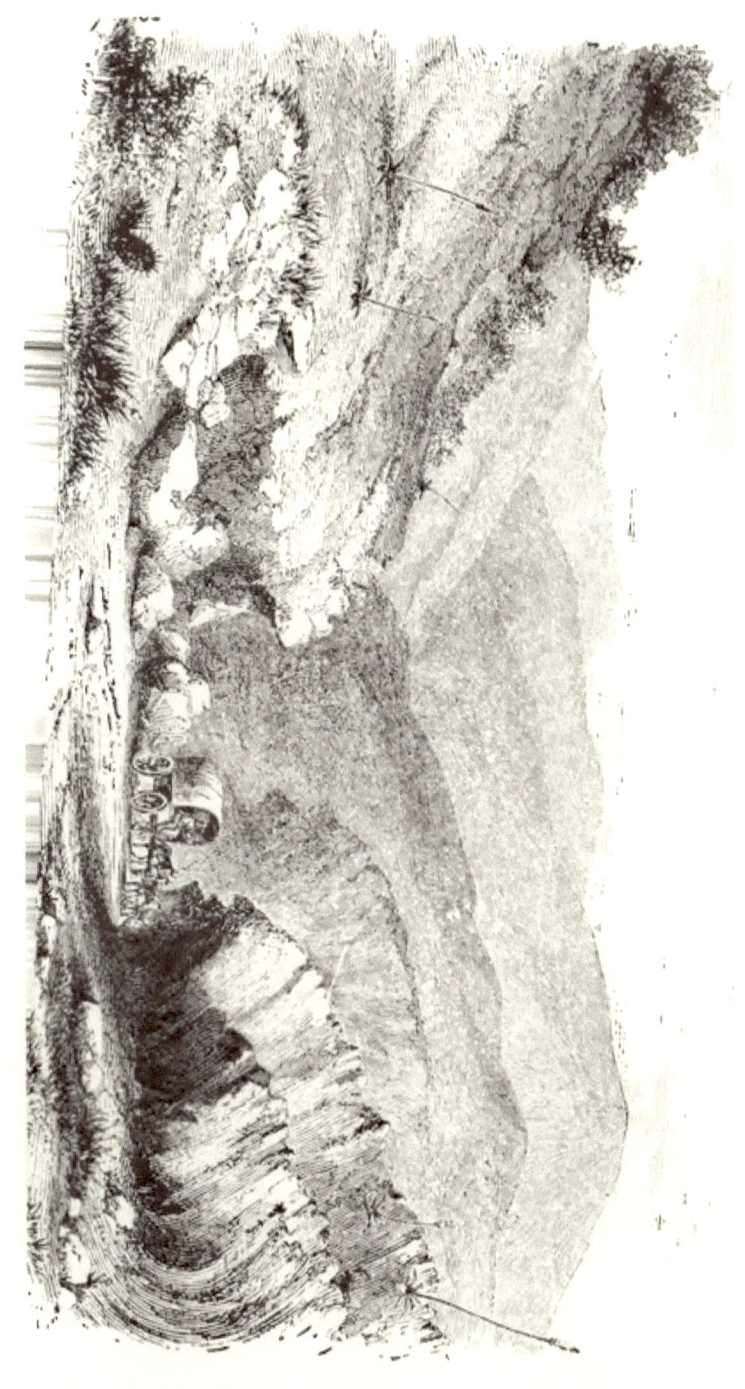

Sumner met with many adventures, but escaped his pur
suers, and considered himself nearly safe, till he arrived
at Leroy county, Arkansas, where he met a Texas recruit
whom he had known before. This soldier reported Mr.
Sumner to headquarters. He was arrested on the 29th
of October, 1862, and sent to Little Rock. General
Holmes turned him over to the provost-marshal, and ordered him to be locked up in an iron cage. He was the
only white man put into the cage. The others had "the
liberty of the prison."

Some time afterwards, nineteen young men, who had
belonged to Hart's Texan company, who had been cut
off from their comrades, were brought and put in the
cages. One, who had been forced into the Rebel ranks,
and whom they claimed as a deserter, was hung. The
rest were put into iron cages, which were originally made
for negroes. Their irons were taken off.

In a few weeks disease began its work. The jailor
told General Rema, if they were not taken out of the
cages they would die. The General said, "Let them die
and go to hell; they are only Yankee jayhawkers." In
about three or four months the prisoners were asked to
volunteer in the rebel army, "to make good soldiers, and
redeem their character." Some volunteered, others
chose to endure the privations of prison, rather than it
should ever be said of them, that they rose in arms
against their country. Finally, when the Union cannon
were within sound of Little Rock, Mr. Sumner and an
old man were released, to go home, on the representations of the jailor, that they were not in physical condition to be of any use in the army; Mr. Sumner went
to the Union lines. He described the stocks and instruments of torture which were applied, as horrible in the
extreme; they compelled him to sustain a weight of

forty pounds, to keep him from choking. When a man became exhausted and fell senseless, the common restorative was the whip, which the rebels said was "the best means of starting the circulation of the blood."

An old man, who was dying, requested to have his son, who was also a prisoner, with him during his last moments. But his keeper said, "If you want to die, why can't you die, and not make such a fuss about it?" The old man was compelled to conceal his groans as best he could, and soon after expired. A prisoner who passed the cell of his son a few days after, whispered through the gates that his father was dead. The son was soon found shedding tears. They said they would give him something to cry for, and gave him seventy-five lashes. After alluding to like and worse instances of fiendish cruelty, the speaker asked how men who had been treated in that way, could go back and live with those who had practised upon them such barbarities, until justice had been meted out to them. Until the rebellion broke out, he was a pro-slavery man, but it was certain, that we could never have peace, until the cause of the rebellion—slavery—was destroyed.

Said Judge Baldwin of Texas, in a speech delivered in Washington, D. C., October 3, 1864: You can scarcely form an idea of the wrongs inflicted on the Union men of Texas. They surpass in cruelty the horrors of the Inquisition. In that State, from two to three thousand men have been hung, in many cases without even the form of a trial, simply and solely because they were Union men, and would not give their support to Secession. Indeed, it has been, and is, the express determination of the Secessionists, to take the life of every Union man. His life is no more regarded than that of a wild beast, and he is shot down or hung without ceremony. Nor are the Secessionists always particular to ascertain what a man's real sentiments are. It is sufficient for them, that a man is a d—d Yankee.

A Massachusetts man, at the commencement of the rebellion was procuring subscriptions for Audubon's Ornithology. As he was passing along one day, some one dropped the remark, "There goes a d—d Yankee," whereupon the bystanders took after him, seized and hung him, although affirming his innocence, and claiming to have done or said nothing against the South. Soon after, a gentleman passing by, and seeing what had been done, inquired, "Why have you hung that man? I know him well. He was no abolitionist." "No matter," said his murderers, "he was a d—d Yankee."

One day a Secessionist said to the Governor of Texas, "There is Andrew Jackson Hamilton, suppose I kill the d—d Unionist." Said the Governor, "kill him or any other Unionist, and you need fear nothing while I am governor." In this way has been produced that utter disregard of the lives of Union men so prevalent at the South.

As I was passing through one place in Texas, I saw three men who had been hung in the course of the night. When I inquired the cause, I was told in the coolest manner, that it was to be presumed that they were Union men. It seemed to be taken for granted, that all Union men were to be hung, and the hanging of them was spoken of as an ordinary affair.

Judge Baldwin said further—He had heard a great deal, since his arrival from rebeldom, of the habeas corpus and free speech; but he could assure his audience, he had seen little of either in Texas. For long months he had been confined in a loathsome dungeon without trial, without even knowing the charge against him, and upon remonstrating, had the consolation of learning, that it was a "d—d sight too good for an abolitionist."

On the 9th of October, 1863, I was waited upon by a Confederate officer, who said to his squad of soldiers: "There's your prisoner, take good care of him; if he attempts to escape shoot him." No explanation was given for my arrest, nor was I permitted to communicate with my family and friends, but the next day was hurried off to San Antonio, where I was thurst into a dungeon, the air of which was so foul, that you could cut it with a knife. I remained in prison ten months, suffering every species of horror. But I thank God, that the shackles are now broken, and I can look once more on the flag of my country and enjoy its protection.

On my way to San Antonio, I was informed by the officer in charge, that I was in danger of being lynched by the populace. I said to him, "If you allow any such thing you are a coward, and I will haunt you as long as you live." This, I believe, saved my life.

General A. J. Hamilton affirmed in a Union meeting, in the Cooper Institute, New York, in 1863, that two hundred men were hung in Texas during the canvass for the Presidency in 1860, because they were suspected of being more loyal to the Union than to slavery.

CRUELTY TO AN OHIO SOLDIER.

A SOLDIER belonging to the Forty-fourth Ohio Regiment, which was then stopping at Sandy, Virginia, having just recovered from a severe sickness, was on his way down the Sandy Valley, to join his regiment. As he was passing leisurely along, he was surprised by a party of rebels, who rushed upon him and robbed him of the last cent he had, and also of all his clothing. After this, they took him off a short distance, and compelled him to stand up, saying they were not going to kill him, but were only going to wound him a little. When everything was in readiness, they fired at him with his own gun, wounding him so seriously in his leg, below the knee, that at one time amputation was thought necessary to preserve his life.*

HORRIBLE MURDER OF A SAILOR.

On or about the 5th of September, 1862, as one of Admiral Farragut's men was wandering very imprudently along the shore, a few miles below Vicksburg, Mississippi, a party of guerrillas, belonging to the same State, who were waiting in ambush, rushed upon him. They carried him a short distance from the shore, and actually disembowelled him while still alive. This statement comes from both prisoners and deserters, known to be perfectly truthful.†

AN INTENDED WHOLESALE MURDER.

As a freight train on the Covington and Lexington Railroad was passing by Garnett's Station, on the night of the 19th of April, 1862, it was precipitated down a

---

* T. L. Moore.
† Joseph P. Evans, of Jackson, Mississippi.

23

steep embankment by obstructions laid on the track by some rebel fiend or fiends, thinking that a portion of the troops, who were expected to pass over the road that night, would be precipitated down the embankment, and a great many be killed and wounded, and that by so doing, they would aid the cause of the rebels; but through the good providence of God, the troops did not go that night. As it was, Henry D. Smith, engineer, and Abraham Tanner, brakesman, were instantly killed, and the locomotive and eleven cars dashed to pieces.*

GUERRILLA BARBARITIES IN VIRGINIA.

ON or about the 19th of July, 1863, as two Federal soldiers were sauntering along the road, within a half mile of their camp, which was near Laura, Virginia, they were pounced upon by a party of guerrillas, who took them into the woods until they thought they were beyond reach of interference, tied them to a tree, and bid them good-by, saying, "that they meant to do them no harm, only to let them starve to death." One of them, by a desperate effort, succeeded in freeing himself, and when free, set about liberating his brother soldier. This done, both started for camp, determined not to be caught in another such trap. A few days afterwards, several soldiers were fired at as they were passing by the woods, but escaped uninjured. These attempts at murder were committed by the rebel sympathizing citizens in the neighborhood.†

---

* W. B. Jones, of Louisville, Kentucky.
† J. C. Stubbs, of Pennsylvania.

RAISING THE BLACK FLAG.

REPLY of Colonel Paine to a letter of General John C. Breckinridge, C. S. A., in which he alleges the perpetration of acts of violence by our forces, and threatens, in certain contingencies, to raise the black flag, and neither ask nor take quarter :—

HEADQUARTERS, U. S. FORCES,
Baton Rouge, August 14th, 1862.

Major-General John C. Breckenridge, C. S. A.

GENERAL: In reply to your communication of this date, I have the honor to make the following statement:

None of the acts therein referred to, have been committed, to my knowledge, in this part of the United States, under the order of our officers.

No private houses have been wantonly burned. Since your attack of the 5th instant disclosed your purpose to drive this army from the public property of the United States, I have determined to adopt such measures as will enable me, in strict accordance with the laws of civilized warfare, to maintain my present position. The accomplishment of this purpose compels me reluctantly to burn a small number of houses, including those of the United States Government and of private persons. While it is not impossible that, through mistake, injustice may have been done in individual cases, and although the vigilance of officers may not always suffice to prevent wrong on the part of subordinates, yet I believe that no unarmed citizen has been seized or carried into imprisonment on false or frivolous pretexts. No negro slaves, have been armed against you in this department. I have no information respecting the order alleged to have been issued to the Mayor of Bayou Sara.

In future I shall permit no wanton destruction of private property. I shall permit no unarmed citizen to be seized on false and frivolous pretexts. I shall not arm negroes, unless in accordance with the laws of the United States. But I am informed that a corps of blacks fought against us in the recent battle of Baton Rouge, and that our pickets were found tied to the trees, shot through the head. And I am sorry to remind you that a most barbarous system of guerrilla warfare is authorized by your officers and practised by your men in this department. While we saved your drowning men at Memphis, you shot ours at White River. I am informed, too, that occasionally you have raised the black flag at the commencement of an action. Nevertheless, I shall never raise the black flag, which all civilized nations abhor, but I shall try to maintain the flag which you have so often promised to defend.

Very respectfully, your obedient servant,

HALBERT E. PAINE,

Colonel commanding U. S. Forces

FIRING ON SHIPWRECKED SAILORS.

ON Wednesday, January 14th, 1863, as the United States steamer "Columbia" was returning from the fishing grounds to her old anchorage, near New Inlet, South Carolina, at 6 o'clock P. M., when within twelve miles of her destination, she was wrecked in the following manner: She was steaming along near the shore when the acting-master, in charge of the deck, sent word to the captain, who was below, that they were only in ten fathoms of water, and near the shore. The captain sent word back not to drop anchor until she was in seven fathoms of water.

Shortly after the captain appeared on deck, and had been but a short time, when Acting-Master Morse, who was in the forecastle, cried out, " White water ahead!" The captain immediately ordered the engine to be reversed, but before this could be done, the ship struck hard and fast on a sand-bank. The yards were braced around and set on the foremast, in hopes of getting her off; a portion of the coal in bags was thrown into the sea, but she still stood immovable; as the last resort the engines were brought into requisition, but they soon became out of order, by a large quantity of sand getting into the boiler, and all hopes of getting her afloat vanished. The captain ordered a boat to be lowered, and sent in search of some vessel of the blockading fleet. The boat was in charge of Acting Ensign Williams and ten men. At twelve o'clock, the ship continuing to pound and thump very heavy, the foremast was cut away, which somewhat eased her. At daybreak, Thursday, January 15th, the small boat, with Acting-Ensign Williams, appeared in sight, about three miles from the ship, and the hopes of the distressed crew began to fail them; they then sent up rockets, and fired signal-guns, but received no response. At 10 o'clock A. M. a shout of "Sail ho!" thrilled every heart, as it came ringing from above, and a cheering prospect of escape gleamed before them. As soon as the sail was distinctly made out, the signal-guns were again fired, when the unknown vessel made for the wreck. The rescuer proved to be the United States gunboat Penobscot, which anchored very near the ship, right on the edge of the breakers. At three o'clock the Penobscot's boat came alongside of the ship, and took a line out to her launch, at anchor, between the two ships.

23 *

The "Columbia" then commenced to send the crew, one by one, on a life-line to the launch. Up to dark they had rescued thirty-two men; during Thursday night the wind increased to a gale, and the sea made a clear breach over the ship, and she pounded and thumped fearfully. About midnight Acting-Master Balch sent word to the men to look out for themselves, that the ship was going to pieces.

During the night the Penobscot sailed further out, for fear of being wrecked; she made signs to the distressed vessel, but they failed to understand them. Early next morning, after the crew had suffered everything but death, a party of incarnate devils, commonly called Rebels, fired upon these suffering and defenceless men of a wrecked ship, struggling with the winds and waves, and almost overcome with hunger and fatigue. The captain ordered the white flag to be displayed, a signal of surrender, when the rebels ceased firing for a short time, fully making manifest that they saw the signal, and were aware of the helpless condition of the crew. Their reckless malice, however, could restrain itself but for a little time, and they renewed the firing. The United States flag was then run up, Union down, a signal of distress. It mattered not. These blood-thirsty fiends continued hurling their missiles of death at the devoted band of wrecked and wretched men. Nor did nor would they cease, until the captain, risking his life amidst the fury of the breakers in a small boat, landed and remonstrated with the semi-savages for their cowardly, brutal conduct. Their only reply was, that "they knew nothing about it;" whereas they had been firing one full hour after the flying of the white flag, and that in full view.*

---

* From a letter of H. H. Fanning, Paymaster Marine Corps, to Lieutenant J. E. De Haven, commanding the United States gunboat "Penobscot." January 17th, 1863.

BARBARITIES OF THE REBELS TOWARDS THEIR OWN SOLDIERS.

THE barbarism of the rebellion is not confined to the treatment of Union men. Here, indeed, it manifests itself in the most odious and revolting forms—in forms that would make a savage blush—but here it does not stop. It is seen in the discipline of the rebel army—in the means to which it resorts to secure unquestioning obedience—and in the atrocious manner in which offences are punished. As an illustration of this, we give the following extract from the Richmond Examiner of January 20th, 1864:—

The times when the cat-o'-nine-tails was the instrument of naval discipline, and soldiers were strapped to the ground and their backs mangled with the scourge, have passed—for us at least—into the traditions of another generation. We are shocked, however, to hear that a naval punishment has been invented in our army which surpasses the horrors of the scourge, and has borrowed its suggestion from the punishment of the Inquisition. It is the thumb-torture.

The mode of punishment is to hang the soldier by straps on the thumb, so that his toes may scarcely touch the ground, and the weight of his body depend from the strained ligaments. We are informed, by testimony that does not admit of question, that this horrid punishment has been practised in a portion of the army on the Potomac, and has been witnessed in the case of two or three men subjected to the torture.*

---

* Rebellion Record.

THE CONVERSION BY THE REBELS OF THE BONES OF SLAUGHTERED UNION-MEN INTO PERSONAL ORNAMENTS.

MUCH has been said on this topic, and much needs to be said. The theory is so hideous and revolting, so opposed to all true refinement, and so indicative of a barbarous state of society, that men are slow to believe it, and many sympathizers with the rebellion absolutely deny that it has been done. Surely, it is one of the last things to be expected of a people claiming to be high-minded and chivalrous. But that it has been done, in numerous instances, is a well-established fact. To the evidence already furnished by these pages, we add the following special Order (152) of Major-General Butler.

SPECIAL ORDER (152).—John W. Andrews exhibited a cross, the emblem of the sufferings of our Blessed Saviour, fashioned for a personal ornament, which he said was made from the bones of a Yankee soldier: and having shown this, too, without rebuke, in the Louisiana Club, which claims to be composed of chivalric gentlemen,—

It is therefore Ordered, that for this desecration of the dead, he be confined at hard labor, for two years, on the fortifications at Ship Island; and that he be allowed no verbal or written communication to or with any one, except through these headquarters.

B. F. BUTLER,
Major-General Commanding.*

---

* Rebellion Record, Vol. V.

BARBARITY OF GENERAL FORREST.

HEADQUARTERS, FIRST DIVISION, FOURTH ARMY CORPS,
Department of the Cumberland, Blue Springs, Tenn., Apr. 21, 1864.

THE late massacre at Fort Pillow, by Forrest, seems to have filled the community with indignation and surprise. To those in the front of our armies, who know Forrest, there is nothing at all astonishing in his conduct at Fort Pillow. I know that this very much respected Confederate hero has, upon former occasions, condescended to become his own executioner.

To show the style of man Jeff Davis and the Confederacy delight to honor, I will relate the following, which was stated to me last summer by a rebel citizen of Middle Tennessee, a man of high standing in his community, who had it from his nephew, an officer serving under Forrest.

About the middle of the summer of 1862, Forrest surprised the post of Murfreesboro', commanded by Brigadier-General T. T. Crittenden, of Indiana. The garrison was composed mostly of the Ninth Michigan and Second Minnesota Infantry, and the Seventh Pennsylvania Cavalry. After some little fighting, the troops were surrounded.

A mulatto man, who was servant to one of the officers of the Union forces, was brought to Forrest on horseback. The latter inquired of him, with many oaths, "What he was doing there?" The mulatto answered, that he was a free man, and came out as a servant to an officer, naming the man. Forrest, who was on horseback, deliberately put his hand to his holster, drew his pistol, and blew the man's brains out.

The rebel officer stated that the mulatto man came

from Pennsylvania; and the same officer denounced the act as one of cold-blooded murder, and declared he would never again serve under Forrest.

This murdered man was not a soldier, and, indeed, the occurrence took place before the United States Government determined to arm negroes. Of the truth of this there is not a shadow of doubt, and it can be established any day by living witnesses.

Your obedient servant,   D. L. STANLEY,
Major-General.

UNIONISTS OF ARKANSAS.

THE persecutions of the Unionists of Arkansas are nearly if not quite equal to those practised upon the Unionists of East Tennessee. The rebels, after driving all the Union men out of the country or hanging them, fell upon the innocent women and children, torturing them in every way that fiends could devise; they even went so far as to steal the provisions from them, and after burning their houses, and laying waste their lands, compelled them to leave the State without means, barefooted and half clad.

The following is a letter from General Fisk, asking the steamboat-men and others to aid one of these poor refugees in reaching her friends:—

HEADQUARTERS, DISTRICT OF S. E. MISSOURI,
Pilot Knob, October 19th, 1864.

To Railroad Agents, Steamboat-men, and others whom it may concern.

The bearer of this note, Mrs. Maria Sharkley, has been robbed of all her possessions, and driven from her home in Arkansas.

She is especially commended to the sympathy of charitable people, as one upon whom kindness and Christian benevolence would not be wasted, and any favor conferred, will truly be worthily bestowed, as well as thankfully appreciated. She is a refugee from the terrors of the murderous rebels who invest the northern portion of her native State, and is of the most devoted loyalty.

C. B. FISK,
Brigadier-General Com'g.

W. T. CLARK,
Lieutenant and A. D. C.

MURDER OF TWO UNIONISTS IN ARKANSAS.

IN the month of October, 1863, two Union citizens, named Joseph Birchfield and Joseph Pound, of Arkansas, were brutally murdered by a party of Confederate soldiers, belonging to Marmaduke's command, in the following manner:—

Stealing upon their victims while they were at home, they arrested them and took them a short distance, at the same time ordering their families to follow; in the mean time telling their prisoners that it was their intention to murder them, and they must prepare themselves for death, as they had but little time to live. The families of the doomed men pleaded and begged for the lives of their husbands and fathers, but to no avail. The villains had come to murder, and nothing but blood would satisfy them. The fiends then actually made the families of the two unfortunate men stand up and look on as they proceeded to murder their innocent friends and kept them there until they had finished the job, when they sought new fields for crime; and left the distressed and weeping families to bury their murdered husbands and fathers.

The same cruelties were practised upon numerous other Union families in the immediate neighborhood, and their crimes were that they loved the old Government and its flag better than they did the Confederacy. These actions were committed by Confederate soldiers, and sanctioned by their commanders.*

BARBARITY OF JOHN LETCHER.

THE following is a letter from the arch-traitor, John Letcher, Governor of Virginia, to a Unionist named Fitzgerald, who was arrested upon suspicion, and confined in one of the loathsome dens, called prisons, in Richmond. The letter will fully show how corrupted and dead to all sense of justice and humanity the minds of the leaders of the rebellion are; they think death is none too good for a man who is even suspected of being a Union man. We give the letter, and leave our readers to judge for themselves :—

EXECUTIVE DEPARTMENT, RICHMOND, VA.,
June 25th, 1863.

Mr. William Fitzgerald—Sir: I was aware before the receipt of your letter yesterday, that you were still in prison, and I can assure you that it shall be no fault of mine if you do not remain so during your natural life. When I promised to intercede in your behalf, I believed

---

* Mr. Ward, of Arkansas.

your assurance that the suspicions against you were without foundation; but on calling on General Winder, I found that it had been reported to him by a gentleman of undoubted loyalty and veracity, that you have been for years an enemy and vilifier of Southern institutions. In 1856, you voted for the Abolitionist, Fremont, for President. Ever since the war, you have maintained a sullen silence in regard to its merits. Your son, who, in common with other young men, was called to the defence of his country, has escaped to the enemy, probably by your advice. This is evidence enough to satisfy me that you are a traitor to your country; and I regret that it is not sufficient to justify me in demanding you from the military authorities, to be tried and executed for treason.   Yours, &c.,

JOHN LETCHER.

CAPTURE OF THE STEAMER LEVIATHAN.

On the 23d of September, 1863, the United States Steamer Leviathan, was seized at South West Pass in the Mississippi river, by a band of rebel pirates, who stole on board by means of row-boats, and overpowered the crew before they could get their arms to defend themselves. Then having put all on shore but eight men, they raised steam and immediately put to sea; the eight men were in the mean time heavily ironed and put below.

As soon as these facts were made known to the United States authorities, the United States Steamer De Soto was sent in pursuit; she came up with the eight men in a small boat, who stated that after they had been at sea some time, the rebels put them in this small boat, without

24

oars, sail, or any food; beside, the wind was blowing a
fearful gale at the time, and had not the De Soto providentially crossed their path when she did, they would
certainly have all .gone to the bottom, or starved to
death, as they were at the mercy of the waves. This
intended murder was committed by the high-toned
chivalry of New Orleans.*

MURDER OF MAJOR WILEMAN.

ON or about the 5th of October, 1863, a party of rebel
soldiers went to the house of Major Wileman, which
was in Pendleton county, Kentucky. Major Wileman
belonged to the Eighth Regiment, Kentucky Volunteers,
and was a gallant and brave officer, and was wounded in
the battle of Chickamauga. He had just returned home
to recruit his health, when the rebels, like thieves,
silently stole up to his house, and surrounding it, so that
all chance of escape was cut off, they rushed in upon
their unsuspecting and defenceless victim, and took him
out, and then commenced stripping him of his clothing, telling him that they had come to kill him, and
were now getting ready to do it. The major protested against such barbarity, and told them, that they
should treat him as a prisoner of war, because he was an
officer in the United States Army. They cursed him
for a d—d tory, and told him they never took prisoners.
They then proceeded to tie him to a tree, and when this
was done, they deliberately shot him. We have since
learned, that four or five of his murderers have been
captured, and it is to be hoped that they will meet their
just reward.†

---

* Colonel William McNair.
† From Colonel J. O. Morrison.

PROCLAMATION OF ANDREW JOHNSON.

NASHVILLE, TENNESSEE, MAY 9th, 1862.

WHEREAS, certain persons, unfriendly and hostile to the Government of the United States have banded themselves together, and are now going at large through many of the counties of this State, arresting, maltreating, and plundering Union citizens wherever found,

Now, therefore, I, Andrew Johnson, Governor of the State of Tennessee, by virtue of the power and authority in me vested, do hereby proclaim that in every instance in which a Union man is arrested and maltreated by the marauding bands aforesaid, five or more rebels, from the most prominent in the immediate neighborhood, shall be arrested, imprisoned, and otherwise dealt with as the nature of the case may require, and further, in all cases where the property of citizens, loyal to the Government of the United States, is taken or destroyed, full and ample renumeration shall be made to them, out of the property of such rebels in the vicinity as have sympathized with, and given aid, comfort, information, or encouragement to the parties committing such depredations.

This letter will be executed in letter and spirit. All citizens are hereby warned, under heavy penalties, from entertaining, receiving, or encouraging such persons so banded together, or in anywise connected therewith.

By the Governor,   ANDREW JOHNSON.
EDWARD H. EAST, Secretary of State.*

---

* Rebellion Record.

PROCLAMATION OF GENERAL LOAN.

HEADQUARTERS, DISTRICT NORTH-WEST MISSOURI,
St. Joseph, May 26th, 1862.

IT has become manifest, that rebels returning from the armies of the insurgents, and other disaffected and disloyal persons, are, throughout this military district organizing bands to act during the ensuing season as guerrillas and banditti. It is intended to resort to the most vigorous measures to suppress these outlaws, and to this end it is enjoined upon all commands, scouting parties, officers and soldiers, when these outlaws are detected in bushwhacking, marauding, and committing other depredations, as guerrillas or bandits, upon peaceable inhabitants of the country, to shoot them when found.

All ablebodied men in the vicinity where acts of murder, marauding, robbery, or larceny, shall be committed by guerrillas, or bandits, are required to make immediate pursuit, and render all the assistance in their power to secure the destruction or capture of the criminals.

Those who are known to have heretofore sympathized with the rebels, and who fail to render such assistance, will be arrested, and the facts reported to these headquarters for final disposition.

Murderers, robbers, and thieves have become so numerous on the border, and so bold and daring in the commission of crime, that it is utterly impossible for the civil tribunals to punish the perpetrators of crime with sufficient promptness and severity, to deter them from committing further outrages, and to furnish protection to the citizens.

Hereafter, the perpetrators of such crimes, when

arrested, will be tried and punished at the discretion of a military commission.   By order of

Brigadier-General LOAN.

JAMES RAINSFORD, Assistant Adjutant-General.

GUERRILLAS OF KENTUCKY.

HEADQUARTERS, DISTRICT OF KENTUCKY,
5th Division, 2d Army Corps,
Lexington, Ky., July 16th, 1864.

GENERAL ORDERS, No. 59.—The rapid increase in this district of lawless bands of armed men, interrupting railroads and telegraphic communication, plundering and murdering peaceful Union citizens, destroying the mails, &c., &c., calls for the adoption of stringent measures on the part of the military authorities for their suppression.

Therefore all guerrillas, armed prowlers, by whatever name they may be known, and rebel sympathizers, are hereby admonished that in future stern retaliatory measures will be adopted and strictly enforced, whenever the lives or property of peaceful citizens are jeopardized by the lawless acts of such men.

Rebel sympathizers, living within five miles of any scene of outrage committed by armed men not recognised as public enemies by the rules and usages of war, will be liable to be arrested and sent beyond the limits of the United States, in accordance with instructions from the major-general commanding the military division of the Mississippi.

So much of the property of rebel sympathizers as may be necessary to indemnify the government or loyal citi-

24*

zens for losses incurred by the acts of such lawless men, will be seized and appropriated for this purpose.

Wherever an unarmed Union citizen is murdered, four guerrillas will be selected from the prisoners in the hands of the military authorities, and publicly shot to death in the most convenient place near the scene of outrage.

By command of Major-General S. G. BURBRIDGE.

J. B. DICKSON, Captain and A. A. General.

JEFF DAVIS AND MAJOR-GENERAL B. F. BUTLER.

FROM the Proclamation of Jeff Davis against Major-General B. F. Butler, for the hanging of W. B. Mulford, for pulling down the United States flag, after trial and condemnation by court-martial :—

Now therefore I, Jefferson Davis, President of the Confederate States of America, and in their name do pronounce and declare the said Benjamin F. Butler to be a felon, deserving of capital punishment. I do order that he shall no longer be considered or treated simply as a public enemy of the Confederate States of America, but as an outlaw and common enemy of mankind, and that in the event of his capture, the officer in command of the capturing force do cause him to be immediately executed by hanging.

And I do further order that no commissioned officer of the United States taken captive, shall be released, or paroled, or exchanged, until the said Butler shall have met with due punishment for his crime.   *   *   *

Now therefore I, Jefferson Davis, President of the Confederate States of America, and acting by their authority, appealing to the Divine Judge in attestation that their conduct is not guided by the passion of revenge, but that they reluctantly yield to the solemn duty of redressing, by necessary severity, crimes of which their citizens are the victims, do issue this my proclamation, and by virtue of my authority, as commander-in-chief of the armies of the Confederate States, do order,

First. That all commissioned officers in the command of said Benjamin F. Butler be declared not entitled to be considered as soldiers engaged in honorable warfare, but as robbers and criminals deserving death, and that they and each of them be, whenever captured, reserved for execution.

Third. That all negro slaves captured in arms be at once delivered over to the executive authorities of the respective states, to be dealt with according to the laws of said states.

Fourth. That the like orders be executed in all cases with respect to all commissioned officers of the United States when found serving in company with said slaves in insurrection against the authorities of the different states of this Confederacy.

In testimony whereof I have signed these presents, and caused the seal of the Confederate States of America to be affixed thereto, at the city of Richmond, on this twenty-third day of December, in the year of our Lord one thousand eight hundred and sixty-two.

By the President,　　　　　JEFFERSON DAVIS.
J. P. BENJAMIN, Secretary of State.

HANGING OF UNION CAPTIVES.

WE have had occasion to speak repeatedly of the treatment of Union men in Tennessee by the rebel forces. All that we have said of the inhumanity practised towards them is confirmed by the following extract from the Richmond Dispatch.

According to the Dispatch a band of Unionists, styled tories by the Dispatch, about seventy in number, under the command of one Taylor, were attacked by a body of rebels under Colonel Folk, in Johnson county, East Tennessee, January 23d, 1863.

The Dispatch, in describing the affair, says: "The tory cavalry and infantry were parading in a field near the Fish Springs; Colonel Folk ordered his men to swim the river and charge them. The tories, seeing this, abandoned their horses and took shelter upon the summit of a large ridge. Folk's men were then dismounted, and charged up the ridge, completely dispersing the tories. All of their horses were captured. Four of the tories were killed, and a number wounded and captured. The captured *were immediately hung,* by order of Colonel Folk."

MASSACRE OF NEGRO SOLDIERS.

HEADQUARTERS, ARMY OF THE JAMES,
In the Field, October 12th, 1864.

GENERAL : I have the honor to forward the report of Colonel Draper, Thirty-sixth United States Colored Troops, commanding brigade, as to the information furnished by Lieutenant Veirs, who· was wounded and captured at Fort Gilmer, in charge of the Twenty-ninth.

Lieutenant Veirs has been paroled or exchanged, and has gone to Annapolis, so he can be examined upon the matter by the Judge Advocate General.

Please forward the report to the Hon. Secretary of War, for investigation, and instruction as to how I shall act in the premises.

I have the honor to be, very respectfully,

Your obedient servant,

B. F. BUTLER,

Major-General Commanding.

U. S. Grant, Lieut.-General U. S. A.

FIELD-HOSPITAL, ARMY OF THE JAMES,
In the Field, October 12th, 1864.

Major: I have the honor to transmit herewith a communication from Major William H. Hart, Thirty-sixth United States Colored Troops, in which he reports the statement made to him by Lieutenant Veirs, Fifth U. S. Colored Troops, concerning the murder of colored soldiers by the men of the Fifteenth Georgia, after the repulse of Brigadier-General Foster's troops at Fort Gilmer.

Lieutenant Veirs's regiment, the Fifth U. S. Colored Troops, supported a brigade of General Foster's division in the assault on Fort Gilmer, on the 29th ultimo.

Lieutenant Veirs was wounded and captured—was exchanged—and made his statement to Major Hart, on board the steamer City of New York, on Sunday, October 9th.

Major Hart is reliable and accurate, and his report of the conversation is without doubt correct.

Lieutenant Veirs is now, probably, in the hospital at Fort Monroe.   I remain, very respectfully,

Your obedient servant,

ALONZO G. DRAPER,
Colonel Thirty-sixth U. S. Colored Troops.

Major R. S. Davis, A. A. G., Department of Virginia and North Carolina.

CAMP THIRTY-SIXTH U. S. COLORED TROOPS,
Army of the James, in the Field, October 12th, 1864.

Colonel: The following is a correct statement of the conversation held by me with Lieutenant Veirs, Fifth U. S. Colored Troops, who was wounded and taken prisoner in the assault on Fort Gilmer on the afternoon of the 29th ultimo.

I saw Lieutenant Veirs on board the City of New York, at Riker's Landing, on her last trip down the river, October 9th. He stated to me, that after the assaulting party had retired, the rebel soldiers (who he afterwards learned belonged to the Fifteenth Georgia regiment) came out of the fort and bayoneted all the colored soldiers who were so badly wounded that they could not walk. They also flourished their bayonets over him, called him the vilest names they could utter, and would probably have killed him on the spot, had not the officers of these men come to his rescue. They (the officers) ordered the men to desist, and had Veirs conveyed inside the fort, where he was again subjected to the vilest insults, from the lips of a Confederate naval officer. This officer admitted, however, that the "d—d niggers fought like devils!"

I remain, Colonel, very respectfully,

Your obedient servant,   W. H. HART,
Major Thirty-sixth U. S. Colored Troops.   .

Col. A. G. Hart, Thirty-sixth U. S. Colored Troops, Field Hospital, Eighteenth Army Corps.

DEVILISH TORTURE.

On or about the 3d of September, 1863, a party of rebel fiends visited the house of a well-known Union man (whose name we refrain from mentioning from obvious reasons), in Jamestown, Russell county, Kentucky. Rushing into the house, they arrested him and his wife, and, after some private consultation, took them out of the house and carried them to a place where they knew they were beyond pursuit.

The fiends then threw the woman down upon the ground, and compelled a negro who was with them to hold her down. The negro protested, and declared he would not do it, when a pistol was presented to his head and held there until he consented to do it; and then the brutes actually violated her, compelling her husband to stand up and look at them while they committed their devilish work. She plead and begged them to kill her before they thus treated her, but they only cursed her, and told her that she deserved more, and ought to consider herself lucky in getting off so easy for being a d—d Unionist.

They then released her and her husband, to go home and mourn over the wrongs that were inflicted upon them, for no other reason than that they loved their country and would not desert it.*

MURDER OF CARTER FOSTER.

In the latter part of the summer of 1863, a party of rebels made a raid into the neighborhood of Conyersville

---

* Captain J. D. Hale, of Kentucky.

Kentucky, and after robbing the Unionists of the country, and committing numerous other depredations, they went to the house of a man named Carter Foster, whom they arrested, and after calling him a d—d Unionist, and heaping every species of abuse upon him, they told him that it was their intention to kill him. He begged and plead with them not to take his life, and said that he had always been quiet and attended to his own business, and had said nothing to injure them or their cause. "You are a d—d Lincolnite," said they, "and that is enough; besides, it is our business to rid Kentucky of such men." They then drew their pistols and brutally shot him; after the body fell, the fiends actually kicked the corpse. This is but one of the many atrocious murders committed by this same band upon the unprotected Unionists of Kentucky. At one time it was worth a man's life to be even suspected of being a Unionist.*

THE DOCTRINE OF STATE RIGHTS PRACTICALLY REPUDIATED BY THE REBEL AUTHORITIES.

One of the principal grounds on which it has been attempted to justify the rebellion, is the mischievous doctrine of State rights; yet, this doctrine, which they profess to hold so sacred, for which they claim they have taken up arms, and submitted to the greatest sufferings, has been uniformly disregarded in practice by the rebels in the pursuit of their fiendish purposes. Maryland, and Kentucky, and Missouri, they have sought to force into the rebellion. Several of the seceded

---

* J. P. Dunlap, R. Pollard, and others.

States, to say the least, were actually forced into the rebellion against the will of a majority of the people, by the inauguration of a reign of terror. The practical disregard of this doctrine by the rebel authorities in North Carolina, is thus set forth in a speech of Hon. C. J. Barlow, of Georgia, delivered in the Cooper Institute, New York, October 15, 1864:—

In all my reading, I have not found in history so barefaced an attempt to deceive an intelligent people as this of Davis, to set up a claim that he is fighting the battles of the American people, and that he is the champion of State rights. Now let us come to the doctrine of State rights, and Mr. Davis's rule. The people of North Carolina proposed to meet in convention to nominate a candidate for Governor. They proposed, as a part of their scheme, that inasmuch as Mr. Davis evidently did not desire to make peace with the United States Government, it was competent for the "sovereign State" of North Carolina to withdraw from her "agent," Mr. Davis, that portion of his power delegated to him, and which gave him the control of the subject of peace, believing that the State could negotiate a peace better than Mr. Davis. The convention met in a building used for camp meeting purposes, and I suppose was as large as this. It was a body composed of the first men of the State, men of intelligence, wealth, and many of whose names were historic, and among them were many of advanced age. What did Mr. Jefferson Davis, the exponent of State rights, who is so exceedingly sensitive on that point, do? He sent an armed force to disperse the meeting and arrest its leaders; and, fellow-citizens, to-day, in the North Carolina prisons, are many aged and respected and intelligent citizens languishing and dying, because they had the audacity to nominate a candidate for Governor upon certain principles which they thought would redound to the benefit of the people. But that did not do. The agitation went on. The Georgia peace party kept pressing Mr. Davis. We held our Congressional elections and turned out of Congress what were called the "Forty Thieves." These were forty members of the so-called Congress at Richmond who always voted compactly as Davis wanted them to, and always in secret session, for there never had been an open session of that body upon any question that interested the people. We knew them, and in our election, what the *Richmond Examiner* called the "Forty Conscripts," and others called the "Forty Thieves," was turned out. But when Mr. Davis found that he had lost them, he induced them before their final retirement to pass a law, some of the features of which I will detail to you, because they are quite novel and original, and particularly as coming from a State Rights Democrat. In the first place, that law sets forth that any man who uses language calculated to lead anybody to suppose that he can possibly be in favor of the idea that a State has a right to secede from the Southern Confederacy, it is treason. [Laughter.] Then a clause gives to Mr. Davis the power to construe the language and motive of a man, and any lawyer knows the extent to which tyranny can be carried under such a clause. Then he is empowered by this to appoint military courts and the officers who compose it, the law having abolished the civil tribunals. What is the result? When a citizen is brought before the military court, he is tried with closed doors, is refused legal counsel, is refused the benefit of testimony, is refused correspondence or communication with his family, and all for what? To try and to shoot him, if, after getting all the evidence that can be got together, it can be shown to the mind of

Mr. Jefferson Davis, by direction or indirection, that this man could possibly entertain the idea that under any circumstances a State had a right to secede from the Southern Confederacy! * * * * * *
* * * In the southwestern part of North Carolina, in the mountain region, there is a valley corresponding to the Valley of East Tennessee, which is grand and beautiful in its appearance. The inhabitants of this valley are almost entirely small farmers—many of them farmers who have quietly pursued their industries without slaves, in the midst of a picturesque country and fertile soil. They were simple and rural in their characteristics, patriotic, and they voted *en masse* against all the schemes and propositions for disunion. [Applause.] When at last the trial came, when Mr. Davis's conscript law was passed, those unfortunate people sent a commission to Richmond, asking that they might be absolved from the operation of that draft. The petition was, of course without avail. They then resorted to other means to avoid taking up arms against the Government under which they were reared and which they loved. They petitioned for expatriation. That, too, was refused by Mr. Jefferson Davis, this modern representative of civil liberty and defender of the rights and liberties of localities. [Laughter.] On the contrary, this champion of State rights sent North Carolina troops to that region for the purpose of having the conscript law executed against that unfortunate people, and to force them to take up arms against the conviction of their consciences. But the North Carolina troops fraternized with their fellow-citizens, and Mr. Davis was forced to send other troops, who also failed to effect the purpose. What next did he do? He enlisted a brigade of Cherokee Indians, numbering, I think, from 3500 to 4000, of as desperate

and lawless ruffians as a hybrid population ever produced, and these miserable wretches were turned loose upon the population, and from that day to this that valley has been the scene of battle, of violence, of assassination, and of crime. The history of the massacre of the people of La Vendee, in France, the murder of the Innocents, or any tale of atrocity related in imaginative literature, or in history, hold no comparison with the cruelty and crime perpetrated upon the Innocent and unoffending people of that region, because they loved the country of their birth.

GENERAL SHERMAN.

THE following is a letter from General W. T. Sherman to the rebel General Hood, in relation to the removing of the citizens from the city of Atlanta, after its capture by the Union army:—

General J. R. HOOD: I have the honor to acknowledge the receipt of your letter of this date, at the hands of Messrs. Ball and Orr, Esquires, consenting to the arrangements I had proposed to facilitate the removal south of the people of Atlanta, who prefer to go in that direction. I enclose you a copy of my orders, which will, I am satisfied, accomplish my purpose perfectly.

You style the measure proposed "unprecedented," and appeal to the dark history of war for its parallel, as an act of "studied and ingenious cruelty." It is not unprecedented, for General Johnston himself very wisely and properly removed families all the way from Dalton down, and I see no reason why Atlanta should be excepted.

Nor is it necessary to appeal to the dark history of war, when recent and modern examples are so handy. You yourself burn dwelling-houses along your parapet, and I have seen to-day forty houses that have been rendered uninhabitable, because they stood in the way of your forts and men. You defended Atlanta on a line so close to the town, that every cannon-shot and many musket-shots from our line of investment that overshot their mark, went into habitations of women and children. General Hardee did the same at Jonesborough, and General Johnston did the same last summer at Jackson, Mississippi. I have not accused you of heartless cruelty, but merely instance those cases of very recent occurrence, and could go on and enumerate hundreds of others, and challenge any fair man to judge which of us has a heart of pity for the families of a brave people.

I say it is kindness to those families of Atlanta to remove them now, at once, from scenes that women and children should not be exposed to, and a brave people should scorn to commit their wives and children to rude barbarians, who thus, as you say, violate the laws of war, as illustrated in the pages of its dark history.

In the name of common sense, I ask you not to appeal to a just God in such a sacrilegious manner; you, who in the midst of peace and prosperity, have plunged a nation into civil war—dark and cruel war—who dared and badgered us to battle, insulted our flag, seized our arsenals and forts that were left in honorable custody of peaceful ordnance sergeants, seized and made prisoners of war the very garrisons sent to protect your people against negroes and Indians, long before any overt act was committed by the, to you, hateful Lincoln Government.

You tried to force Kentucky and Missouri into rebel-

25*

lion spite of themselves, falsified the oath of Louisiana, turned loose your privateers to plunder unarmed ships, expelled Union families by thousands, burned their houses, and declared, by an Act of your Congress, the confiscation of all debts due Northern men for goods that had been received. Talk thus to marines, but not to me, who have seen these things, and who will this day make as much sacrifice for the peace and honor of the South, as the best-born Southerner among you.

If we must be enemies, let us be men, and fight it out as we proposed to-day, and not deal in such hypocritical appeals to God and humanity. God will judge us in due time, and he will pronounce whether it be more humane to fight with a town full of women, and the families of "a brave people," at our back, or remove them in time to places of safety, among their own friends and people.

I am, very respectfully, your obedient servant,

W. T. SHERMAN,
Major-General Com'g.

BUSHWHACKING AND THE BLACK FLAG ENCOU-
RAGED AND COMMENDED BY THE REBEL PRESS.

THE atrocious character of the rebellion, and of the men who are conspicuous in it and give it tone and shape, manifests itself in the utterances of the rebel press. In the newspapers of the Confederacy, deeds of violence, acts of rapine and murder, and cruelties supposed to be characteristic of savages only, are commended, encouraged, and urged. As an illustration, we give the following extracts:—

Now is the time for bushwhacking, and the black flag. Now is the time to punish, with the full measure of retributive justice, the vandals who have dared to desecrate our soil for the purpose of rapine, murder, and every manner of cruelty and outrage which illustrates the depravity and wickedness of human nature in its most degenerate form. It is not improbable that, by means of iron-clad boats, they will succeed occasionally in effecting landings upon the Mississippi river, with a view to predatory incursions into the interior. Nothing better could be desired. It will give each man, of whatever age, calling, or occupation, an opportunity to become an efficient soldier.

He can take his gun, ascertain the places most likely to be frequented by the Yankee thieves, conceal himself in ravine, thicket, or undergrowth, and pick them off by the wholesale. This will be fine sport—better indeed than hunting wild-game; and those engaged in it will have the satisfaction of knowing that whenever they bring one of these prowling beasts to the dust, the number of our remorseless enemies will be that much less. We know of one quiet, but shrewd and resolute citizen, in a certain region infested with these plunderers from Yankee land, who has bagged about a dozen of them. His example is commended especially to the people of the river counties; but not to them alone. Where the base hoof of the Yankee leaves its impress, there let his carcass be made to enrich the soil which he has come to plunder.

Nor must their coming be awaited. Every part of our territory should, alike, be held sacred from such a loathsome presence. The Yankee generals, dreading the guerrilla and bushwhacking system of war, have indicated their purpose to retaliate by seizing non-combatants, and destroying property indiscriminately. It is not for our people to be deterred by this expedient.

We must remember, that our condition cannot possibly be made worse than it will have become should the Yankees succeed in their scheme of subjugation.

As for the rules of civilized war, we have this to say. A people who, for no justifiable cause whatever, have come to place a yoke of iron on our necks, are not entitled to their benefit. Moreover, these rules, as well as the ordinary obligations of humanity, have been entirely disregarded by the Yankees wherever they have succeeded in obtaining control. Witness their inhuman conduct at Nashville, Huntsville, New Orleans, and elsewhere. * * * *

In addition to pitched battles upon the open field, let us try partisan ranging—bushwhacking—and henceforward, until the close of this war, let our sign be "the black flag, and no quarter."*

The Northern vandals have invaded our State, not to confront our armies and decide the chances of war in pitched battles, but have come to rob and steal—to plunder—to burn—and to starve to death our women and children. Under such circumstances, we should meet them as we would meet the savage, the highwayman, or the wild beast of the forest.

Partisan bands should lie in wait for them, on the roadside, in fence-corners, and behind trees; and, in short, they should be hunted down in any and every way that can be made efficient and effectual, until the State is relieved of their presence. Not observing the rules of civilized warfare themselves, they cannot expect its observance from us. We need more Colonel Blythes in the woods, all over the State. A dozen well-directed shots from the bush, will at any time put a brigade to

---

* Jackson Mississippian, June 10th, 1862.

flight; and this is the most sure and certain method of putting a stop to the marauding expeditions that are from time to time sent out through the country. In Colonel Blythe's district or field of operations, it has proved most efficacious in holding the enemy at bay, and we hope to see the plan put more extensively in practice.*

Our people were greatly surprised, on Saturday morning, to see the black flag waving over the depot of the Virginia and Tennessee Railroad Company. We are for displaying that flag throughout the whole South. We should ask no quarter at the hand of the vandal Yankee invaders, and our motto should be, an entire extermination of every one who has set foot upon our sacred soil. Let that flag then float over every hilltop and valley throughout the whole South, and as the breezes fan its folds, let it tell to the Hessian scoundrels the welcome they will have on Southern soil—death to each, one and all !†

We could give numerous other extracts from their own papers to prove this point, but we think the above will suffice.

GUERRILLA WARFARE SANCTIONED BY THE REBEL AUTHORITIES.

It may be said that some of the atrocities recorded in this book are the work of guerrillas, and therefore the rebel authorities are not responsible for them. But when or where have these atrocities been rebuked by the Confederate authorities? and it is an old maxim that silence

---

* Charleston Mercury, 9th May, 1863.

* Lynchburg Republican.

gives consent. In how many cases have these so-called guerrillas been actually enlisted in the rebel service, and drawn pay from the rebel treasury, and have been led by men holding commissions from the rebel government! Yea, more, in how many cases has this guerrilla warfare received the direct sanction of the rebel authorities, and been organized under them! The evidence on this point is abundant. From the mass of evidence that might be adduced, we select the following official documents, among which, as will be seen, is an Act of the Rebel Congress, approved April 21st, 1862. The Act reads thus:—

Section 1. The Congress of the Confederate States of America do enact, That the president be and he is hereby authorized to commission such officers as he may deem proper, with authority to form bands of Partisan Rangers, in companies, battalions, or regiments, to be composed each of such members as the president may approve.

Section 2. Be it further enacted, That such Partisan Rangers, after being regularly received into service, shall be entitled to the same pay, rations, and quarters, during the term of service, and be subject to the same regulations, as other soldiers.

Section 3. Be it further enacted, That for any arms and munitions of war captured from the enemy by any body of Partisan Rangers, and delivered to any quartermaster at such place or places as may be designated by a commanding general, the Rangers shall be paid their full value in such manner as the secretary of war may prescribe.

Extracts of an official correspondence between J. B. Clark, Confederate State Senator, and Geo. W. Randolph, rebel Secretary of War, in relation to the treatment of guerrillas, if taken prisoners by the United States forces:

EXTRACT OF J. B. CLARK'S LETTER.

SPOTTSWOOD HOTEL, RICHMOND, VA., July 15, 1862.

Hon. George W. Randolph, Secretary of War.

SIR: I respectfully desire to know from you whether the several partisan corps of Rangers, now organized, or that may be organized in the several States of the Confederacy, are to be regarded as part of the army of the Confederacy, and protected by the government as such; and whether, if any of said corps are captured in battle, *or otherwise,* while in the line of their duty, by the enemy, this government will *claim* for them the same treatment, as prisoners of war, which is now exacted for prisoners belonging to our provisional army.   *   *   *   *

With great respect,

JOHN B. CLARK.

REPLY.

Confederate States of America, War Department,
RICHMOND, VA., July 16, 1862.

Hon. John B. Clark, C. S. Senate.

SIR: I have the honor to acknowledge the receipt of your letter of the 15th instant, and to reply that Partisan Rangers *are* a part of the provisional army of the Confederate States, subject to all the regulations adopted for its government, and entitled to the same protection as prisoners of war. Partisan Rangers are in no respect different from troops of the line, except that they are not brigaded, and are employed oftener on *detached service.* They require stricter discipline than other troops to make them efficient, and, without discipline, they become a *terror* to their *friends,* and are contemptible in the eyes of the enemy.

Very respectfully, your obedient servant,

GEORGE W. RANDOLPH,
Secretary of War.

PROCLAMATION OF GENERAL HINDMAN.

HEADQUARTERS, TRANS-MISSISSIPPI DEPARTMENT,
Little Rock, Ark., June 17th, 1862.

For the more effectual annoyance of the enemy upon our rivers, and in our mountains and woods, all citizens of this district, who are not subject to conscription, are called upon to organize themselves into independent companies of mounted men or infantry, as they prefer, arming and equipping themselves, and to serve in that part of the district to which they belong.

When as many as ten men come together for this purpose, they may organize by electing a captain, one sergeant, and a corporal, and will at once commence operations against the enemy, without waiting for special instructions. Their duty will be to cut off Federal pickets, scouts, foraging parties, and trains, and to kill pilots and others upon gunboats and transports, attacking them day and night, and using the greatest vigor in their movements. As soon as the company attains the strength required by law, it will proceed to elect the other officers to which it is entitled. All such organizations will report to these headquarters as soon as practicable. They will receive pay and allowances for subsistence and forage for the time actually in the field, as established by the affidavits of their captains.

These companies will be governed, in all respects, by the same regulations as other troops. Captains will be held responsible for the good conduct and efficiency of their men, and will report to these headquarters from time to time.   By command of

Major-General HINDMAN.

R. C. NEWTON,
     Assistant Adjutant-General.

A. LINCOLN,
Assassinated in Washington, April 14th, 1865.

THE ASSASSINATION PLOT.

The rebellion, which began with falsehood and perjury, and was prosecuted with the most hideous acts of barbarity, at length culminated in a deed which has scarcely a parallel in the annals of crime. The plot contemplated the assassination of Secretary Stanton, President Johnson and Lieutenant General Grant, as well as President Lincoln and Secretary Seward, but through the good Providence of God was limited in its execution to the beloved Chief Magistrate of the nation, and his illustrious Secretary of State. That one so good, so kind, so forbearing and so forgiving as Abraham Lincoln, pre-eminently a man "with charity for all, and malice towards none," should have been stricken down by the assassin's hand, and that the life of one so inclined to conciliation and moderation towards the rebels as the sagacious Secretary of State, should have been so ferociously assailed, must be forever a source of astonishment and indignation.

It is a well known fact that secret meetings were held in the armies of the so-called Confederate States, and in them was discussed the propriety of sending certain persons on detached service to the Northern States and Canada, to release rebel prisoners of war, to lay northern cities in ashes, and, to use their own terms, to get after the members of the United States cabinet, and finally murder President Lincoln. At one of these meetings, held in the camp of the 2d Virginia regiment, Booth and others concerned in this damnable conspiracy were present.

The rebel officials went so far as to offer large sums to different persons to enter into this conspiracy ; one of the most influential men of Richmond remarked at a public dinner, that he would give ten thousand dollars in addition to the *Confederate amount to have the President assassinated.* Booth held a commission as one of their detailed men ; the commission was given to him by Jacob Thompson, rebel agent, stationed in Canada.

The following is a letter found in a box purporting to contain a part of the archives of the War Department of the so-called Confederate States of America, delivered up to Major General W. T. Sherman after the surrender of the rebel army under General Jos. E. Johnson in North Carolina :

MONTGOMERY, WHITE SULPHUR SPRINGS, VA.
To his Excellency the President of the Confederate States of America :

DEAR SIR : I have been thinking for some time, I would make this communication to you, but have been debarred from doing so on account of ill-health. I now offer you my services, and if you will favor me in my designs, I will proceed, as soon as my health will permit, *to rid my country of some of her deadliest enemies, by striking at the very heart's blood of those who seek to enchain her in slavery.* I consider nothing dishonorable having such a tendency. All I want of you is to favor me by granting the necessary papers, etc., to travel on while within the jurisdiction of this government. I am perfectly familiar with the North, and feel confident that I can execute anything I undertake. I have just returned from within their lines. I am a lieutenant in General Duke's command. I was on a raid last June in Kentucky, under General John H. Morgan. I and all my command, except two or three commissioned officers, were taken prisoners, but finding a good opportunity while being taken to prison I made my escape from them in the garb of a citizen. I attempted to pass through the mountains, but finding that impossible, narrowly escaping two or three times being retaken, I directed my course north and south through the Canadas, by the assistance of Colonel J. P. Holcomb. I succeeded in making my way round through the blockade, but having taken the yellow fever at Bermuda, I have been rendered unfit for service since my arrival. I was reared up in the State of Alabama, and educated at its University. Both the Secretary of War and his Assistant, Judge Campbell, are personally acquainted with my father, W. J. Allston, of the fifth congressional district of Alabama, having served in the time of the old Congress, in the years 1849, 1850 and 1851. If I do anything for you, I shall expect your full confidence in return. If you give this, I can render you and my country very important service. Let me hear from you soon. I am anxious to be doing something, and having no command at present, all or nearly all being in garrison, I desire that you favor me in this a short time. I should like to have a personal interview with you, in order to perfect arrangements before starting.

I am, very respectfully, your obedient servant,

Lieutenant W. ALLSTON.

(Address me at these Springs, in hospital.) On the letter were the following indorsements:

Brief of letter.

Respectfully referred by direction of the President to the honorable Secretary of War.

BURTON W. HARRISON,
Private Secretary.

Received November 29th, 1864. Record Book A. G. O., December 8th, 1864. For attention. By order.

J. A. CAMPBELL,

Assistant Secretary of War.

This letter was taken from the box marked "Adjutant General's Office; letters received from July to December, 1864." While Jeff. Davis was trying to make his escape South, after the fall of Richmond, Va., he stopped on the way at the house of Lewis F. Bates in Charlotte, North Carolina, on the 19th of April, 1865, where he made a speech to the people off the steps. Near the close of his speech he received the following telegram:

GREENSBORO, April 19, 1865.

His Excellency President Davis : President Lincoln was assassinated in the theatre in Washington on the night of the 14th instant ; Seward's house was entered on the same night, and he was repeatedly stabbed and is probably mortally wounded.

JOHN C. BRECKINRIDGE.

At the close of his speech he read the telegram to the people, and made the following remark : "If it were to be done, it were better that it were done well." In a few days after, Breckinridge and a few other leading rebels called at the same house to see Jeff. Davis. The subject of their conversation was the assassination of President Lincoln. Breckinridge remarked that he regretted it very much ; that it was unfortunate for the people of the South at that time. Davis replied, "Well, General, I don't know ; if it were to be done at all, it were better it were well done ; and if the same were done to Andrew Johnson the beast, and to Secretary

Stanton, the job would then be complete." What man with common sense, after seeing such evidence, will deny that Jeff. Davis and the members of his cabinet were themselves the assassins ; and Booth and his associates no more nor less than hired tools, subject to the orders of the War Department at Richmond, or its authorized agents in Canada?

On the evening of the 14th of April, 1865, President Lincoln and wife started from the Presidential Mansion, between the hours of 8 and 9 o'clock; in their private carriage, for Ford's Tenth-street theatre, going by the way of Senator Harris's house for Miss Harris and Major Rathbone, to accompany them. Arriving at the theatre about 9 o'clock, the presidential party proceeded to the box designated for them, it being the left-hand upper private box. On the President's entering the box, he was received with cheers and shouts of joy ; bowing in acknowledgment, he took a seat, and was soon absorbed in the play, "The American Cousin," laughing heartily at the comic remarks of Asa Trenchard.

In the mean time the assassins were at work ; having by agreement met at the Herndon House, they matured their plans and started on their mission of blood. Booth having been designated to murder the President, started for the theatre, stopping on the way for his horse, which was in a stable rented by him in an alley in the rear of the theatre. Opening the door, he led the horse out, and up to a small door in the back of the theatre ; opening it, he called three times for Ned Spangler, one of his tools employed as a stage carpenter at the theatre. In a short time Spangler came running across the stage to the door where Booth was standing. As he came up

Booth remarked, "Ned help me all you can, won't you?" "Oh yes," returned Spangler, at the same time taking the reins of the horse from Booth, and handing them to John Burrows *alias* Peanuts. Booth then started for the front of the theatre, where he met and commenced talking with a very rough-looking man (one of the conspirators.) Soon another of the conspirators joined them, a small well-dressed man, and the three stood at the end of the passage leading to the stage conversing together ; in the course of their conversation Booth remarked, in a loud tone, "I think he will come now," (referring to the President) In a short time Booth, leaving the other two, stepped into the drinking saloon below the theatre and took a drink, and came out in a style that indicated that he was becoming intoxicated ; stepping up to where the other two were standing, he whispered something to the roughest one, and then went into the passage and remained a few minutes. The third or smallest one of the party stepped up toward the door leading in front of the theatre just as Booth came out of the stage passage, and called the time, then started up the street toward F street. Remaining a short time, he returned and called the time ; shortly after, he stepped up toward the door and called the time again louder than before, ten minutes after ten, then went up the street on a fast walk. At the same time Booth entered the theatre by the front door leading to the audience, and the rough-looking man went into the passage leading to the stage. After Booth went into the theatre, he inquired the time of the doorkeeper, who told him to step into the lobby leading into the street, then he could see the time. Stepping out, he walked in at the door leading into the parquette ; coming out immediately, he walked up the stairway leading to the dress circle ; passing around the circle by the passage behind the seats, he walked up to the door leading into the box where the President and party where sitting, and stood there a few minutes meditating whether to enter. Presently the fiend slowly opens the door, and entering, fastens it behind him with a small bar made for the purpose ; then turning towards where his unconscious victim sat, he softly draws a one-barrel Derringer pistol from his pocket ; raising his arm, he takes sure aim and fires the deadly shot ; the ball entering the back part and left side of the President's head, passes through and lodges in the left side of the brain. The ball was an unusually large one for a Derringer. As soon as the fatal shot was fired, Major Rathbone sprang from his seat, and looking around, saw through the smoke the desperate murderer, with a haggard and devilish look upon his countenance, standing between the door and his unconscious victim. As soon as Major Rathbone saw him, Booth shouted "Freedom." It is also reported that he cried "Revenge for the South." Major Rathbone made a spring toward him and seized him, but Booth was too strong and wrestled himself from the grasp, and made a violent thrust at the breast of Major Rathbone with a large knife. Major Rathbone parried the blow by striking it up, receiving a flesh wound several inches deep in his left arm between the shoulder and the elbow; the orifice of the wound was about an inch and a half in length, extending towards the shoulder. Booth, after stabbing Major Rathbone, rushed towards the front of the box ; Major Rathbone tried to grasp him again, but only succeeded in tearing his clothes as he leaped over the railing of the box. Finding that he was about to escape, Major Rathbone cried out in a loud voice, "Stop that man." Miss Harris also cried out at the same time, "Stop that man; won't somebody stop that man?" After Booth leaped on the stage, Major Rathbone turned toward the President. His position was not changed; his head was slightly bent forward, and his eyes closed as if in sleep ; the Major supposing him to be mortally wounded, rushed to the door for the purpose of calling medical aid. On reaching it, he found it barred by a heavy piece of wood ; one end was secured in the wall, and the other resting against the panel of the door. In the mean time Miss Harris assisted two persons, wearing the uniform of naval surgeons, to climb into the box by reaching her arm down and pulling them up from the stage into the box. Major Rathbone having managed to get the door open, the President was carried out of the theatre, in an unconscious state, across the street to the house of Mr. W. Peterson, No. 453 Tenth street, where he was laid on a bed in a small back room on the first floor. In a few minutes Dr. R. K. Stone, the family physician, arrived and pronounced the wound mortal. The President, lingering in a state of unconsciousness, died at half-past seven next morning (15th of April,) mourned by all who knew him—the first martyr of universal liberty. After the President had been carried out of the box, Major Rathbone assisted Mrs. Lincoln, who was exceedingly excited, to leave the theatre. On arriving at the head of the stairs he was compelled to call Major Potter to assist him to carry her over to the house where the President was lying. She remained with her husband until he breathed his last. The wound on the Major's arm bleeding profusely, he fainted after leaving Mrs. Lincoln, and was carried home in a carriage.

As Booth jumped from the box, his spur caught the flag and tore off a piece, which stuck to his spur until he passed over nearly half of the stage. As he came down he fell on the stage, his back slightly towards the audience; but as he was rising, his face came in full view, when he cried "Sic semper tyrannis," at the same time flourishing his knife. He ran behind the scenes, where he met William Withers, jr., leader of the orchestra at the theatre, whom he struck upon the leg, and turning him around, made two thrusts at him with the knife he held in his hand, one on the neck and one on the side, as he went past him, rushing for the small door in the back of the theatre. Opening this, he rushed out, and striking the boy who held his horse with the but of the knife, he mounted the horse, and putting spurs to him, galloped down the alley and es-caped. When J. Wilkes Booth left the Herndon House, Payne started for the house of Mr. Wm. H. Seward, Secretary of State; arriving before the time appointed, he stepped into the square just opposite, and there waited for the time to roll around. At ten o'clock the watchman at the square going his rounds, seeing Payne still sitting there, requested him to leave. Going out at the southeast gate he mounted his horse, and riding up to the Secretary's house, which stood in the middle of the block, dismounted, and stepping up to the door, he rang the bell. In a few minutes it was answered by the waiter. On the opening of the door, Payne walked into the passage, carrying a small package in his hand, which he said was medicine from Dr. Verdi, (the Secretary's family physician;) he said he was sent by Dr. Verdi with particular directions as to the man-ner the Secretary was to take the medicine, and must

go up to the Secretary's room; the servant told him
that he could not go up. He (Payne) then replied that h
must go up; must see him—must see him. The servant
still persisted in his refusal, telling him it was against
his orders, and that if he would give him the medicine,
he would tell the Secretary how to take it, if he would
leave him the directions. Payne said that that would
not do, and started to go up the stairs. The servant
finding that he would go up, ran up past him to excuse
himself if he was wrong in not letting him pass. Payne's
step being heavy on the stairs, the servant requested
him not to walk so heavy, or he would disturb Mr. Seward. When he reached the landing of the first floor,
Payne met Mr. Frederick Seward, who asked him his
business. He answered that he wanted to see the Secretary. Mr. F. Seward told him that he could not, as
his father was asleep at that time, and to give him the
medicine, and he would take it to his father. "That will
not do" returned Payne, "I must see him; I must see
him." Mr. F. Seward answered, "You cannot see him."

Payne continued, "I must see him." Mr. F. Seward
still refused, saying "I am proprietor here; I am Mr.
Seward's son ; if you cannot leave the medicine with me,
you cannot leave it at all." Payne finding that he could
not pass, started toward the stairs as if to go down.
The waiter started down before him, and had gone about
three steps when, turning around, he remarked, "Do not
walk so heavy." By the time the servant had turned
half way around, Payne jumped back and struck Mr.
Frederick Seward on the head ; on his repeating the
blow, Mr. F. Seward fell, throwing up his hands ; after
Payne struck Mr. Frederick Seward the second blow,

the servant ran down stairs and into the street to give the alarm.

Sergeant George F. Robinson (the Secretary's nurse) hearing the scuffling in the hall, opened the door of the room, where the Secretary was lying sick from wounds received a few days before by being thrown out of his carriage, to see what the trouble was. As he opened the door he saw Payne standing close up to it. As soon as the door was opened wide enough Payne rushed in, striking Sergeant Robinson as he passed, knocking him down ; rushing up to the bed where the helpless Secretary of State lay, he drew a large knife and made a lunge at the Secretary's head. The Secretary was sitting partially up in the bed, his head reclining a little to one side, so that as the knife descended it cut his face down on the left side and ran into the neck. Payne, to make sure that the job was complete, made another strike, cutting the Secretary on the other side of the neck. As soon as the nurse regained his feet, he ran to the bed and endeavored to pull the murderer off his helpless victim. As the nurse came up Payne turned upon him. They clinched, and while they were scuffling Major A. H. Seward came into the room, having been attracted by the screams of his sister. The gas being low as he entered the room, he saw what appeared to be two men, one trying to hold the other ; his first impression being that his father had become delirious, and that the nurse was trying to hold him, he ran up and took hold of Payne, and at once saw from his size and his struggles that it was not his father. He then thought that the nurse had become delirious, and was striking about the room at random. Knowing the delicate state of his father's health, he endeavored to shove the person he had hold of to the door ; as he was doing this, Payne struck him five or six times over the head with what he had in his left hand (a pistol,) supposed at the time to be a bottle or a decanter that he had seized from the table.

During the scuffle Payne cried out "I am mad, I am mad." As the three neared the door Payne clinched his hand around the neck of the nurse and knocked him down with his fist; then giving a sudden turn, he broke away from Major Seward and rushed down the stairs to the front door, leaving his hat behind. On reaching the street he mounted his horse and rode rapidly away. Major Seward did not realize the situation until after Payne was out of sight.

As soon as the nurse could regain his feet he went to the bed and found the Secretary lying on the floor weltering in his blood ; assisting him in bed he sent for a surgeon. Surgeon General Barnes, hearing of the affray, went to the house and found the Secretary wounded in three places, and Mr. Frederick Seward insensible in the adjoining room, badly wounded in the head. Both the Secretary's and his son's wounds were considered very dangerous, but they have since recovered. The vengeance of a just God is swift and sure.

After Booth escaped from the theatre he was tracked through the south of Maryland, across the Potomac river into Virginia, to the barn of a man named Garrett, in Caroline county, where one of his accomplices, Herold, was captured, and Booth met his death, being shot in the head (by Sergeant Boston Corbett, of the 16th New York cavalry) very near the spot where he (Booth) shot the President. After having been shot, he was ta ken out of the barn, it having been previously fired to make him surrender, if possible; and having been laid down on the porch of Mr. Garrett's house, he lingered about three hours, when he died, paying the debt he owed both God and man.

When Payne escaped from the house of the Secretary of State, he wandered about the streets for two or three days when he was arrested at the house of one of the conspirators, Mrs. Surratt, on H street, near Sixth, dressed in the attire of a laborer. Having been fully identified, he was tried by a military commission, was fully convicted, and suffered the penalty of his crime on the gallows, with three other of the conspirators, Atzerott, Harold, and Mary E. Surratt, in the yard of the old Penitentiary building, at the foot of Four-and-a-half street, Washington, D. C., on the seventh day of July, 1865, between the hours of one and two o'clock p. m.*

FIRING INTO A CHURCH.

Comment is unnecessary on such an outrage as this. The mere fact of men firing into a church, indiscriminately, upon unarmed men who were gathered together to worship God, without the demand of surrender, is enough.

The following is a statement of Walter E. H. Fentress, acting master, commanding United States steamer Rattler, who was captured during the affray:

On the 12th of September, 1863, as the steamer Rattler was lying off Rodney, Miss., I went on shore

---

* See official record of the conspirators at Washington, D. C.

to attend divine service, which was performed in a
church not two hundred yards distant from the steamer,
and in open view. * * * * We had just entered,
and were seated in the church, when a squad of fifty
cavalry dashed upon us, and opened fire from the windows and doors. I endeavored to stop this brutal fire
upon unarmed men, but was fired upon by the fiends,
and slightly wounded in the back. My hands were
tied, and I was made fast to a horse and compelled to
keep pace with them five miles. My treatment since
my capture has been brutal.

ANDERSONVILLE PRISON.

[From the official report of the trial of Henry Wirz.]

This horrible pen of misery and death will ever be
remembered by those poor unfortunate creatures, who,
through misfortune, were unlucky enough to be confined there; but who, through the kind providence of
a merciful God, were snatched from the very claws of
death, and permitted once again to breathe the pure
air of freedom.

Much has been said, and much will be said, about
this place of woe. Fiction cannot, in its most extrava-
gant rhetoric, overrate the sufferings and privations
endured by our patriotic soldiers, who, at the tap of
the drum, tore themselves from their homes, their
wives, their children, and all that they held dear, and
shouldered the musket to battle for the preservation
of this great and glorious republic. Time may moul-
der and decay other republics, but, with such soldiers,

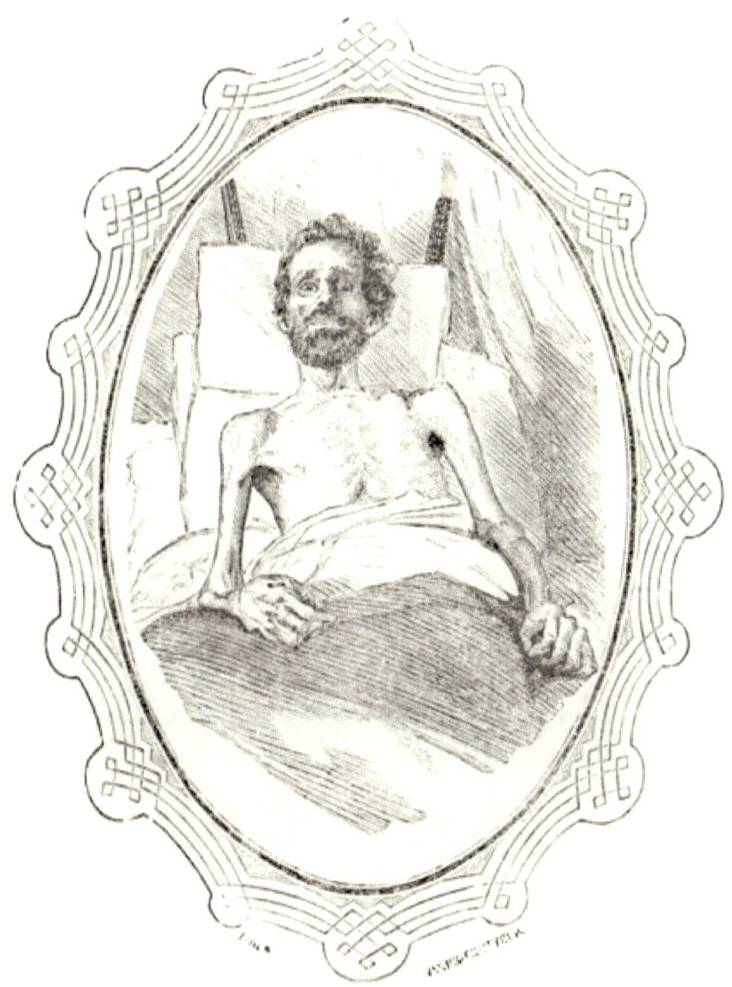

PRIVATE FRANCIS W. BEEDLE,

Company M, 8th Michigan Cavalry, Admitted per Steamer New York, from Richmond, Va., May 2d, 1864. Died May 3d, 1864, from effects of treatment while in the hands of the enemy.—U. S. General Hospital, Div. No. 1, Annapolis, Md.

ours will stand as long as God permits this planet to be inhabited by man. They needed not the second call to rally and sustain the honor of that flag that now, thank God ! waves proudly over every foot of soil from the great St. Lawrence to the noble Rio Grande, and from the angry Atlantic to the calm Pacific; and proudly may it wave over that soil, made twice dear to us by the blood of thousands upon thousands of heroic men, who bravely laid their bosoms bare, and fearlessly marched to the cannon's mouth to sustain its honor. Palsied be the arm and withered the hand that dare pull down that proud emblem of human liberty and lay it in the dust.

The stockade, inside of which the prisoners were confined, was located by Captains R. B. and W. S. Winder, and was commenced in the latter part of November or early part of December, 1863, and was built of roughly hewn pine logs, about eight inches in diameter, inserted in the ground about five feet, and projecting above the ground fifteen feet, enclosing an area of five hundred and fifty by two hundred and sixty yards, and surrounded by earth-works, with six and twelve-pound guns mounted on them, all pointing towards the stockade, for the benefit of the prisoners if they attempted to escape.

The fiend who commanded this famous prison (whose name will go down to posterity as one of the blackest-hearted villains that ever was permitted to breathe God's pure air) was one Henry Wirz, a fugitive from justice, who held a commission as captain in the army of the Jeff. Davis oligarchy, and a fit subject to carry out the damnable designs of such men as Jeff. Davis and his satellites. It appears that he had absolute control over the whole prison. He issued all

orders, and such was his tyranny that he would not
even allow a surgeon to enter the stockade to see the
sick without first applying to him for a pass, and this
it appears he seldom granted. His office was above
the stockade, and was a frame building, over the door
of which were the following words : "Officer in Command of Andersonville Prison."

The villain's soul was so deadened to all feelings of
humanity, that it seemed he took delight in inventing
schemes to torture the poor creatures who were so
unfortunate as to be placed in his hands, after being
captured while battling for the most sacred rights of
man. The following are the names of the most prominent tortures :

Dead-Line, Stocks, Chain-Gang, Thumb-Torture,
Bucking, Gagging, Vaccination, Sun-Torture, Whipping, and Starvation ; which I will endeavor to describe as far as my knowledge of them extends, commencing with the—

DEAD LINE.—This place of torture was a slight-
made railing, which ran parallel with the stockade (inside) and at a distance of about twenty feet from it.
Wirz, with a half dozen other men, layed it out in the
latter part of April, 1864, it is said, by authority of
the Rebel General Winder. Wirz issued the orders
to the guards to shoot the prisoners if they were seen
crossing, or even reaching over it. The guards designated to commit these willful murders were stationed
on a platform, which ran around the stockade on the
outside of it near the top, enabling the guard to look
over into the prison. An inducement, in the shape of
a thirty days' furlough, was offered to the guards to
commit these murders. Whenever a new guard was
put on, Wirz could be seen going around giving them

special instructions in regard to shooting the prisoners. On one occasion he was seen going up to one of the guards, who was on the platform near where a small creek ran across this accursed line, and, in tones loud enough to be heard, told the guard to shoot any d——n Yankee that even reached over the line. Just as he had finished giving the order, one of the prisoners reached over the line for some water; the guard seeing him, raised his gun and fired, killing the poor fellow instantly. As a matter of course the guard was immediately relieved. The guards, before entering upon duty, received special instructions not to warn any of the prisoners to go back if they attempted to cross the line, but to shoot them down like dogs. If the guards did not strictly obey this order they were severely punished. The prisoners on entering the stockade were not informed of the existence of the dead line, and thereby a great many of them were launched into eternity while ignorant of committing any trespass or violating any order. Whenever a prisoner was shot Wirz could be seen mounting the platform, and going up to the guard, would congratulate him for being so prompt in carrying out his orders; and, as a matter of course, he would be relieved for his brave act by this humane commander !

When any of the prisoners were shot inside this line, his comrades were afraid to go over and get the body; for, if they did; they would suffer the same penalty. Therefore the body would lie there until ordered by Wirz to be taken away.

The guards were not restricted to shooting of the prisoners, even if they were not near the dead line; but, if they were so inclined, they were permitted to fire into the stockade among the prisoners. It was a

frequent occurrence for the prisoners to hear the report of a gun in the night, and when they awoke
in the morning would find one or more of their
comrades lying dead on the ground with a bullet hole
in him.

The first man who suffered death after this accursed
line was established was an insane German. He had
just drawn his ration, and was returning with it, when
he dropped his bread, which rolled inside of this line.
He was in the act of stooping under the line to
pick it up, when, one of the guards seeing him, he shot
him, killing him instantly. At the junction where the
creek ran through this line of death the railing was
broken down. The prisoners used to congregate there
in large numbers to get water, as it was clearer there
than at any other place on the stream, and there many
a poor creature suffered death, by being accidently
crowded over the line by his comrades, unintentionally,
in their eagerness to get pure water. The prisoners
had also dug a number of wells inside the stockade,
and one of these was near the line; and here also
many a poor fellow paid the penalty of death by being unfortunate in reaching over or getting too near
this line. None but fiends could be guilty of such
brutality.

THE STOCKS.—These instruments of torture, it appears, were situated between the stockade and Wirz's
headquarters, and were composed of thick boards or
planks, two of which were placed upright with another across the top of them, in which was made a
hole large enough for a man's head to protrude. When
a prisoner was brought out to be put in the stocks, if
he happened to have a hat on, it was taken away by
the guards, and his head thrusted through this hole,

with his face turned towards the sun; and, thus secured, the arms of the victim would then be streched out to their utmost extent, and placed in holes made in the uprights for that purpose, and there fastened. In most instances the feet of the poor sufferer would scarcely touch the ground, and in this position he would be kept all day long. Food would generally be withheld from them while they were in the stocks, thus hastening death. Some who had constitutions like iron would live through it. It is known that this incarnated devil (Wirz) has kept men in these accursed things for two and three days at a time, and very often they would become senseless, and remain in this condition a long-time before they were taken out; and often they would not be taken out until they were quite dead. The faces of those who died in the stocks were quite black, as if they had been strangled or choked to death. There were as high as eight men in these stocks at one time. It did not matter whether it was raining or not, the victim's face would be turned upwards. A great many of the poor sufferers, after they were taken out of the stocks, would linger for a short time and die from the effects of it.

The stocks designated as the spread-eagle stocks, were constructed on the same plan as the others, only with an addition of holes for the feet of the prisoner; his arms and feet would be stretch to their utmost extension, and then fastened. These stocks would hold two persons.

There was still another mode of stock torture. These I designate as the feet stocks, and were constructed of plankst with holes in them about a foot from the ground. The feet of the prisoner would be placed in these holes and there fastened. Through great exertions, the person thus punished could sit up ; but in most cases they were compelled to lie down, with their backs upon the ground, and their faces exposed to the sun. The person placed in these stocks generally had a ball and chain attached to his arms.

CHAIN GANG.—This mode of torture like the stocks was of a varied nature, there being different gangs, and these varied in numbers. The first, or main gang, consisted of twelve or sixteen men, and these were subdivided into fours, which were placed in double files or two ranks. Iron collars were fastened on the necks of the men, then a small chain extended from the collar of one man to that of the other, and so on until the whole four were linked together. A chain was then attached to the inner leg of each of the four men, one end of which was secured to a sixty-four pound ball which they were compelled to carry. Then a small ball and chain was attached to the other leg of each man. To complete this net-work of chains a large chain ran between the ranks, extending the entire length of the gang, thus uniting the several subdivisions. This chain was secured to the smaller chains which connected the several files. It mattered not whether the prisoners were sick or not they would be put in the gang. There was a case where one poor creature was put in one of these gangs, who was very ill with the chronic diarrhœa, and who was kept there until he was so weak that he could not move; he was then taken out, but a ball and chain was kept on him until he died, which was a few days after he had been taken out of the gang.

The second gang was composed of about five men, who were chained to a large ball and kept standing in the sun. At times one man would be chained to a hundred pound ball. The men were kept in the chain gang from twenty-five to thirty days, being liberated one hour out of every five, so that they could endure the torture the longer.

When the men were sentenced to the chain gang they were taken to the blacksmith's shop, where collars and shackles would be riveted on them. This damnable torture was in full operation until General Stoneman made his raid toward Andersonville, then Wirz, through fear, broke it up. ·

THUMB TORTURE.—This mode of torture was as follows: The prisoner's hands were placed together, and a stout cord tied tightly around their thumbs, then their arms would be raised as high above their heads as they could reach, the cord thrown across the limb of a tree or post, erected for that purpose, in this manner the victim would be drawn up until he was compelled to stand on his tip-toes, and they barely touching the ground, and would be kept in this position for a long time with noth'ng to lean against. The poor sufferer when cut down would drop down on the ground entirely exhausted; after being released he could not use his hands for months, they being much swollen.

BUCKING.—This punishment was inflicted in the following manner: The prisoner's wrists would be tied together with a stout cord; they were then obliged to sit down and bend over in order to thrust the knees between the arms, a stick was then put over their arms and under their knees, and in this position they were compelled to sit. The effects of this torture upon the persons thus punished was terrible; their limbs would become perfectly paralyzed, and remain so for some days.

GAGGING.—This torture was inflicted as follows : The prisoner's arms would be tied behind their backs with a cord secured around their elbows, and drawn as tightly together as possible, without absolutely breaking their limbs, so that the sufferers could not reach their mouths with their hands; then they would be compelled to open their mouths, a and bayonet or a strong stick (the bayonet is generally used) would be inserted between their teeth. A cord was then fastened to one end of the bayonet or stick, and run around the back of the head, and generally drawn so tight that it compelled the victim to keep his mouth wide open, causing him the most excruciating pains. While enduring this torture the victim's tongue would become so swollen that when let loose he would not be able to speak for many days. In many instances the prisoners would be bucked and gagged at.the same time, thereby the torture became almost unindurable.

VACCINATION.—This torture was one of the most damnable of tortures that fiends could devise. As the process of vaccination is known to almost every person it is useless to explain it here. Suffer me to say that all the prisoners were ordered by Wirz to endure this torture. If any of the prisoners refused they were immediately put into the stocks or chain gang, and kept there until they consented to submit to undergo the process of vaccination. It is well known that the art of vaccination has in all preceding ages been used for a blessing to mankind, but in this case the villain used the rankest of poison, thus reversing this humanly intended purpose, making it a curse, and causing the most excruciating tortures.

The surgeons would congregate together in the evening and exult over the number of prisoners that

PRIVATE CHARLES R. WOODWORTH,
Company G, 8th Michigan Cavalry, Admitted from Flag-of-truce boat
April 18th, 1864.—West's Building Hospital, Baltimore, Md.   51

each had poisoned during the day by vaccination, saying that they had been ordered by Wirz to do it, and they were in for killing or disabling as many of the d——d Yankees as possible. This vaccination produced different results; on some it would create sores (such as are produced by the disease itself) on their bodies and under their arms as large as a man's hand. On others the flesh would .rot all round the place where the vaccine was inserted, gangreen would very often set in, and then the arm of the prisoner would have to be amputated.

Vincent Halley, of the 72d New York volunteers, saw, at one time, one hundred and fifty cases where gangreen had set in; he remarks, that the sores on their bodies were awful to behold.

Samuel Andrews, saw men who had become insane from the effects of vaccination, and would wander around, suffering the most intense agony until they fell down and died.

Wirz visited the grave-yard one day with some visiting surgeons, who examined the bodies of some of the men who had been brought out to the grave-yard that day, by cutting their heads open, &c.; the surgeons remarked to Wirz that, some of the men whom they had examined had died from the effects of inoculation, which had spread in green streaks from the arms of the victims to their bodies. Wirz laughed, and said, the G—d d—d Yankee s—s of b—s, I am giving them the land that they came to fight for—just six feet. The sores on the arms of some of the poor sufferers would become alive with larvae before they died.

SUN-TORTURE.— This torture was, to compel the prisoner to stand in the hot sun for hours at a time, without allowing them a drop of water to quench their thirst. For minor offences, Wirz would keep a whole squad, of ninety men, standing in line in the sun for a whole day at a time. The reader may easily imagine what effect this treatment had upon the poor unfortunate creatures, who through starvation and sickness, were already so reduced as barely to be able to support their emaciated frames. When a squad was compelled to stand up, Wirz would order the guards to shoot any of the prisoners who stepped out of the ranks, under any pretext whatever; and if any of the prisoners would fall down from the effects of a stroke from the sun, there they would have to lie and suffer, where their comrades could see them in the last struggles of death, and could not offer them any assistance, or be allowed to carry them in the shade, because this fiend of torture wished to satisfy his satanic appetite by taking their lives.

When a new squad of prisoners were brought to Andersonvile as an introductory iniation to the tortures they were to endure in this minature hell, they were taken to Wirz's headquarters, and there they would be compelled to stand in the hot sun for hours, (probably after having walked for many miles before they got into his hands,) until it suited his fiendish convenience to order them to be counted off and sent into the stockade.

WHIPPING.—In whipping the prisoners they generally used hickory switches about four feet long or a leather strap about two-and-a-half feet long and from two to two-and-a-half inches wide. When a prisoner was to be whipped he was stripped to to his waist, and tied across a log or barrel, and then whipped from head to foot, generally receiving from one hundred to two hundred and fifty strokes. Almost every blow would cause the blood to flow. After being whipped the poor creatures would be let loose, and turned into the stockade, and their wounds, no matter how serious from the effects of this flogging, were left to heal the best they might. The screams of the poor creatures while enduring this torture could be heard for a great distance.

STARVATION.—It seems almost beyond belief that in this enlightened age there should live men so devoid of feeling, so deadened to all sense of humanity, so inexorable to the duties of nature's first law as to compel human beings to undergo the frightful horrors of starvation, but this, I regret to say, has been done by Wirz and his coadjutors to the unfortunate men who were prisoners at Andersonville. It is useless to deny this, because it has been established beyond doubt by the testimony of hundreds of witnesses during the trial of the heinous monster who had direct control of the prisoners. Would to God that this was the only evidence that we had to offer to establish the truth of this assertion. The mind recoils back in horror in contemplation of the scenes that are now witnessed throughout the entire land where the forms of thousands of decrepit and emaciated beings are scattered. Look at these and you will see living examples of this hellish attempt upon their lives ; the effect of the treatment that they received has so broken down their constitutions as to render them totally unfit for either menial or physical exertion. Having been by this hellish torture deprived alike of their reason and every other manly qualification which kind Providence had bestowed upon them, they wander about, abject and miserable beings, without the hope of ever being restored to themselves or their families.

Kind reader imagine to yourself all the comforts of a good and plentiful home, and then accompany me, as it were, to Andersonville, and there behold the scenes of woe and misery caused by the most wicked and un-heard of treatment. Oh! what a contrast.

There you could see men, or rather shadows of men, wandering about in a state of lunacy, (the ef-fects of starvation,) with their eyes bent on the ground vainly seeking for something wherewithall to sustain life. Some could be seen with out-stretched arms, and without addressing themselves to any particular object, imploring for something to eat; others too much reduced to walk would crawl upon their hands and knees, lifting or scattering about any object under which they thought they might, perchance, find something to eat. Some of these help-less creatures were entirely nude, and to such a de-plorable condition were some of them reduced, that to satisfy the cravings of fierce hunger, they would pick up and greedily devour beans, &c., that had passed through the bowels of the other prisoners un-digested, others would search through the offal and refuse matter of the camp for food, wash it, and then eat it. At length some of the poor creatures, entirely despairing, would deliberately walk over the dead line to be shot, or put an end to their miseries by commit-ting suicide.

Wirz has repeatedly said that he would starve every d——d Yankee in the stockade, and exult over the number that were dying of starvation, saying that he was killing more men than Lee was at the front.

So great were the cravings of hunger that the poor sufferers would reach under the dead line in search of crumbs when they knew it was almost certain death to do so. The prisoners were neglected in every respect. You could see at all times poor cripples crawling upon the ground. A great many could not move at all; these were left lying on the bare ground without the slightest attention being paid to them.

Doctor Thornburg, a rebel surgeon, stationed at this prison, testified that a large majority of those who died could have been saved had a proper quantity of food been furnished them. And the small quantity that was furnished them was entirely unfit for human beings to eat, it being at times full of vermin.

I will now cite the case of a poor young man who was shamefully treated by this fiend. To give the reader a better view of the frightful sufferings of these unfortunate creatures confined there, the poor creature referred to was lying sick on the ground, almost dead with the chronic diarrhœa, while he was lying there suffering, Wirz happened to pass near by, the poor sufferer seeing him, called, and asked him for a piece of bread, saying that he was starving, and that he was too weak to go after his ration; when he was done Wirz turned around and struck him on the head with a large whip he had in his hand, the poor sufferer swooned, he was then taken to the hospital and died shortly after.

The cry put forth by some, of the scarcity of provisions at Andersonville, is simply an invention to excuse or palliate this damnable crime, as it is well known from the evidence given that there were large storehouses at the depot, which was but a short distance from the prison, and these were always filled with

provisions; furthermore, the whole world is acquainted with the noble efforts of the Sanitary and Christian
Commissions to relieve the sufferings of the soldiers
confined there, by sending to them large quantities
of good and substantial food, yet this was never given
them for fear they would derive too much nourishment
from it, and this would have been inconsistent with
their original idea of treating Yankees.   Wirz and
others were seen very often eating their provisions,
and it has also been clearly proven that a great quantity of these provisions were permitted to lay there
until they spoiled, rather than they would allow the
prisoners have them.   To prove more conclusively
that provisions could be had for the prisoners if they
chose to furnish them, I will refer the reader to the
act of the rebel congress, requiring the farmers to pay
as tithes one-tenth of all the produce raised on their
farms.   The Georgia legislature also passed a law, the
second year of the war, prohibiting the farmers from
planting more than two acres of cotton, all the rest
had to be planted in provisions.   By summing up the
amount thus accumulated in but a few counties it will
be seen that a sufficient quantity was collected to enable them to furnish the prisoners the proper quantity
they required.   In October, 1864, the confederate
authorities slaughtered at Oglethorpe from 50,000 to
60,000 head of hogs.

Each county in Georgia, like every other of the
southern States, had a ware-house where the county
tithe collector would have all the produce collected,
and from there it would be shipped to the points where
it was needed.   In 1863, a good crop of corn and
vegetables was raised in Georgia, and a large quantity of this was sent to Andersonville, still the prison-

ers were insufficiently fed. It is also proven that a good crop, yes, a surplus, was raised in Georgia in the year 1864. · In this year, it is said, that there was an unusual large supply of vegetables ; there was also large cornfields within sight of the prison.

I will here give you an account of the produce collected by one of the tithe agents (Walter D. Davenport) in the counties of Sumpter, Webster, Marion, and Schley. Marion and Schley are very small counties, in fact, none of these counties are very large: 247,768 pounds of bacon, 38,900 bushels of corn, 3,567 bushels of wheat, 3,420 pounds of rice, 817 bushels of peas, 3,700 gallons of sirup, 1,166 pounds of sugar. The foregoing were for the year 1864, and from January 1, 1865, to April, 1865, the time of the surrender, there was collected 155,726 pounds of bacon, 13,591, bushels of corn, 86 bushels of wheat, (remnant due on old crop,) 2,077 pounds of rice, 851 bushels of peas, 5,082 gallons of sirup, 56 pounds of sugar, &c., &c.

So horrible was the treatment of the prisoners at this place that it even created the sympathy of the ladies in the vicinity, they went even so far as to collect together a large quantity of provisions, and carried them to Andersonville, when they arrived there they were refused permission to carry them to the prisoners by General Winder, who happened to be there when the provisions were brought up by the ladies', he positively refused to let them pass, saying that he believed the whole country was becoming Yankee, and the effort to relieve the prisoners was a slur upon the confederate government, and he was going to put a stop to it; it was best for the Yankees to die. And this companion in guilt of Wirz's had the gal-

lantry to use language to the ladies, (God bless them,)
that a blackguard would be ashamed to utter.   During this villain's conversation with the ladies Wirz
remarked that if he had his way he would build a
house at Andersonville, and the ladies' should be put
in it for a vile purpose.   These men are mere specimens of the villains who so long deluded the minds of
the southern people.

If the prisoners happened to get a few vegetables,
&c., when they were allowed to go out of the stockade
for wood, they would be searched at the gate, and
the vegetables taken from them.

For very simple offences Wirz would stop the rations of a whole squad of ninety men, (the prisoners
were divided off in squads of nineties.)   Sometimes
for his own devilish gratifications, he would stop the
rations of all the prisoners in the stockade for days at
a time; for instance the rations of the prisoners were
stopped from the third to the fifth of July, because
the Fourth was regarded by the prisoners as a day of
national rejoicing.   When one of the prisoners escaped, the rations of the whole squad that he was in,
was stopped for four or five days.   On one occasion
Wirz ordered a squad of prisoners to move from one
place in the stockade to another, some of them walked
faster than it suited his pleasure, and as a revenge, he
stopped the rations of the whole squad, which had the
effect of starving to death Hugh Lynch, Wm. Keizer,
and Wm. Waterhowers.

It has been stated in the evidence before the commission, by the men who were then confined in this
place of woe, that they could eat all the rations that
were allowed them in a day at one meal, and then be
hungry.

PRIVATE JOHN BREINIG,

Company G, 4th Kentucky Cavalry, Admitted April 18th ,1864. Improved a little for two weeks, then gradually failed and died.—West's Building Hospital, Baltimore, Md.

35

There was as high as 33,000 prisoners in the stockade at one time, and these were in the most horrible condition, being filthy, naked, and swarming with vermin, and without shelter, some were crazy; in fact, the horrors of the place are indesirable. I will here insert that portion of the report of the rebel Col. D. S. Chandler to the authorities at Richmond, which refers to the condition of the prisoners confined there, and let the reader form his own conclusion from the facts stated by one of their own officers. After describing the locality of the prison he goes on to say thus :

The federal prisoners of war are confined within a stockade fifteen feet high, enclosing an area of 550 by 260 yards, about $3\frac{1}{4}$ acres, near the centre of the enclosure, are so marshy as to be at present unfit for occupation, reducing the available present area to about $23\frac{1}{2}$ acres, which gives something less than six square feet to each prisoner. Even this has been constantly reduced by the additions to their number.

A small stream passes from west to east through the enclosure at about 150 yards from its southern limits, excepting the edges of the stream, the soil is sandy, and easily drained, but from thirty to fifty yards on each side of it the ground is muddy, marshy, and totally unfit for occupation, and having been constantly used as a sink since the prison was first established, it is now in a shocking condition and cannot fail to breed pestilence.

No shelter whatever, nor materials for constructing any have been provided by the prison authorities, and the grounds being entirely bare of trees, none is within reach of the prisoners. Each man has been permitted to protect himself the best he can, by stretching his blanket, (if he had one,) or whatever he may have about him on such sticks as he may procure. * *

The whole number of prisoners is divided into messes of two hundred and seventy, and subdivisions of ninety men, each under a sergeant of their own number and selection, and but one confederate States officer; in consequence of this fact the absence of all regularity in the prison grounds, and there being no barracks or tents, there are, and can be no regulations established for the "police consideration for the health, comfort, and sanitary condition of those within the enclosure," and none are practicable under existing circumstances.

There is no medical attendance furnished within the stockade. The sick are directed to be brought out by the sergeants of squads daily, at sick call, to the medical officer who attends at the gate. The crowd at these times is so great that only the strongest can get access to the doctors. And the hospital accommodations are so limited that though the beds (socalled) have all, or nearly all, two occupants each, large numbers who would otherwise be received are necessarily sent back to the stockade. Many are carted out daily who have died from unknown causes, and whom the medical officers have never seen. The dead are hauled out daily by the wagon load, and buried without coffins. Their hands, in many instances, being first mutilated with an axe in the removal of any finger-rings they might have.

The sanitary condition of the prisoners is as wretched as can be; the principle causes of mortality being scurvy and chronic diarrhœa. Nothing seems to have been done, and but little, if any, effort made to arrest it by procuring proper food. Raw rations have been issued to a very large portion who are entirely unprovided with proper utensils, and furnished with so limited a supply of the fuel, they are compelled to dig with their hands in the filthy marsh for roots, &c. No soap or clothing has ever been issued. After inquiry I am confident that, by slight exertions, green corn and other anti-scarbutics could be readily obtained. It is impossible to state the number of sick, many dying within the stockade, whom the medical officers never see or hear of till their remains are brought out for interment. The ratio of deaths has steadily increased from 37-4-10 per cent. during the month of March last, to 72-7-10 per cent. in July. This report was dated Andersonville, Aug. 5, 1864.

Inside the stockade the prisoners, through great exertions, had managed to dig a few wells, for the purpose of getting drinking water, with plates, spoons, &c., as they were not allowed spades or shovels to dig them with, for that would be helping the poor creatures too much, who were so unfortunate as to be confined there, to sustain life, and thereby totally reverse the principles of the so-called Confederate government. There were also a number of small springs inside the stockade, but these wells and springs furnished very little water, and thereby the greater portion of the thirty-three thousand prisoners confined there were compelled as a last resort to get the greater part of their drinking water from a small stream of filth, (the creek referred to in Col. Chandler's report.) It cannot be called water.

The first-cook house was situated in the northwest part of the stockade, the second one in the northeast part; the last one was erected in September 1864. The first one was a large frame building, with brick bakeries. All the drainage from these places, they being situated on sloping ground, were washed into this stream and ran down through the stockade. At first all the rations, such as meat, beans, &c., for the whole number—thirty-three thousand prisoners—were cooked at the first bake house. Dr. Barrows, in his evidence before the commission, stated that the condition of this place was horrible, and beyond description, that no one could live in the vicinity of it and enjoy good health. The stench from this place was awful in its best days.

The guards of the prison, numbering some four or five thousand men, were encamped on both sides of this stream, just above the stockade, and whenever it rained the washings from their camps and sinks would wash down into this stream, and run through the prison.

The ground on the east side of the stockade, outside, was marshy and blocked up with logs, having been thrown or fallen into it and all drebis and vegetable matter would naturally congregate here, thereby producing a large quantity of maggots, white ants, and all such insects as result from the decay of an accumulation of vegetable or animal matter in such places, and these necessarily washed into this stream.

Martin T. Hogan, in his evidence, stated that the filth of the camps, inside the stockade, washed into this stream during each rain; the water, he says, was not suitable for use either for washing or drinking purposes, as he had seen a large mass of maggots and filth of every kind in it. James H. Davidson stated that he had seen plenty of vermin in it. There were not sinks enough inside of the stockade to accommodate one-twentieth of the men, and they therefore were compelled to use the swamp, which occupied about one-fifth of the enclosure, and this was at one time a foot deep with maggots and human excrement, and the drainage of this swamp ran into the stream.

John H. Stevens stated that he remembered a case of a man, where the maggots from the stream got on his clothes and attacked his nose and eyes, penetrating the victim, causing him excruciating pain and after a few days resulting in death, he also stated that he had seen a number of other cases similar to the above; other witnesses state that they have seen the same.

Who would ever imagine that human beings, men created after the image of God, and the noblest piece of his handiwork, would have been compelled to drink such filth; yes, and here at this stream, which must have been, at times, a living mass of maggots, filth, &c., could at all times be seen poor unfortunate prisoners who, through starvation, and bad treatment were unable to walk, crawling up to it on their hands and knees, with pails and cups in their mouths, to get this filth to drink; there were a great many who were encamped away from it who were too weak to get to it to quench their thirst, yes, and hundreds who through great exertions had managed to crawl up to the side of it and there die.

There seemed to be a regular system of robbing instituted by the prison authorities. It seemed they were not satisfied in robbing the poor prisoners of their lives, but would take everything of value from them while living, and then strip them of their clothes after they were dead. When a new squad of prisoners were brought in they would be drawn up in line before Wirz's headquarters, then they would be ordered to take off their knapsacks, haversacks, canteens, &c., and pile them up in front of the ranks; after this was done, Wirz would tell the guards to take what they wished; then this prince of thieves would tell the prisoners to take what was left, (nothing.) When the men who were captured during the raid of General Stoneman near Andersonville were brought in, they were stripped of nearly all their clothing, and turned into the stockade almost naked. The guard it seems were as light-fingered as their commander, they would rob the prisoners every chance they could get, and the robbing became so general that the prisoners applied to Wirz for protection. After hearing their protest he laughed at them, and said, that it served them right, and bully for the guard, or something to that effect.

The letters of all the prisoners were broken open, that is the letters that were sent to them from their friends in the north, and everything of value, such as money, &c., taken from them, and the letters given to the prisoners. At all times could be seen sanitary goods, that had been sent to the prisoners, on Wirz, and, in fact, upon all the rest of the rebels around the prison, even to the guards. The shoes that were sent to the prisoners by their friends in the north were seen on the feet of Wirz's slaves.

One of the prisoners, a Mr. Stevenson, died shortly after entering the stockade. He had respectable clothes on; Joseph Adlen asked Wirz that he might be buried in them. This Wirz promised should be done. Shortly after, Wirz with two guards, went to where Mr. Stevenson laid, and stripped him of all his clothing, and he was thus buried.

A prisoner belonging to a Michigan regiment, (name forgotten,) had taken from him a daguereotype likeness of his dead wife, and his two children. While Wirz was looking at them, he asked him to be kind enough to return them when done looking at them; without making any answer, Wirz threw the likeness on the ground and stamped upon it. This thief took another likeness of a young lady from one of the prisoners, after looking at it for some time he made vulgar remarks about the young lady; the prisoner remonstrated. Wirz drew out his pistol, and placing it to the man's head, said that he would blow out his brains if he uttered another word.

About the last of June, 1864, a wounded prisoner named Underwood, of company L, 7th Indiana cavalry, who had managed to secret about his person a $10 bill, went to the sutler and asked him for some medicine; Wirz was standing by when he came up; he said to Underwood "no you can't have it, except you pay me one dollar;" Underwood pulled out the ten dollar bill, and handed it to Wirz; after waiting sometime he asked Wirz for his change. This, it appears, aroused the brutish anger of Wirz, who kicked the poor fellow out of the shop. He died shortly afterwards.

There were hounds kept at this place to aid in capturing the prisoners if they attempted to escape; these were regularly mustered into the service as horses, and drew rations under Wirz's signature; they were the common plantation hounds such as were used in tracking slaves; at one time it appears there were two packs, one under a man named Harris, and the other, or more notable, under one Turner, a fit subject to control a pack of canines; it would be a hard matter to tell which was the most ferocious, Turner or the hounds; the pack that Turner had charge of contained about fifteen hounds, including a leader, or catch dog, which was a sort of a bull terrier. This man Turner was a detailed soldier, and it appears owned the pack he controlled, and he has repeatedly said to the prisoners that he was making more money with his hounds than he could make on his farm.

Every morning Wirz and Turner used to go around the stockade, with the dogs, to see if any of the prisoners had escaped during the night, and if a trail was found they would gather together a party and start off in high glee; it may have been sport to them but it was misery, and sometimes death, to the poor fellows, for the dogs were invariably allowed to bite the prisoners. When the prisoners knew they were tracked they generally would climb a tree, and when the party came up they would order the prisoner down, and as soon as his feet touched the ground the dogs would fly at him and commence to bite him, and when the fiends were satisfied with this hellish sport the dogs were taken off, and the prisoner taken back to the stockade, and generally put in the stocks or chain gang. On one occasion, one of the prisoners, a lad, seventeen years of age, escaped from the stockade, but was brought back by the dogs and literally torn to pieces by them. Wirz and Turner were there and witnessed it but would not take the dogs off of the poor unfortunate boy. It has been proven that Wirz gave Turner positive orders not to bring any of the prisoners back alive, but let the dogs tear them to pieces.

One of the witnesses stated that he saw one man, who had been caught by these dogs, brought into the stockade, his throat being frightfully lacerat d, he died the same day. Wirz, Doctor's White and Stevenson were standing by when the dogs were tearing the poor fellow; while they were doing it Wirz remarked that, it served the d——d dog, meaning the prisoner, right.

PRIVATE LEWIS KLEIN.

Company A, 14th New York Cavalry, Admitted from Steamer New York,
from Richmond, Va., April 18th, 1864.—West's Building Hospital, Balt. Md. 51

The hospital, or more properly, the slaughter-house, was situated outside of the stockade, within a stone-throw of it, and consisted of rows of old moulded and ragged canvass tents, so that when it rained the water would run down on the patients; the tents having no flooring the ground inside of them would become very muddy; there were very few bunks in the hospital and the majority of the patients were compelled to lay on the bare ground without any covering. The sick were treated inhumanly; in a great many cases they had no medicine or attendance for days. In the month of June, 1864, they were without medicine for fifteen days; there they would lay, some of them completely covered with vermin, and too weak to clean themselves, and in this condition they would suffer until death relieved them. The stench from this place was awful, and could be smelled for a great distance. It has been stated that if a prisoner happened to scratch his hand, and stay in this place any length of time, he would be reported, the next day, as a gangrene patient. Very few who had their limbs amputated in this place ever escaped with their lives, as gangreen generally set in. The poor fellows were almost destitute of food and would, beg the doctors to bring them bones so that they could break them up and suck the nutriment from them, and thus prolong life. Dr. J. C. Bates, a Union prisoner, stated that he would slily take things to the patients and drop them down where they could reach them. Seventy-five per cent. of the patients alone could have been saved had proper food been given them. The prisoners, confined in the stockade; had such a dread of this place, that when one of their comrades was to be taken to the hospital, they would flock around him and bid him good bye, never expecting to see him again alive. Thomas Walsh, 74th N. Y. vols., says that he only knew of one man, (named Kelley, a seaman, belonging to his squad,) whoever came out of this place alive, but was taken back again, and there died.

The grave-yard contained about twenty-five or thirty acres of land, and was situated a short distance from the stockade. The dead were buried in trenches about two-and-a-half feet deep, and a slight layer of dirt thrown over them. The grave diggers were Union prisoners, and numbered from twenty to thirty men. These were kept digging all the time. The dead were brought out to the yard by the wagon loads, as high as fifty to seventy-five a day. They would be piled up in the wagons like cord-wood, one on top of the other. In the month of August alone there were buried in this place 2,700 prisoners; in fact, the mortality was so great that the wagons could not haul the dead out fast enough, and some of the bodies would lay in the dead-house until they became mortified and alive with vermin, and would burst while being taken out. Many were buried inside the stockade. Wirz got in one of these wagons one day, and rode to the grave-yard; while riding he remarked to the driver that he was killing more d——d Yankees than Lee was at the front. On one occasion a party of rebel officers visited the grave-yard, and while there, remarked to some of the grave-diggers that the Yankees would make good manure. That it would be a good idea to plant a vineyard there, and invite their northern friends down to eat the grapes raised from these Yankees bones.

I will not detain the reader any longer, in describing this horrible pen, but will proceed to give a synopsis of the evidence of those men which refers to personal cas· s.

Thos. C. Alcoke, 72d Regiment, Ohio Volunteers, was a prisoner at Andersonville during the summer of 1864. On his arrival there he was robbed of every thing of value he had upon his person. The fiend Wirz officiated at the ceremony, and took from him $430, $150 of which was in gold. On one occasion he saw Wirz going through the stockade, when a sick prisoner called him, (Wirz,) and said "Captain I am very sick, may I go out and get some fresh air." The only reply this monster deigned to make to so humble a request was to draw his revolver, ask the man what he meant, and in the same breath saying, "I'll give you air," then shot the unfortunate sufferer dead. After the shot was fired, Mr. Alcoke, who was standing close behind him, remonstrated, and said something about the cruelty of the deed, when Wirz turned around and reminded him, tauntingly, of his situation as a prisoner, and intimated that any attempt to correct him (Wirz) was a sure way of drawing upon himself a like fate. Nor did the affair end here; this fiend in human form had deadened his heart to every feeling of humanity, and consequently could not brook this reproach. The next day Mr. Alcoke was ordered to the blacksmith shop, where a ball and chain was fastened upon his leg, which he wore all the time he was confined there. But finally managing to get the irons off he made his escape from this second hell.

When he testified before the commission in Washington, a piece of paper was shown him, on which were drawn the most important points of that den of woe, where he had suffered so long, but was so near blind from the treatment he received that he could not recognise anything.

Thomas Hall, U. S. Marine Corps, testifies, that while he was confined in this prison Wirz ordered the prisoners to fall into line, but as they did not move fast enough to suit him he drew out his revolver and threatened to blow out the brains of every one if they did not move faster. On a certain occasion he threat-ened to pour grape and canister among the prisoners if they did not desist from huddling together in the stockade. This was about the time that they (the rebels) were expecting a visit from General Kilpat-rick, who was then spreading terror and consternation throughout south-western Georgia.

Mr. Hall had charge of one of the squads of ninety men, and the greater part of these died from the ef-fects of ill treatment. One day Wirz ordered Mr. Hall's squad to stand in line, a great many of them protested, telling him that they were to sick to do it, whereupon he drew his revolver and threatened to blow out the brains of every d——d Yankee that did not comply immediately, of course the demand was complied with. He saw one poor crazy creature shot while in the act of reaching under the dead-line in search of some crumbs of bread that had been thrown there, he died immediately after being shot.

James Clancy, 28th N. Y. vols., was confined in this place from June until November, 1864, and while there he says he saw Wirz beat a sick boy under the following circumstances: A number of prisoners were ordered into line in front of Wirz's head-quarters, and with them was this youth. While standing there he was taken very ill, and was compelled to leave the ranks and sit down on a pail near by. Wirz seeing him, ordered him to take his place in the ranks imme-diately; this the poor sufferer was unable to do; find-

ing the boy did not move, he walked up to where he
was sitting, and pulling out his revolver, he struck
the lad a powerful blow on the head with it, which
caused the poor sufferer to lean over on his elbows,
he had hardly leaned over before Wirz gave the pail,
upon which he sat, a kick throwing him to the ground
and causing him excruciating pain; subsequently the
boy was brought into the stockade by two of his comrades; he died shortly after. I saw a man shot at on
the dead line while in the act of reaching under it for
a chestnut burr, which he intended to use in cooking
his rations; the shot missed him and killed a man who
was sleeping on the ground behind him.

O. B. Fairclough, member of company E, Ninth
New York cavalry, testified, that he was taken to
Andersonville in the month of February, 1864. When
Wirz first took command of the prison, he deprived
the prisoners of their rations because he could not find
out the exact number of prisoners confined there; one
of Wirz's favorite speeches toward the prisoners was
to call them d——d Yankee s—— of b——s. On
one occasion he kicked witness' stepfather when he
was in a helpless condition, his arms and legs being
drawn up with the scurvy. He could not get into
line soon enough, when Wirz come up and kicked
him in the side, remarking as he did it, "You d——d
Yankee s——of b—— if you don't fall in I'll give you
nothing to eat for a week." The kick caused a very
severe pain in the side of the poor sufferer who died
in a month after he received the kick. Just before
he died he told his stepson that he was dying of sheer
starvation, and implored him not to tell his mother
how he died. Witness then wrote down what his
stepfather said, and had him sign it, it reads as follows :

CAMP SUMPTER,
Andersonville, **Ga.**, *August* 21, 1864.

OLIVER: I die from sheer starvation, and don't for the world tell your mother of the awful condition I am compelled to die in.

RICHARD FAIRCLOUGH.

He died ten minuets after he signed the paper.

On one occasion witness went to the hospital to see his father, who was taken there after he had been kicked, when the surgeon came to him and told him that he was going to vaccinate him, he refused to submit to the operation, as he had seen the effects of it, and believed it to be poisonous; on his refusing he was taken before Wirz, who called him a G--d d----d Yankee s—— of a b——h, and asked him why he had disobeyed orders. As soon as Wirz s anger had subsided, he asked to speak to him, telling him that he knew that the matter used was poisonous and that was his reason for disobeying orders. Wirz told him that it would serve him right if it did kill him, and the sooner he died, the sooner he would get rid of him. After a little further conversation, Wirz ordered him to be placed in the chain-gang and to be kept there until he consented to be vaccinated. Having observed that some of the surgeons were very careless in performing the operation, and that by taking some soap, and carefully washing the arm, he would (and did) prevent any serious effects. He then proceeded to inform the other prisoners of the mode of, preventing serious consequences from this outrageous villany; but up to that time nearly all who had been vaccinated had died from the effects of the operation. Witness saw Wirz knock down one of the prisoners with his pistol, because he was man enough to complain of his rations.

Frank Maddox, 35th U. S. colored troops, was sent to this den of misery in the month of April, 1864. This unfortunate man had been severely wounded previous to being sent there, and while there his wounds were never attended to, yet, notwithstanding he mended slowly, and when he had nearly recovered, he was taken out of the stockade and put to work. On one occasion he saw this agent of Lucifer (Wirz) knock a man, named Isaac Humphries, out his tent, at the same time calling him a d——d smoked Yankee s—n of a b——h. Calling a guard he ordered Humphries to receive five hundred lashes. The guard seizing him hurried him away, and stripping him, they laid him across a log, and whipped him from head to feet. The rebel sergeant designated to do the whipping made a mistake, and gave Humphries only two hundred and fifty instead of five hundred lashes.

Maddox with a squad of others was ordered to go into the swamp to work. The majority of them objected, because it was so filthy, when Wirz told the guard that was with them to knock them all in the head, and let them lay where they fell for the buzzards to eat.

On one occasion a prisoners blacked himself and went out of the slockade with the negroes, bnt he had not gone far when his absence was discovered. Wirz hearing of the occurrence ordered the man to receive thirty-nine lashes, saying that he had placed himself in a negro's place he should receive a negro's law; the order was promptly executed. He saw one man who attempted to escape, but was recaptured by the hounds, who had frightfully lacerated him about the neck, breast, and legs ; in this condition he was placed in the stocks, where he shortly after died. Turner, the king of the prison canines, went to the grave-yard one day, where Maddox was working, and remarked that the other man who attempted to escape, with the one that had been placed in the stocks, resisted, and he allowed the hounds to tear him to pieces, and that he had left the body in the woods.

The usual mode of punishing the colored prisoners was by whipping them; they were, as a general thing, placed by themselves in the stockade.

James H. Davidson. 4th Iowa cavalry, arrived at this place of torture in the month of March, 1864, and remained inside the stockade until the 11th of May, when he was taken out by Wirz, and detailed as teamster part of the time. He states he was employed in hauling out the dead to the grave yard, which he says was three quarters full, when he left, (September 11, 1864.) In many instances, after hauling out the dead, he was ordered to haul into the stockade a load of rations for the living. Saw one man who had been placed in the chain-gang die while in it, and he was buried with the iron collar around his neck; saw a man shot while in the act of picking up a piece of clothing which he had washed and hung up to dry, and which had blown under the dead-line; and while reaching over to get it was shot, and killed. On one occasion, in the month of April, as Wirz was coming into the stockade by the south gate, he walked close by one of the prisoners, who was lying sick on the ground, who asked him something which he did not like, turning around, he drew his revolver and shot the poor crea-ture, killing him instantly.

Martin T. Hogan, 1st Indiana cavalry, arrived at Andersonville in August, 1864, and made his escape in the month of October, but was caught by the

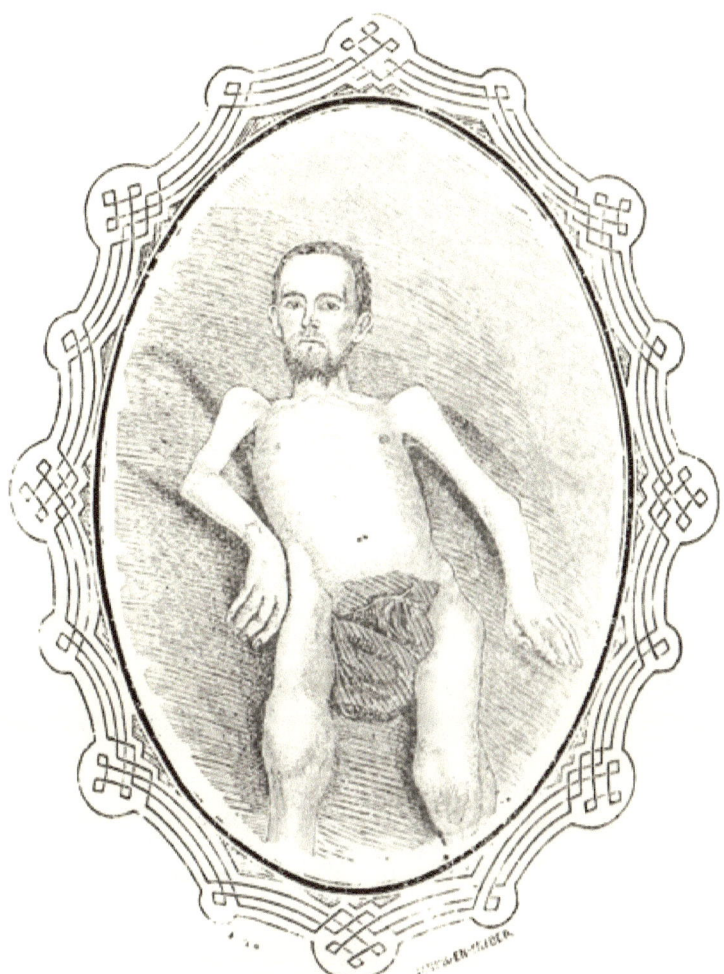

PRIVATE JOHN Q. ROSE,

Company C, 5th Kentucky Volunteers. Admitted per Steamer New York, from Richmond, Va., May 2d, 1864. Died May 4th, 1864, from effects of treatment while in the hands of the enemy.—U. S. General Hospital, Div. No. 1, Annapolis, Md.

hounds, brought back, and taken before Wirz, who, after heaping all sorts of oaths upon him, ordered him to be put in the spread eagle stocks, for sixty eight hours, without food. Had it not been for a few comrades, who were bold enough to bring him food secretly, he would have died. He thinks that Wirz put him in the stocks through personal revenge. Saw Wirz knock a sick man down, and stamp upon him because he did not walk fast enough to suit him. The man was too weak to walk any faster; the poor fellow was taken up bruised and bleeding, and died shortly after.

O. S. Belcher, 16th Illinois cavalry, says that while confined in this prison he saw many acts of cruelty committed by Wirz, one of which was the murder of "Chickamauga," a cripple, under the following circumstances. One day Wirz came into the stockade, and passed near Checkamauga, who called him, and asked him to take him out of the stockade, as he could not live in such a place, as the other prisoners tormented him. Wirz positively refused Chickamauga, who then remarked that he would sooner be shot and end his miseries than stay in the place any longer. As soon as Wirz had left him he deliberately walked over the dead-line, Wirz seeing him crossing, ordered the sentry to shoot him, but it appears he had some humanity left, and refused to execute the order, then Wirz went to another of the sentries and ordered him to shoot Chickamauga; he hesitated, when Wirz drew out his revolver to shoot him, (the sentry,) but he fired before Wirz could shoot him. The shot struck Chickamauga in the head, killing him instantly. After he had been shot some of the prisoners were attracted to the spot by the report of the gun. Wirz coming up ripped out an oath, and ordered the guard to fire into the crowd if they did not disperse imme diately. Mr. Henshaw, after Chickamauga was shot asked Wirz to allow him to remove the body; Wirz replied take him and go to hell with him.

Saw a prisoner shot while he was going out for some wood under orders; saw another shot while he was trading with one of the guards; they were not near the dead-line.

W. W. Scott, 6th West Virginia cavalry, testifies that on the 26th or 27th of August, 1864, that a sick prisoner was sitting on the ground near the gate, Wirz came along, and asked him if he could get up; the man answered that he could not; Wirz then pulled out his revolver, and beat the poor fellow over the head and shoulders with the butt end of it. It is not known whether he ever survived it. He says, one day as Wirz was passing around the prison, between the stockade and the dead-line, one of the sentries sta tioned on the platform threw a brick at him, which struck him in the back; Wirz after being struck, wheeled his horse around, and drawing his revolver, fired the contents of it among the prisoners. One of the shots struck a man on the head, but as luck would have it, it only took away part of the skin and hair.

Rufus Munday, 75th Ohio vols., states that on or about the 21st of February, 1865, the prisoners man aged to borrow a few spades, when they were returned, one of them was missing; next morning Wirz ordered the squad into line; one of the men being sick did not get into line soon enough to suit Wirz, and he picked up a brick and struck the poor sufferer on the head with it, knocking him down. On the 10th of March the men were ordered into line again, one of the men who was sick, after standing one hour, was compelled to sit down through weakness and pain, Wirz ordered him to take his place in the ranks, which order he did not hear, Wirz then walked up to him, and hitting him, knocked him down and then commenced kicking him, through great exertion the prisoner regained his feet, and took his place in the ranks; his face bleeding and terribly lacerated.

A. A. Kelley, 40th N. H. vols., says that on or about the 10th of July, 1864, he saw one of the prisoners faint and fall under the dead-line; one of the guards seeing him, shot him, killing him instantly. In August, 1864, saw a man lying at the gate, sick, with a large sore on his back, and it full of vermin; one of the sergeants standing near by asked Wirz to let the man be carried to the hospital for treatment; Wirz refused, saying "let him lay there and die." In a short time the man breathed his last.

W. H. Jennings, 8th U. S. colored troops, says that he was put to work at digging a ditch about a month after he arrived at this place; being badly wounded in the thigh, after he went to work it commenced bleeding so bad that he was compelled to stop work. Wirz hearing of this ordered him to receive thirty lashes, which were given to him by Turner; after receiving the lashes he was put in the stocks, and kept there a day and night without a thing to eat or drink. This occurred in the month of March, 1864.

S. B. Brown testifies that when he was first taken to Andersonville, he was robbed of his watch, and all his money, one hundred and seventy-five dollars; while in this place he saw a crippled prisoner crawl up to where Wirz was standing and asked him to take him out of the stockade, as his leg would never heal in that place; after hearing the pleadings of the poor man, Wirz turned to a sentry standing near by and said, "shoot that one-legged Yankee devil." The sentry fired, the ball striking the poor sufferer in the head, killing him almost instantly.

A. W. Barrows, surgeon, formerly a member of the 27th Mass. volunteers, was taken to Andersonville in May, 1864, while there, heard Wirz say that he was of more service to the Confederate Government by being in command of that prison than any four regiments at the front, also, that he would starve every d——d Yankee he had in the prison; has seen men who had attempted to escape, but was caught by the dogs and brought back, one of the men had his ear bitten off, and his face terribly lacerated, another, he says, was so badly bitten in the thigh and neck that gangrene set in, and he died from the effects of it. He saw one poor fellow shot in the hip, by one of the sentries, through a hole in the fence while he was crawling, (being too weak to walk) up to a fire that some of the rebel soldiers had made, to get warm, the fire was six feet from the fence; Dr. White amputated the leg the next day, the poor fellow died a short time after the operation had been performed. In September, 1864, while some of the prisoners were being removed to Savannah, Ga., one of them, through sickness, was unable to walk fast enough, to keep up with the others, and fell behind, Wirz seeing him, came up to where he was, and after cursing him, knocked him down and then trampled upon him; it is said that he died shortly after.

Jos. E. Keyser, 120th N. Y. vols., arrived at this slaughter-pen in the spring of 1864, in the month of April, he says a few of the prisoners received boxes from their friends in the North, and in them was some moulded bread, which they threw under the dead-line; one of the poor starved creatures passing by shortly after, seeing it laying there, could not resist the temptation, and ventured under the dead-line for it; he had hardly grasped it when he was shot by the sentry in the head, killing him instantly, his body lay partly inside and partly outside of the dead-line. He says while confined in this place he only know of one instance where a man was warned back from the dead-line. He knew one man who died in the guardhouse with a ball and chain on him, heard Wirz give orders to the guards to shoot any man that came within fifteen feet of the gate.

J. Nelson Clark testifies that he has seen a great many of the prisoners, in the stockade, insane; saw one man who had become deranged go up and down the creek with his clothes off; when his meals were taken to him he had not sense enough to cook them; he finally died. One morning when he got up he saw a prisoner, who had hung himself near the place where he (Clark) slept; he had previously heard. the poor fellow say that he would rather die than live in such wretchedness. He saw a prisoner go over the dead line, the guard fired upon, and missed him, the ball struck another prisoner confined in the stockade; the next morning the poor fellow was reported dead. He saw another man shot, about the last of July, while they were drawing rations. Also, saw another shot, near the gate, where the dead were carried out.

Edward L. Kellogg, 20th N. Y. cavalry. says that he was bucked six hours at one time, because he failed to report the escape of one of the prisoners to Wirz. A new prisoner who had just come in and who knew nothing of the existance of the dead-line, went to the brook, across which there was no railing, two sentries fired at once, killing him instantly.

J. R. Achuff, 24th Ohio vols., and a few others, who got one of the guards to take them out to get wood, after he had taken them a short distance, they pounced upon him, took his gun away from him, and then ran, but the rebels were soon on their track, and Achuff was captured by the dogs, and taken back to Wirz's head-quarters. Wirz ordered him to be put in the stocks, where he was kept thirty-six hours without any food, and but two drinks of muddy water. He appealed to Wirz, who said "dry up or I'll blow your brains out." After thirty-six hours he was taken out of the stocks and put into the chain-gang and kept there thirty-two days. Saw Wirz strike a boy, who was a prisoner, over the head with a revolver; the boy was shortly after taken with fits, and died. He had a fit 'at the time he was struck, and two or three every day afterward, until death ended his sufferings. Saw Wirz kick and beat a sick man who was a mere skeleton. About the middle of July as the men were carrying out the sick, there being a great many, the stronger in their eagerness to get to the doctor, crowded around the gate. Wirz seeing this, ordered the guard to shoot the d—d Yanks, if they did not stand back. A sick man named Hicks was taken to the hospital; the doctor said nothing was the matter with him; Wirz commenced to curse him and told the men to carry him back to the stockade; the man died before he got back. One of his comrades, by the name of Geo. White, was taken to the hospital, he went up to him, saying, "good bye George," knowing that it would be the last time he would see him alive; a few days after he saw his body in the dead-house. He asked Wirz, who was present, to allow him to cut a lock of George's hair. Wirz, pointing to the dead man said, "If you go there I will blow your brains out." In July some of the men were in the creek, bathing; a young sentry was on post, and with him a rebel woman. The sentry fired into the party of men, to amuse his companion, killing one of their number—they were not near the dead-line—after he had fired the woman jumped, cheered, and waved her handkerchief. Also saw a crazy man, who was naked, shot and killed.

Mr. Achuff states that, when he was first captured, the rebel Gen. Wheeler took from him his pocket-book, containing thirty-five cents, and three postage stamps. Gen. Hindman took his hat and put it on his own head. This occurred near Dayton, Georgia.

Thos. N. Way says, that while he was confined in this place, he was tied up by the thumbs, because he was sick and he was not able to stand up in line with the others that had been ordered to stand up. He says, that after he was let down he could not use his hands for two months; one time he tried to escape, but was captured, and brought back, and put in the stocks for four days, at the end of which he was taken out, and four men ordered to carry him into the stockade, he being too weak to walk; as the men were carrying him they passed by where Wirz was standing, Mr. Way seeing him remarked jestingly, "I am very much obliged to you, captain, for having me carried as I am not able to walk;" Wirz remarked, "I will put you in the stocks four more days for that, and if you give me any more lip, I will shoot you;" he then ordered the guards to take him back and put him in the stocks. He says he was bucked and gagged one time for being late at roll call; he was also put in the chain-gang, and kept there twenty-five days, for trying to escape the second time.

B. Colligan says that while he was confined in this horrible hole he was kicked, and beat over the head, by that prince of fiends, (Wirz) because he did not answer to the name of Carrigan, his name being Colligan; at one time he was bucked three hours for committing a minor offence. At one time the men crowded around the gate, and Wirz ordered the quards to fire into the crowd; one of the prisoners who had been out to get some medicine for his comrades was shot dead by the guards during the affray.

Henry C. Lull, 146th New York vols., states that he saw a man by the name of Howe, belonging to a western regiment, shot on the 18th of August, 1864. The man, when he was shot, was about ten or a dozen yards from the dead-line. After he was shot the prisoners sent word to Wirz, and asked him to request the guards to be more careful, and not fire into the stockade at those whose who were not near the dead-line, but there was no notice whatever paid to this request, not even an answer sent back. Saw another poor creature shot and killed on the 28th of May, on the east side of the stockade; he accidently stepped on the dead line in trying to avoid stepping into a mud-hole.

Felix de la Baum saw a man belonging to a New York regiment, tied up to a post with an iron collar around his neck. This happened in December, 1864, and it was very cold at the time. The neck of the man was much swollen and bruised, and he was in a dying condition, being reduced to a mere skeleton by starvation. The man died two days after he was seen by this witness. Mr. Baum states that when he was captured he weighed 155 pounds, and when he was released he only weighed 98. When he was first taken to the stockade, he, being badly wounded, asked Wirz for a bandage to dress his leg; Wirz asked him his name, after having told it to him, he called Mr. Baum a d——d Frenchman, and asked him why he was fighting against the south? Mr. Baum did not reply-

Prescot Tracy saw, during the month of August, a prisoner, by the name of Roberts, arrive, who, not knowing the regulations, went to the brook to get a drink, the ground being wet, he slipped, and fell in, as he fell his head went over the dead-line; Wirz saw him fall, and yelled to the sentinel, "why don't you shoot that Yankee." The sentry fired and killed the man. Mr. Tracy had a comrade who died of starvation; this man asked Wirz for rations, he replied, "I'll ration you in hell."

John E. Marshal saw a man shot, in the early part of April, while the dead-line was being established; it was marked out, but the railing was not up; he also saw, about the same time, a German killed, in the north part of the stockade, while in the act of picking up a piece of bread which was lying beyond the dead-line; the sentry who shot him said, "I will soon have another furlough."

William N. Peeble testified that he was a detailed as a clerk, under Col. Farman, and acted in that capacity about three months. One day while there he went up to the stocks; it was raining very hard; he saw one of the prisoners fastened in them, with his face turned upwards, and the rain beating in it, nearly drowning him. Mr. Peeble held his umbrella over him; subsequently he went to Wirz and requested him to relieve the man; Wirz replied let him drown and be d——d, I don't care.

W. W. Crandall, 4th Iowa infantry, saw a man belonging to his regiment badly bitten in the calves of his legs, by the dogs, while attempting to escape. When he was brought back to the stockade Wirz had a ball and chain placed on each leg, and this, notwithstanding the swelling that had taken place; Mr. Crandall requested a surgeon to have the ball and chain taken off. The surgeon took one of them off, remarking that he could not conscientiously take off the other. The remaining ball was kept on the man nearly three weeks. He saw one man put in the stocks for expressing a desire to see his brother.

Lewis Van Buren, 2d N. Y. cavalry, says, when he arrived there, Wirz told him to count off his men; he d d so, and found a surplus of two men; this he reported to Wirz, who commenced swearing and said they were flankers, at the same time putting a pistol to Mr. Van Buren's head, and threatened to shoot him if he permitted flankers to get into his squad. On one occasion one of the men stepped out of the ranks to get a stick of wood, Wirz ordered the guard that was with them to shoot him; the man returning quickly thus saved himself; remembers seeing three men shot at once, in the brook at one shot, while they were getting water; one of the number was killed outright; saw another shot near the north side of the stockade. The night previous he had attempted to go over the dead-line for the purpose of being shot; witness tied him to keep him from seeking his own life, but as he begged hard to be let loose, and promised not to go over the dead-line, witness complied with his request. Soon after he walked across the line and was killed.

Father Hamilton, a Roman Catholic clergyman, of Macon, Georgia, went there to find out the number of Roman Catholics that were confined there. The stockade was swarming with vermin. He has administered the consolation of religion to the dying at the rate from twenty-five to thirty a day. He seen men walking about the stockade entirely nude. They seemed perfectly lost to all sense of shame and morality. He had administered the sacrament to prisoners who were covered with vermin. Some of the men were so far gone that they were unable to stand, and he was obliged to lie down beside them. Has seen them covered with all kinds of sores, and the sores covered with flies and maggots.

Charles E. Tibbles saw Wirz take a man by the throat, and drawing a pistol threatened to shoot him. Mr. Tibbles while there was branded by the doctor in charge with caustic on the back with the initials U. S. The doctor remarking at the time "they will know you when they see you again."

Robert H. Kellogg says he went to the swamp, sat down on the bank, and commenced to wash; he heard the report of a gun; looked up, and saw the gun of one of the sentries levelled at him. Shooting by the sentries was of such frequent occurrence that after a time he became used to it, and paid but little attention to it. Out of four hundred men that were in his squad, three hundred are dead. The greater part of them died while in this prison.

A. D. Blair, 22d N. Y. vols., heard a man ask Wirz for a ration. He replied, with an oath, that they would get all they deserved, and that would be little. Had seen Wirz at the gate when sick men were being carried out; they not moving fast enough to please him, he would kick them and push them along. Mr. Blair escaped, and succeeded in getting about thirty miles, was recaptured, carried back, and put in the stocks. On one occasion he went down to the brook to get water; when he reached over the dead-line the sentry fired at him; the ball passing by his head, striking two other men, one of whom was mortally wounded, and the other slightly.

Hugh R. Sneed, 39th Illinois vols., who was confined in this place, states that he smuggled himself out the stockade with a party of prisoners who were leaving the prison for exchange, as agreed upon between Generals Sherman and Hood. The men were ordered to march at the rate of eighteen miles a day, and all those who could not comply with this order were to be shot. One of the prisoners fainted at the brook, which was between Wirz's head-quarters and the depot, Wirz coming up fired the contents of his revolver at him, killing him instantly. The lieutenant who had command of the squad remarked at the time that it was a brutal act. Saw Wirz push over one of the men, who was in the squad, and the poor fellow was trampled upon by the crowd, and when taken up was in a dying condition.

C. H. Russell states that he saw one James Duncan, the quartermaster of this vile hole, come into the stockade one day with a load of bread, a piece of which broke off and fell on the ground, one of the poor starved creatures standing by, seeing it, stooped down and picked it up, and greedily devoured it; this man Duncan seeing him, jumped down off the wagon, and beat the poor creature so unmercifully that he died in a few days after. On another day saw this same fiend beat a half witted fellow who had come to him and asked him for bread.

Geo. C. Smith, 4th U. S. cavalry, saw three men killed in this horrible place by one shot; saw another poor fellow killed while in the act of picking up some crumbs under the dead-line; Wirz being on the platform, pointed the man out, and told the sentry to fire at the man. The sentry hesitated, when Wirz drew out his revolver, and told him if he did not fire immediately he would shoot him. The sentry fired, killing the poor starved creature instantly.

Robt. Tait, 53d Pennsylvania vols., testifies that on or about the 1st of May, 1865, he saw Wirz inhumanly kick one of the prisoners who was too weak to stand up when he ordered the squad in which the poor creature was to stand in line. Wirz compelled the men who were in the chain-gang to manœuvre for the amusement of some of his friends who had come to the prison on a visit. Wirz fired his pistol at Mr. Tait one day for being out of line at roll call. Mr. Tait had a very sore leg, and was sitting down to rest it, when he heard Wirz coming, and he got up and started to run and get in line before he (Wirz) saw him; but the fiend saw him before he reached the line, and called on him to stop, at the same time fired one shot at him, but it missed him, and he got into line safe, then Wirz came up and asked where Mr. Tait was, and said the whole squad should have no rations until the man was found. Mr. Tait stepped out and said he was the man, and the reason that he was not in the ranks was because he had a very sore leg, and could not stand long on it. Wirz, after some threatening remarks, said that he wished every d——d Yankee's leg would rot off, then ordered him to take his place in the line.

John A. Kane with a squad of others arrived at this place from Richmond, Va., on the 10th of March, 1865. When they arrived there it was raining very hard; they then were drawn up in line, four ranks deep, and then marched through water knee deep for about a half mile, and then turned into the stockade. Mr. Kane became so sick from the effects of it that in a few days he could not attend to roll-call, and his rations were stopped. When this was done he made up his mind to die, but his comrades helped him all they could, and in a short time he was able to attend to the call. On the 25th of July, 1865, he saw a rebel hospital guard shoot a sick prisoner through the thigh, for coming near a fire he had built to cook his rations, without giving the poor fellow the slightest warning, and in a few days after the poor fellow died from the effects of it. He says John Burk, 96th N. Y. cavalry, was shot in his right cheek; his tongue and upper teeth and three of his fingers were carried away by the same shot. He was taken to the hospital where gangrene set in, on the root of his tongue, which killed him. After he was taken to the hospital he wrote, on a piece of paper, that he was lying down when shot. The shot, he says, was fired at another man, but missed and struck him. The hospital book shows that he died the next day after entering the hospital.

Sergeant Geo. W. Gray, 7th Indiana cavalry, while confined in this place tried to escape in the latter end of August, 1864, but was caught by the dogs and brought back, and then put in the stocks, and there kept for eight days. One day Mr. Gray, and a young man named Stewart, belonging to the 9th Minnesota cavalry, were sent out of the stockade, under guard, with a dead body. They had just carried it to where they were directed, and had just laid it down when Wirz came up and asked them by what authority they were there. Young Stewart replied by proper authority. Wirz not liking such an answer, pulled out his revolver and shot young Stewart, killing him instantly. At one time there was received an order to parole some of the sick prisoners. Mr. Gray testifies that while those who were to be paroled were being taken to the cars, one of the sergeants asked Wirz to allow him to help some of them that were too weak to gain the cars; Wirz would not allow him to do it, but issued an order to bayonet all those who fell between the stockade and the cars. He also stated positively that he had seen many a poor fellow bayoneted while he was trying so crawl to the cars.

J. B. Walker, 141st Pennsylvania infantry, says that while confined in Andersonville, he helped to take a man, who was dying to the hospital. Surgeon Russell was there when the man was brought in. After looking at the man the surgeon ordered them to take him back to the stockade, remarking that he would live until to-morrow. He says that on the 14th of September, 1864, he saw Morris Prinville, belonging to company H, 7th Indiana infantry, shot in the head by one of the sentries. He says his brains were scattered around on the ground where he fell. Mr. Prinville, it appears, had been badly wounded at the battle of the Wilderness. Mr. Walker says that he pinned a paper on his breast, after he had fallen, saying that he was shot; he also made a report to Wirz of the fact. The following is a report taken of the affray from their own record book, which will show the reader how accurate they were in keeping their records :

"Mr. Prinville admitted in hospital on the 6th day of September; died same day. Cause of death unknown."

Mr. Walker says that he saw two men killed by one shot from a sentinel's gun. On the 26th of October he was paroled, and put at cobbling shoes. He was very much afflicted with sores at the time, and Captain Wright, whom he was then under, said he should stay there until he got well. The captain gave him many things which he needed. The men outside the stockade were informed, on the 4th of March, 1865, that the rebel General Cobb would make a speech on that day, and that they could go and hear him. Gen. Cobb, in his speech, said he was sorry the prisoners at Andersonville had been captured. He would have hanged them. He said if the prisoners should speak to the southern ladies they should hang them. He knew if Lincoln got him he would hang him; and if he ever got Lincoln he would hang him. In referring to Wirz, he said he was glad to find things at Andersonville as they were. Wirz was an efficient and meritorious officer. He said to the rebel troops, at the same time pointing over to the Andersonville prison, "look over to those men, and then go home and kiss your wives and daughters, and then strike again to gain your independence." He said he would feed and shelter the prisoners well, and he would (speaking in a deep-meaning tone, and pointing to the grave-yard,) treat them well.

William Balser, assistant surgeon U. S. vols., testified that he was on duty at Jacksonville, Florida, where he was engaged in treating the diseases of the prisoners who came from Andersonville prison. The prisoners, he states, were in a most horrible condition, and many of them were merely living skeletons, filthy and lousy. The principal diseases were scurvy and diarrhœa. The arms and legs of the poor unfortunate men were much swollen and drawn up, and upon the thighs and calves of their legs there were ulcers three and four inches in diameter. Pieces of bone and teeth fell from the mouths of his patients; their eyes were sore, and many were idiotic; and in many instances there was a softening of the brain. These diseases were attributed to exposure, bad food, and ill treatment in sickness. He had treated several thousand of these poor fellows, and does not believe one-half of them will ever be able to perform their usual avocations again. Has also treated cases of gangrene; has never met with similar cases in our army; in many instances he could not make amputations, the patients being too far gone. During his practice in the United States army, which was three years and eight months, up to the time he testified, he never met with but one case of scurvy.

The above conclusively proves to what extremes bad men will go to accomplish their ends. Allow me to say that Andersonville prison is only a fair example of the way that all the prisons in the south have been carried on. The smaller ones have been worked on a smaller scale, and therefore have not gained the notoriety that this one has. The commander of this prison, Henry Wirz, suffered death for his crimes, on the gallows, in the yard of the Old Capitol prison, in Washington, on the 10th day of November, 1865, at twenty-seven minutes past 12 o'clock, thus ending a life of infamy and crime which has scarcely a parallel in the world's history.

YELLOW FEVER PLOT.

The gun-powder plot of Guy Fawkes sinks into in-
significence, when compared with the hellish attempt
of one Dr. S. P. Blackburn, upon the lives of the innocent men, women, and children throughout the then
loyal portion of this country.   It is useless to comment
upon it, the mere facts are horrible enough.   I will
therefore only give the evidence of those men who
were acquainted with the secrets of the plot.   God-
frey J. Hyams, a resident of Toronto, Canada, testified
that he made the acquaintance of this Dr. Blackburn,
about the middle of December, 1863, and knew he was
doing work for the confederates.   He says: I was introduced to Dr. Blackburn by the Rev. Stewart Robinson at Queen's Hotel, Toronto ; Dr. Blackburn was
about to take south some soldiers who had escaped
from northern prisons ; I asked him if he was going
south himself ; he asked me if I wanted to go south,
and serve the confederacy; I said I did ; he then told
me to come up stairs, that he wanted to speak to me;
I went up stairs with him into a private room; he offered his hand to me, as a freemason, in friendship, and
said he would never deceive me ; that he wanted to
place confidence in me for an expedition; he asked me
if I would like to go on an expedition ; I told him I
did not care if I did ; he said I would make an independent fortune by it—at least one hundred thousand
dollars—and more glory than General Lee ; that I
could do more for the southern confederacy than if I
had taken one hundred thousand soldiers to reinforce
General Lee ; I considered after a time, and told him

I would go ; he then told me he wanted me to take a certain quantity of clothing—he did not say how much (coats, shirts, and underclothing)—into the States, and dispose of them at auction; he wanted me take them into Washington city, into Norfolk, and as far south as I could go, where the general government held possession; he wanted me to sell them on a hot day or night; it did not matter what money I got for the clothes, I was just to dispose of them for what I could get; if I left, I was to inform Dr. Stewart Robinson where I was, and he was to telegraph or write to me; on the 8th of June, 1864, I was out in town attending to some business, and on my return my wife had a letter in her hand from Dr. Robinson, which he had just called and left there ; I called on Dr. Robinson and asked him what I was to do; Robinson said he did not know anything about it; he did not wish, himself, to commit any overt act against the United States government; that I had better take only enough money to carry me down to Montreal; I had a letter to Mr. Slaughter, who gave me directions to proceed to Halifax, where I was to meet Dr. Blackburn ; the letter was dated May 10, 1864 ; from Havana I went down to Halifax ; Dr. Blackburn arrived there about the 12th day of July, from Havana ; he sent down to the hotel where I was staying, and I went to see him; he told me that he had clothing there, which had been smuggled off, and in accordance with his directions I took an express wagon, belonging to the hotel, down to the steamboat landing, and got eight trunks and a valise; he directed me to take the things to my hotel and put them in a private room, which I did, and notified Dr. Blackburn ; he asked me if I would take the valise into the States, and send it by express, accompanied with a letter, as a

present to President Lincoln; I objected, and the valise was taken to his hotel ; he ordered me to scratch
the marks off the trunks ; they had Spanish marks on
them ; he told me a man would go with me the next
morning, to make arrangements with one or two vessels going to Boston, to smuggle the trunks through; I
went down to the barque Halifax, Capt. J. O'Brien;
the officer, who was with me, said I had some goods I
wanted to take to my friends as presents—silk and
satin dresses, &c., and that he wanted to make an ar-
rangement to smuggle them into Boston; the captain
and he had a private consultation ; when they came
out he consented to take them on the Halifax, and
smuggle them in ; he took them on board his vessel
that day; on arriving at Boston it was five days before
we got an opportunity of getting them off, but he succeeded at last in doing it, and expressed them through
to Philadelphia ; from there I brough them to Baltimore, and brought five trunks to Washington; four of
them I gave to a man representing himself as a sutler
from Boston, by the name of Myers ; I understood at
the time he was a sutler in Sigel's army; he said he
had found some goods that he was to take to Newbern,
N. C.; my instructions were to make a market for the
goods, and I turned them over to him. (The disas-
trous effects of this plot was felt more at Newbern
than at any other place, the cases at one time reaching the startling number of one hundred a day.) Dr.
Blackburn stated, to deponent, that he would have
about $100,000 worth of goods got together, that sum-
mer, to be disposed of ; he also stated that the goods
that were in the trunks had been carefully infected
with yellow fever, and the object in sending them was
to destroy the army and every body in the country;

Blackburn also stated that the goods in the valise, intended for President Lincoln, had been infected with yellow fever and small pox; the trunk I took to Washington, known as big No. 2, I turned over to W. L. Wall & Co., commission merchants, and they give me an advance of $100 on it, and after receiving the money I went back to Canada; on my way I met Mr. Holcomb, and C. C. Clay, at Hamilton; they both shook hands with me, greeted me heartily, and congratulated me on my safe return, and on my making a fortune; they told me I should be a gentleman for the future; I telegraphed to Dr. Blackburn, who was staying at Montreal, (as Mr. Holcomb had told me,) that I had returned; the next night between 11 and 12 o'clock, Dr. Blackburn came up and knocked at the door; I was in bed, but looked out of the window, and saw Dr. Blackburn: he told me to come down and open the door, that I was like all other rascals after doing something wrong, afraid the devil was after me; he was accompanied by James H. Young; he asked how I disposed of the goods, and I told him; he said it was all right if "big No. 2" had been disposed of; that that would kill at sixty yards distance; I then told him that everything had gone wrong in my business there since I had been away, and that I needed some money; he said he would go to Col. Thompson and make arrangements to draw on him for any money I desired; he said the British authorities had solicited his attention to the yellow fever raging at Bermuda; that he was going on there, and, as soon as he came back, he would see me; I went to see Jacob Thompson, on the next morning; he said that Dr. Blackburn had been there and made arrangements to pay me one hundred dollars when the goods had been disposed of according to his directions ; I told him I needed the money; he said "I will give you fifty dollars now, but it is against Dr. Blackburn's request ; when you show me that you have sold the goods, I will pay the balance; I gave him a receipt for fifty dollars on account of Dr. Blackburn ; this was the 11th or 12th of August ; the next day I wrote a letter to Mr. Wall, saying I had gone Canada, since he sold the goods, and asked him to remit to me the proceeds at Toronto ; when I got the letter of Wm. L. Wall, I took it to Col. Thompson ; he said he was satisfied with it, and gave me a check for fifty dollars on the Ontario Bank of Montreal; I gave him a receipt for fifty dollars on account of S. P. Blackburn. Jacob Thompson, rebel agent in Canada, had a perfect knowledge of the character of the goods, and told deponent that the confederate government had appropriated $200,000 for that purpose; I went under the assumed name of J. M. Harris while in Washington.

Mr. A. Brenner states that he was employed in the commission house of Wall & Co., in Washington, and says that a man, calling himself Harris, brought a package of goods to the store for sale ; I thought him a sutler returning home, and I advanced him one hundred dollars upon them and sold them the next day ; he said there were twelve dozen shirts, but there turned out to be more ; I rendered an account of the sales to him at Toronto, Canada, with the balance of his money, in accordance with a letter received from him directing it, which I have here; it is dated at Toronto, September 1, 1864, and he states that he had written to me previously in respect to five trunks, containing one hundred and fifty woollen shirts, and twenty-five coats, but had received no response, and asked me to send him a check on New York for the proceeds.

Through some unknown cause the plot did not succeed in Washington.

Sanford Conover, of Montreal, Canada, testified that he knew Dr. Blackburn employed a man by the name of John Cameron, for the purpose of taking charge of infected goods, to take them to the cities of New York, Philadelphia, and Washington. Heard Blackburn say, about a year before this time, that he had endeavored to introduce yellow fever into New York, but from some reasons unknown it failed. Blackburn went from Montreal about January, 1863, to Bermuda, or some of the West India Islands, for the express purpose of attending cases of yellow fever, and collecting infected clothing, and forwarding it to New York city.

Jacob Thompson, C. C. Clay, and Lewis Sanders, rebel agents, all favored the enterprise, and seemed very much interested in it. It was also proposed to destroy the Croton dam in, New York, and poison the reservoir. They even went so far as to take the measure of the reservoirs, and the amount of water that was generally kept in them, and had made a calculation of the amount of poisonous matter it would require to impregnate the water so far, as to render an ordinary draught poisonous, and the deadly kind of poison to be used was strychnine, arsenic, and prussic acid, and a number of other acids which Mr. Conover did not remember. This scheme was spoken of in January, 1864, but for fear of detection was not carried into effect.

BOAT BURNING.

RICHMOND, *February* 11, 1865.

His Excellency JEFFERSON DAVIS, President C. S. A.:

When Senator Johnson, of Missouri, and myself waited upon you, some days since, in relation to the project of annoying and harrassing the enemy by means of burning their shipping, towns, etc., etc., there were several remarks made by you upon the subject, that I was not fully prepared to answer, but which, upon subsequent conference with parties proposing the enterprise, I find cannot apply as objections to the scheme. First, the combustible material consists of several preparations, and not one alone, and can be used without exposing the party using them to the least danger of detection whatever. The preparations are not in the hands of Mr. Daniel, but are in the hands of Professor McCullogh, and are known to but him and one other party, as I understand.

Second. There is no necessity for sending persons in the military service into the enemy's country, but the work may be done by agents, and in most cases by persons ignorant of the facts, and, therefore, innocent agents. I have seen enough of the effects that can be produced to satisfy me that in most cases without any danger to the parties engaged, and in others but very slight, that is: First, we can first burn every vessel that leaves a foreign port for the United States. Second, we can burn every transport that leaves the harbor of New York, or other northern ports, with supplies for the armies of the enemy in the south. Third, burn every transport and gunboat on the Mississippi river, as well as devastate the country of the enemy, and fill his people with terror and consternation.

I am not the only one of this opinion, but many other gentlemen are as fully and thoroughly impressed with the convictions as I am. I believe we have the means at our command, if promptly appropriated, and energetically applied, to demoralize the northern people in a very short time. For the purpose of satisfying your mind upon the subject I respectfully but earnestly request that you will have an interview with General Harris, formerly a member of Congress from Missouri, who, I think, is able, by conclusive proofs, to convince you that what I have suggested is perfectly feasible and practicable.

The deep interest I feel for the success of our cause in this struggle, and the conviction of the importance of availing ourselves of every element of defence, must be my excuse for writing you and requesting you to invite General Harris to see you. If you should see proper to do so, please signify to me the time when it will be convenient for you to see him.

I am, respectfully, your ob't serv't,

W. S. O'LAHM.

On the back of the letter are two indorsements, the first being "Hon. W. S. O'Lahm, Richmond, February 12, 1865. In relations to plans and means of burning the enemy's shipping, &c. Preparations are in the hands of Professor McCullogh, and are known to only one party. He asks the President to have an interview with General Harris, formerly M. C. from Missouri, on the subject." The other is "The Secretary of State, at his convenience, will please see Gen.

Harris, and learn what plan he has for overcoming the difficulty heretofore experienced. J. D. 20th February, 1865. Received February 17, 1865."

The confederate government partially carried this incendiary scheme into effect. Lewis Harkins testified before a military commission, in Washington, D. C., that he had at one time a large claim against the confederate government, for the burning of some steamers on the Mississippi river. The hospital in Nashville, Tenn., was burned by one these incendiaries. Kennedy, the New York incendiary, was another of their agents. The Robert Campbell, Imperial, Daniel Taylor, and others were burned by men employed by the confederate government.

The many lives lost by this scheme will never be known. If the war had not closed as soon as it did, no merchantman, or any other vessel which carried the American flag, could leave any port with security. As it was a great many sailed under the colors of other countries through fear of this plot.

THE END.